CW00767317

Tangled
Roots

Tangled Roots

Maria Turtschaninoff

TRANSLATED BY A.A. PRIME

PUSHKIN PRESS

Pushkin Press
Somerset House, Strand
London WC2R 1LA

Original text © 2022 Maria Turtschaninoff

UK edition published by agreement with Maria Turtschaninoff, Elina Ahlbäck at the
Elina Ahlbäck Literary Agency, and Abigail Koons at Park & Fine Literary and Media.

English language translation © 2025 A.A. Prime

Tangled Roots was first published as *Arvejord* by Förlaget in Finland, 2022

First published by Pushkin Press in 2025

FINNISH LITERATURE EXCHANGE

This work has been published with financial assistance
of FILI – Finnish Literature Exchange

ISBN 13: 978-1-80533-013-4

A CIP catalogue record for this title is available from the British Library

The authorised representative in the EEA is
eucomply OÜ, Pärnu mnt. 139b-14, 11317, Tallinn, Estonia,
hello@eucompliancepartner.com, +33757690241

Designed and typeset by Tetragon, London
Printed and bound in the United Kingdom by Clays Ltd, Elcograf S.p.A.

Pushkin Press is committed to a sustainable future for our business, our readers and our
planet. This book is made from paper from forests that support responsible forestry.

www.pushkinpress.com

1 3 5 7 9 8 6 4 2

Tangled
Roots

For Malin, my pomodoro partner

CONTENTS

Whose Daughter   9

THE 17TH CENTURY

Nevabacka   17
Border Folk   33

THE 18TH CENTURY

The Chaplain   57
Johannes   78
The Trial   101
Forest Sister   112
Nettles   130

THE 19TH CENTURY

Bitter Herbs   157
Shadow Song   191
Bread and Stone   201
Bird Girl   220

THE 20TH CENTURY

Pests 267

Maps 297

Sleigh Ride 318

Summer with Doris 333

THE 21ST CENTURY

Decay 363

Inventory 391

Instructions 409

WHOSE DAUGHTER

I place the urn on the porch table when we unpack the car
pour a glass of Talisker
For a brief moment
I want to open the urn lid and pour some inside
You were the one who taught me to drink whisky
Instead I toast to the evening sun
the lawn yellow with dandelions before the house
lilacs and bleeding-heart flowers by the woodshed
All this is mine now
because you are gone

even though I live so far from here
and don't know how I'll manage
how it will work
with the forest and the land
I don't know anything
can't do anything
and don't belong to anyone

Finishing the last of your mother's lingonberry jam
that's when you're no longer anyone's daughter

This place was never
my summer paradise
like it was yours
when you were little
You had memories here
friendships with
people animals land
some place you went dancing
went camping with your cousin
competed in ski races
you pointed, I listened with one ear
You didn't live here
but you did belong

I don't even know where the cellar key is
why the radiator is making that strange clanging
when the mobile library comes
who to call to get the roof fixed

But
you have left a list
instructions
Bearing in mind
just in case
for such time as it might be needed

Three months before your death
you were here and
wrote in your logbook
Thank you dear Nevabacka for everything

This place was so important to you
I want to understand why

Your routines have seeped into the walls
gently, I introduce my own
shift
move
adjust
Apologize for reordering the kitchen
you had your systems
I wasn't to disturb them
else you would get angry
I try to take solace from the thought that you would love me
    being here
(wouldn't you?)
I remove your clothes from the closet
can't bring myself to get rid of them
take them out into the shed
standing askew with peeling paint and flaking window frames
yet another thing for me to deal with

I can use your rubber boots
and Doris' old jacket

Otto's rucksack from the war is hanging on its hook
next to the mangle board with the year 1683 in slanting
    numerals
and a gimlet with a horn handle
The bedsheets still hold your scent
and your grandmother's monogram

This is the first time I've been here
without you
without any older generation
the dialect familiar to my ear but not my mouth

When I get a punctured tyre
I call the village car service
(you wrote the number on a scrap of paper and pinned it
    next to the corded phone)
The man on the other ends says:
"You're at Nevabacka, right?"
Even though my surname is different from yours
And neither of them is Nevabacka

When I go into the bakery
to order the sandwich cake for your funeral
the woman behind the counter says:
"I can tell whose daughter you are"
before I even state my business

When I drive into town to buy new mattresses
for the children
the man in the furniture shop wants to know how come the
    delivery address
is for Nevabacka
"Sure I knew Eva-Stina to be sure"
You had a summer job together back in 1967

Strands spread out in all directions
roots I never noticed when you were here
You sort of stood in the way
But now they are clearly visible, luminously obvious
now that I am the eldest
am the one to carry things forward
hold onto these strands
until the next generation takes over

My ten-year-old's hand in mine
as the urn is lowered into the ground
my six-year-old kneeling by the hole
watching his grandmother
disappear
into the soil

There is something in the earth here
that knows you
and now it is getting to know me

13

catching my scent

I walk through history
on paths my ancestors trod
past cairns they built
sheds they filled with hay
barns they raised
fields they farmed
year after year after year after year
The traces of their lives
are overgrown
receding
covered with weeds and brushwood and moss

I walk through the sunlit June night
with the taste of Talisker on my tongue
the scent of mown hay
potatoes fresh from the earth
tar burning and midwinter snow

the sound of my steps on the ground
which listens
and whispers
I know your steps
I know whose daughter you are

THE 17TH CENTURY

The first law of nature is this: that man might live, build and dwell on the land, support himself and his kin, marry and procreate.

ANDERS CHYDENIUS,
POLITICIAN, WRITER AND CURATE

NEVABACKA

A SOLDIER FROM THE WESTERN HALF of the kingdom
had been promised a plot of land in the east as a reward
for faithful service to the crown. He travelled by ship over the
sea to the young town of Kokkola, then followed a river until
he came to a small village. There was no church, and in the
whole village, which was spread over a wide area, there were
only fifteen smoking chimneys. He was advised where to go by
the locals he met, who spoke Swedish, his native tongue, but
there were those who spoke Finnish as well.

At the furthest eastern edge of the parish, he found the land
that was now his to farm. He knew he would have to build a
cabin by himself, but this did not bother him in the slightest.
The woodland he walked through was dense and dark; nothing
like the deciduous forests of his home. Here there was timber
enough for a fine cabin. The treetops whispered like the sea
he had traversed on his way to fight in the war. He had done
well for himself in the war and earned the trust and respect of
officers and fellow soldiers. But he was not made for killing and

17

plundering. He was made to hold a shovel, hoe and plough. He imagined the weight of the tools in his hands as he walked.

He spent the night in the forest and set off again before daybreak. When he reached the hill where he was to build his croft, it was still early morning. The full moon hung low above the treetops, white against the pale spring sky. It had risen before the sun. He stood for a long time gazing at the hill. The forest was thick, and at the foot of the slope flowed a stream, swollen with rippling meltwater. He could picture where his house would stand and where he would create his first field. He could fetch his water from the stream until he dug a well. The forest would provide more than enough firewood. Here was everything a man could ever need. This was virgin soil, and he was primed to tame it, to sow his seed and make the land bear fruit. He would be as tireless as the May moon and rise before the sun to begin his labour. Many of the place names in these parts were a mixture of Finnish and Swedish, and sometimes more languages besides. This plot was called Nevabacka, for it was on the only hill—*backa* in Swedish—in a sunken area filled with bogs—*neva* in Finnish. And as was the custom, he would henceforth be named after his croft. Matts Mattsson Rask became Matts Mattsson Nevabacka.

A robust and hard-working man was Matts Nevabacka. He felled large firs and built himself a cabin at the top of the hill with a magnificent hearth that kept the single room warm even on the coldest winter days. He burned out a field next to the cabin. He sowed his first seeds and, though it was not much, he knew that this was his chance to finally be his own man. To shape his own destiny and make his own decisions, no longer beholden to officers and kings. Never again would he follow orders, never again would he risk his life on someone else's whim. He would use his life as he saw fit. Every swing of the axe, spear of the skewer and strike of the spade brought him profound satisfaction.

Yet the forest was not easy to tame; it resisted. The trees were resinous and difficult to fell. The stumps refused to be torn from the ground, no matter how he pried. And the earth was stones, stones and still more stones. He heaved them out of the soil and stacked them into cairns around his little field and fell asleep in the evenings dreaming of stones. He dug and skewered up roots that clung to the rocky soil as stubbornly as if they had minds of their own.

For a while he was content in his solitude and even preferred it to the enforced company of soldiers. But then a new desire was born in his breast: he dreamed of a son to assist him in his labours. Perhaps two sons, strong and capable. Surely with their help this forest would bend to his will. With sons by his side, the rocks would almost fly out of the muddy earth.

Yet he had neither sons nor a wife, and there were very few womenfolk out here in the wild woods. The nearest hamlet had but two chimneys and no women of marrying age at all. Matts had no time to visit markets or other places where he could imagine coming upon eligible maidens.

Then one day an idea struck him. North of his croft was a treeless marsh. He was loathe to go that way, for something

19

was there watching him every time he drew near, he was sure of it. It was sacrilege to say so, but the surrounding woods were inhabited by more than birds and beasts alone. The villagers made sure to stay on good terms with the forest folk, or else stayed well away from them, according to the customs of the times. It happened that people brought them offerings, though always in secret, for it was against the teachings of the church. Yet sometimes there was simply nowhere else to turn for help in the face of famine or disease.

Being a stranger to these parts, Matts knew very little about the forest folk. He knew nothing of their names or ways. He always carried steel with him when he ventured into the forest and sang hymns loudly if necessary. He had a deep and resonant singing voice. The forest folk had no love for the Christian God; everyone knew that. It was not that he was afraid, but he knew to be cautious.

If only he could drain that marsh, he would have the finest, softest, most arable soil, completely free of stumps and roots. What a lot of work that would save him! He could already picture the land filled with abundant swaying rye. Prosperity—that was what the marsh would mean for him. During his time abroad, he had learned a little about draining lakes. He knew how it could be done, though he also knew how difficult it would be for one man to accomplish alone. Once he had made up his mind, he did not tarry, but set out for the marsh with his shovel and hoe.

It was a hot summer's day, and a dense swarm of mosquitoes and gnats hummed above the sedge tussocks. The sky was a sharp blue. No birds sang. A single red-crowned black woodpecker drummed out its rhythm against a hollow tree trunk at the edge of the marsh. As he put down his shovel and hoe, Matts caught sight of some small flowers with golden petals growing along the boundary of the wetland. He had never seen anything like them before. He thought they must be a good omen. Here, this was where he would dig the first dyke.

Matts set to work. He was aware of the vast difficulty of his impending task, but this did nothing to curb the power of his thrusting shovel or the zeal with which he swung his pick.

He worked hard and did not pause to swat away the flies and mosquitoes. When the sun was at its highest and hottest peak, he drank water and lay down to rest awhile in the shade of a fir tree.

He dreamed that someone came to him, some sort of being it was, with long dripping hair and eyes like golden petals. The being smelled of moss and marsh water, its hands were twisted and gnarled like a mountain pine, and its clothes were woven from cottongrass. In the dream, Matts crossed himself, for he understood perfectly well who had come to him. The being stood in front of the marsh with its hands raised in a defensive position. It pointed to the woods in a way that appeared welcoming, inviting. Then it made deterrent, dissuasive gestures around the marsh.

Matts awoke, dazed and with a dry throat. It was not in his nature to be easily frightened. He had seen much that had hardened him, made him calloused, that had made his soul as tough as granite. He had witnessed his countrymen plundering

21

to slake their lusts: women, food, gold. A dream would not trouble his mind.

He continued with his task. A few days later, again he dozed off by the marsh, with a stump as his pillow. Again the creature came to him. This time it was angry. Its golden eyes flashed. The ground beneath them was boggy and precarious. He understood perfectly well what the creature wanted. He was not to disturb the marsh.

Matts awoke as before and resumed his work. No one could intimidate or instruct him any more. He was his own man and would swing his pick exactly as he pleased! Yet he could not shake the feeling that he was being watched while he worked.

After a week or so of toil, he spent the night next at the marsh in order to continue digging early the next morning. He awoke at dawn when thin veils of mist were drifting across over the swaying sedges. A crane called somewhere nearby. Mistle thrushes and song thrushes chattered in the trees around. The black woodpecker was pecking, as always. A grey-headed woodpecker let out its melancholy wail.

He picked up his shovel.

Then he saw someone walking towards him across the marsh. Or was it just the billowing mist? If it was a person, they were treading in the most sunken, waterlogged patches of land.

Matts crossed himself. Clutched the steel in his pocket.

The mist closed in, took on form—a soft, curving form. The figure was coming straight for him. It was a woman, with long hair as golden as those little flowers that had just surrendered

22

to his shovel. It cascaded down her back, unbound and tangled. Her arms and legs were long and slender like sedge grass. She smiled at him and her eyes were moss-green. Though Matts had seen, and had, many beautiful women on his travels, none could compare to her. She said nothing and simply stood before him in all her nakedness and loveliness. Then she laid her hands on his shoulders, and he inhaled her rich, dark scent. She pushed Matts down onto the boggy ground, untied his trousers and straddled him. He had never experienced anything like it, not even with the strumpets of Prague.

Once they had both finished, she disappeared again across the marsh without a word. Matts was spent and weak, and he struggled to trudge back home to the croft. More digging was out of the question.

He knew perfectly well what kind of creature he had lain with. But no harm was done, he reasoned. He would protect his Christian soul from sin and never falter again. And yet, he found his mind returning to her again and again during the autumn, when he harvested his modest crop, and during the winter, when he skied in the forest and hunted game large and small for survival. He often skied to the marsh, and told himself it was because animal tracks were easier to spot there. He spent at least as much time scouring the landscape for other tracks entirely but did not see the golden-haired woman again.

One stormy, rainy evening on the brink of spring, he was surprised by a knock at his door. He felt for the knife in his belt before lifting the latch and opening the door.

He found himself looking straight into a pair of moss-green eyes. He could not help himself and took her in his arms at once, brought her inside and inhaled her scent of forest and lichen and stone. But then he noticed she was holding something in her arms, between their two bodies, and when he looked down he saw that it was a baby.

"He is thine," she said. "I bequeath to thee this heir, if thou swearest to leave the marsh untouched."

The crofter gazed down upon the chubby little hands, the big blue eyes that looked curiously into his own, and something swelled in his heart that he had never felt before.

"I swear," he replied. "I shall break ground anywhere save the marsh."

Satisfied, the woman left.

The boy grew rapidly and looked in all ways like an ordinary child, except that he was remarkably healthy and strong. Naturally, the inhabitants of the surrounding crofts wondered whence their new neighbour had suddenly acquired a son. That men sowed their wild oats was hardly a novel or unusual concept, but it was unusual for a man to raise his offspring alone. When Matts first visited his neighbours to request milk and clothes for the little one, there was a great deal of talk. Nevertheless, he simply claimed that the mother had died, and when people saw how well he cared for his son, the gossip gradually stopped. Matts had his son christened in Kokkola, home of the nearest church, and named him Henric.

Matts cared for Henric as tenderly as any mother. Henric had the very best food and slept in bed with his father. He grew quickly, much more so than other children, and in a few short years he was big enough to help Matts with his labour on the land. They grew turnips and barley and rye, and it was not long before they could afford a cow for milk as well. If Matts ever spared a thought for the marsh, it was one of pure gratitude for the wonderful gift he had been granted.

However, when Henric became a young man approaching adulthood, already as tall as his father, Matts started to change his mind. His thoughts turned more and more often to the marsh. What treasure was there, right under his nose! What fine, rich farmland it would be! The marsh belonged to him. It was his to decide over.

One spring, when the fields around the cabin were sown, he set off with his shovel and hoe and Henric, down to the marsh to drain it.

On the first night they slept out, Matts enjoyed a deep and dreamless sleep, but when morning came, Henric appeared sullen and grave. Matts asked him what was wrong.

"Mother came to me in a dream. She said that thou art breaking the promise thou made to her. What promise was that, Father?"

Matts ignored his son's question. They resumed their work and made rapid progress now that they were two.

The next night, Matts slept well again but Henric awoke with sorrow in his heart. "Mother says she shall take back what she gave thee, if thou breakest thy promise." He squeezed his father's hands. "Father, my heart is gripped by anguish. Tell me, what was thy promise to Mother?"

25

But Matts dismissed his son's concerns once again, saying that dreams were not to be believed. They continued to dig and toil in the warm pre-summer sun, which reminded Matts of the summer when his son had been conceived; his broad-shouldered son who now walked beside him. The boy belonged to him. He had sown the seed and the fruit was his. He stood up straight and looked out across the marsh as before, wiping the sweat from his brow. This was where his kingdom would flourish, this was where his gold would grow, where he would create something for his son to inherit one day.

A black woodpecker at the edge of the forest drummed relentlessly.

The following night was not dreamless for Matts. This time he was visited by the being with the golden eyes. Just like fifteen years ago, it uttered no words, but its sorrow and anger filled his dreamscape and flurried around him like a dark, all-consuming storm. The being reached for him with its claw-like hands, and its rage flowed into him through his nose, mouth and eyes until he felt as though he might suffocate.

He awoke gasping for air. The place where his son had lain was empty. Matts leapt to his feet and looked around the still, silent marsh, dressed in the pale half-light of the summer night. He called for Henric but no answer came. Terror-stricken, he ran all around the marshland, shouting and calling, but no answer came, and he saw no trace of his son. He fell to his knees and bellowed out across forest and marsh, begging for the return of his son—he would do anything asked of him, he promised, if only he could have back the only being he had ever truly loved.

The marsh was silent and dark. No birds sang, no woodpecker drummed. The only sounds came from mosquitoes in their thousands, thirsty for blood.

The crofter returned to his cabin a broken man. He never returned to the marsh. He died not long after, for though he had never yielded to the horrors of war, he succumbed now to his grief and loss—his spirit and strength were broken until eventually he was unable to work the land. He withdrew from his neighbours and lived on home-made schnapps and game he hunted in the forest. He died before his time, bitter and alone.

The croft stood empty, and the forest began to creep its way back into the small fields. The forest is always quick to reclaim land. It sends in a shoot or two, a few feelers, then by the following year, fresh shoots abound, grown to man-height already, until there is no trace that there ever was a field that someone once ploughed and harrowed and sowed.

Several years passed. The village grew along the riverbank. The low-lying fields were easier to work and yielded more crop than the stony little forest plots. The river was used to transport the tar burned in the forest, animal skins, butter and barrels of rye that had to be paid in taxes. There were fish to catch, and in winter the villagers could walk or ski along the river all the way to the coastal town of Kokkola.

In a tiny hillside cottage, half buried in earth near the river's shore, there lived an old woman with her youngest daughter Estrid Johansdotter. The mother was a strict, God-fearing woman who taught her daughter the catechism and prayers, and kept her under a watchful eye. Once she realized that Estrid had a knack for learning things by heart and a clear, beautiful singing voice, she taught her all the hymns she knew. Estrid liked to sing, and when she had learned all the hymns there were to know, she sought out anyone in the area who could teach her further songs and ballads. She had to do this in secret, however, for the old woman considered such things worldly and sinful. Through these songs, Estrid gained a wealth of knowledge about the world that she would never have learned from her mother, and a great deal about the faerie folk, trolls and other many unseen creatures of the forest. Soon they were as familiar to her as the Twelve Apostles and the Holy Mother of God. Estrid became known as the girl who forever had a song on her lips, while she washed in the river, while she herded the village sheep for a small fee, while in the sauna or sweeping the cottage.

When Estrid's mother found out that she had been singing heathen songs, she flogged her with a broom to cleanse her of her sins, which was not the first time she had resorted to the broom to keep her daughter on the narrow path of the Lord.

Estrid did as she always did and fled to the forest to sit under a rowan tree. The wisdom of the ancient songs had taught her that rowan trees offer protection. She sang to the rowan of her sorrows, and the tree and forest listened. Estrid sang all the songs that her mother had forbidden, and the rowan held them for her.

If she suspected someone was in earshot, she sang only psalms.

One day Estrid's mother died, but rights to their cottage on the hill did not pass to Estrid. Once the burial was over and the cottage was empty, she sat down on the stone outside her old home. She should have been devastated, motherless and homeless as she was. And yet she felt gloriously light. She held in her hand a bunch of rowanberries, for it was September and the trees were changing colour.

She could take a position as a farm maid. That is what most poor girls did. If she found no work she would have to move from farm to farm and live on the mercy of others.

But Estrid did not want to be a maid.

She stood up and left her home behind without looking back. She walked north, into the forest where she knew she could be alone. Soon the forest was dense and dark around her. Tall pines rustled overhead. The moss was soft and yielding beneath her feet. She came to her friend the rowan and sat beneath it. She leaned her head back against its smooth grey trunk. A flock of nutcrackers chattered in its branches. There she sat for a long time. The rowan whispered and sang back to her all the ancient songs and ballads that she had entrusted to the tree. Estrid listened. Once she had retrieved them all, she stood up and continued deeper into the forest. She came upon a path, trodden by the forest folk, and followed it without a plan. When a new path crossed the first, she took it. And so she travelled further and further from her former home, and was soon completely lost.

When she came to a dell with several storm-felled pines, she had no idea where she was. She sat down on one of the fallen trunks, grey and smooth as silk. The ancient songs trembled inside her, but she did not sing. Not yet, she thought. Not yet.

She saw a beetle crawling over the dead tree trunk. It bumped into an ant with flailing antennae. A little further along the trunk there grew some tiny yellow mushrooms, and when she leaned closer she saw that they were teeming with beetles and insects of various kinds. A playful breeze danced through the trees. The light was fading, evening was falling, but still she continued to wait.

A woodpecker cawed at the edge of the clearing and Estrid looked up. She searched until she caught sight of the bird's red head. She remembered a story her mother had once told, about a miserly housewife whom the devil had turned into a woodpecker with a black widow's robe and red cap on her head. She also recalled one of the songs an old man had taught her, which told of how woodpeckers were related to bears, and humans were related to both. A woodpecker could herald death. Though death had already visited Estrid's house.

The bird did not fly away, as expected, but flitted lower down the tree trunk and peered at her with one shiny black eye. Then it flapped higher among the trees and settled on a nearby birch trunk. Estrid stood up at once to follow. Each time she had almost reached the tree where the bird was sitting, it flew away further into the forest.

The daylight began to fade. It was autumn and darkness fell very quickly. She walked and walked, without really knowing where to put her feet next or how far she had come. She could not explain why she was following the black bird with its eerie caw; it was like wandering through a dream. Much of her life over the past month had felt unreal, and following a bird into the depths of the forest felt neither more nor less real than anything else. Her sense of lightness remained, or was it more a feeling of emptiness, or freedom, or being utterly alone in the world?

The bird guided her with such gentle cunning that she barely noticed herself emerge from the woods out to a large marsh.

When she became aware of her surroundings, the bird let out a screech, flew straight as an arrow across the marsh and disappeared. A gibbous moon hung above the forest edge. Estrid stood for a while gazing at the moon and the marsh. The night was quiet and still. It was waiting. She knew that whatever she decided to do next would determine everything.

Estrid closed her eyes and began to sing.

> *"I robe myself in human guise*
> *Slip over to the shadow side*
> *The moon knows that the night is wise*
> *And all the cows in the pasture*

"No one guesses, no one sees
The changeling's secret mystery
The night-time feels so light and free
The cows graze in the pasture"

She heard the sound of someone walking towards her but kept her eyes closed. Only when she came to the final verse did she open her eyes. There before her stood a young man with long fair hair and a beard. He was observing her curiously. She ought to have been scared, yet she felt no fear. She felt nothing at all.

"In the woods are guises shown,
Hidden, changed or never known,
The cup neither empties nor overflows
Night falls in the pasture"

Henric had been lured by her song. He had never heard anything like it in all his years with the forest folk. He was as though enchanted. The moment he looked into Estrid's eyes, memories of his years in the wilderness began to fade.

"I am Estrid," said the girl. "What hast thou to offer me?"

"I have nothing," Henric replied. "Nothing but a strong pair of arms and my youth."

Estrid looked at the man before her and thought that here was a future she could live with.

She held her hand out to him.

BORDER FOLK

ONE AUTUMN, RUMOURS SPREAD OF A robber hiding in the woods. Someone was breaking into storehouses in the villages along the riverbank and stealing from the barrels of saltfish and rye. One farm found that they were missing a shovel, and the farm wife of another lost all the round breads she had hung from the rafters to dry before the family set out on the long journey to church in Kokkola. A pair of sewn mittens and a small pail disappeared from Nevabacka farm, and Skogsperä croft lost an axe and some salt.

People had grown accustomed to enemy attacks in these parts, and to the King's soldiers showing up and forcing young men into service, but it had been several generations since they had had a robber to deal with. Now they no longer dared let the women walk alone between the villages, and preferred to travel in groups to church and market in town. One Saturday, men from almost every farm in the parish set out with spears, clubs and crossbows to see if they could hunt down the villain. They found traces of someone having felled trees in the forest very close to the Vittermåsa marsh but they lost the trail, despite having a hound with them, and came home with nothing to show for their efforts.

Every day, Jon Henricsson Nevabacka's wife Karin Hansdotter entreated her husband to put locks on all the sheds and buildings of their homestead. Jon doubted the situation was dangerous enough to warrant such action—no one had been hurt, after all. His wife narrowed her eyes and warned that he would change his tune when their cow and calf went missing from the barn.

Old mother Estrid, who was feeding porridge to the youngest member of the family, sat and listened in silence. She was used to keeping quiet in her eldest son's house. There were fewer quarrels and disputes with her daughter-in-law that way. At the Skogsperä croft, her youngest son Elim Henricsson Skogsperä and his wife welcomed her warmly with open arms. The same could not be said for Nevabacka. She preferred not to intrude on them too often. Her middle son Abraham Henricsson, who had always been happiest out in the woods and fields, had been conscripted to the King's army the year before. No one had heard from him since. In her mind, Estrid had accompanied him as he marched south towards great unknown wars. What was he eating and wearing? Who was he talking to? What did the trees look like where he was?

At home in the tiny grandmother cottage where she lived on her son's land, Estrid liked to tell Jon and Karin's children all about how their great-grandfather had once met a forest nymph out by Vittermåsa, and how she herself had met their grandfather there, one autumn day when the marsh was water-logged and dangerous. She could not tell these stories if her daughter-in-law was in earshot. Karin would not stand for it.

Something was weighing on Estrid, and as soon as everyone had finished eating, she left her son's warm house and walked across the yard to her own little cottage. She stood outside for a while and looked up at the starry sky. It was almost Martinmas. Winter was at the door. She thought about the items that had gone missing nearby: gloves, food, utensils.

Necessities to survive the winter.

She opened the door to her cabin and laid more wood on the fireplace before rummaging through her few belongings in the glow of the growing fire. Finally satisfied, she sat down on the bench by the hearth. There she sat for a long time, gazing into the dancing yellow flames. The next morning, Estrid got up very early. Before the sun rose, she packed a small bundle and set off down the path that started behind the barn and led into the forest. Estrid found it easily, for the moon, though not quite full, shone a cold light upon the forest, and the trees cast long shadows on the snow.

She came to Vittermåsa just as the sun came up, colouring the moss golden and pink and causing every frosted grass blade to glisten and sparkle. Mist rose from the ground and Estrid crossed herself. It looked very much as though the forest folk were out dancing this morning. She must be careful. She did not suppose that she was invulnerable to the wiles of creatures of the wilderness just because she had married one of them.

35

She had brought with her the only silver coin she had and held it tightly in her hand. She blew on it and sang over it, ancient words she had learned and her own words as well, mothers' words, to protect and shelter. Then she threw the coin far, far into the marsh, and heard it drop into a pool of water with a tinkling silvery sound.

The mist surged, like a curtsy or a bow. The old woman was filled with calm. She had done all she could.

She felt the steel in her apron pocket and made the sign of the cross again, just in case. Then she sat down to wait.

She was good at waiting. Something always happened sooner or later, if only she waited long enough.

The sun crept up into the pale blue sky of late autumn. The old woman was cold but did not move. She looked out over the marsh and thought about that day long ago when she had stumbled upon this place and chosen her future. She had thanked the marsh for the gift of her Henric. And their children. Many times. It was sinful to thank the land. So the church priest said. One must not say prayers or make sacrifices to the forest-dwellers. Everyone was supposed to pretend that they did not exist.

Yet they knew otherwise. They knew they were close by. Estrid had always made sure to stay on good terms with them. When she sheared the sheep, she always hung a tuft of wool on the fence for the forest folk to card, as thanks for keeping the sheep safe from wolves. When she baked bread, she always put a piece of bread out for the forest folk on the smooth flagstone at the edge of their land, as thanks for keeping the reindeer and moose out of the rye. When she churned butter and made cheese, she left some out for the forest folk, next to the stone step outside the barn, as thanks for keeping the cattle safe from bears and wolves when they grazed in the forest.

When her Jon had married and his wife Karin had come to learn Estrid's ways, she was outraged and forbade her from making such offerings now that she, Karin, was the farm wife of Nevabacka.

Nevertheless, Estrid continued to do as she pleased. She stayed out of sight and performed her rites in secrecy.

Finally, Estrid saw what she had been waiting for. In the distance, a wisp of smoke curled skyward from the marsh. It was a sure sign that something was hiding there—something other than wild animals, wood nymphs or elves.

The old woman stood up and smoothed her skirt. Then she took a deep breath and called out, much like she used to call for her cows out in the woods, every year that they were in her care. The first had been Yellow Cheek, Red Goose, and now Sea Tern and her little calf. Estrid had her own special way of cooing, and her voice was still strong and carried far and wide. The cows were in the barn for the winter. It was not to them she called.

She began to walk around the marsh, trying to get as close to the smoke as possible while paying heed to the soggy, treacherous terrain. She saw cranberries lying scattered on the ground, a sure sign that a brown bear had been there. She was not afraid of the bear, which would be fat and sated after the summer and soon make its winter nest. She cooed once more. And there, across the marsh, a tall, thin figure emerged and came carefully walking towards her on two marsh skis.

She met him on a small stony mound. He was bearded, and his hair was long and tangled, but his eyes shone just like they used to when he was a little boy.

He was not in some far-flung place fighting in the great wars. He was here. Close. Home.

He had an axe slung over his shoulder, which he let down and leaned against a rock.

"Here thou art," the old woman said, and the words came out much more harshly than intended. "Why has thine old mother never received a visit? And that belongs to thy brother." She nodded at the axe. "He lost that and salt last summer."

"Aye." His reply came out as a growl, not unfriendly, but gruff. This man seemed unpractised in using his voice. As if it had been a very long time since he last spoke to another human. "He can spare it." Abraham looked his mother in the eye. "Tell him it is payment for the knife of mine he broke when we were small."

"If thou hast something to say to thy brethren, canst thou say so thyself. I think it is better if no one knows thou art here."

"Aye, Mother." He cleared his throat and scratched his beard. Glanced at the bundle she had placed by his feet. The old woman ignored it.

"Thou hast deserted the army."

"War was not for me," he replied. "Disease. Death. Here is better." He gazed out across the sedge grass and mountain pines, where the sun was chasing away the last of the mist. But steam still rose from the mossy stones at the forest edge slowly becoming sun-warmed after the night's frost.

"Hast thou been here long?"

"I came with the cuckoo," he said. "I got by with what I had for a while, but then I needed tools, and when the hunt was meagre, I had no choice but to help myself to some bread and fish."

"Dost thou intend to stay?" She inspected him closely. He had some new scars on his cheeks and hands and more lines upon his face. Otherwise, little had changed. His gaze was still distant, like when he was a child. He had always been looking elsewhere, at something no one else could see.

"I cannot say," he answered slowly. "We shall see. I am happy here."

"They shall keep searching for thee if the thefts continue," she said. "Karin nags Jon every day. She believes the cow and calf are in danger."

Abraham scoffed. "What would I do with a cow? Milk and make cheese out here?"

"Or sell her. Earn some copper."

He spat in the marsh. "I want no further dealings with people. They create nothing but misery."

"Art thou not lonely?" She remembered holding him in her lap when he was little. Feeding him first with her own breasts, and later with gruel and chewed bread.

"Never." He smiled and his teeth shone out of his beard. "I have plenty of company."

She shook her head. "Be careful. They are not Christians, like us."

"Thou hast not seen what we Christians do to each other out in the world, Mother. Else thou wouldst not be so quick to judge those who have never wronged thee."

"It is in thy blood," said Estrid, thinking of how she had lured Henric out of the forest with her song all those years ago. He too had been half wild back then. Abraham must be allowed to choose his own path, just as she had herself. She bent down to pick up the bundle she had brought and held it out to him. "So that thou needest not steal. Something warm to wear. A little salt."

"Many thanks, Mother," replied Abraham solemnly. "Winter is coming and any help is welcome."

She left her middle son in the marsh and made her way home. Now she knew where he was, at least. She could be grateful for that.

Abraham knocked on her door sometimes, always at night. Estrid was never frightened, for she knew at once who it must be. One night he came with a large pike he had caught before the ice set in, and asked for some yarn to patch his mittens with. Another time he had cut his thumb badly, and she dressed the wound and muttered incantations over it. Then he stayed all night and only left at dawn.

"Dost thou recite thy prayers?" she said as they sat together by the hearth, warming themselves on the glowing embers.

"I pray and make offerings," he answered thoughtfully and gazed into the glow. "There is much that is holy in the forest, Mother. The water, which quenches my thirst. The animals, which give their lives so that I might live. The trees, which provide me with shelter and fuel. Indeed, every day the forest bestows blessings beyond measure upon me."

"God created the forest," she said. "And it is His will that we cultivate the Earth and tame the wilderness." Estrid had psalms and folk tales in her blood in equal measure. "And that we go to church and hear the word of God."

"I can hear His words so well out in the forest," he replied and patted her hand. "I cannot hear them in church over the ramblings of the priest. But in the forest... Mother, hast thou never heard the first lark sing after a long winter? Is that not the word of God in its purest form?"

"Dost thou not miss companionship out there, in any case? A girl. It is high time thou tookest a wife—no one is made for solitude."

"Oh, there are girls of all sorts who do not deny me," he said, and she did not care for his tone. "I need no priest's blessing for that."

Nothing she said could reach him.

Years passed. Nothing more was stolen from the village, and the old woman knew that if her son needed something, he would travel further afield to get it, so as not to be caught.

*

Skogsperä's youngest was forever getting into adventures and mishaps. When she was born—swiftly, as she did everything—there happened to be an old beggar woman at the croft. She glanced at the girl, drew a deep puff on her clay pipe and said: "That girl shall bring much fortune and misfortune to Skogsperä." And so it was. She was the one who found the best spots for berry-picking in the forest, but ripped her only skirt in picking them. She was the one who managed to find the cow and heifer when they had strayed too far grazing, but also screamed so loudly that she spooked the cow, causing her to flee to the marsh and drown before the adults could reach her. She had more strength in her scrawny arms than any of her older siblings and could churn for much longer than they, but she often stumbled and kicked over the butter churn, spilling all the buttermilk onto the ground.

The girl's name was Kristin Elimsdotter.

One warm and sunny summer morning, Kristin was playing with one of the croft's kittens down by the stream that ran between Skogsperä and Nevabacka. The fireweed and marsh marigolds growing there attracted butterflies, and Kristin sat on a rock for a long time watching the kitten chase them. No longer a little baby, the animal was long, lithe and swift.

Swallows darted to and fro overhead, catching insects. The air was warm and still. After a while, Kristin became thirsty and took a drink from the stream. Then she felt hungry. She remembered that she and Mother had seen raspberries growing along the path a few days ago. Might they be ripe by now? She left the kitten and stream behind and scurried up the hill to the meadow where the cow trail began. She followed the trail into the forest. The air trembled with heat, still warm in the shade of the trees. There were the raspberries! A whole thicket full. Kristin picked and ate. It was only once all the raspberries were gone that she felt a pang of guilty conscience. How selfish and greedy she had been. She had eaten up all the raspberries that Mother had intended to pick. How disappointed she would be!

There must be more raspberries in the forest, Kristin reasoned. If these were ripe then surely there were more. She would pick an apron full and take them home to Mother! She followed the cow trail further into the forest but, strangely, saw no raspberry bushes anywhere. She walked and walked, quite far from home now, but still did not find any raspberries. She knew she ought to go home so as not to worry Mother. She could follow the same path back, but it was a winding route—if she cut straight through the forest, she would get home much quicker.

So off she marched on her little six-year-old legs. She was familiar with the forest surrounding her home and was certain that she had never wandered this far before. There were no paths to follow between the tall, rustling firs. But the moss was soft beneath her feet, and she would surely be back home with Mother soon.

On she walked, and the sun followed its course across the bright blue summer sky, but the shingle roof of home did not appear between the trees. She must have gone too far to the left, so she swerved to the right and continued walking. Presently, she passed a beautiful grove of birches where the friendly trees waved their green leaves, then she passed a little fen covered in willowherb and cottongrass. Kristin knew that cottongrass was what troll mothers used to make beds for their troll babes. But it was broad daylight, and she was most certainly not afraid of trolls. Not in the slightest. She picked up her pace, though her little legs were weary.

When she came to a small pond that she had never seen before, she had to admit to herself that she was well and truly lost—and tired and hungry and frightened, besides. Exhausted, she sat down in the moss by the pond and sobbed for a good long while. Then she leaned down to slake her thirst with the cool pond water.

She saw her own face reflected in its surface. But then she saw something else there too, something shining and shimmering underneath. Was it a silver coin? Imagine how happy Mother and Father would be if she, Kristin, came home with a silver coin! She reached into the water, but the glittering thing was further away than she had thought. She had to reach further. Before she knew it, she had slipped on the slimy, wet stones on the shore and fallen headlong into the dark water. It was not very deep, yet she sank straight to the bottom and was unable to figure out how to get back up to the surface. Something was down there, drawing her in, wanting to drag her down into the depths. Its lure was powerful, clinging at her limbs and preventing her from fighting back. She surrendered to the embrace of the cold darkness. Maybe it was not all that dangerous, maybe…

Something grabbed her. A firm, steady hand wrapped around her arm and pulled her back up to the surface, to the light.

Kristin sat on the shore, dripping wet, coughing up water. Sitting beside her was a troll—yes, it must have been a troll—with bushy grey eyebrows and tangled hair and beard. The troll glowered at her with a dreadful frown, and Kristin was more frightened now than she had been in the pond.

"Did thy Mother and Father never warn thee about the Nix?" growled the troll in a deep and terrible voice.

"I saw a coin," Kristin replied. "I wanted to take it home to make Father happy."

"Fool's gold," snapped the troll. "That is what the Nix uses to ensnare little children and drown them. Do not fall for his tricks again, promise me!"

Kristin nodded, terrified. She was shivering in her wet skirt, for evening had fallen and brought cool shadows with it.

"We must get thee dry," muttered the troll. "Wilt thou promise not to tell anyone what I show you?"

Kristin dared not disobey, and the troll scooped her up in his arms and carried her with long strides along invisible paths that he clearly knew well. By the time they arrived at a wooden cabin hidden in the marsh, Kristin had come to the conclusion that he was not a troll after all, for he had no tail. Besides, here he was living in a little hut with a stone fireplace, whereas everyone knew that trolls lived in caves and hollows and were afraid of fire. She took off her wet skirt and warmed herself by the fire that was soon blazing, then the man wrapped her up in a blanket from his own bed.

Kristin sat there in silence for a long time, fiddling with the blanket. She recognized it. She had seen it in Grandmother's cottage last year, but then it disappeared. Kristin was a clever girl, and slowly she started to piece together things she had heard the grown-ups talk about.

"You are the robber." She looked up at his hideous face, but it no longer scared her. He had shown her nothing but kindness. Now he was carving dried meat into thin strips for her. She popped a piece in her mouth and chewed. "Auntie is terribly afraid of you. She wants Uncle to find you and chase you away."

"And who is thine aunt?" grunted the robber.

"Karin of Nevabacka, of course."

The robber became very still, then turned his big shaggy head to look at her in a new way. "Art thou the daughter of Elim of Skogsperä?"

Kristin nodded. The robber laughed. "Well, how about that? In that case thou oughtest to have more sense than to be lured by the Nix." He paused. "Tell me, is thy grandmother well?"

"She mainly just sits at home. She cannot see very well, so I help her sometimes."

Truthfully, it was Kristin's elder siblings who usually helped their old grandmother. But Kristin liked running home to Grandmother and sitting with her as dusk fell. Of course, during summer there were so many other exciting distractions and Kristin and her siblings tended to forget about Grandmother.

46

"That is good," said the robber. He sat quietly for a few moments. Gazed into the fire and pondered.

"I ought to get thee home for the night," he said at last. "So they do not begin to fret at Skogsperä." He looked over at his bed, where Kristin had fallen asleep with a piece of dried meat in her hand. "In the morning, then."

He sat for a long time that evening, observing the sleeping girl: her thin eyelashes, the long fair plaits coiled around her head, her little mouth, her parted lips gently pouting in her sleep. His breast filled with the same tenderness he used to feel when he found baby birds that had fallen out of their nests or fox cubs that had strayed too far from their dens. He would help them get back to where they belonged. He knew all the dens and nests of this marsh and for miles around, and could guide each and every animal home if need be. He did it because he pitied them, but also because those fox cubs would grow into animals he could hunt for their fine furs. In the autumn, he hiked up to the town of Kalajoki to exchange furs for necessities: salt; a new cooking pot or knife blade; fishing hooks; sometimes tobacco. There was little risk of him being recognized or arrested there. He never lingered longer than was strictly necessary, never drank ale with other pelt-hunters, never conversed with locals. Likewise, people kept their distance from him. It was clear from his appearance what he was: a robber and a savage, who smelled of smoke and poorly tanned animal hides. All who encountered him must have known what breed of man he was, but the traders gladly accepted his fine wolf, fox and reindeer skins.

Now, the tenderness he felt for this little girl sleeping so soundly, so trusting, in his hideaway, was far greater than anything he had felt for those defenceless baby animals. It was mixed with something else as well. A longing—a melancholy he could not define. He got up and went to the open door to look out at the marsh in the summer night, where gnats sang and danced over the grass, bog-myrtle and cottongrass.

The only person he had spoken to in many years was his mother. He could forget her for long periods of time, and not miss their conversations, but sometimes he thought of her when he came into the vicinity of their old homestead or saw something that reminded him of her: cloudberries ripening on the marsh; a song on his lips that she had sung to him when he was small. Then he made sure, under cover of darkness, to walk silently to her door and wake her with his special knock. He often brought something for her to help with or fix: a wound to bandage; a garment to mend. He knew her provisions were meagre in her little grandmother cottage, so he tried to bring things that would be of use but not raise too many questions: a deer he had snared or fish he had caught. He might whittle her a new butter knife or weave a vessel from birchbark. Sometimes he brought ready-chopped firewood for her hearth.

He was often restless when he came to her door. He shifted his weight, eager to leave, to get away. To be home. He was curt and blunt with his mother, responding to her with single words. He was not one for overthinking and did not care to question his ways. He just took his newly darned socks as soon as she was done with them and disappeared into the night. Home to the forest, marsh and stars. To his world. His mother called it the wilderness, the backwoods; she did not understand why he stayed there, year after year. "Thou couldst start a new life elsewhere," she would say. "Where nobody knows thee. Get thyself a croft and a girl. A real home."

Even as a child, when Abraham returned home from yet another of his long forest excursions, the only one who seemed to understand him was his father. It was Henric who had shown him how to survive and behave in the forest. How to honour those that dwell there and live alongside them. When Abraham absconded from a soldier's life, he headed directly for the place where he always felt most secure, most at peace. The marsh and forest behind the old homestead. Here he was his own man; here he wanted for nothing. He roamed far and wide but always returned, if only for winter when his little cabin was essential for survival. He had no desire for human companionship—he had never got along with his brothers—and the forest provided everything he could ever need. If this was the wilderness, well then, he was a wild man and proud of it. His mother was his only remaining connection to human life and society, yet it was an inseverable bond. This was what he felt when he visited her. That bond remained and prevented him from being fully free. He turned in the doorway and took another look at the sleeping child. It tugged at him again: the longing, the feeling that he had given something up after all. Something that all the foxes and birds got to experience, every spring.

49

*

The next morning he brought Kristin back to Skogsperä but took his time getting there. He showed her where polypody ferns and wild strawberries grew. He taught her how to find her way in the forest. He warned her about the Nix and other sprites, advised her always to carry steel in her pocket and told her that rowan-berries offered protection from unseen forest folk. He showed her the spring he had discovered, unknown to any villager, and birds' nests full of chicks with hungry, gaping beaks, and the flower meadow where the cows grazed when they were let out to pasture, and the beautiful birch grove where wood violets bloomed in early summer. The little girl held the big, bearded man's hand all the while and plodded curiously by his side. She was fascinated by everything and wanted to learn more.

"You know, when I first saw you I thought you were a troll," she confided to him. "I wondered where you were hiding your tail."

"What dost though think thy mother and father shall say when they hear that thou wast spirited away by a troll?" He smiled down at the bright little face that looked up at him so earnestly.

"Oh, they shan't believe me," she said glumly. "They never do."

"Well, let them doubt. But tell thy grandmother and see what she says."

"May I visit you again?" the girl asked gaily. "It was such fun in your cabin! I think I could find it again, you showed me the way!"

"No, it is much too far to walk for someone so small. And tell no one where I live. Canst thou keep a secret?"

The little girl looked disappointed, and her lower lip began to tremble. Abraham could not risk his brothers searching for him in the forest. He did not know how they would react if they knew that the robber stealing from them for the past few years was their very own brother.

"Promise to tell no one where I live, and I shall give thee something." He reached into the pouch he carried on his belt, where he kept a little tobacco, a firestriker, a few coins and other small items. His fingers found the small lump of amber he had got from a merchant who had come sailing to Kalajoki from distant lands. He pulled it out and crouched down, holding it up to the light. "Look. I can give thee this piece of sun that I captured."

The girl looked at the stone with wide eyes. It caught the sunlight and glistened and shimmered like honey. She held out her hand and nodded in awe. "I promise. Is it hot?"

"No, the sun has hardened it and it has become firm and cool. When winter comes, look at this to remember that the sun always returns, every year, no matter how distant she feels when the winter storms blow and she hides her face for weeks at a time."

The girl took the stone, and the man stood back up straight and looked around.

"We are very close to home now. See? There, between the trees, we are coming up to the farmyard fence. Now be a good girl and run along home, very fast now, so thy mother need not worry any longer."

Kristin held the sun stone ever so tightly in her tiny fist. She quickly curtsied to the robber before running barefoot between the trees towards the croft and her worried parents. Abraham stayed on the path for a while, watching her. She did not turn around. "I must go away, at least for the summer," he said to himself. "I cannot expect her to keep my secret."

But Kristin told no one where the robber's cabin stood. When her parents asked her where she had been all day and night, she said only that the Nix almost got her, but that she was rescued by a friendly troll who gave her dried meat and a stone made of sunshine.

For many years to come, tales were told throughout the parish of the little girl who was saved by a troll, and people marvelled that trolls could be so helpful. Then there was always someone who reminded everybody of the child once born of a soldier and a forest nymph, and that such things were not as uncommon as people would like to believe.

That evening, Kristin ran to her grandmother's little cabin. She tiptoed into the darkened room and over to the bed where Grandmother was resting. She was resting more and more these days, though she had never sat idle during all her years as farm wife of Nevabacka.

"Grandmother!" Kristin said eagerly. "I was given a piece of sun by a troll!" She crawled into bed next to the old woman and held out the yellow stone, which had captured the setting sun's last shimmering rays. It was the most beautiful thing either of them had ever seen.

"A troll," Grandmother said slowly. "How frightening."

"No, not at all. He was very kind and saved me from the Nix, and he was not really a troll after all, he was a robber. He had your blanket, Grandmother. He let me sleep in his cabin, and then he brought me home and gave me this." She put the stone into her grandmother's hand.

"Well, that is a relief," murmured the old woman. "What a relief." She held the stone tightly and patted her granddaughter on the cheek. "What a relief that he was kind."

Abraham steered clear of those parts after that, afraid that someone might find him and take him prisoner or conscript him into the King's army again. That autumn, he built himself a small, much simpler cabin in another forest and stayed there all winter. He often thought of the little girl, and on occasions he thought he could hear her chirping voice beside him as he walked in the woods, and feel her little hand in his.

This was what his mother had meant when she said he was lacking something, because he had chosen the forest over people.

On the verge of spring, a woodpecker came thrice to his cabin and pecked at a stately pine that grew nearby. After the third time, Abraham took his small pack and began the long trek back to his home marsh. He knew a harbinger of bad news when he heard it.

He did not make it back in time for the burial. Not that he would have attended anyway. But he could have stood in a hidden spot and watched the funeral procession go by. Seen the little girl again. He laid a cross he had carved from juniper wood on the burial mound. "Farewell, Mother." Then he adjusted his pack and turned away. Left the graveyard and continued to walk.

THE 18TH CENTURY

But through darkness and silence
strong invisible bonds bind generation to generation,
bind them so tightly that they can never be undone.

HELENA WESTERMARCK

THE CHAPLAIN

T HE CHAPLAIN HAS JOURNEYED to the marshland to go into hiding. It is far from his chapel. He hopes it is far enough.

He is alone. His wife is dead, as are so many of his parishioners. He knows not where his sons may be or whether he shall see them again. They have been taken by the Russians. The Russians who have burnt towns and villages to the ground, who have stolen weapons and silver from the church, plundered every settlement they have come across and torched the remains. Butchering, slaughtering, kidnapping children and defiling women. The Russians who bound the parish priest of Ilmola to the Cossacks' horses and forced him to run from Ilmola to Närpes in the bitter cold. The priest survived but shall never walk again.

This chaplain can still walk. Though he walks with the heavy steps of a man who wishes he too were dead. He has prayed to God for liberation from this earthly life. God has not listened. God requires him to continue caring for his flock. They have no one else to turn to now.

He may be a chaplain, but he was born on a farm and knows how to work with his hands. He is prepared to build himself a shelter; he has an axe with him. When he comes to the edge of the marsh, a woodpecker lets out a catlike screech. Or is the sound more reminiscent of a screaming infant, soon to have its skull crushed by an enemy boot?

The chaplain must rest briefly to allow his pounding heart to slow before he can continue along the edge of the marsh. He has a goal in mind. His housekeeper Kristin told him of a robber who lived hidden in these woods for many years. He was never caught, and his hiding place was never found. But Kristin knew that the robber had a little cabin on Vittermåsa marsh. She packed the chaplain's haversack and urged him to flee under cover of darkness. "You must save yourself," she said. "In the name of God, away with you!"

The chaplain was raised to be wary of the wilderness. God put man on Earth to civilize nature, cultivate the soil and make it fertile and fruitful. The wild lands hold nothing but darkness and danger. The devil's domain. A dwelling fit only for faerie folk and thieves.

And now the chaplain, fleeing from human evil.

He searches for half a day before he comes upon the cabin. There it stands, on a hillock in the middle of the marsh. A few young pines grow on the mound, obscuring most of the cabin, so he does not see it at first. But then he sharpens his focus; it helps that he knows what to look out for. A roof. A smooth grey wall. He sends a grateful thought to Kristin.

There is yet space in his heart for gratitude. He is surprised.

He starts to make his way towards the cabin. There must be a dry path to get there, if someone was able to build it in the first place. He walks slowly. He missteps, falls to his knees in the boggy ground, rises with great effort. If only he had his marsh skis. Eventually he discovers a subtle trail he can follow. There is a plant with dark, smooth leaves that only grows in the drier places. By following its growth, he eventually reaches the cabin.

It is old but solid. The roof was covered with grass and moss, but there is not much of it left now. The walls are built with sturdy logs—they shall withstand the storms of winter. If he must stay so long. Which he believes he must.

He puts down his haversack and sets to work sealing the roof.

A few evenings later, the chaplain is sitting by a fire he has built outside the cabin. He eats no supper, for the food he brought with him has run out. He was lucky to get anything at all. He has his Bible and hymn book, an axe, a knife and his father's old wolfskin coat. It is not yet autumn. But soon the cold shall come. He has his coat loose over his shoulders now, more for companionship than for warmth.

The chaplain is not old. His hair is still golden like the sun and his eyes are clear. Sharp. Sharpened by all that he has been forced to witness. Hence, he catches sight of the old man walking towards him across the marsh straight away. He reaches for his axe, then stops. This man does not belong to the enemy. Nor to his parish. The old man is stooped and grey and difficult to focus on. His fingers are long and bent, and his beard looks as dry and grey as the lichen growing on the towering firs around the marsh. His body is gnarled and shrivelled like a marsh pine. The chaplain crosses himself, which makes the old man stop in his tracks. The chaplain plucks up his courage. He has God on his side. God has not appeared to the chaplain for a long time, but he has not lost faith. Not yet.

"Good evening, uncle," says the chaplain. "Would you warm yourself by the fire for a spell?"

The old man nods shortly and sits down on a rock on the other side of the fire. It is difficult to see his features clearly through the flickering light and smoke. He appears at first as though he is impossibly small and then as a giant, thrice the chaplain's size. When the firelight flashes in his eyes, they glow red. But the chaplain knows that this man who has come to sit by his fire is not the devil. He has seen the devil in the eyes of the Cossack who made him watch as he defiled his wife. He has seen the devil in the eyes of the soldier who took his two sons, aged seven and eleven.

It is clear that the old man wants something. He has come with a mission and the chaplain allows him to take his time in presenting it. Just like the old days, when a parishioner would come to the parsonage with an important matter, but needed to be coaxed into revealing what it was. In those cases, the chaplain would ask Kristin to bring out beer and bread, to loosen his guest's tongue. Perhaps he would read a little from the New Testament. Ask how things were at home. Now he cannot tell whether the old man wants to ask a favour or make a threat. The chaplain does not know what sort of encouragement he needs.

"I would offer you something to eat, uncle," he says. "Alas, my stores are bare."

"Times are hard," the old man says eventually. His voice is neither loud nor soft. It is more like a whisper, a rustle in the trees.

"That they are, uncle. Have you been spared from the enemy's advance?"

"Humans do not tend to involve themselves in my affairs," says the old man. "Yet I see what is happening. I see all that happens. I see that a blackcoat has come to my marsh and settled here."

"Your marsh?" says the chaplain, realizing who this man must be. None other than the guardian of the marsh, to whom some of his parishioners still bring secret offerings. They think the chaplain is oblivious, but such stories always reach the parsonage sooner or later. He has tried to warn against such practices in many a Sunday sermon, has spoken from the pulpit with passion and fervour of the dangers of impious superstitions. He knows about such things, for he has read Agricola's Psalter. Even two hundred years ago, Agricola was appalled by the ignorance and gullibility of the people. Still to this day, false gods and folk beliefs must be quashed.

However, his parishioners have stubbornly maintained that this is not mere superstition. That the forest folk are real, and it is important to maintain a good relationship with them. The woods are the workplace of the common people. They cannot afford to clash with those who dwell there.

"What are you doing here?"

"I am in hiding," replies the chaplain. "If you will allow it. I need somewhere to hide where my flock can find me if they need me, but where the enemy cannot."

The old man nods at the word "flock", as if this is something he can understand.

"You must look after your people."

"Yes," says the chaplain. "They have no one else to turn to."

"And I must look after mine, blackcoat." The old man sits for a long time, unspeaking and unmoving. In so doing, he almost fades into the background, as a rock or a stump, grey-green and ancient. The chaplain can only see him because he knows he is there. Eventually the old man speaks again.

"My folk must be safe from you and what you bring here. You may take what you need, but no more. And no shovels."

The chaplain is not sure what the old man means. He does not know what promises he can make now.

"I mean no harm to your flock," he says carefully. That is a promise he believes he can keep.

The old man leans forward and spits into the fire, as a sign of the agreement made between them. The flames flare and a swarm of sparks swirl up into the starry sky above.

By the time the sparks have turned to flakes of soot and sunk back down again, the chaplain finds himself alone by the fire.

The next day he finds three hares outside his cabin, their hind paws tied neatly together. They are enough to feed him all week. He is not sure whether this counts as a sin. He knows where they came from. Yet he has had no luck with hunting and is starving. The more he thinks about the conversation he had by the fire, the more he convinces himself that the person he encountered was some kind of robber. Maybe even the robber from Kristin's stories, if he has lived this long. Yes, so it must be. The chaplain tells himself this until he is beyond doubt. He made a bargain with a woodland robber and to accept his gifts is no sin. Even a thief is a child of God. Unlike the forest folk.

On Sundays he conducts holy service in his cabin but makes sure to pray silently. To be on the safe side.

A woodpecker drums against a rotten pine trunk. It sounds like a message, like a herald announcing news to the townspeople.

Many have fled their homes in this parish, but more have fled the villages and parishes nearer the coast. There is a waterway to the west for those who have been severely tormented by the enemy. But here, inland, they do not have access to the same escape route. There are no boats. There is no way of reaching the coast without encountering enemy Cossacks. They plunder all they can lay their hands on and burn all that remains, so that the King's army cannot move south into the country again. The chaplain did not want to run away, did not want to hide; he wanted to lie down in the shell of his destroyed home and die, as his wife had. But Kristin forced him up and away—she was the one who packed the bread and saltfish she had managed to hide from the enemy, and told him where to go.

*

When the chaplain has been hiding in the marsh for a month, Kristin's younger brother, a boy of thirteen or so, comes to find him. The chaplain has been kept alive by the gifts that occasionally appear on a rock outside the cabin: a fat salmon, a wood grouse, some perch. The chaplain has blessed each gift, thanked God and asked for His forgiveness. He feels he should give a gift in return for all the hospitality he has been shown, but does not know how.

The boy, Anders Elimsson Skogsperä, is serious and taciturn. He has a small bag with him, which he places in the chaplain's hands. It contains bread and salt. Kristin has made it home to her father and mother at the Skogsperä croft. It was she who sent Anders to find him.

"Bless you, Anders," says the chaplain and touches the boy's head. His smooth hair reminds the chaplain of his sons. He withdraws his hand. "What news?"

"The Russians have plundered Nevabacka. They burned the barn to the ground, but the house still stands."

Nevabacka is Skogsperä's neighbouring farm. The chaplain recalls a family connection between the two homesteads. It is natural that the boy is primarily interested in what happens in the vicinity of his ancestral home.

"They came to ours too, but the farm wife of Nevabacka warned us they were coming, and we had time to escape to the woods. The cows, too. We have them there still. Father went down to the croft to look and said that all the buildings were still standing, but that the enemy had been inside. They

64

took everything they could carry, he said. And burned the hay. But Mother said the most important thing was that we were alive."

"Your mother is right about that. Do you know anything of what has happened in Forskant?"

His chapel is in Forskant, the heart of the parish.

"We have seen no one from Forskant, save you."

Please let the chapel be safe, the chaplain prays silently. Let them not have desecrated God's house.

The boy does not stay for long. He wants to return home to his family.

"Pass on my greetings to your father and mother, and tell Kristin that the fewer people who know where I am, the better. But if anyone is in need and could benefit from God's word or sacraments, let them come to me."

These words echo in his head. *Let them come to me,* as if he were the son of God. He blushes and lowers his head.

The boy turns around. He has already gone some distance out on the marsh, along the path the chaplain pointed out for him. The chaplain looks at his thin, lanky outline against a backdrop of golden sedge grass. "Kristin says to stay on good terms with the folk who live here."

The chaplain watches him until he disappears into the woods at the edge of the marsh. A woodpecker takes off from a mountain pine and its red crown stands out from the grey forest.

The chaplain makes sure to toss a piece of bread in the marsh that evening. Then he regrets it and writhes in spiritual anguish all night. A servant of God making offerings to the old gods? Is there any worse sin?

Little by little, people start finding their way to the marsh. The young mistress of Nevabacka comes with a newborn to be baptized, with a farm maid as companion and the boy Anders as guide. He knows the best route by now. It is a bitterly cold winter though snow has not yet fallen. The women are wrapped in grey wool from head to toe. The maid carries the child on her back under shawls. The chaplain receives them with a blessing, invites them to sit down inside the smoky little cabin. The mother is weak after childbirth, pale beneath her shawls.

"You ought not to have come. It is plain to see that you are frail. Anna could have come alone with the child. You are yet to rejoin the congregation since the birth."

The young mother is pallid, but her gaze is focused. "And if they came upon Russians on their journey?" she says. "And I never knew what became of them?"

"If we should have to hide here, Sigrid is the only one with milk for the little one," Anna says pragmatically and quickly unwraps the shawls to expose the baby. "The breast is the only thing that keeps her quiet."

"Did you see anyone on the way hither?"

Anders takes off his cap. He is still standing at the cabin door. "No. But... I thought I heard something. It might have been a gunshot."

"Have you heard word from Forskant?" The chaplain cannot

stop thinking of his chapel. He lies awake at night and imagines it desecrated, up in flames. His dear, beloved chapel.

"The Russians are there. We know nothing more. No one dares go there."

Anna hands the baby to her mother, who brings her to her breast. The girl has chubby little hands that wave around as she suckles.

"She looks strong," says the chaplain.

"They burned the barn. Slaughtered all our animals. We have no livestock left, and nothing with which to buy animals or milk. I hardly know how we shall survive the winter."

"You must put your faith in God," says the chaplain. He gets a strange, bitter taste in his mouth as he utters these words. He swallows, runs his tongue around his mouth to get rid of the taste. "Our Lord God reigns over life on Earth, not we humans." Now it is almost as though the words burn his tongue. The chaplain rises to his feet and goes to the water pail, where he drinks a scoop of water to wash away the bitter taste in his mouth. The other three watch him. The baby lies with her eyes shut in her mother's arms, nursing and half asleep.

The chaplain performs the baptism in haste. He tells them it is because they must be home before dark. They cannot stay there, it is too dangerous. But it is also because, with every moment that he rushes through the recitations, he fears that the words of prayer are going to burn, become caustic lye in his mouth.

When the baptism is over, the chaplain is in a cold sweat. He accepts the gifts the women have brought: bread, turnips, groats for porridge. Anders has brought him a small cooking pot. The chaplain has had nothing to cook with until now.

"Kristin thought you might need this," says the boy. The chaplain looks at him. His straight fringe, his bright young eyes. So like Kristin's honest grey eyes. His narrow shoulders in a knitted jumper. He is suddenly afflicted with a ghastly premonition of some terrible fate awaiting the boy. "God bless you, Anders," he says ardently, and these words do not burn. Anders bows awkwardly. The women have wrapped their shawls around themselves once more. The child is sleeping. "Many thanks," says Anna. The young mother says nothing. Her gaze is already distant, on the other side of the marsh. He wants to say something to her, give her comfort, inspire her to recognize the Lord's grace. He dares not speak. He has no words.

When they have gone, he cooks porridge over a fire on the cabin floor. But the porridge, cooked with these good Christian people's grain, tastes rancid in his mouth. He cannot force down a single spoonful. He has allowed himself to taste meat and fish that came to him in ungodly ways, without God's blessing, and now he cannot eat what God has blessed.

At night he hears the wolves howling. It is a desolate, lonely sound. He feels a sudden urge to rise from the wolfskin fur on which he lies as protection from the cold, to put it on, run outside and cry: Brothers! Take me with you!

He resists. He wants to pray yet cannot remember the words to a single prayer. In wordless torment, his heart turns to God, though he knows that God will not listen to one so far astray. A man of the cloth who has lost his faith.

Finally he falls into a restless sleep, with troubled dreams of running away from the marsh, through the forest, along the fields. Swift as the wind he is, silent and invisible. He runs on all fours, with his brothers and sisters beside him. Their eyes shine yellow in the night. He sees the enemy in the village, but the chapel is still standing. It is no longer his chapel. He runs away from the village, back out towards the marsh, with the winter wind in his nostrils.

When he steps out of the cabin the next morning, he finds a young girl sitting on a rock outside. He cannot see her clearly in the half-light, just her silhouette in the rising mists of the marsh. The mist appears as though full of barely visible forms, gliding along in silence. And she is but one of many such forms, who has happened to sit down for a while.

He stands still for a moment. Wonders whether to address her or wait for her to speak first. From the forest on the other side, he hears the rhythmic pecking of a bird searching a tree trunk for food. The girl looks as though she is listening to the sound. She shakes her head angrily and gets up. Catches sight of him. Curtsies uncertainly, a little bob. Does not speak.

"Good morning, my child," he says. "What brings you here at this early hour?"

"I saw others come here yesterday," she says. "They asked for your counsel and guidance. Is this something you will grant me?"

"Yes, my child." These words, like yesterday's, taste bitter. Give counsel? What gives him the right? Wretched lost soul that he is.

"Even to someone like me?"

Now he understands who she must be. A fallen woman. *God has led a fallen woman to my door*, he thinks. *He is giving me an opportunity to prove that I am worthy, that I can save her soul.* The chaplain convinces himself and gazes at the girl as if she were the Holy Mother Herself. And lo, is that not a halo shining around her head? Yes, so it is, shining through the mist! He cannot see her face at all, but her dress is grey and modest, as befits a woman of her rank. She may have sinned, but she has the right mindset. Humility. He can save her, and in so doing, save himself. He wants to touch the hem of her skirt, to reach out to his saviour, but he controls himself.

"It is for sinners such as yourself that God sent us His only Son. To redeem and save the lowliest, the meekest, the most sinful among us. God loves us all." There. He managed to say the words, they did not hurt him; he believes in them. He believes in God's love.

She appears to ponder what he has said. Something in her posture makes him think that she is not fully satisfied with his answer. It is not what she wanted to hear.

"What does this love look like?" she asks, leaning forward, anticipating his answer. He can see that his response is very important to her. He searches through all the words in his mind, all the sermons he has written, all the advice he has shared as solace and encouragement for his parishioners, fluttering past, all the words, he sees them as though they were butterflies, like flies, leading him all the way back to his seminary days; he hears himself speak vehemently of God's infinite, merciful love, how each and every person who puts their faith in this love shall come to the Kingdom of Heaven, that they may reach heaven even here on Earth. The words get stuck in his throat, gather there, condense into a lump, air cannot flow freely past them, he cannot breathe, his throat tightens, he is suffocating, he falls to the ground...

The woman drops to her knees at his side. She loosens the clothing around his throat, lays her hand on his head and chants over him, a rhythmical rhyme, rising and falling.

He is on the verge of losing consciousness when he finally manages to gasp for breath. He lies on the ground for a long time and pants for air with his head in her lap. He does not dare look up.

He knows now that this is no fallen woman. No, this is a sorceress. A witch. One who adheres to the old beliefs and follows the old ways. She has no doubt come to the marsh to make sacrifices to the old gods, those who dwell in the forest and marsh and lake. He must protect his immortal soul from her influence, but he has lost the ability to utter the word of God. All his past beliefs suffocate and strangle him. Is he any better than she? No. He remains lying on the ground as wave after wave of shame and despair floods over him.

Eventually, he lifts his head. He would rather not set eyes on the witch and instead sits and stares at the marsh and forest beyond. Presently, she speaks again.

71

"They used to love me. Leave offerings for me. They saw me as a mother, a sister. But now…" —her voice breaks—"Now I encounter only fear and greed. All the humans want is to force me into submission." Her voice is as clear and deep as her sorrow. "They defile me and mine. They rob and take, giving nothing in return. So I question this love of which you speak. For I see none of it."

He is not sure he understands. But he must find a way to respond, if not for her sake, then for his own. He must find new words. The old ones have become shameful and poisonous. If he tries to hold them in his mouth again—those old, outdated, outworn words—they shall kill him.

He realizes that he must find the words within himself. Not from scripture. Neither Agricola nor the Bible. They must be his own words. And they must be absolutely true.

"My wife died from the injuries inflicted upon her when she tried to prevent the enemy from taking our sons away," he says slowly. "My boys, Mikael and Mattias, were seven and eleven years old. I tried to offer money, but they only chased me away, and I ended up here, in the marsh."

He takes a deep breath. It is not easy to speak of such darkness and not let it snuff out the tiny flame that burns yet within him. "I do not believe that was God's will. Nor do I believe it was God's punishment. I know that is what I ought to believe. It is how I am expected to see it. These are the words I have spoken to my congregation when their fathers and mothers, brothers and sisters, sons and daughters have died. When they were chased from their homes and land. This is God's will, I have said. God is all-powerful. God…"

He looks around. The mists are still gliding gently and secretively across the marsh. A singular bird calls from the forest.

"God's love is this. The existence of a marsh. Of a bird. That a forest exists, and morning dawns upon the world. God's love is that He never withdraws His hand from me, no matter how much I grieve and weep and rage. Whatever I do, whatever happens in my life, there is always the morning, and the marsh, and God."

The words do not burn or choke him. He sits and gazes across the landscape and slowly begins to feel this love. It flows into him from the marsh, from the morning; it fills his whole being with its warmth. It tells him that he has the strength to bear this too, and that what he needs more than anything is to love the world and love his neighbour, and spread this love as far and wide as he can. Because such is the nature of this love: that the more one shares it, the more one is filled by it.

"You mean to say that this love can also be found in the forest?"

"Yes, it exists everywhere," says the chaplain. He hears that his voice has changed now. It is steady, full of conviction. "Yes. Beneath the forest trees, on the open marshland, on the still surface of the forest lake." He chuckles. "This is where God is, no matter what name or face one might attribute to Him."

He knows that he is speaking heresy. It goes against the teachings of the church. He also knows at once—it dawns as him, as clear as water—that he cannot continue as chaplain. That path is closed to him now; more than a closed door, it is a wall rising all the way up to Heaven. He knows that many priests fulfil their role out of convenience, to make a living, but lack faith, and do not care whether what they teach is true or not. He cannot be one of them. He absolutely refuses.

This realization ought to fill him with deep spiritual distress. Who is he if not a priest? Which path shall he walk, if not that of the church? Yet he feels no suffering. He draws air into his lungs. He feels free.

For the path to God is yet open to him.

"Then spread the word to your brothers and sisters." She is deadly serious, but the sorrow has left her voice. "Tell them this. That there is nothing to fear here. Only love."

"I shall. I do not know who is going to listen, but proclaim this message I shall." He is certain that it is true. Until the day he dies, he shall spread this wisdom to whomever he meets. Proclaim this love.

She stands up. He looks up at her face and sees her clearly for the first time. She has a smooth, high forehead, cloudberry-coloured hair and deep green eyes. When he looks into them, it feels like being embraced by the forest, like lying on the marsh on an autumn day and inhaling the scent of cloudberry and wild rosemary, like running barefoot among wood anemones, like a rustling spruce forest on a midwinter night.

Like a dream of running with wolves.

Then, as the sun rises, she turns around and makes her way across the marsh. She walks straight across, where it is wettest and most treacherous, where no human can walk. Without hesitation, without sinking, she walks, and he does not see her reach the forest edge. Suddenly she is simply not there.

For two years the chaplain, who is no longer a chaplain except in appearances, hides in the cabin on the marsh. He performs baptisms and weddings. One person comes to the marsh again and again, without asking anything from him. It is Kristin, and she comes for his sake. Seeing her walk carefully along the dry, safe passage through the marsh fills him with light and joy every time.

He no longer uses those old, outworn, sullied words. He finds new, bright, light ones. Words to convey the truth he has found within. He reads the New Testament, he reads the word of God. He understands them in a new way.

Every day he prays to God, while he ploughs the little field he has dug in the forest, next to the marsh, while he fishes in the pond a short distance away, while he chops his wood and cooks his fish, while he harvests his turnips, and he knows that God has not forsaken him.

When the enemy retreats and it is safe to emerge into the open again, he does so. The first thing he does is visit Skogsperä. Kristin is waiting there. The years have been cruel, but the people at Skogsperä and Nevabacka have not abandoned their homes. Kristin receives him on the steps of the small croft.

"Kristin," he says and takes her hands in his. "I can no longer be a priest. If you will have me, I would be yours and share my life with you."

She squeezes his hands. She will.

He never speaks of the two beings he met out in the wilderness. It is best not to speak of the forest folk much. Let them be and they shall let us be, people say.

Though the man who once was chaplain remembers the feeling of getting lost in those green eyes. In his dreams he walks in their woods, swims in their clear lakes and runs across the fragrant marshland. And he says nothing more about the wilderness being dangerous or ungodly, or that it ought to be cleared and cultivated.

One spring day, when the birch leaves have newly sprouted, the man who once was chaplain is out ploughing the field. He is helping his father-in-law and young brother-in-law with the spring farm work. The burden is so much less when shared among many hands. He knows that he and Kristin must find a home of their own soon, but this year his father-in-law is happy for the extra help. He is old and has a leg injury from the Cossacks that is unlikely to ever recover.

The man who once was chaplain has rolled up his shirtsleeves and is dusty with earth. His Kristin comes walking across the field carrying a pail of water. He gratefully stops working and drinks from the bucket of cool well water. Then he rinses the dust from his eyes and face.

A woodpecker calls from high in the forest. Like a child, it sounds. They both raise their eyes skyward and see it darting over the forest's edge and away.

"Who goes there?"

It is Kristin that notices them first. The man who once was chaplain dries his face on his shirtsleeve and looks. Someone is indeed approaching along the path. Two wayfarers, not fully grown. Two youths, no longer children but not yet men. Fair-haired, ragged and barefoot, they walk along the path.

Just before he realizes who they are, he sees another figure. A young woman dressed in grey stands at the forest edge and watches the boys as they walk. She ensures that they arrive safely at their destination.

Then he cries out, a loud, wordless cry that rises above the treetops and soars up to the heavens, as he runs with open arms to greet his sons.

JOHANNES

A NEW FARMHAND had been hired on Lammas Farm. A youth of twenty or so, tall and handsome with dark hair and big dark eyes. "Cow eyes," the men said disdainfully. The women, however, were not disdainful. It soon became apparent that this Johannes Andersson had learned exactly how to beguile womenfolk. Not that he was calculating, bawdy or fawning. No, it was rather that he was so evidently enraptured by women, by all women, and foremost those nearly twice his age, that the women could not bring themselves to be annoyed by his attention and flirtations. There was no malice in him; he was like a kitten or a lamb, frolicking around, eager to please and entertain and be rewarded with affection. He showed earnest appreciation for qualities of women that had not received compliments before: their round hips, dimples, their long shiny hair, their laughter or the dainty hollow where their throat met their ribcage. He leaned over them as they churned, carded and knitted, interested in their work. He leaned in so close that they could feel his hot breath on their bent necks. He ran to meet them on the path, helped them carry their loads of wood, water, milk and the little children they were dragging along. And he always had a smile for each and every woman, whatever her age. Grandmothers chuckled and clapped their hands: *The way he talks, to an old crone like me!* Mothers blushed and shooed him away: *The things he says to me, a married mother of five!* The little girls ran around in giggling flocks and hid behind buildings to spy on him and whisper.

The women who had been unmarried for a long time were most bewitched by his attention; women wise to the ways of men's wooing, who thought they knew what they wanted: marriage, a home of their own, a husband to support their family. Women who were waiting for a good man to marry. Who may have already turned down some presumptuous farm boy with no prospects, or a widower with too many children to care for. They were defenceless against Johannes' warm smile, helpless against his hand creeping around their still slender waists on summer evenings, at the mercy of that burning admiration in his eyes.

The first to fall was Anna-Maria, a milkmaid at Lammas, who worked with him on a daily basis. She was over thirty and had never been considered comely before, but under Johannes' gaze she shone like the midsummer sun. All the other men started looking at her differently as well, realizing all of a sudden that she was not so plain after all. Eventually their union produced a child and in the spring Anna-Maria gave birth to a daughter named Anna, and Johannes was named as father in the church register.

But by that time, Johannes had already moved on to the village of Såka and had got a girl with falling sickness pregnant, which was improper indeed, because people with the falling sickness were prohibited from marriage in order to prevent inheritance of the disease. She lived on the little support she received from the congregation, but any recipient of such support must necessarily live a blameless life, and now there was a little daughter, born in the same year as Anna Johannesdotter, as proof that she was certainly not without sin.

The following year it was the daughter of the village shepherd, Liisa, who could not resist Johannes' embrace and honeyed words, and later that year she also gave birth to a daughter, Juliana. People in the parish shook their heads, baffled by the youth's behaviour. Three children with three women in less than two years? Johannes hardly understood it himself. He simply could not resist women—their soft flesh, smooth skin, heady fragrance, and all their lovely places to touch and caress and love. He never entertained the idea of marriage, and so was obligated to pay the fine for defiling a maiden, earned a bad reputation in the community and was forced to move on.

Next, he ended up at Nevabacka, under the roof of the widowed farmer Erik Jonsson. Erik had four children: a young daughter and three even younger sons. Two of the sons were just old enough to start helping on the farm but did not yet have the strength of full-grown men, and as his previous farmhand had left the parish in October, he was in need of a new one.

Perhaps his daughter momentarily slipped his mind, or perhaps rumours of Johannes' behaviour in the neighbouring parish had not yet reached his ears. Or perhaps it was because Brita was still only a child in her father's eyes that he employed Johannes so heedlessly. Besides, the boy's affections had hitherto been focused on older women, while Brita was but seventeen years old.

She was a serious girl with straight eyebrows and a little frown line between them, young though she was. Since her mother's death five years earlier, she had taken on the farm wife duties, together with her grandmother Karin, who was still alive but losing her sight. Brita's three brothers were most dear to her, almost like her own children. According to rumour, the people of Nevabacka had a hint of magic in their blood, because one of their ancestors had lain with a woman of the forest folk, and it was said that uncanny abilities manifested in family members from time to time, or that the occasional child might be born with six fingers or a tail. Indeed, it was even rumoured that Brita's cousin on her father's side had seen Huldra, the Lady of the Forest herself, escort two boys home to their father after they had been kidnapped by the Russians during the Great Wrath.

As for Brita, she had a number of skills, young though she was. Her family were grateful for her ability to staunch blood and reduce fever. Envious tongues gossiped about the time she had saved a child from the Nix by referring to their kinship, while others said that was not Brita at all, but a relative of hers, and that it was not the Nix in any case, but a troll. Lisa of Smalabacka

81

swore that she had seen Brita conjure away rain on a haymaking day, but there were few who believed her.

Brita did not attach much importance to her appearance, wanting only to help and serve her family in all she did. Taking on her mother's roles at the tender age of twelve had been no easy feat, but it had given her a deep understanding of her own worth. She had never received a proposal, but she was still young. As the only daughter of a large farm, she would receive a good dowry, and would not have to settle for just anyone. The farm had been ravaged during the war, when Brita was born, but they had subsequently been granted a few years' tax exemption by the crown, and now they could boast no fewer than seven cows, ten sheep, a horse and a mare. She would marry a rich farmer's son, she had decided, and kept a close eye on the best farms in the area, the boys growing up there and their skills with knife and axe, plough and spade. Did they go to church? Were they good to their father and mother? Did they remove their hats in the company of women, or did they whistle at the girls they saw on the church hill? Were they eager to help with community roofing efforts and haymaking? Since she had a knack for healing, she was often called to other farms, and got an idea of how they lived, how many cows and sheep they had, how many barrels of grain and herring, and bread cakes hanging from the rafters. She listened to the other girls talk about their nocturnal courtships when the boys would visit the girls and sleep by their side in hay barns and sheds. She learned who used a silver tongue to charm his way inside, who could not keep his hands to himself and who was turned away and not allowed in at all. She stored all the information behind her serious forehead and pondered it carefully. However, she had not yet let any boy in to spend the night with her. She had decided that she would only invite in the very best.

She caught Johannes' eye at once. He had previously been drawn to older women, with soft flesh and fine lines around their eyes. And yet there was something about Brita that immediately attracted him. She was so small and stern. He wanted to elicit a twinkle in those dark eyes; he wanted to make that rosy mouth smile; he wanted to unbutton her blouse to see if the same rosy hue adorned her breasts. He could not get enough of her, of the shiny braid that hung all the way down to her round rump, of those pretty arms and incredibly slender waist. She was like a bird, he thought, one he wanted to catch and tame.

Alas, she proved very difficult to approach. She was cold and dismissive, even in the face of his most ravishing smiles. No matter how helpful he was, he got only a polite thank you in return—but it was a smile he wanted, dimples in girlish cheeks, a slight flutter of the eyelashes. He went out of his way to be in Brita's presence as much as possible, coming to meet her when she brought the cows in from the forest, helping her carry the washing from the stream, offering to bring water into the cabin and then lingering while Brita cooked porridge or baked bread or whatever she happened to be doing indoors.

Brita was so young and inexperienced that it took a while before she realized she was being courted. Johannes was new and she thought this was just his way. It was not until she received a visit from Eva of Skogsperä that her eyes were opened. Eva watched Johannes strut away to perform his chores in the barn and finally leave them alone. "Now there's a man who only has eyes you," said Eva.

Brita looked up from her carding in surprise. "Johannes?"

"It's a wonder he gets any work done. He can't stop staring at you."

There were family ties between Nevabacka and Skogsperä, and Eva was Brita's older cousin. The relationship between the larger farm and smaller croft was not always harmonious, because the crofters thought Erik Jonsson demanded too many days' labour. But Eva and Brita had always been good friends, despite Eva being almost a decade older. Since Brita had taken responsibility for her brothers after her mother's death, she had had no time for leisure and companionship, and the girls rarely got the opportunity to sit together and talk. For Brita, it was much needed. Eva had a sister, whereas Brita had so few women in her life. And there was something about Eva that drew Brita to her, so that she sought her out whenever she had a little time to spare, however rarely that was.

After that, Brita paid close attention to Johannes and soon realized that Eva was right. But Brita was not swayed by this—she was a farmer's daughter and would not marry a lowly farm boy. If she did she would became a maid or at most a croft wife, if her father chose to give them some land on the farm property. This was not the life Brita intended for herself.

Sometimes, at night, she had different thoughts entirely. Once, when she and Margareta the milkmaid were out in the forest with the cows, they had to spend the night under a fir tree, because they could not find two heifers that had gone astray. Nils, Margareta's betrothed, came looking for his fiancée. While Nils and Margareta thought Brita was asleep, she heard them making love. The sounds she heard echoed in her ears at night, and she tossed and turned in her bed. She had no words for what she felt, but her body burned so hot that she could not sleep at all.

She paid no heed to such thoughts during the day. They would have no influence on her plans for a sensible marriage. She would not name them; they belonged to the dark of night and there they would stay, forever.

Summer came, and with it the traditional nocturnal courtship. Brita slept out in the barn, and this time several groups of boys came and drew lots to see who got to spend the night beside Erik of Nevabacka's beautiful daughter. But Brita rarely invited anyone in, and Johannes did not have the honour, try though he might, again and again. Johannes spent the whole summer trying to win Brita's favour through acts of service, jokes and flattery, but to no avail. He managed to steal a dance during one of the barn dances that summer, but Brita remained distant and withdrew when he tried to put his arm around her and draw her near. And so it might have continued, had the plague not come.

It came, as it often did, without warning. This time it was smallpox, and it afflicted the children the hardest. Brita, to whom everyone turned in times of need, had to rush from farm to farm, trying to help and heal. But in so doing, she brought the disease home to Nevabacka. All three of Brita's brothers fell ill, as did her father. Brita fought like a mother bear to take care of them all, using every trick she had learnt, praying, hardly sleeping, brewing concoctions and reciting spells. But no matter how hard Brita worked, employing all the knowledge and skills in her possession, she could not save them all. Her two elder brothers died after only a week. The third, her youngest brother, went blind. Her father survived but was very sick and weak for a long time.

Johannes, who was spared the disease, found Brita sitting on the stairs the night after her second brother Daniel had died. She turned her pale little face up to him, and once again he felt the same intense tenderness that gripped him every time she fixed her serious gaze upon him.

"You have shown that you care for me, Johannes," Brita said slowly. Johannes sat down next to her on the stairs and took her hands in his. Yes, he did, he confirmed. He was so desperately fond of her. While she had never given him so much as a smile. He had never dared hope…

"We can marry this autumn. Before the snow comes. It shan't be a big wedding."

She looked out over the fields on the other side of the stream. They were golden now. It was harvest time, but the farm had lost two young men and the third was blind. They could not afford a farmhand. A son-in-law, someone who could take over the farm, that was what was needed now.

She barely noticed Johannes' hands holding hers.

*

Johannes was amazed by this turn of events and could not believe his luck. Brita was fair to behold, and he was fond of her, so he was. She was so different from the other women he had wooed. Quiet, serious and always so clear about her intentions. There was no shame in marrying into the Nevabacka family either. It was much more than Johannes had ever expected from life. From farmhand to farm owner, indeed.

Erik was not against Johannes becoming his son-in-law. He was certainly surprised when Brita came to speak to him where he lay in bed, still weak from illness. His body no longer suffered as much but his heart was in anguish. He had lost two fine sons. And the third would be a dependent for the rest of his life. Erik had truly been harshly afflicted.

"Father, I have decided to marry Johannes," Brita said from the doorway. She stood with her hands clasped in front of her apron and her long plait over one shoulder.

"All right," said Erik slowly. "Are you obliged?"

Brita blushed and quickly shook her head. "No, Father. But we need him on the farm."

She was right, as usual. Now that the matter was settled, she entered the room, brought him a drink and laid her cool hand on his brow. She was skilled at nursing the sick, whether human or animal. She would make an excellent farm wife. He sighed softly. "You should announce the engagement then."

"Yes, but not just yet. After the harvest."

And they spoke no more of it. Brita did not need to prepare

the traditional items for marriage, for she had all she needed already on the farm. Prior to her brothers' death, she would have had no inheritance, but now everything would be passed down to her. The youngest brother would also be her responsibility until the day one or the other of them died. So work continued as before, and as soon as Erik was strong enough, he took part in the harvest.

The residents of Skogsperä, who worked as day labourers on the Nevabacka land, also came to help. The crofter Anders, his wife and their daughters, Eva and Marja, all pitched in, working side by side in the fields. Erik was still weak and had to take breaks to sit in the shade. Brita did as much with them as she could, but also had to go home to look after the youngest brother and see to the cows. One evening, when she had gone home to do the milking and Erik became too dizzy to work beyond noon, Johannes and the Skogsperä family were left in the field. Eva and Marja were doing the farm chores that day. News of Johannes and Brita's engagement had not yet reached Skogsperä. Johannes walked with the scythe and Eva gathered the crop behind him. Johannes chatted and joked with Eva, who was quick-witted and always had a response to everything. How he had missed this! Joking and jesting with comely women. Eva was his ideal woman, he thought, glancing over his shoulder. Plump and ripe as rye. Round, dimpled cheeks and a sunny, playful disposition. He saw the fabric of her blouse tighten across her breasts and felt desire rise in him.

Eva, who was no stranger to men and their ways, could see what was on his mind. She noticed how he looked at her, and that his jokes became increasingly brazen and saucy. She was flattered. Of course she knew of his reputation, for gossip had spread around the parish by this time. She did not mind. It made her feel special. That this young man, who had known so many women, now saw something in her. What harm was there in playing along? She could certainly control herself if need be. And she was curious about this man who had seduced so many seemingly respectable women. So she answered his jokes with jokes of her own. Gave him a taste of his own medicine! She watched his broad shoulders shake with laughter as the scythe whistled through the rye.

They did not stop working until evening fell, bringing coolness with it. She was going home to the croft and he to the loft where he slept during the summer. She was hot, tired and hungry; supper and rest awaited her at home.

"Meet me by the lake," he whispered as they parted. "A swim before supper?" The look he gave her was warm and beseeching.

Surely there can be no harm in that, she thought. *A whippersnapper like him. I am woman enough to resist him.*

She went home with Marja and helped her mother put the pot on the stove. Then she set off for the lake. There was no need to explain or apologize, for she was a grown woman, and not yet married. She worked hard and had never caused her parents any trouble.

It was a warm, windless evening when Eva set off for the lake. She lifted the braid off the back of her neck to cool herself down and thought longingly of the cool water. She temporarily forgot all about Johannes' brown eyes and broad shoulders. She ran her fingers along the tansies and fireweed that grew along the path up to the lake, enjoying the sun shining on her back but not in her eyes, while humming an old harvest song. She saw the lake shining between the birch trees, its water dark and mysterious.

She was so deep in thought that she was startled when Johannes slipped his arm around her waist. There he was, shirtless, his hair dripping wet, standing beside a white birch and laughing at her.

"You frightened me!" Eva said reproachfully. But Johannes drew her close to him.

"I wasn't sure you would come," he whispered. "Oh, Eva, I can't stop thinking about you at night. Your neck." He moved to kiss it, and she let him. "Your breasts." He pressed his mouth on her breasts, and she put her hands on his chest, which was tanned and muscular, and though she thought about pushing him away, his lips sent a rush of warmth through her. It felt nothing like all those other clumsy caresses from boys during the nocturnal courtships of summers past. She sighed and remained motionless, yielding, allowing his lips to wander wherever they pleased, his hands to do as they pleased. *Why not?* she thought. *I want this, I have a right to live my life.*

Afterwards, they lay side by side in the lakeside grass that had been nibbled short by the croft's cow. Eva fell asleep in Johannes' arms and awoke to find him gazing at her. He caressed her cheek. "Eva, beautiful, beautiful Eva," he whispered hoarsely. "You are magnificent, you know that?"

A thought came to her like a breeze across the lake: she was not the first he had called beautiful, not the first he had considered magnificent, and probably would not be the last. Then he leaned forward and kissed her, and was upon her again, young and insatiable as he was. Johannes, her Johannes, and she let him do it all over again and it was even better the second time around.

She washed herself in the lake while he sat on the shore with his arms around his knees, following her every move with his eyes. But the cool lake water did something to her. His gaze no longer felt like pleasurable caresses. It clung to her. She wanted to be alone with the water and the gentle evening. The water was lovelier, cooler, more refreshing on her skin than were his gaze or hands.

I cannot abide him, she thought. "Go home, Johannes," she said, loosening her braid. His cow eyes turned sad, and she smiled to soften her harsh words. "We mustn't be seen walking together, you understand."

He stood up and pulled his shirt on over his head.

She turned away from him to face the lake, dipped once more under the dark surface of the water and stayed there for a long time. When she opened her eyes, she saw only darkness.

On Sunday, Eva saw Johannes in church. Harvest time was over and the rye awaited threshing. She sat on the women's side, on the bench behind the Nevabacka family, and Johannes sat on the same row across the aisle. When she caught his eye, he smiled briefly and turned his head away, as though ashamed. *Is he ashamed? For my sake?* She directed her gaze straight ahead towards the pulpit. She thought about it. Was she ashamed of herself? No. Even here, in church, she could not bring herself to feel ashamed or sinful. *Now I know what it's like*, she thought. *Now I've tried it, and know that there are many ways to feel alive. To lie with a man. To bathe in a lake.*

The sermon was followed by hymns, and then came the announcements. There was one for the engagement of Johannes Andersson and Brita Eriksdotter Nevabacka.

It must have been agreed upon before the evening at the lake. Long before. She could not see Brita's face, only her slender neck, down-bent slightly in prayer or contemplation, with her grandmother by her side. But she was free to stare openly at Johannes, as everyone was looking at the newly engaged youths. He was sitting up straight with his dark curls falling over his brow, staring ahead with red-flushed cheeks. He looked like a little boy caught sucking eggs in the henhouse. Ashamed, yet a little proud, Eva thought. It seemed strange to her how detached she felt, as though their engagement were nothing to do with her. Which, of course, it was not. *A brief spell by the lake, one evening and no more. Brita has promised herself to him for the rest of her life.* She looked at the girl on the bench in front of her and felt pity. For she knew, suddenly and without a doubt, that she would not be the last woman pursued by Johannes.

*

Brita and Johannes' engagement was announced twice more in the church, and autumn advanced, with the smoking and threshing of the rye, and the haymaking, ploughing and slaughtering. The days were filled with work, as always, and the autumn was beautiful. By the end of October, the wedding of Brita the farmer's daughter and Johannes the farmhand drew near.

Even before the wedding, Eva knew for sure: she was with child. It was still early, but there was no doubt that she was carrying. Johannes had impregnated her that evening, and now he was going to marry another. She did not know what to do.

It was not that she wanted Johannes for herself. Not now that she knew what sort of man he was. But she would have to face the shame. A fallen woman with an illegitimate child. And should the baby happen to die during childbirth, everyone would surely believe that she had killed it, and she could be hung as punishment. She did not want Johannes, but she did want a father for her child. He must acknowledge the child as his own and take responsibility, with a fine for fornication, or marriage.

She had not yet told anyone, even Marja. On the night before the wedding, she went to Nevabacka to talk to Johannes.

She preferred not to enter the cottage; it would seem improper for the crofter's daughter to seek out the groom-to-be. So she sneaked around the back of the house, trying to stay out of sight, though there were people everywhere. It had not occurred to her that naturally their home would be full of guests. Far-flung relatives had come to stay in anticipation of the wedding.

Eventually she found him, sitting behind the barn with some other farmhands, having a drink. She watched him from the shadows for a moment. He brushed his dark hair away from his eyes, drank from the flagon and passed it on. She tried to recall the way she had felt about him during the harvest and by the lake. The lust, the attraction to him, to his body. But she felt nothing at all, except fear of birthing this child and having no father for it.

The flagon must have been empty by now, and while all the other farmhands swayed as they got to their feet, Johannes rose steadily. He appeared less inebriated than the others, which was good. He said something and the other young men laughed before disappearing around the corner of the barn. Johannes turned to the barn wall and relieved himself. Eva averted her gaze. Then, when he started walking towards his loft, she hurried out of the shadows.

"Johannes," she said quietly, and he turned around.

"Eva!" He stopped in his tracks, clearly delighted to see her. When she approached him, he reached his hands out towards her, and without thinking, she walked over and grasped them. Then he quickly let go of her hands and wrapped his arms around her waist instead. He pulled her closer towards him and for a confused moment she thought, *he knows—how could he know?—and everything is going to be all right*, and she leaned on him and the burden that had been weighing on her immediately lightened.

Then she felt his lips on her throat. His hands squeezed her waist, crept up to her breasts. She froze and tried to shoo him away.

"Please, Eva." He was panting heavily, his breath smelled like schnapps, and now his hands were fumbling with her skirt. "It was so good last time, was it not?"

Anger swelled in her. She pushed him away, hard.

"Johannes, I am with child."

He stood there with his arms by his sides and looked at her, still panting.

"Then it can't hurt to do it again, one last time…" He held out his arms and tilted his head. He tried to use his dimples, his sweet words and flattery.

Slowly, his words sunk in.

"One last time? You still intend to marry Brita?"

He looked taken aback. "Why, yes, we are engaged."

"And the child?"

He ran his hand through his hair in what looked to her like a girlish, coquettish gesture. He shrugged his shoulders and looked helpless. "Not much to be done about that." Then something seemed to occur to him. "Or perhaps there is? You're not far gone. Brita knows about these sorts of things. Maybe she could…"

"You want your betrothed to get rid of our baby?" He nodded eagerly, like a puppy. She could not believe he would suggest such a thing—it was a sin. How could he fail to see how absurd his words were? She had to make sure she had understood correctly. "You want to tell your betrothed, the woman who is to become your wife tomorrow, that you have impregnated me during your engagement, and ask her to employ the dark arts to get rid of the child?"

"I shall help you."

Eva turned around. There by the granary stood Brita, holding a flagon and a loaf of bread. She had come to deliver them to her husband-to-be and his friends. Her face was very pale beneath the shawl wrapped around her head and shoulders. The autumn evening was cold.

"Brita, I didn't know. When Johannes and I... I thought he was unattached. I swear it."

"I believe you." Brita's voice was expressionless. Lifeless. A cow lowed from inside the barn. A solitary bird screeched in the forest. "I know what we must do. But we must do it now, tonight." She held the flagon and bread out to Johannes. "You take these. We're going out to the marsh. We can find what we need there."

The look Brita gave Eva was cryptic, but made Eva inclined to obey despite not understanding. She followed Brita, with Johannes stumbling close behind. Eva could not think straight. It was all so dreadful, so awful. The woodpecker squawked, the night was dark and cold, and surely there were bears and wolves in the forest. She did not want to follow her at all, she did not want any of this, but what choice did she have? Johannes would not marry her or take responsibility for the child. Should she have it alone? Bring shame upon her parents? She imagined her father's face, how he would look at her with disappointment, perhaps even contempt.

Suddenly she remembered the maid she had once seen in the shame stocks outside the chapel when she was a child. A Russian bride, they had called her. The Cossacks had taken her by force when she tried to hide in the forest with her brothers. Her brothers were tortured to death, while the maid wound up pregnant.

In her despair, the maid had killed the baby at birth. It was a terrible crime, the worst imaginable. Then she drowned herself and her body was buried with that of the child outside the cemetery wall.

All at once, Eva reverted to her eleven-year-old self, being told this terrible story, but she was also the maid with the illegitimate child, floating in the water, denied consecrated ground for all eternity. The same fate could await her. If she got rid of it now... But that was also a sin. The forest around her rustled and whispered of her sins, and it felt as though everyone must know of her wickedness. She sobbed, and stumbled, but did not stop following Brita's pale figure along the path. She could barely see Johannes in the darkness, but Brita was visible, walking in front of her, with her back straight and her shawl wrapped several times around her. When she heard Eva's sobs, she stopped and turned, and when Eva, in her desperation, tripped on the path, she rushed to catch her.

They continued through the forest, hand in hand, like two children on their way to pick berries for their mother. And like a child, Eva felt small and helpless, and lost in the darkness. The only thing she had to hold on to was Brita's warm hand.

They arrived at the marsh, a vast and colourless expanse stretching out before them. The moon had risen and was reflected in the larger pools of water. Then Brita straightened her back and, without a word, took the flagon and bread from Johannes and flung them far out into the marsh. They disappeared into a pool of water with a faint splash.

"A gift for you." Her clear girlish voice rang out crisply over the marsh, which was silent as though listening. Johannes had sat down on a rock. He yawned widely. Brita turned to Eva and Johannes.

"I shall help you, as I promised. But first I must know. Johannes, would you not do the proper thing: break our engagement and marry the woman carrying your child instead?"

Johannes shuddered and looked up in surprise. A wrinkle of worry appeared in his brow.

"Is that what you want, Brita? They have announced our engagement in church and everything."

"What I want is of no importance. The question is which path you choose."

Johannes hesitated. "No, I think keeping my promise to you is the right thing to do." He seemed content with his decision and stood up from the rock. "Sometimes children are born into this world, and sometimes they are not, and that is in God's hands."

He is thinking of other children he has fathered, Eva thought. He has never cared about them, or the girls he has got into trouble. He thinks only of himself.

This realization gave her a feeling of peace. She could not have a child with such a man, and on the neighbouring farm besides. She looked at Brita and gave her a quick nod. Brita began to undress in the moonlight and gestured to Eva to do the same. Delighted, Johannes sipped his drink. He certainly had not been expecting this, but he was not going to say no.

Soon the two women stood naked before him, side by side.

Then Brita showed Eva what they must do.

It was Brita who saved Eva's honour. She swore in front of the lawman and the priest that Johannes had broken off their engagement with her the night before the wedding and promised to marry Eva instead. And even though a babe conceived during engagement was still legally illegitimate, in the eyes of society it was the same as if it were within wedlock. Johannes had been a philanderer, that was for sure, and had brought hardship upon many women's lives. What he had done to Brita of Nevabacka was wrong. But in the end he did right by Eva of Skogsperä. What happened to him after that, no one knew. Perhaps he was taken by a wolf or a bear, perhaps he changed his mind and moved on—that was what the young men of the parish thought, anyway. In any case, he was never seen again.

In the spring, when Eva's labour pains set in, it was Brita she wanted by her side. The baby was born in the croft sauna, a fine and healthy child. He was named Johan Johannesson. But some of the womenfolk looked askance at Brita. Anyone who could staunch blood flow and heal afflictions as well as she could must have other knowledge as well. Since time immemorial, everyone had known that people like her could cast spells and curses. And there were some who claimed that a slender young rowan tree had started growing very suddenly at the edge of Vittermåsa, one that Lisa of Smalabacka swore had never been there before. Greta of Backsjö, who had come to the marsh to meet her suitor Juuso from the neighbouring parish—of whom her parents did not approve—swore she heard a man's voice whispering sweet words in her ear while she rested under the rowan.

It was a beautiful rowan tree that bore red berries, even when all the other rowans around had long since dropped theirs.

THE TRIAL

J URYMAN NILS FORSHÄLLA was on his way home from the council meeting. He was tired and hungry, and a long, dark path stretched before him. He lived by the river, a fair distance from the church. His wife and supper awaited him at home. The children would be asleep by now. Nils Forshälla had served as juryman for over ten years and was accustomed to a broad range of disputes and settlements. But today's case had been particularly distressing.

Last autumn, Evert Wilhelmsson Nevabacka had accused his crofter Johan Johannesson Skogsperä of arson when Evert's granary burned down. Evert claimed that Johan had set fire to the barn when he, Evert, refused to abstain from draining a marsh on Nevabacka land. Johan was the last person to be seen in the vicinity of the grain store, and there was no obvious explanation for how the fire started. Johan swore his innocence, but when several witnesses attested to his numerous attempts to prevent the Nevabacka farmer from draining the marsh, Johan was sentenced to prison and a fine, and it was a heavy fine for a humble crofter.

This time, Evert Wilhelmsson had returned to the council with another case: he was accusing Johan's wife Fredrika of dabbling in the dark arts. She had set a snake on him and afflicted his six-year-old grandson with rickets and his daughter with a raised rash. She had also supposedly summoned ghosts to prevent him from carrying out his work in peace, and it was her fault that all the calves born that year were sickly and wasted away. Indeed, many were the accusations he brought to the council.

It had been a hundred years since the great witch trials in these parts, in which shackles and many other dubious methods were used to get women and men to confess that the devil had bitten them on the shoulder and breast, promising them gold and riches and everything they desired. So when the council was assembled, there were more attendees than usual. District Judge Sturesson considered this a very special occasion and took his time describing the case in detail for those present, starting with all that had happened last autumn. Meanwhile, Johan's wife Fredrika sat quietly and calmly with her black headscarf tied tightly around her fair head and looked straight at Nils. She was younger than her husband, and their only child, a daughter of about seven years, sat on her lap. Nils had never seen Fredrika before. Or perhaps he had from the other side of church, but had never noticed her. She was no beauty, but neither was she unpleasant to look at. She was very thin—food must have been sparse at their croft—and dressed all in black, in her Sunday best. Yet there was something about her eyes; Nils could almost feel them boring into him. Why had she chosen him specifically to focus on? Might she have heard rumours of his mercy that had given her hope?

Evert listed all of Fredrika's sins. He never called her a witch, but he pointed out one misfortune after another, all of which occurred when Fredrika had visited Nevabacka. She had praised his cows, saying that they were fine creatures. Then all the calves born that spring wasted away and died! Not a single one survived. Then, one day when Evert came across Fredrika down by the stream, where was she washing clothes with her daughter by her side, she gave him such a wicked look that he knew some terrible mishap was awaiting him. And sure enough, later that day, a snake came slithering straight towards him as he was going to the outhouse and bit him on the calf. Everybody knew that there were folk who had the power to set a snake upon someone in such a way that nothing, not water nor fire, not any obstacle it might encounter on the way, could prevent the serpent from finding and biting its victim. Evert had lain sick in bed with a bad foot for several weeks after, incapacitated and unable to help with the spring tasks, which was a great misfortune.

Now it was the committee's job to decide whether Fredrika was guilty or not guilty, and the judge's job to decide on the submission of evidence and punishment. But first Fredrika must say her piece. She lifted her daughter from her lap and stood before the committee, straight-backed and dignified. She looked directly at Nils.

"I have no dealings with snakes or strange beings. I have neither the power to cure disease nor cause it, though I wish I

103

did. I heard that Evert's own mother Brita was skilled in such arts, so I fail to understand why he should fear them so. All I have done since last autumn is try to keep myself and my little daughter Ingrid alive. What would I gain by Evert of Nevabacka being bitten by a snake? He has enough venom in him as it is."

This brought a smirk to many a juryman's face, but not Nils. Something about this story brought to mind a rumour he had heard about Evert which he could not fully recall now.

"If you must know, gentlemen, I was at Nevabacka to beg for alms." She stood just as tall as before, though a little redness burned on her cheeks. "Milk, for Ingrid. Their maid has a kind heart, she took me to the barn, out of her master's sight. When I saw what fine cows they had, I spoke a few words of praise. Surely that is no crime. And I always do my washing down at the stream; everybody in the village knows that. It was Evert of Nevabacka who had no honourable business there." Now her gently blushing cheeks had become large red roses. "He probably thought that a poor unaccompanied crofter's wife like me would be easy prey, now that I have no man at home. But he was wrong. Many people can testify to the fact that he was dripping wet when he returned from the stream that day. I pushed him in—yes, I did and I am not ashamed—to protect my honour. He has a weakness for womenfolk, you need only ask the milkmaids at his farm."

The jurymen exchanged glances. Just a few years ago a case had come to the council about a maid at Nevabacka who claimed her illegitimate child had been sired by the farmer.

"Naturally, his pride was hurt and so he invented the story about the snake. His horse was bitten by a snake last summer and a farmhand two years before that. There are many snakes at Nevabacka."

"And that's your fault, you bitch!" Evert slammed the bench with his fist. "You have cursed my farm since the day you arrived at Skogsperä!"

"In which case I have done a very bad job, considering all the good fortune Nevabacka has enjoyed since I have been at Skogsperä," said Fredrika bitterly. "Which farm in the village pays the greatest tithe to the crown? Is it not Nevabacka?"

Nils knew that this was the case. Nevabacka had fifteen cows, twenty sheep, and both oxen and horses. Last summer's harvest had produced fifteen barrels of barley and five barrels of rye.

"And as for the ghosts plaguing the master of Nevabacka, may I remind you that hauntings are usually brought about by something in one's own conscience."

The pastor, who sat on the committee, nodded thoughtfully.

Suddenly Fredrika turned very grave, and her voice softened.

"I was greatly saddened to hear of little Tomas' ailments," she said quietly. "But my own Ingrid was very sick also. It was a cruel disease that plagued these parts last winter. I had nothing to do with it. And Kajsa has suffered from rashes every winter, even I know that."

"And how do you explain so many misfortunes tormenting Nevabacka ever since Johan and Evert's dispute over the marshland?"

105

"What about the misfortunes that have tormented Skogsperä?" Fredrika straightened her headscarf, which had slipped to one side, revealing a single lock of long fair hair. She did not seem to notice. The curl of hair gave her a girlish appearance, Nils thought. He wondered if this would be to her aid or detriment in the minds of the other jurors. "My husband is in jail. My only child was at death's door over the winter. I shall have to sell my only cow for grain to make bread this winter. No seed, no milk. Soon I shall have to rely on church handouts, or else we must leave the croft."

As she uttered these final words, Evert leaned back on his bench contentedly and rubbed his hands on his trousers.

"Nobody believed my Johan when he said it was the faerie folk that burned down the Nevabacka granary, as a warning."

She hesitated, glanced at Evert. Nils Forshälla watched her curiously. There was something she was not saying. Something relevant to this case. He was sure of it. She swallowed and returned her gaze to the committee. "I say the same thing now as Johan did then: the people of the forest are issuing their final warning. Evert of Nevabacka is continuing with his plan to drain the marsh in the approach to spring. Soon they will stop warning and start taking from him that which he holds most dear."

"Do you hear?" Evert leapt to his feet again. "She threatens me, just as her husband did!"

The judge made him sit down again, but he refused to calm down.

106

"Is that so? Are you threatening the farmer?" the judge asked severely.

Fredrika shook her head. "I only speak the truth, so that when misfortune does arise, you cannot blame me."

She is wrong about that, thought Nils. *She believes that by warning him of impending disaster she will be able to prove her innocence. In reality she is doing the opposite.*

Now it so happened that District Judge Sturesson was not raised in the countryside, but was a town pastor's son. He was ignorant of the sorts of creatures and beings that might live in the forest, land and water. What he saw was a woman trying to blame incidents on fairy tales. He was a man of science and had studied in Turku. She must have given the cows something, he thought, some herb or plant that caused the calves to die. And she admitted that the illness last winter had affected her daughter— perhaps she had deliberately spread it to Nevabacka. He did not believe that she could be blamed for the snake attack, however. He intended to sentence her to pay a fine for her wicked deeds.

But the pastor knew that Skogsperä could never afford to pay a fine, and should the croft be further burdened, the church would have yet another family to support with alms and charity. Johan would no doubt come out of prison eventually, and then there was a chance that they could get back on their feet. It would be better for the village that way. Therefore he was inclined to find Fredrika not guilty of all accusations.

As for Nils, he could not shake the feeling that something was not right at Nevabacka. He agreed with the pastor.

It ended with the committee acquitting Fredrika Karlsdotter Skogsperä of the accusations Evert Wilhelmsson Nevabacka had levelled against her. And without established guilt, the district judge could not impose a fine on her, and thus he went home in a bad mood.

When the committee dispersed, Nils saw a scene unfold, which he was not supposed to have witnessed. He had come out ahead of everyone else, but was subsequently stopped by the pastor down at the crossroads to discuss the annual road inspection. So it was that Nils was there to see Fredrika and her daughter begin their long walk home through the forest. It was already dusk. But when Fredrika and her daughter reached the foot of the hill, where a large hedge grew that would soon be in flower, a shadow detached itself from the tree and approached Fredrika. Nils was too far away to see the face, but he recognized Evert of Nevabacka by his hat and posture. He stopped in his tracks. Evert might be up to no good, and Fredrika might need help.

"You know you cannot continue living here without Johan," Evert growled from under his hat. "You may as well give up now. Take your child and move into the poorhouse. You have no son to help work the land. Skogsperä must return to the ownership of Nevabacka."

Fredrika, who had been so straight-backed and proud throughout the trial, so collected and dignified, suddenly grasped Evert's arm with both hands and leaned towards him. Her pale face almost shone in the darkness.

108

"Please, Evert, get a hold of your senses! Leave the marsh alone, before it's too late. Think of the children, of Gösta's and Kajsa's children. Of your little Arne! You don't want anything to happen to them!"

The farmer seemed surprised by her sudden outburst. He backed away, momentarily speechless. A small hesitation, a doubt, made the tall figure tremble. Then he shook off her hands. He turned to the little girl, who was standing next to her mother, and grabbed her by the chin. The child stood completely still, and her mother also appeared as though frozen to ice. The farmer ran his fingers along the girl's neck. Slowly.

"You ought to be careful that nothing happens to your sweet little Ingrid," he said quietly, and something in his voice made Nils head towards the three of them at once. But before he could reach them, Evert turned around and disappeared up the hill with long strides.

Nils continued towards Fredrika, who had pulled her daughter close. They stared straight at him but Fredrika did not seem to recognize him at first. Then she half-turned away, as though ashamed, and pulled her daughter behind her.

"I must leave the croft."

"I am sure I can help you with some seed, if that is what you need."

"No. No." At first that was all she could say, then after a few moments she turned to him. Her eyes were in shadow.

"We are no longer safe there without Johan."

She took the girl by the hand and started walking along the path.

109

Nils lingered awhile to make sure that Evert did not return. Then he followed the river home, with a heavy, brooding heart.

He thought of Nevabacka. Of the maid that had worked there last summer, a young slip of a girl, she was. Evert had bid a paltry sum for her at the poorhouse auction. Thirteen or fourteen, she was. She had disappeared quite suddenly last autumn. Nils' wife had heard rumours that she was with child.

As he stepped inside the door of his home, he took a deep breath. It felt like the darkness outside still clung to him for a moment. But there was his wife in her cap and striped skirt, and there were candles shining in their holders, and there on the table was a steaming pot of porridge. He took off his coat and sat down at the table.

She handed him his porridge spoon. "How did it go tonight?"

"I fear Fredrika of Skogsperä and her Ingrid will end up in the poorhouse. Evert of Nevabacka will see to it. There is something not right there."

"At Nevabacka?" His wife sat down at the table and looked gravely at her husband. "I feel the same way. I have wondered whether the granary fire was an accident." He looked at her in surprise. She shook her head. "I don't know anything for certain, and I never even heard a rumour about it, but... Well, you remember the maid who disappeared last autumn? Everyone thought she took advantage of the chaos of the fire to run away. She was with child, I know that much. Evert can't keep his hands off his maids. I heard that she had been to Tobacco-Maria to ask for advice."

Nils helped himself to porridge and waited. He knew his wife would get to the point soon enough. She just had to give him all the details first, to let him form his own opinion. She knew that was what he wanted—it was a habit he had acquired from being on the council for so long.

"One trick for a woman who wants to get rid of a baby she is carrying is to squat over a tub of very hot milk." She quickly looked up at him. "Now, I know that it is a crime and a sin. I am only repeating what I have heard. That is what Tobacco-Maria advised the maid to do. And I have been thinking about it ever since. Where would a maid go to secretly heat up milk? Where is there a kiln that often goes unused?"

"You mean to say that the girl lit the kiln in the granary to heat the milk, and when the fire spread she fled in fright?"

His wife looked at him.

"Maybe. Maybe she got out in time."

"Nothing was found in the barn," Nils said slowly. He put down his spoon. He had gone off his porridge. "It burned to the ground."

He thought about how difficult it had been getting Evert Nevabacka to pay the fine for his deed the first time around. He thought about the farmer's hand on Ingrid's tender throat. He thought about how quickly fire could spread, and how often granaries and barns and crofts burned down.

FOREST SISTER

WHEN THE SNOW HAS MELTED and the ground is bare, finally, Ingrid goes out to greet her sister. She runs barefoot while everyone else is still wearing shoes. At first her feet ache from the cold. But she cannot find her sister with her boots on. In footwear they are strangers to each other, she and her sister. They could cross paths without even recognizing one another.

When she is barefoot, everything is different. There is a path leading from the cottage to the forest. She has bounded along that path every day of her summer life. She usually first goes barefoot around the end of April, and it is as if her feet come alive. They greet every root and rock. They know where the land is rough and where it is smooth, where it is wet from wild-running streams and where it is soft with springy moss. She walks slowly at first, enjoying the sensations as her bare skin comes into contact with pine needles, soil and leaves. A sense of awakening rises through her body. She breathes in the scent of rot and decay, of water and waking earth, of rising sap and sun-warmed bark. Her ears, filled all winter long with the wind whistling in the treetops and storms sneaking around the house, can now hear cranes calling loudly above the forest canopy, and flies waking from sleep, and little birds chirping everywhere. At night, she hears eagle-owls hooting, and early in the morning, she hears black grouse frolicking outside the house. The trees drip and the wind sounds different through snowless branches. Once her whole body feels fully awakened, she begins to run, overjoyed that her feet know the way as surely as they did last summer. She does not need to look down.

She and Ma lived at Forshälla for a year. That was when Pa was in jail. Ingrid missed her sister terribly during that time and was so afraid that they might forget one another. But as soon as Ingrid came to see her once again, it was as if they had never been apart.

Her sister is waiting for her by the forest lake, in the den they built together under the dense branches of an old fir tree. At last, they are reunited.

Ingrid is so grateful for her sister. She has no siblings at home in the Skogsperä croft, and Arne of Nevabacka is too big to want to play with her. All the other farms are too far away to walk to.

But Ingrid's forest sister always has time for her. They play such wonderful games. Her sister shows her where polypody ferns grow, and they nibble on the bittersweet roots after washing them in the lake. Whenever Ingrid is with her sister, she always seems to have some tasty treat or other in her mouth: wood sorrel in spring; sap when the warm sun makes the trees bleed; wild strawberries and blueberries and raspberries and cloudberries in summer; and then, later in the year, lingonberries and cranberries. Even the willow flute she carved all by herself has its own special taste. They taste everything: mosses and birch leaves, spruce shoots and ground elder, blueberry leaves and dandelion buds.

When Rosie the cow goes out to graze, it is Ingrid's job to take her into the forest and bring her home again, which she loves to do because it means she can spend all day with her sister if she likes. Ma was worried at first.

"She is so little," she said to Pa on the May day when the ground was finally turning green again, when the last of the hay and grain stores were finished and the skinny cow and tiny calf could be set free to find their own food.

But there was no one else to do it, because Ma and Pa were busy with the spring chores, and Pa gave Ingrid a horn to blow in case she saw wolves or wolverines or other dangers. She wore it proudly over her shoulder but never had cause to use it. They made enough noise to keep predators at bay—her sister made sure of that—and besides, they had better game than little girls to hunt in summer. Once a forest reindeer doe and fawn passed by very close to their lakeside den, and Ingrid and her sister lay silent and still, watching the little fawn's slender legs step as soundlessly as the doe's through the moss. Ingrid could see the gnats buzzing around its soft muzzle and its little ears flapping to swat them away from its large eyes.

"We shan't say anything to Pa," whispered Ingrid, once the animals had moved to the other side of the lake. "Else he'd shoot them." She knew that Uncle Ivar had shot a forest reindeer last winter and been boasting about it ever since. Her cousins, Lauri and Anna, said the meat was delicious and they could all eat their fill many times over. Ever since then, Pa had been keen to shoot one too, but it had been a long time since anyone had seen one. There used to be many, according to Great-grandpa Anders. His father used to go reindeer hunting every autumn and winter, and rarely came home empty-handed.

"No, we shan't say a word," she confirmed resolutely and sat up. She wanted that little fawn to live in peace.

She and her beloved sister fished in the little lake—while Rosie nibbled on the sedge grass—and sometimes they got a bite. Ingrid did not know how to make a fire, so she took the fish home to her mother, who made them into a delicious soup with turnips. On these occasions, Ingrid received praise, which she was not used to. Ma would send her out with the cows in the morning with a piece of bread, and if she got very hungry she could always take a sip from Rosie's teats.

Ingrid's sister gifted her a tame little greenfinch, which always came to say hello when she was up by the lake. It sat on her fishing rod, which she had made herself, and watched as she fished. She fed it breadcrumbs and enjoyed listening to its squeaking trill and watching it as it flew.

Ingrid's sister could do anything. She could swim underwater with the loons, she could fly high in the sky with the ravens, and she could burrow into earth dens with the foxes and badgers. The only thing Ingrid could do almost as well as her sister was climb the dense pines, with her toes curled around the branches and her hair full of ants and needles.

Sometimes Ingrid wasn't allowed to go out to see to her forest sister. Then she would leave her messages and gifts at the forest edge outside the croft: a lovely smooth stone and a feather from one of their hens in a hollow tree by the cairn; a piece of eggshell on the magic stone behind the outhouse; a small wreath of dandelions over the gnarled stump on the path up to the lake. Ingrid knew her sister found these little messages and understood their meaning: I am thinking of you, I miss you, you are important to me.

Then one spring, Ingrid finally got what she had been longing for—a little brother. Ma had been as big as a barn door for a long time, and then one day Haapa-Kajsa came, and Ingrid was not allowed to be there when Haapa-Kajsa helped deliver the baby. It was early spring, and she had to go with her father to Uncle Ivar and Aunt Elna's house in the neighbouring village and have supper there. Ingrid was too excited and curious to eat. Pa looked concerned, and Aunt Elna shook her head and said something about hoping everything would be all right this time. Ingrid did not understand why she could not be at home with her mother. When they finally set off, Ingrid danced all the way home with her father walking behind.

Back home in the cottage, Haapa-Kajsa was waiting with a little bundle in her arms. She muttered something to Pa, who took one look at the bundle and went straight out to the barn. Haapa-Kajsa laid the bundle next to Ma, who was lying in bed.

Ingrid walked over to the bed and looked down curiously at her little brother. He looked a little different from the babies she had seen before, but then again she had not seen very many. Ingrid sat there for a long time, gazing at her brother, while Ma looked tired and sad.

"What's his name?" she asked.

"Lars," Ma replied wearily. "We shall see how long he lives."

But Lars did live, and grew big, and Ingrid understood from the way the grown-ups spoke that he was not like other children. His head was too big and he had trouble holding it up on his little neck. His limbs looked like skinny twigs compared to his large head. But his eyelids were as thin as wild pansy petals, and his skin was soft like coltsfoot leaves. He looked up at Ingrid with big dark blue eyes and gripped her finger with his surprisingly strong and stubborn little fist. And he was hers, her own little brother, whom she had so longed for.

Ingrid was happy.

However, she could see that her parents were not. Pa barely looked at Lars, and though Ma took good care of him, she did so without joy. Ma had never had much joy in her heart, and all the times she had laboured only to bring forth early-born, stillborn babies had stolen the smile that Ingrid could remember seeing when she was very small and Ma used to sing "Dear Goose" to her and bounce her on her knee. Now that smile seemed to have gone forever and Ma's lips were eternally fixed in a thin, firm line. It was not until one Sunday in winter out on the church hill that Ingrid understood why.

Ma and Pa were standing at the church door, talking to the priest. Ma had Lars in her arms. Ingrid had run over to Tar-Mattas' horse, harnessed to a sleigh, while Tar-Mattas and his brother were talking to some of the old men of the village. Tar-Mattas' horse was very friendly and didn't frighten Ingrid at all. She stood by his head and scratched his neck and spoke affectionately to him. Then three old women of the village came walking past, whom Ingrid recognized as Walborg, Mårten's wife Elin and Tobacco-Maria. They lived in the main village, close to the church, and Walborg in particular lived very close by and took pride in knowing all about the comings and goings of the village. At least that is what Uncle Ivar said. The old women did not notice her, but stopped by the church steps when they saw Ma and Pa. Walborg pulled her woollen shawl tighter around her neck and scoffed.

"A little late now," she said. "Trying to appeal to God's mercy and forgiveness. You can see by that child of hers how hardened her heart is. That is punishment for her sins."

Ingrid froze. Had Ma sinned? One must not sin. Else one ends up in hell, as the priest had said many a Sunday.

"Haapa-Kajsa said that she turned to sorcery to cure her childlessness," said Tobacco-Maria, taking a puff on her pipe. The smoke billowed up into the clear winter sky. Ingrid stood as still as she could so that the old women would not hear the snow crunch beneath the soles of her shoes. "She went to perform witchcraft down by the Johannes-rowan on Vittermåsa. You know the one. The one that grants fertility."

"Well, if she resorted to magic it's no wonder the child looks like a changeling," Walborg nodded.

"He's not a changeling, he's a punishment from God!" Mårten's wife Elin said in a bitter voice. "One mustn't consort with the forest folk. The pastor said…"

Ma and Pa came down from the church steps and the old women stopped their gossiping and hurried through the gate. Ingrid stood pressed up to the horse and sucked on her braid.

A changeling? She knew what that meant but it did not apply to Lars. He was a normal little human person, even if he did look different. Could his enlarged head be a punishment for Ma? Ingrid could not make any sense of this. She wished she had never heard the old women's malicious talk and spat angrily at them in the snow.

Lars was no punishment. He was her beloved little baby brother.

About a year after Lars' birth, Ma gave birth to live twin boys. They were strong and healthy and everything that babies should be. Yet no joy returned to Ma's speech or behaviour. She was very busy with the twins, and caring for Lars increasingly became Ingrid's responsibility. As the years passed, the twins grew and soon surpassed Lars in both strength and intelligence. Lars never learned to speak, and he had to be carried everywhere and fed and looked after like a baby, even when his brothers were already walking and eating by themselves. Ingrid could see that

Ma found this a great burden and had no patience with Lars at all. Ingrid made sure to keep him out of her way as much as possible. She fed him before she fed herself and took him with her when she worked and played. She could usually tell what he wanted. She taught him to point to things he wanted to look at more closely, and she knew that if he moved his arms in a certain way, it meant he was happy, while another movement meant he was sad or in pain.

They played with her sister out in the forest every day. Her sister did not judge Lars or say that he was a punishment or had anything wrong with him. Together they would come up with all sorts of ways to amuse him: Ingrid lured the greenfinch over with breadcrumbs, and Lars gurgled happily and waved his fists at the bird as it hopped around by their feet. Sister made it rain on the other side of the lake, and Ingrid held Lars up to let him see the beautiful rainbow arching over the marsh beyond. The girls picked all possible treats from the forest and took turns spoiling Lars with sweet wild strawberries, raspberries and blueberries. Sister helped Ingrid find beautiful yellow flowers that grew at the edge of the marsh, and Ingrid hung them as decorations from the roof of their den so that Lars could lie on a bed of soft, dry moss, look up at the yellow blossoms and enjoy their sweet, mild fragrance. Sister led a family of foxes past their little hideaway so that Lars could watch the funny little fox cubs leaping and playing on the lake shore. Lars was always utterly content and at peace out in the woods with his sisters, and Ingrid could not imagine him being a burden in any way whatsoever.

It was harder in winter, when the short, cold days forced them to stay indoors. How harshly the cold would nip at them if they dared venture out. Then it was a struggle to keep Lars happy and entertained and out of everyone else's way. Ingrid's heart grew so heavy when Ma would snap at Lars if he spilled food on his frock, and if Lars cried and fussed Pa would grumble from his corner of the room that someone had better quieten that child. Wherever the twins were, Lars wanted to be too, doing the same thing as they were, which often infuriated their mother.

"Can't you keep him out of the way?" were words Ingrid often heard. And she did her best. But she longed for spring when she and Lars could go outside again, to the freedom of the forest.

This year, however, spring was biding its time. The spring months came, bringing lighter days, and the calls of migratory birds could be heard across the land, but still the snow remained. The time for sowing came and still the snow remained. Pa went out every morning to look for signs that warmer days were coming, and the frown lines in Ma's brow deepened. The times when Ingrid had to go to bed with hunger clawing at her belly, like an angry little animal, became more and more frequent.

Ma baked bread that was more tree bark and chaff than barley and rye.

By May, the snow was still deep, and there was not a single blade of hay or dried birch twig to feed the animals. Father had no choice but to slaughter them all. First the sheep, then

121

the cow. It put food on the table, and since they didn't need to survive on bread, they saved some seed to sow when the ground eventually thawed.

Ingrid understood what was happening. She saw how weak their poor diet was making Lars and the twins. And yet, in some ways the worst part was not being able to see her sister, whom she missed so.

It was not until June that meltwater began to drip from the roof. It was not until June that Ma and Pa could sow seed in the soil, and not until June that Ingrid could take Lars out into the forest. This time Ingrid built another shelter in a forest dell behind the croft, so she did not have to carry Lars as far as before. He was getting a lot heavier these days. From the new shelter she could also hear if Ma was calling for her. She was older now and really ought to be helping with the farm work, but for the most part Ma let her run free because she took such good care of the boy and kept him out of the way.

Her legs ached to run, jump and climb after all those long months indoors. She was weak after the winter famine, but knew that she would soon grow strong again if only she was allowed to play with her sister to her heart's content. Once the shelter was ready, she left Lars on a soft bed of last year's grass and moss and scurried off. She knew he would be safe there; he could not go anywhere, there was nothing dangerous in hand's reach that he could put in his mouth, and no predators would venture so close to the house in the middle of summer. There was so much to discover and explore, so many paths her bare soles must tread, so many places she must visit to see if everything was the same as before. Were bluebells growing down by the river? Where were the first birch leaf sprouting? Had the flycatchers already built their nests? She ran through the forest with her skirt fluttering around her spindly legs and her heart fluttering like a baby bird in her chest. There was so much to taste and stuff in her mouth: the wood sorrel and polypody ferns and fir shoots tasted wonderful after all that bitter bark bread.

She was away from the shelter for a long time.

When she finally came back, she saw a figure hurrying away from the den. A flash of a skirt hem between the trees, or was it a thin tail—or maybe a wing? Ingrid's heart began to pound. Had a wild animal come and hurt her brother, mauled him? She heard no screams of pain. As she crawled into the shelter, her heart pounding, she heard her brother making noises of pure contentment, and when he saw her he made the sign with his hand for *more, more!*

Now, Ingrid had never actually seen her forest sister. She knew that she was there; she knew that she was the one showing her all the wonders and miracles of the forest, singing to her through birdsong, leading the greenfinch and foxes to her path. Ingrid could feel her presence as vividly as she could feel Lars in her arms, and she never felt alone in the forest, for her sister was there to keep her company, and Ingrid spoke to her and knew how to listen for her answer.

But on this occasion she was sure that she had really seen something—some*one*—running away from the shelter. And it

123

filled her with such a great many emotions that she did not know what to do.

She had a guilty conscience for having left Lars alone for so long.

She was afraid of what she might have seen.

And she was profoundly envious.

She gave Lars some fir shoots to chew on and sat for a long time, staring out through the opening of the shelter. She strained her eyes, trying to make out a movement in the forest, a face, anything that was not just trees and rocks and stumps. All she saw were ants marching across the path, an early bumblebee buzzing around the blueberry bushes, and the birch trees' slender shadows slowly shifting as the sun moved across the sky.

After this, she began to see signs that someone, or something, was visiting Lars as soon as her back was turned. She would come into the house after helping with the milking and see that the boy, whom she had left lying on a patch of rug on the floor, was holding a dandelion. She could not understand how he had got it and grabbed it away before their mother could see it. When it was time for haymaking and everyone on the farm had to help gather the sparse grass that had grown over the cold summer, Ma laid Lars down in the shade of a rowan tree. He lay there contentedly all day long, gurgling and making noises, and every time Ingrid glanced over she thought she saw someone else in the shadows, but as soon as she approached, whatever or who-ever it was disappeared, and the boy emitted loud, angry howls.

She often found small gifts in his hands or beside him: flowers, berries, smooth pieces of wood. Never anything that could harm him if he accidentally put it in his mouth. She started asking her sister—though she could not be entirely sure that it was her forest sister—to look after Lars when she had to help with the milking or when her mother called her. And she knew that Lars would be completely safe until she came back.

Try as she might, she never caught a glimpse of Lars' visitor. And this filled her with sorrow.

"You have known me for longer," she whispered one August evening as she sat with Lars in her lap up by the cairn behind the house, watching the first stars begin to shine in the rapidly darkening sky. Lars was playing with her braid. The bush crickets were chirping, and the scent of fresh hay was seeping out of the nearby barn. The swallows had another brood of chicks and flew like little black arrows across the scythed field behind the house, on the hunt for their final feed of the day. Ingrid could feel her sister all around her, her breath on her shoulder, her voice in the bats' squeaks and evening birds' song. "You were my sister first."

But her sister did not answer, or she did, but only with squeaks and songs and star shimmer. Suddenly Ingrid felt old. Ancient, like the very rock she sat on. She jumped down with Lars in her arms and walked back home with determined steps.

Summer was short and cold, and winter came early. The harvest was meagre, and hunger came once again, knocking at every door in the land—indeed, the whole world seemed to suffer this year, when cold caused widespread crop failure. Pa managed to shoot a forest reindeer with his gun. It was a lone, young animal. Usually the forest reindeer moved in herds at this time of the year, but Pa managed to ski out to Vittermåsa and shoot this animal all on its own. It had been a long time since anyone had seen a herd of forest reindeer.

The carcass was left to hang in the shed and freeze, and the meat was a welcome addition to their austere diet of thin barley gruel and bark bread.

"We shall be spared from Korpholm yet," Ma said with relief. She always spoke of the institution in Kronoby when starvation was on their doorstep. That was where the sick, feeble-minded and destitute ended up—those who could no longer take care of themselves.

Ma glanced at Lars and then at Pa.

"Perhaps the child would fare better there. Here he is taking food from the mouths of the other children."

"But it would cost us," said Pa, putting down the knife he had been sharpening. "We haven't the coin for it, after a year of selling neither wool nor butter."

Ingrid went over to Lars and lifted him up off the floor where he had been sitting with his little brothers and playing with her wooden cow. She took him into the bedchamber and showed him the frost patterns on the window to distract him from his departure from his playmates. She did not want him to hear Ma and Pa's conversation. They thought he understood nothing of what they said, but Ingrid knew better.

Alas, Ma's words reached them in the bedchamber as well.

"What about the tar? You got two barrels from Tar-Mattas. If you could sell them this winter…"

"If we transport them to town and sell them, there are taxes to be paid."

Ma went silent. Ingrid knew that once she got an idea in her head, she did not give up on it easily. She could carry it with her for many years, if need be.

Ingrid clutched Lars close to her breast and kissed his crown. If they decided to send Lars to the hospital, she would take him into the woods and hide. She could fish and pick berries. Grandma Eva had told her about a chaplain who had hidden from the enemy out on the marsh during the Great Wrath. She knew where the remains of his old hut were—maybe she could rebuild it, and then they could live there together, she and Lars. If they were no longer a burden on their family, they might not bother looking for them.

"No one is going to take you away from me, little Lars," she whispered and blew gently in his ear. "You are mine, no matter what Ma does."

As is so often the case, bad harvests are followed by pestilence. Winter brought a terrible fever that swept through the country-side and claimed many lives, what with the population weakened from hunger and malnutrition. Hardly a home was spared from losing at least one soul, and it was mainly the youngest and oldest who succumbed. At Skogsperä, everyone got sick, but everyone recovered except the underdeveloped little boy. They had to bury him before the raging winter was through.

Mercifully, spring came early that year, with bare ground and birdsong and freshly sprouting grass by Easter.

On these budding days of spring, Ingrid regained her strength, and she went out to her den, where dry birch leaves on the branches of the shelter rustled mournfully in the wind. She could not weep. It was as if all the tears inside her had evaporated when her body was ridden with fever.

She sat on a stump, surrounded by patches of tired old snow, and rested her chin on her knees. She drew the crisp spring air into her lungs, which still ached after her severe cough.

Then she spoke, out loud to the spring and the forest and whoever might be listening, about her brother's final days. About how she took care him, fed him, tried to coax him into drinking something. About how she was the one holding him when he died.

"They said it was an act of mercy, that God was taking Lars."

She sat quietly awhile. She plucked a little of last year's grass and twisted it around her stiff fingers.

"Everyone seems to think I ought to be relieved that Lars is gone. Now that I don't have to drag him around with me any more." She sniffed. She was not crying. She had no tears. "But he was my brother. I miss him."

She sat still and listened, really listened for an answer. But she could not hear her sister singing in the treetops, or smell her on the southerly wind or feel her breath against her bare neck. There was no one there. Had there ever been? Had she imagined it all?

She never returned to her forest shelter after that. She was a big girl now and had no time for play; Ma needed her to watch the twins and help with the daily chores. So she did not see the dry birch branches sprout tiny green leaves the following night. She did not see the white windflowers poke their heads up through the snow, or the spruce covering the roof of the shelter grow bright green shoots. She did not see the dry grass that had been her brother's bed become suddenly green and lush, as if it had been gathered on an early summer's day. Nor the butterflies and bumblebees fluttering amongst the saplings while the rest of the forest remained deep in slumber, grey and seemingly dead.

NETTLES

MANY WERE BAFFLED as to how Arne of Nevabacka managed to win the hand of Kristiina Mikaelsdotter, a priest's daughter from Oulu. That Arne had a magnificent farm could not be denied. Since the Great Wrath, the Nevabacka family had enjoyed increasing prosperity, and their farm now boasted fifteen cows, thirty sheep, several pigs, no fewer than three horses and several mares and foals. Arne was a well-respected farmer in the parish, with many important responsibilities, and was known as a serious, honest and god-fearing man. He also earned a fair sum from selling timber to the shipyards in town. He had long been unmarried, and his potential bride had been a subject of much speculation. No one at Nevabacka would ever forget their first impression of Kristiina. She came to the farm dressed more elegantly than even the parish priest's wife Elisabet. It was winter, and Kristiina wore a green damask coat with grey fabric lining. On her head she wore a blue velvet cap. Under her coat she wore a black satin skirt, which must have cost as much as a cow, and a striped jacket of Russian damask. On her feet were blue shoes with high white heels.

When old mother Serafina of Nevabacka helped her daughter-in-law unpack her belongings, she was amazed at all the head-wear, hoods, collars, cuffs, half-sleeves, muffs, stockings and slippers. There were colours and materials she had never seen before in her life and did not even know what they were called.

"Such frivolity is unbecoming of a farmer's wife," said Serafina to her son. "It may be all very well for the pastor's daughter, but she has married a commoner, and we're not ashamed of who we are. She needs to accept her place."

Arne said nothing and his mother wondered once again what had possessed him to take this dainty priest's daughter as his wife, when he had all the robust farmers' daughters of the region to choose from.

As it turned out, Kristiina not only accepted her place, she committed herself to it wholeheartedly. Everyone expected her to be a pampered little doll, who would be of no use on the farm at all. But Arne must have known differently before he proposed, or else was incredibly lucky. The young mistress of the farm turned out to be strong and capable in most things concerning the household. Of course, she did not deal with the outdoor agricultural work, but neither did Arne expect her to. What Kristiina was good at was all forms of women's work, and once her mother-in-law and sister-in-law had shown her where everything was and how things were done, she was soon busy from dawn till dusk: milking, skimming, curdling and churning, salting and smoking, boiling and preserving. New dishes appeared on the Nevabacka table, because the young matron was used to smoked and grilled salmon at her childhood home in the city, and she had a taste for all sorts of herbs that were completely foreign to the Nevabacka household. Kristiina also saw to it that Nevabacka started growing potatoes—only the second farm in the parish to do so. Otherwise, it was only the pastor in the church village who grew exotic things like potatoes and herbs. The master of the house seemed more than satisfied with their new fare, but Jöns Eriksson, the farmhand, often grumbled to his friends about the strange provisions.

Whenever she was not busy in the larder or raised storage shed or cold cellar, Kristiina could be found at the carder, spinning wheel or loom. She spun flax as well as she spun wool, and she encouraged her husband to grow even more flax and buy sheep with extra fine wool, and spent much of her time spinning yarn, weaving cloth and sewing garments for herself and her husband. And occasionally she might sew a little lace onto a hat for herself too. Thus, Kristiina remained among the best-dressed ladies in the parish, except that now her Sunday best was all woven and knitted by her own hand, and the lace in her hat home-made. And though she used fine *ras-de-sicile* silk trim on her hats, so did many of the peasant women.

Yet Kristiina's most remarkable accomplishment for Nevabacka was probably the garden she planted. The pastor was the only other person in the parish to have such a garden. Turnips and onions were grown in the field, and that was all.

Turnips and onions were enough. But Nevabacka's new farm wife saw opportunity in the long south wall of the house, protected as it was from cold northern winds. This was where she would put into practice everything she had learned from her father.

The first thing to do was gather seeds. She wrote to her old friends in Oulu, where there was a lot of trade with cities across the Gulf of Bothnia, and to a cousin who lived in Stockholm. They all sent her bags and packets of seeds.

Most of Kristiina's inspiration and seeds, however, came from the rectory. She and the pastor's wife Elisabet soon became dear friends, though Elisabet was much older than the young mistress of Nevabacka. The pastor and his wife were childless, and perhaps she saw Kristiina as something like a daughter, being from a priest's family as she was.

Pastor Alexander was an enterprising man. He had studied in Turku and drained a marsh next to the rectory to plant a garden, which grew all sorts of rare and wonderful things: parsley, carrots, red onions, swedes, parsnips, celery.

"Yes, he orders and plants the seeds, but I do all the upkeep," said Elisabet good-naturedly. She had accompanied her husband to Nevabacka for the catechism review, in which the pastor guided his parishioners in matters of morals, scripture and literacy. "My Alexander likes the idea of gardening more than the actual ongoing labour. But he often has very clever ideas. He has built a dam to channel water from the stream to our little herb and vegetable garden, which saves me a lot of carrying." She looked around and nodded approvingly. "You have done a great deal in a short time, dear Kristiina. Do you fetch water from the stream? Would it not be easier to plant the garden closer to the water source?"

"It would be easier, but this spot is warmer and better protected from wind and frost," answered Kristiina. "Many of my herbs and crops would not grow down by the stream, which emits frosty vapours even in early autumn. Though perhaps I could grow hardier plants there."

"Have you heard that Gabriel Aspegren planted a garden in Pedersöre some years ago, with the first ever apple trees in Ostrobothnia? But few survived the cold winters."

"There are no fruit trees at all in Oulu," said Kristiina. "But we had many currant bushes in my father's garden, and I brought cuttings here. They are yet to produce berries, but next year I hope for a good harvest."

"I think gooseberries could do well too," said Mrs Elisabet, nodding at the berry bushes. "It is warmer here than in Oulu, I dare say." She adjusted her green taffeta sun hat and glanced over to her husband preparing the horse for departure in the yard. "Here's hoping we arrive home safe and sound. The last time Alexander went out for a catechism review, he drove so hard that he broke the cart shaft."

Kristiina bade farewell to their distinguished guests and set about tidying up after the many refreshments they had offered the pastor and his wife.

*

When Kristiina became pregnant with her first child, Arne told her to hire a farm maid. They had only had one farmhand before, and old mother Serafina and Kristiina were used to taking care of all the women's chores themselves. Arne cared deeply about his young wife, even if he did not always show it, and was keen to employ a milkmaid to help her with the animals.

There was an uncommon shortage of help available that year. Most servants preferred to stay in their existing posts, or take positions in the town, where it was said that the labour was lighter and the pleasures greater. Kristiina gave up hope of ever finding someone to hire. Michaelmas came and went, and no suitable girl could be found during the one week of the year when servants usually sought out new positions.

Then, one day in October, Kristiina went out into the forest to bring the cows in for the evening. Kristiina sensed that this might be the last day they could go out to graze. The fields had seen several nights of frost already and there was precious little left for the animals to eat. They had roamed much further from the farm than usual. The leader cow White Hoof was old and wise and knew where the last blades of grass could be found and where the last leaves clung to the shedding bushes. Kristiina had been walking for several hours and was sweaty and irritable. Her back ached, for her belly was swollen and heavy by now. The baby would be born around Christmas, she guessed. She was not especially afraid of giving birth. Kristiina Mikaelsdotter was used to getting what she wanted, her heart's desire having only ever been denied once before. She had chosen Arne, not the other way around, though no one knew this but her and her sister Catariina, who had married their father's assistant priest Timotheus the year before. Poor, young and handsome, Timotheus had stolen both sisters' hearts the very first time he stepped foot in the rectory. But it was Catariina who emerged victorious and won the beautiful man of God as her husband. Kristiina could not bear to see them walking side by side through Oulu, on their way to see the rapids shed their ice crust, or to Lötan to spot the first lark of spring. Seeing them together made her sick, and she made two decisions: firstly, that she would marry someone who did not live in Oulu or the surrounding villages, and secondly, that at least he would not be poor like Timotheus.

She was content with her choice, for she had gained a magnificent farm to run and decide about, with a mother-in-law who was easy to manage and rarely stood in her way. Arne was something of a mystery, but he was sober and obliging, and that was enough for her. Sometimes she almost thought he was afraid of her. On their wedding night he had not dared touch her. They spent the night simply lying side by side in bed. He had drunk a little that day, which she later realized was a very rare occurrence, and which loosened the lips of this otherwise taciturn man. He held one of her hands between both of his and, obscured by shadow, he dared to shine a light on the darkness inside his heart. His father Evert had been a real devil, he said. He had beaten his wife and children, when he was drunk and when he was sober. And he did not hit them only once, nor only

136

with his hands. Arne's voice trembled in their marital bed, and Kristiina stroked his cheek with her free hand. Arne's father had forced him to beat the others as well. His sisters. And Arne had done it, for he was only small and terribly afraid of his father. He could never forgive himself for this, he whispered.

Evert was a philanderer as well. He was unfaithful to his wife. Once—no, Arne could not bring himself to say what had happened—but once his father had done something so unforgivable that Arne knew he had to be stopped.

"He took me out to Vittermåsa," he whispered. "He had been drinking for several days. I was fourteen then, not yet grown to my full height and strength. We were going out to hunt, he said. I was so scared, but I knew what I had to do."

Kristiina could guess what happened next. She knew she ought to feel frightened, appalled, horrified, but she did not.

"I said he drowned. It had rained a lot that autumn, the marsh was treacherous, and everyone knew he was a drinker. But it was I who drowned him, Kristiina. You are married to a murderer. I am sorry for deceiving you as I have. I imagine you must feel very frightened now."

Once Arne had spoken his piece, he lay completely rigid and still.

Kristiina leaned on one elbow and looked at him in the darkness of their chamber. "I have married a man who does what he must to protect his family," she said. "Why should that frighten me? And I have married a man who would never beat me or our children. Is that not so?"

"Never," said Arne. "On this I swear." He embraced her and rested his head on her breast.

Kristiina felt strangely relieved. Now she understood why he had never married before, though he was wealthy and had a farm in need of a wife. It had worried her a little that a man of his age had remained unmarried so long. Now that she knew the reason, she felt reassured.

Kristiina soon became the most important woman in the parish, second only to the pastor's wife. If the next pastor was unmarried, she would certainly ensure that she became the most influential woman in the community. With a little hard work, she could encourage Arne to take on all the most important and respectable responsibilities, and then she could sit in the front row at church and wear her finest, most precious garments without appearing vulgar or inappropriate.

But now she could not even find her cows, let alone a milkmaid. It was frustrating, and Kristiina was not usually one to give way to frustration.

She called for the cows and thought she heard distant lowing and cowbells coming from Vittermåsa. She found the right path and soon arrived at the marsh. It was a familiar place, where she and Arne had picked cloudberries earlier in the year. She had already fetched the cows from the lake by the marsh once before.

She spotted the cows, gathered along the edge of the marsh, nibbling on the last blades of grass and a few withered flowers. Someone was there, standing beside White Hoof's pale head. A young woman—or was she young? In any case, she was tall and slender, and dressed in a simple grey dress that shimmered in the deepening dusk. She wore her fair hair twisted in a thick braid around her head and stood stroking White Hoof's muzzle. When Kristiina came to meet her, she nodded politely. Kristiina was about to ask who she was and what she was doing with her cows. It was not every day that one came upon a stranger in the forest.

"I helped her out of the marsh," said the stranger, giving White Hoof a final pat. "She had got stuck and couldn't get herself out."

Now Kristiina saw that White Hoof was wet and dirty up to her flanks. She looked gratefully at the stranger. She never would have been able to pull the cow free with her heavy belly, and would have had to go and fetch Arne, by which time the creature might have drowned.

"I owe you thanks." She pressed her thumbs into her lower back and stretched. "I could not have accomplished such a task on my own. How did you manage?"

"I simply told her what to do," answered the woman, looking White Hoof in the eye. "Showed her where the ground was dry and safe to walk on." She turned to Kristiina, who realized that she might not be as young as she first thought. There was more life experience in her eyes than her flaxen hair suggested. "Would you like help bringing her home?"

"Yes, please," said Kristiina. "Though surely you must have been on your way home? What brings you to the marsh so late in the day?"

Kristiina could sense something unusual and remarkable about this woman. She stuck her hand down into the loose pocket tied around her waist—yes, the scissors were still there. They should protect her from phantasms and getting lost in the woods.

"I was picking golden bloom," the woman replied. She gestured to a little pouch lying at the edge of the marsh. "It only grows here. I use it to dye my yarn." She pointed out an inconspicuous little plant that Kristiina had never noticed before, with pointy little leaves.

They walked back to the farm as darkness fell. The woman said her name was Myrsky, and when Kristiina asked where she came from, she pointed north. On the other side of the marsh and forest was an entirely Finnish-speaking parish, and Kristiina assumed that was where she must have come from.

Myrsky helped her milk the cows. They had not produced this much milk since high summer when the grass was at its lushest. Kristiina watched Myrsky sitting on the milking stool handling the cows and their teats with strong, steady hands.

"I am looking for a milkmaid," she said slowly and lit a dark lantern to illuminate the back of the cowshed. "Have you held such a position before?"

Myrsky pressed her cheek against White Hoof and replied that she was no stranger to hard work, but had never been servant to another.

"In which case you shall not be paid a wage until your second year," said Kristiina. Her mother had taught her how to deal with servants, and she knew the proper procedure. "Food and board the first year, then a salary as well in the second."

Myrsky nodded slowly. "I shall stay for two years," she answered in her deep voice, which sometimes sounded more like a man's. "I should like to see what life is like here at Nevabacka." There was something odd about the way she said this, Kristiina thought, but she was in desperate need of a maid and could not afford to be too picky. This is what she told her mother-in-law when Serafina scolded her for hiring a stranger they knew nothing about.

"She could be a madwoman for all we know! She could poison the well or set fire to the barn!" Old Serafina spat into the hearth. "An unmarried woman, not in service—she is bound to be a woman of loose morals, to say the least. You know what happens if someone like that so much as looks at you while you are with child!"

These words made Kristiina somewhat uneasy. Old Serafina was right—letting a harlot so much as look at a pregnant woman, let alone live under her roof, could cause the child to develop rickets, or whore's legs, as it was often called. But she had already let Myrsky look at her, so the damage was done. Besides, Kristiina found it hard to believe that Myrsky could be a loose woman. She was so serious, so clean and tidy, not at all like the whores she had seen pointed out in Oulu.

Arne accepted the situation placidly. Granted, Myrsky was a stranger, but he saw how well she handled the cows and sheep, and carried pails of water and stacks of wood as well as any man, and spared Kristiina the heaviest chores. That was enough for him.

Kristiina's only concern was that their farmhand Jöns Eriksson, having a weakness for women, might cause problems with a new young maid at the farm. But Kristiina noticed that any time he tried to tease her, or playfully pinch or squeeze her, Myrsky had a way of looking straight at him that deflated him at once. Which was good—it meant there would be no wedding or illegitimate children.

Myrsky was very independent and performed many tasks without orders or advice from Kristiina. She was good with the animals, who gave more milk than usual when Myrsky milked them and never upset the pail or misbehaved in any way. She was very tidy, always sweeping and cleaning. Yet there were many other things she knew next to nothing about. She had never churned butter before, nor could she bake bread.

"We don't grow rye where I come from," she said simply when Kristiina enquired as to the maid's poor kneading technique. But she gutted perch with skill when Jöns had managed to catch some at the lake. And she had incredible stamina; once Kristiina had taught her how to handle the butter churn, she could keep churning and churning until all the butter was ready, without complaint of tired arms or an aching back.

When Kristiina had got married, she had brought to her new home a tea table that now adorned the large cottage, and a mirror that was hung in one of the bedchambers. Kristiina would often spend a little time in front of the mirror, checking her outfit and making sure her hair was neat. On Sundays, when they took a sleigh or cart to church, she devoted even more care to her appearance, often bringing out her finest velvet karpus hat and damask coat. The sumptuary laws were not upheld as strictly in the countryside as in the towns, but silk could not be imported except in certain special cases, so any existing silk garments were even more valuable to their owners. Kristiina always knew exactly how far she could push her displays of finery without causing offence. A rule of thumb was never to dress in more stylish or expensive garments than the pastor's wife. Not that Mrs Elisabet would have said anything about it, but it would certainly raise eyebrows among the parishioners.

Kristiina could often be found out in the forest, picking mosses and plants to dye yarn and thread, and spent much of her time weaving and knitting, especially now that Myrsky, the maid, could see to most of the laborious animal care. Much of what she wove, sewed and knitted was for the baby. When the time came, just before Christmas, it was Myrsky who helped her with the birth, and she was so calm and knowledgeable that the whole thing went more smoothly than Kristiina had ever dared hope. Serafina muttered something about witchcraft, but the baby boy Karl was born healthy and strong, without whore's legs. Kristiina devoted most of her time that winter to her son but was sometimes found at the spinning wheel and loom, as daylight allowed. Sometimes she sewed garments from cloth bought in town, and she ordered a jacket and dress set for herself and a wadmal overcoat for her husband from a tailor. Her sister Catariina and brother-in-law Timotheus planned to visit in the autumn, after the next harvest, so Kristiina was looking forward to showing off such abundance in clothing and food that her sister would return home with envy in her heart. The dispute between the two sisters had been about more than the battle for Timotheus' favour. Kristiina's infatuation with him had not been particularly deep, and it was more a question of rivalry and spite than jealousy.

With spring came gardening work. Kristiina used precious manure to fertilize her plot, and dug and turned, sowed and toiled. She had decided that this year she would have a beautiful, well-tended herb garden to rival the parsonage, and she counted and measured out the seeds she had been given by the priest's wife and her friends around the country. Myrsky helped her cart manure and pry away the biggest rocks that were getting in the way of where she wanted to grow parsley. Myrsky said nothing—she rarely spoke—but Kristiina thought she was looking at her strangely.

"Have you ever seen a herb garden before?" she asked one day when their work was done and they were washing themselves before going to milk the cows.

"Of course, but the one I know is much bigger and doesn't require this much work for a good harvest."

"Does such a magical herb garden exist?" Kristiina asked with a chuckle.

"It is my father's herb garden," Myrsky replied calmly.

Kristiina was most angered by this response and hastened to the barn to get the milking done. Most of the cows were pregnant and soon to calve, so there was not much to do, and she was quickly back in the house, setting out bread and porridge and saltfish. They only ever had simple fare such as this when their stores were empty on the verge of spring. Soon, however, her table would boast all kinds of delicacies! Her husband had presented her with a real salt shaker from Meissen, which would have pride of place on the table when she invited the parson and his wife for supper this summer, she had decided.

Myrsky entered and began taking the spoons down from the wall. The evening sun shining through the window made the fabric of her skirt shine like silver. Kristiina knew that surely the maid didn't have silver cloth in her skirt. She bent forward and took a closer look at the fabric. She had never seen anything like it. Was it silk? How could a maid own a silk skirt?

Perhaps she had too been rash in employing a stranger with no service experience after all? Perhaps Myrsky was indeed a fallen woman—a trollop, a whore. How else would she have got her hands on such an uncommon fabric for her skirt?

"Where did you get that skirt fabric?" asked Kristiina. Outside, she could hear the men returning from their ploughing.

"My mother wove it," Myrsky answered and smoothed her skirt down distractedly. "She spun the thread herself."

"But where does the plant grow from which one can spin silver thread?" Kristiina demanded suspiciously.

"In my father's garden," Myrsky replied, and Kristiina had no choice but to be satisfied, for now the menfolk entered and it was time to fetch old Serafina for supper.

The spring brought heat, sudden and intense, and soon the forest turned golden-green all around the farm. The cows, calves and sheep were let out to graze, sowing began, and when June came, Kristiina and Myrsky took the little boy out with them to the potato field and planted potatoes all morning. Swallows swooped overhead in search of food for their young, blackbirds sang beautifully, and Kristiina happily hummed a folk song while planting potatoes. She was proud of her potato field, proud of having introduced such a novelty to the area. When they were finished, they rinsed their hands in the stream and both drank deeply of the cold, humus-rich stream water.

Kristiina held Karl on her hip and looked around at the farm and surrounding properties. There was the potato field. There was her little herb garden. There were the currant bushes growing in a neat row. There were the fields, veiled in fresh green. The landscape was cultivated, good and correct, just as God intended. *We are doing God's work here*, she thought contentedly. She looked forward to receiving her parents as guests on her very own farmstead and showing them how she and her husband were working to obey God's commands and transform the wild, heathen forest into civilized gardens and fields. She knew that her father would find this especially gratifying.

"Well, does your father grow potatoes in his magnificent garden?" Kristiina asked playfully.

146

Myrsky stepped up from the stream, hands and chin dripping with the delicious cold water.

"No, no potatoes grow there," replied Myrsky with her usual seriousness. "But there are all sorts of roots, berries and nuts."

"Your father must have a lot of cattle to provide enough manure for such a large herb garden and abundant land," said Kristiina.

Myrsky shook her head. "No, we never fertilize. Our servants do this for us and in exchange they may eat their fill from my father's garden."

"He cannot have many servants then," Kristiina scoffed.

Myrsky smiled, wrinkling her freckled nose.

"More than you or I could count," she replied. "And no matter how much they eat, the garden is never empty."

"Well then, I suppose you never had to lift a finger as a child," Kristiina said sternly. She was perfectly aware that the woman was telling fibs. She could have believed anything else, but not countless servants.

"But of course I did, mistress. Thread doesn't spin itself, nor cloth weave itself. Furs must be cleaned and sewn, and food must be dried and salted for winter. But we do not toil as you do here on the farm. I see how you sweat and struggle to grow a few handfuls of berries in your garden, when my father's garden is full of more berries than could ever be picked." She looked at Kristiina and broke into a smile as she took her mistress by the hand. "Let me show you. Come!"

Myrsky pulled Kristiina along behind her, and Kristiina had no choice but to follow. The firm grip of her warm hand, the eager look in her eyes and the sudden, surprising smile playing at the corners of her lips. Myrsky dragged her to the manure pile where the nettles were now growing in a dense, stinging green carpet.

"Here is the silk my mother uses to spin yarn for skirts!" said the maid. "And it is also my father's finest vegetable, my sisters' and my most important beauty product, and our best and tastiest dish. And here"—she pulled Kristiina further away from the farm and pointed to the grassy slope that led into the forest—"this is where some of my father's best berries grow: wild strawberries. No currants in the world can compare!" Then she dragged Kristiina with her into the forest and wrapped her free arm around a thin birch whose bright green leaves were swaying in the warm summer breeze. "Here is his wine cellar, for we tap the birch for sap to drink, and there is nothing fresher or more delicious, not sweet ale or soured milk. And here!" She plucked some spruce shoots off a tree and stuck one in Kristiina's mouth before she could protest. "Taste this! Is this not more flavoursome than all the herbs of the parsonage?" She crouched among the wood sorrel growing in a light green carpet above the moss under the firs. "Here are more of father's leafy greens. We never drink coffee—our drink is tea made from birch and raspberry leaf." She picked up a stick and bent over a large mossy rock, where the polypody ferns grew with thin lobed leaves. She used the stick to pry up a root which she held up to Kristiina with a laugh. "Here are our potatoes! But no one has had to dig or fertilize or earth them up!"

She dragged Kristiina further and further into the forest and pointed out blueberry and lingonberry bushes, raspberry thickets and dandelions, sprouting yarrow and milkweed, and praised their beauty and abundance, and what good food grew there without anyone needing to cultivate or fertilize any of it. She patted a pine tree and talked about the flour one can grind from the bark, then led Kristiina to a small pond, showed her calla and water lilies and said that they were her father's turnips and rye. Bird cherry, rowanberry, crowberry. She pointed out plant after plant, leaf after leaf, talked about roots and mosses, their uses and nutritional benefits.

Myrsky squeezed her hand and looked at her eagerly.

"There is so much goodness and beauty here, and it is all free to take and use, for you too! Father needs no livestock, for the forest is full of animals. He needs no barn, for the forest provides homes and shelter for his flocks and herds. He needs no larder, for this"—she made a sweeping gesture with her hand—"this is his larder, his shed and cellar, his wetland and grain store. Here there are apothecaries and medicines. The most magnificent flowers abound without anyone having to sow or prune, and their beauty is here for all to enjoy. Everything is as it should be; there is enough food for all who live here and rely on his care, so long as no one takes more than they need and everyone gives back what is required."

Kristiina stood completely still. Myrsky was still holding one of her hands, and she was still carrying the boy on her hip. He was happy and calm, sucking on her apron string.

A breeze came gliding across the pond and lifted the corners of her kerchief. She heard the ripple of a nearby stream and the trees' groans and whispers in the wind. Some hidden owl suddenly produced a *HOo* sound, despite it being the middle of the day, and it sent a shudder down Kristiina's spine. She glanced at Myrsky, standing before her with her shimmering grey skirt and bright shining eyes. Her cheeks had a healthy rosy glow and her thick fair hair glistened in the sun. Even though her dress was much simpler than Kristiina's, just then she looked more elegant than any woman Kristiina had ever seen. Not even the Mayoress of Oulu in all her bridal finery could have been more beautiful than Myrsky in that moment, with the brilliant blue water behind her and such bright eagerness on her face. Kristiina was intensely moved, flooded with so many emotions that she could not tell them apart as they quaked through her body, bringing colour and pallor to her cheeks in turn. One of the emotions was envy. Envy of this humble maid's beauty and vitality. Yet she was also afraid. For she knew now who Myrsky really was. She knew whom she had let into her home, let hold her child.

In the end, fear won over all the other emotions. Kristiina withdrew her hand and held her child tightly to her chest.

"Why did you come to us? What is it that you want? My child? You cannot have him."

The excitement drained from Myrsky's eyes, and she blinked. The hand Kristiina had just withdrawn from hung limply by her side.

"I wanted to see how you live. How you survive. I have always wondered."

"Was it my husband you wanted? Perhaps you thought you could take my place by his side? Well, I see you, witch." She spat in the moss at Myrsky's feet. She was trembling with fear, but was struggling not to show it.

Myrsky took a step back. She furrowed her brows and crossed her arms.

"Is that what you heard me say, mistress?"

"I am no longer your mistress. Never show your face at Nevabacka again. Do you hear me? Your kind have no place under a Christian roof." Kristiina spat again.

With this, Myrsky's eyes darkened like a storm. "My two years are not yet up," she said, and Kristiina could not tell whether this was a threat or a plea. She backed away from Myrsky, away from the pond and marsh. When she came to the forest, she turned around and ran barefoot along the thorny path. She stepped on pine cones, tripped over roots, stubbed her toes on rocks, but she stopped for nothing until she was safely back at home. There, she sat the boy down next to the well and stood still for a few moments, waiting for her racing heart to calm down. She was hot and her scalp and neck itched under her headscarf.

There was the potato field, freshly dug and dark. There were her little herb garden and vegetable patch and berry bushes whose leaves were still only small. She was going to create something spectacular here. A garden with a wider variety of plants than even the pastor's. She was going to grow so many berries and root vegetables that they would never have to resort to picking a single berry from the forest. She would ask for some apple tree seedlings from Aspegren in Pedersöre. She would tend to them as though they were her own children. She would create a paradisical Garden of Eden out of this barren northern land. They would have animals, so many animals, and flowers, perhaps roses.

We are made to toil and sweat, she thought. It is God's will. Not to wander in the heathen wilderness and forage for wild plants.

She tore off her headscarf and scratched her scalp. Now her chest itched too.

She grabbed the well crank, pulled up a pail of icy cold water and drank deeply straight from the pail. The water gushed down both sides of her mouth, wetting her blouse and skirt. Suddenly all her clothes were burning her skin, itching and irritating every part of her body that the fabric touched. She picked up the child and rushed into the house, closing the door behind her and then tearing off her clothes. Her skin was red and inflamed. No matter what she did, the itching would not stop.

The itching did not abate that evening. During the night, her bedclothes burned as though made of nettles. She lay awake beside her husband, writhing in silent agony. The next day she fired up the sauna until the logs were red-hot and stayed in there for longer than ever before, beating herself bloody and swollen with the birch whisk.

Nothing helped the itching. She did not dress after the sauna, but walked naked across the yard, for her skin could no longer tolerate any fabric or clothing. Farmhand Jöns stared, and Arne chased him away angrily and brought his wife into the house. But he could not persuade her to dress again. "It burns," was all she said.

Soon she developed a fever, and old Serafina made her a compress and muttered prayers over her daughter-in-law. Arne had to take care of little Karl, because Kristiina could no longer bear holding him on her lap or at her breast—"it burns".

At night she screamed that she was being whipped by nettles, that her blanket and bedsheets were woven from nettles. She cried that they must burn everything the maid Myrsky had ever touched, it must all be burned. Serafina picked nettles to brew a tea, having learned from her mother that evil must be banished with the same evil.

Nothing helped. The fever intensified and refused to let go. On the third night, Arne fell asleep on the kitchen bench and Serafina had little Karl in with her. Kristiina lay wide awake in her marital bed, staring into the darkness, trying not to move at all lest the mattress beneath her tear her skin with its thorns and barbs. She was naked and without a blanket, but felt as though she were burning. Myrsky had touched everything. Every single thing. The fever made her mouth dry, and her long fair hair was so sweaty and tangled and itchy that she thought she might lose her mind. She got out of bed. She had to find the shears, where were the shears? In her feverish state, she made her way to the barn, where the shears were hanging from their hook, and sliced through her hair as close to the scalp as she could. The cows lowed softly when they sensed her presence. Her long locks fell to the ground. She went out into the yard, out of the warmth of the barn. There was a gentle breeze, and she shook her short-cropped head, moving her bare scalp against the night air. It afforded some relief. A little coolness.

There she stood in the summer night, naked and ablaze.

And everything around her was spinning: the farm, the forest and the pale stars of the June sky.

THE 19TH CENTURY

Slumbering tones from times long past
from homes, from fields, and suffering friends
eerie voices from darkened graves
cheers and laments from erstwhile battles
Awake, arise! The forefathers' message
In bringing to sons, to an illustrious time.

The slanted cabin stands below the rowan,
With moss-covered steps and rife with weeds.
Inside the enclosure of old greenish windows
the memories sleep in silence and peace.
Bow your head! Tread softly!
Holy is the place,
where the sheltered spirits of our forefathers dwell.

We light the dying coal on the hearth.
Carefully we take our loved ones into our care
The spinning wheel hums by the blazing fire,
while we weave on the edge of myth.
Burn ancient fire! Shine our deed!
Shine through the ages
for the sons to return to their fathers' home!

A. SLOTTE

BITTER HERBS

WHEN KARL WAS SICK, Arne insisted that Sofia stay indoors to tend to the boy. These were the only occasions when she was grateful for his existence. It meant she could avoid all the toil of outdoor labour. Karl was a small, skinny child, and often sick.

As was the case again. Karl had a cough. The men were out seeing to the chores of spring while Kajsa was in the barn with the cows. Soon it would be time to let the cattle out to graze, which Sofia was looking forward to. There was less mucking out and other barn chores to do in summer. Karl had just fallen asleep with his little hand in hers. He probably had a fever; his hand was hot and clammy. He would only sleep with her there beside him, stroking his head or holding his hand. It was one of the first mild spring days and Sofia was impatient for an opportunity to sneak out for a while. She often did so when Arne thought she was looking after Karl. She would slip into the forest and wander among the trees, alone with her thoughts.

When Sofia used to live with her father, in their little cabin, with all her younger siblings to take care of after the death of their mother, she had never felt that it was her real life. The grey drudgery, the crowded home, the endless chores and hunger always lurking around the corner. That life was supposed to belong to someone else, it was a mistake. Sometimes she would stand on the beach and gaze out to sea, thinking that her real life was awaiting her out there somewhere. Across the water.

When Arne Evertsson Nevabacka appeared one winter to sell tar to her father, his gaze lingered on Sofia. No one had ever looked at her that way before. She turned her longing away from the sea and directed it inland. Towards Arne's impressive farmstead. Just before spring, he returned, despite all the work of spring sowing, and proposed. He gave her a beautiful shawl as an engagement gift and as she held it in her hands, she thought to herself that now, finally, it was happening. Finally she was about to step into her real life, which was bright and beautiful and free from hunger, snotty noses, sick toddlers, endless laundry, baking bread, cooking and that smoky little cabin on a windswept cliff. Arne would sweep her up into his brawny arms and carry her into a new life, in which she would be loved, cherished and important.

The wedding certainly promised as much. Primped and preening, she sat by her husband's side, under an arch of leaves, and everybody from his village and her family sat at two long tables in the yard at Nevabacka and ate, drank and made merry, and everything was so bright and beautiful and elegant. All eyes were on her and no one was more beautifully dressed than she. The bridal crown she borrowed from the rectory made her feel like a princess in a fairy tale. The wedding night was not uneventful either. Arne seemed most enamoured with her and was playful and affectionate.

Then everyday life began. She moved into the farm with her shawl, her bridal gown and great expectations for her new life. It was not long before she suspected, with growing dismay, that she may have been deceived. This was not a new life after all, but a continuation of the same old drudgery in a new setting.

It was not that Arne was cruel or cold. But he was busy on the farm and expected her to do her share. He valued her in the same way as he valued his plough or horse. Except that the horse received more care and attention than she did. They had two farm boys in employment but no milkmaid. It was Sofia's job, shared with Arne's sister Kajsa, to milk the cows, make butter and cheese, grind flour and bake, prepare two meals a day, take care of everything during the slaughter period and feed all the workers hired for harvest and haymaking. Then there was the house to clean, the sheep to shear, wool to card and spin, dye and weave. There were clothes to be made, washed and mended. Beer needed brewing, and cabbages growing, and berries picking. Kajsa, who was a widow and had moved back to the farm to help her brother with motherless little Karl, was different from Sofia in every way possible. Never in her life had she spent time daydreaming, never imagined an existence other than the one she now lived, on a respectable old farm, filled with hard work.

159

Sofia was sensitive and easily moved to tears or laughter—both expressions of emotion that were considered highly inappropriate at Nevabacka. Her life was nought but work from morning to night, and she had Karl to deal with on top of it all.

Arne seemed to assume that Sofia would naturally take on a mothering role to Karl. The boy slept between them in their bed, so there was little opportunity for cuddles and caresses. Besides, Arne was usually too tired.

She sat with Karl's clammy little hand in hers and thought about the previous night. Karl had been sleeping in his own bed and suddenly Arne had given her a look that almost reminded her of their wedding night. But then, when he lifted the covers and said: "Well, there shan't be any children unless we set about making them," what followed was nothing like their wedding night, when Arne had been full of sweet words and caresses. This was more like when the bull was led to the cows and got on with his job.

Sofia knew that she would not get pregnant. Before she accepted Arne's proposal, she had gone to Packhouse-Ulla in Neristan and begged her for help to avoid having children. She had witnessed her own mother die in childbirth. Nothing frightened Sofia more than bearing a child.

Ulla had eyed Sofia's slim hips and said that there was probably a thing or two she could do, but she must never tell anyone what Ulla was about to teach her. Sofia must spit into a handkerchief, tie the four corners together and bury it under a stone in the cemetery under the full moon. Sofia did as she was told, fighting her fear of the cemetery and its spectres, and then agreed to marry Arne with relief in her heart. She did not feel guilty. Arne already had a four-year-old son and would not need any more children.

Still, if this was how things were going to be from here on in—no caresses, no tender words, only trying to make babies that she had no desire or intention to bear—with all this hard work and Karl besides, well, surely this could not be the life she was meant for either. There had to be more than this!

Suddenly Karo, the farm dog, started barking. Sofia withdrew her hand from Karl's sweaty little fist, carefully so as not to wake him, and walked over to the bedroom window. She saw the stocky figure of the sexton Elias enter the farmyard and brushed a strand of hair away from her forehead, irritably. What was he doing here, and on a weekday? The man was no doubt drunk again. He would settle down on a bench and be impossible to get rid of, imagining himself to appear urbane and charming to the young mistress of Nevabacka with his inappropriate rhymes, lusty glances and busy hands.

But what was this? He was not alone. A tall, towering man followed behind him, his pale, chiselled face half-hidden beneath a hat. Sofia leaned closer to the window before she realized that she might be seen from there and stepped back. She smoothed her hair and checked her apron for stains. Then she strode out of the house to greet the stranger with her head held high.

It was a clear and beautiful spring day with a gentle breeze chasing the cold out of the shadows. The yard had dried up since the snow had melted, and great tits, larks and white wagtails competed to see who could make the most noise from the trees and roof ridges.

"Here we have the young mistress of Nevabacka," said the sexton Elias, dusting off his greasy old hat with an exaggerated gesture. "So young and sweet and gentle, a fine figure of a woman." He nodded to indicate the man behind him. "I have a visitor from Turku, as you can see, Sofia. Per Kollert, a genuine academic. Have you ever met such a person before, madam?"

The man behind him took off his hat and gave a quick bow. "I dare say I am not quite an academic yet, Elias. Although it is my hope that my work here may bring me closer to that coveted title."

Now that he was addressing her, Sofia allowed herself to observe Per Kollert more closely. She saw large, deep-set eyes with heavy lids and a sort of dreamy gaze. She noticed a straight, narrow nose and pursed, determined lips. Pale hands with long, slender fingers—nothing like the men's hands she was used to seeing. For a brief moment she remembered Arne's meaty hands on her skin and suddenly felt her cheeks heat up.

"I do hope we are not intruding," Per continued. He spoke so softly that Sofia had to lean forward slightly to catch everything he said. "Elias has informed me of a rare flower growing on a marsh belonging to this farm, and I mean to study it. We were hoping to go to the marsh today, to see if it is already in bloom." He patted a round leather satchel slung over one shoulder. "I should like to collect some specimens, sketch them and note the location of their growth."

"Which flower? I might know where it grows."

"A yellow one, which grows on the south side of the marsh. Do you know it?" Elias stuck his thumbs inside his waistcoat authoritatively. "I discovered it last year and wrote to my good friend Wallenius at the Royal Academy of Turku."

Sofia had never noticed any unusual flowers on the marsh but did not want to say so and only nodded slowly.

"Yes, I think so. Shall I come and help you find it, perhaps?"

"If you would be so kind," Per looked down at her and squinted, suddenly intensely interested. "That truly would be a great help. As long as we are not taking you away from your work?"

Karl. Suddenly she remembered Karl, and a jolt of disappointment ran through her. She could not leave the feverish child alone. She had done so once last autumn. Karl had contracted some illness or other, as he so often did, and she thought no harm could come from her going to the lake for a brief spell. She liked being alone there with her thoughts and dreams. But then Arne, who had come into the house to fetch something or other during the working day, found the child alone and crying. It was the only time Sofia had ever seen him angry. He was usually a man of even temper, but on that occasion he had met her at the door with clenched fists and lips white with rage.

"I try to look past the fact that you're absent-minded and work-shy. I know you haven't been long at the farm and it takes

163

time to get used to. Or so my mother says every time I bring it up. Give the girl time to get used to it, she says. It's not easy to leave your childhood home and learn new ways. But you have experience with young children! How could you leave him alone? He could have fallen into the well or been bitten by the dog or taken by a troll! I have but one son, and he is your responsibility!"

Sofia had been startled and a little scared. She expected a blow, as her father had often dealt her if she angered him, but Arne simply stood there, pale with anger. It was almost more frightening. It took a long time for him to calm down and Sofia had to work hard to appease him. After that, things had never felt quite the same between them. She was also horrified and ashamed that he had discussed her with his mother. That nasty old crone! She had a way of looking from under her headscarf straight through Sofia that sent a shiver down her spine. It was as though the old woman could see all of Sofia's thoughts and secrets, including what Packhouse-Ulla had taught her to do with the handkerchief. It was forbidden, of course, by God and society alike, to use sorcery to prevent or expel babies. Nevertheless, Sofia thought defiantly, no one else understood how her mother had suffered, first with all her children, and finally with the last baby who tore her apart on his way out.

"I cannot," she said curtly to the two gentlemen standing in the yard, with Karo jumping around their legs. "Little Karl is sick with fever and cannot be left alone." Her disappointment made the words burn in her throat.

"What a pity," Elias said with a deep bow. He thought it made him appear genteel, showing off in front of women in this way. He did not know that everybody saw him as a fool. "In which case, we shall have to find our own way to the marsh without your delightful company, Sofia."

Per Kollert said nothing and only nodded briefly at her before following Elias across the yard, taking long strides with his lanky legs. Sofia watched them go. Oh, how she wished she could go with them! She was sure that Per would be able to hold a much more interesting conversation than any of the farmers around here. He came from Turku. She had so many questions about Turku! She imagined the two of them strolling side by side through the lush spring forest, speaking in hushed voices about… well, she was not exactly sure what, but something other than dung and drainage and lame horses. Elias was not involved in this imaginary conversation at all. Per would look at her with his earnest face as he stopped to hold a birch branch aside so that she, Sofia, could pass, and then she would…

Her reveries were interrupted by a howl from inside the house. She sighed, pressed her lips together and went indoors to see to Karl.

All day, she followed Per's steps in her mind. He must have reached the marsh by now. Now he was taking off his hat, wiping the sweat from his brow and peering thoughtfully out over the sedge grass. Now he was dropping to his knees and taking out a pencil with his slender fingers to sketch a small, exquisite plant.

She remembered the way he had bowed to her, so polite and understated, with none of Elias' ridiculous affectations. Had his gaze lingered momentarily on her? She allowed herself to believe that it probably had. Her head was such a flurry of thoughts that she quite forgot to be blunt and unkind to Karl. Instead, she behaved absently and dreamily with him, leaving the child rather confused and whining much less than usual.

When the men came in to eat, Per and Elias returned from the marsh. Everyone introduced themselves and Arne invited the men to join the family at the table. He assured them that there would be enough food—his sister Kajsa always saw to that. Sofia saw the sexton raise his eyebrows and, for the first time, felt embarrassed by her husband's words. She was the mistress of Nevabacka and by all rights she was the one who should make sure there was food on the table. Arne must have noticed her reaction because he turned to the guests to explain.

"My young son has been sickly over the winter. My wife has had her hands full taking care of him."

Elias launched into questions about what was plaguing the little one, and whether they had tried this or that remedy. Sofia took the opportunity to demurely turn to Per Kollert and enquire as to whether he had found the plant he was searching for.

"Alas, no. It is probably too early for it to bloom."

"What a pity that you didn't find what you came for," said Sofia. He looked at her, just as she imagined he would in the forest, during the walk they had already shared in her imagination.

166

"I intend to stay in the area until it blooms. A botanist such as I must have both patience and persistence, if he is to get what he wants."

Sofia's heart leapt. Did he truly just utter those words to her? He was being almost too obvious! She glanced furtively around the table, but no one else seemed to have found it outrageous or improper. Elias and Arne were discussing the medicinal benefits of cupping, the farmhands were silently eating cabbage soup, and Kajsa was moving quietly around the table laying out bread and meat. Then an idea struck Sofia, something blazing and brazen, and she turned to Per.

"Perhaps Mr Kollert could stay here at Nevabacka? That way you needn't walk all the way from the village to the marsh each day."

Per straightened his back and smiled—a smile that made his pale face shine with an almost blinding light. "Are you quite sure, madam? That it is not too much trouble? It would certainly make my job easier."

"No trouble at all," Sofia was quick to assure him.

Arne overheard and leaned over the table. "As long as you can make do with a hayloft. There isn't too much hay left, but probably enough for one man." Sofia was so ashamed that she wanted to put her hand over his mouth to stop him from speaking. Putting a learned man in the hayloft! But Per shook his head with a smile.

"I have slept in many a hayloft and many a barn on my study trips. That will suit me just fine. If it was good enough for Linnaeus, it is certainly good enough for Kollert!"

167

Elias, on seeing that he was losing his drinking partner, looked frantically from one man to the other. "But who shall show him the way? You cannot possibly find the way on your own after only being there once, dear brother."

"As soon as Karl gets well, Sofia can accompany him," Arne said confidently and leaned back. Kajsa scoffed but he ignored her. "She knows her way in the forest. Even though she only moved here last summer," he said, turning to Per. "She spends a lot of time out in the woods and fields."

"With the cows," Sofia added, so that Per would not think she went out idly rambling. Even though that is exactly what she did. "We have no milkmaid." Sofia could count on one hand all the occasions she had been out with the cows. But there was no need for Per to know that, she thought. Kajsa gave her a knowing look, but kept her mouth shut.

"That would be a blessing indeed," said Per. "No need to go in haste tomorrow, we can wait for the boy to recover. The flowers probably need several more days of spring warmth before I can expect them to bloom in any case."

Several days! Sofia felt as if her whole body was floating. Several days of having Per at their table, seeing his beautiful face, hearing that soft, earnest voice. Perhaps notice his gaze lingering on her body. What joy! It felt as though the whole house was filled with spring sunshine. Finally life was about to begin—her real, genuine life!

After supper, the men returned to the village in the light, mild spring evening. Per was to return the next day with his modest belongings. All that morning, Sofia was in an exuberant mood. She was friendly and playful with Arne, and tender and gentle with Karl. Why worry about all this daily toil and grey tedium, when her life was about to be illuminated with a new radiance? She could see a way out now, the escape she had been waiting for and knew would come eventually. Before Arne left the house for work that day, he paused in the doorway and looked at her.

"It's as if the Sofia I first met in the town has suddenly returned." He appeared to be struck by a thought, walked back over to her and wrapped his large workman's hands around her slender hands. "Have you been very unhappy here with us?"

Sofia was not sure how to answer. She looked down at the floor and blushed. She felt exposed, unable to hide her feelings now that she was floating on a cloud of elation. Unhappy? She could not say for sure. Had she been unhappy?

"Marriage isn't exactly what I expected it to be," she stammered. Arne squeezed her hands tenderly.

"My poor girl. Sometimes I forget that you have never been married before and are practically a child yourself. Perhaps I haven't been the sort of husband a maiden dreams of on summer nights. Forgive me, Sofia. I shall do better, so I shall." And he emphasized his promise with a kiss.

Sofia watched him as he made his way across the sunlit yard. She absent-mindedly let her fingertips rest upon her freshly kissed lips. But it was not her husband's face she was imagining. The moment his lips met hers, she had seen another face before her, with thin lips and melancholy grey eyes. The kiss had taken her breath away, and she felt a strange heaviness in her loins.

Arne's old mother had said that Karl suffered from heart-sickness, a common ailment that afflicted children who secretly wished for something but did not know what. As soon as the morning chores were done and Kajsa had left the house to per-form her outdoor duties, Sofia wrapped Karl up in a blanket and carried him up the hill to old mother Serafina's grandmother cabin.

She had never gone there by herself before. She held Karl close and he wrapped his little arms tightly around her neck and was content, for he loved being cuddled and carried. Sofia thought she would almost rather go to the cemetery at midnight than up to see old Serafina on her own, for the old woman made her feel uneasy, with her smell, her tobacco and the way she looked straight through her. But she was in need of advice. She needed Karl to get well so that she might be free to accompany Per to the marsh as his guide. She saw Arne and the farmhands out in the field sowing seeds. Arne raised a hand in greeting, and, even from such a distance, she thought she could see his face break into a wide smile. She waved back, taking some courage from his greeting.

Serafina's little cottage was at the edge of the forest by a small patch of land that she did not use. Every year she received a barrel of rye and a barrel of saltfish from her son. Sofia found the old woman bent over in her cabbage patch with her rump in the air.

"Have you seen to your cabbage patch already?" Serafina stood up straight and looked at her daughter-in-law. Sofia shook her head.

"Not yet. But I believe Kajsa intends to start soon." Who could think of cabbages when there were beautiful grey eyes in the world?

"Well, no sense in putting it off. Warm days a-coming."

Sofia smiled to herself. Warm days meant nothing would get in the way of her taking Per to the marsh! She adjusted Karl on her hip. "I was hoping that Mother Serafina might know a good remedy for heartsickness? Karl refuses to get better."

Serafina brushed dirt off her hands. "Come inside. We need to do a reading."

Inside the dark, smoky cabin, Sofia sat down on a bench with the heavy boy on her lap. He wrapped his arms around her neck and pressed his cheek to hers. He was clammy and smelled sour. She watched as Serafina took out a pair of sheep shears, which she wrapped in a folded cloth.

"Put the boy down on the floor," ordered Serafina, and Sofia pried his little hands from her neck, unwrapped his blanket and placed him on the floor in front of the old woman.

"Now we shall find out what he longs for," said Serafina. She moved the shears around Karl's little body while naming things she could imagine he might long for: sweet treats, toys, a sibling. When she said the right thing the shears should poke out of the fabric and reveal what the sick child needed to get well again. Karl whimpered and reached out for Sofia.

171

"The shears aren't showing themselves. Can you think of anything he might be longing for?" Serafina stood up with a heavy sigh. "Usually when children get the heartsickness, what they want is a treat to eat. And they only improve once they get it. With adults it's more difficult."

Some special treat that Karl wanted? She looked at the boy. "We've tried rock sugar and butter." She thought about the foods she enjoyed as a child. Blood sausage and smoked ham, which they had once at a party. She thought of her mother's pale arms with flour up to the elbows as she mixed dough for batch baking. The smell of fresh bread, her mother's warm embrace before she had to share it with all her siblings. She sighed. "If only his mother were alive. She must have known what he likes."

Serafina frowned and moved the shears inside the fabric around the boy's body one more time.

"Well then, perhaps he longs for his mother. And lo and behold, now the shears have shown themselves. Mm, 'tis a shame." She took the blanket from Sofia, wrapped the boy up again and picked him up. She looked into his soft little face. Her gaze softened and she pulled him close. "Terrible thing to be motherless at such a young age." She looked over the boy's head at Sofia. "But he has you."

Sofia became suddenly aware of how much she missed her own mother. The feeling was very strong and took her by surprise. She brought her apron up to her face to hide the tears threatening to spill from her eyes. She knew that the Nevabacka family considered crying to be weak and silly. To her great

172

surprise, she felt Serafina sit down on the bench beside her. Karl's tiny fists reached for her at once, pulling on her apron.

"There there now. No one blames you for Karl's ailments. He's been a sickly child ever since that mother of his was taken by the fever."

Sofia's tears flowed freely now. They always had notions of what she might be thinking and feeling, and they were never anywhere close to the truth! This was how she knew that she was stuck in the wrong life, with the wrong destiny. As soon as she found her true path, everything would fall into place. She was absolutely certain that Per would understand her perfectly. He would put his arm around her and say: "Is it your own mother you're thinking of?" And then she would cry on his shoulder.

She wiped her nose on her apron and let Karl crawl onto her lap. "I suppose it will be difficult to cure his heartsickness. What do you think Arne will say?"

"No point in telling him. We can only hope that Karl will get healthy as the warm weather comes in. The heartsickness is usually worst in spring."

Sofia bit the inside of her cheeks. Karl had to get well immediately so that she could take Per out to the marsh.

"The fever is making him weak," she said sadly. Serafina looked at her.

"Bless you for caring so deeply for Karl. Perhaps if you try to take his mother's place, the fever shall break." She patted the curly-haired little boy on the cheek. "'Tis akin to a sin how much joy this child brings me. I do so hope he recovers. And that you give Arne many more children to help with the work on the farm."

Work, always the work. The farm above all things. Naturally, Sofia understood that the land's produce was essential for their livelihoods. Yet somewhere deep down, she had come to loathe Nevabacka. As she carried the child back home, she looked down at the farmstead by the stream: old, grey and slumped. It claimed all their waking hours and crept into their dreams, with its fields, meadows, cabbage patch and barn. There was always something to repair, maintain and check on. It was even more demanding than Karl.

She sat Karl down on the floor, where he immediately clung to her skirt and cried, wanting to be held again. Kajsa was standing by the hearth, cooking porridge for dinner. The words "take his mother's place" echoed in Sofia's mind. She knew very little about his mother. They preferred not to speak of the dead.

"What was she like, Arne's first wife?" she asked Kajsa suddenly. Kajsa shrugged without turning away from the pot. She did not care for chit-chat with her spoiled, unhelpful sister-in-law.

"She was from Oulu. Daughter of a priest, don't you know. She could read. She learned Swedish quickly, but only spoke Finnish to Karl." Kajsa stirred the pot vigorously with the pine porridge crosier.

"Skilled at spinning, weaving and sewing. Her hands were always busy."

"Arne never speaks of her."

"No, can't say I'm surprised. Seeing as how she met such a terrible end." Kajsa closed her mouth tight. It was probably an inappropriate topic of conversation. The dead ought to be allowed to rest in peace. No matter how they died. Kajsa searched for something else to say, something safer.

"Beautiful singing voice. Knew a lot of songs, learned as a child in Oulu. And sang the loveliest herding calls. She sang to Karl all the time, in Finnish. During the brief time she got to be with him."

Sofia looked down at Karl, who looked back up at her with flaming red cheeks and a dripping nose. She knew many songs, but only one in Finnish and it was not a lullaby. She supposed it could not hurt to try. She lifted Karl up, carried him to bed and laid down next to him. He snuggled up close to her and wrapped his arms tightly around her neck. She began to caress his head, just like her mother used to when she was little, and then started softly singing a Finnish ballad, aware that Kajsa could hear.

Karl froze. He stared up at her with wide eyes. Then it was as though a tremor moved through his little body, and his cling-ing grip on her eased. By the time she reached the end of the long verse, he was asleep. Sofia carefully disentangled herself from his arms and got up. Kajsa, who was still by the hearth, said nothing. When the workers came in to eat, she put the pot of porridge on the table, but let Sofia bring out the bread and saltfish. Then she nodded at her sister-in-law.

"Sofia sang to Karl in Finnish and he fell straight to sleep," she said to Arne.

"Yes, Mother Serafina said he is heartsick. She examined him and said that he must miss his mother. Kajsa said she mostly spoke Finnish."

"What a clever idea!" Arne smiled broadly at her. "Now he is sure to get well!" Sofia blushed and looked down. His praise made her feel warm inside, but unworthy, because she knew very well that her actions had not been motivated by care for Karl.

Karl was much calmer and more pleasant for the rest of the day, and whenever he started to frown, she sang to him in Finnish, and he was soothed. By the next day, his fever had subsided, and he ate gruel with a good appetite. Sofia was not expecting Per yet, but was very happy that the boy was healthy so that she would be free to be his guide whenever he did show up. That night in bed, Arne wrapped his arms around her waist and hugged her close.

"You have been so good with Karl these last few days. It makes my heart happy every time I come in and hear you singing to him. You sing so beautifully! I never knew."

"I'm glad the cure was so simple," replied Sofia.

"But you were the only one who thought of it. Neither Mother nor Kajsa ever thought of such a remedy." He brushed away a strand of hair that had come loose from her braid. "My Sofia, I haven't seen you this happy since our wedding."

She smiled at him. "My heart has never felt so light before."

"You've settled in here on the farm now."

"Yes, that must be it. Everything has seemed much brighter these past few days."

"Perhaps you have been a little heartsick too?"

She laughed and blushed at the truth of Arne's words. She had longed for another life and now she was close to getting one—could he not see that this was the reason for her happiness?

That night Arne was as affectionate and tender as he had been on their wedding night. Sofia had desired his caresses for so long that she was almost angry with him for giving her what she wanted now, when she had finally found what she had been waiting for elsewhere. But she hid her feelings.

Per came the next day. It was lunchtime so all the workers were inside eating. When Sofia heard the farm dog start barking, she suddenly felt very hot, then ice cold. He was here! Karl sat with them at the table, on his father's lap. He had been free from fever for two days, with clear eyes and a healthy colour to his cheeks. There was no reason she would have to stay inside with him. Was there? She glanced quickly at Kajsa, who had got up to see who had come.

"It's that botanist from Turku. The one who wants to hang around the marsh looking at grass."

The men around the table laughed good-naturedly, and Sofia looked around in surprise. Were they mocking Per? Suddenly she saw him through their eyes: a pampered fellow who cared for flowers and books, things which had no value to them at all.

"It's good of you to offer to help him," said Arne, wiping gruel from Karl's chin. "I doubt he'd last long alone in the forest."

"No, we'd be pulling him out of the marsh before evening," said Kajsa. "Come in, we're nearly finished." Per's tall, thin figure had appeared in the doorway. Sofia's heart began to pound. "Can I offer you a little gruel?"

"Thank you, I have already eaten," Per replied mildly. "I had a farewell dinner with Sexton Elias."

"In liquid form, no doubt," said Arne.

Per smiled sadly. "Yes, for his part. I little understand how that man can teach the local children to read. He is certainly never sober."

"Well, the children around here can't read," said Arne confidently. "Such things aren't all that important to us, despite the clergy and the authorities' insistence."

"Well, here I am," said Per, looking straight at Sofia. "I should be most grateful for your help in finding the marsh, at your convenience."

Sofia looked down at her hands, which she had clasped in her lap to keep them from trembling. She must not seem too eager, too desperate for his company. No one must guess what was going on inside her.

"Well, Kajsa and I were talking about warping the loom." She looked at her sister-in-law. "And then there's Karl. He seems healthy now, but…"

"I can look after the boy for a while," said Kajsa gruffly. "I did it when his mother died. And the loom isn't going anywhere."

"Well then," Sofia said, finally daring to look at Per. "We are free to go."

*

They were surrounded by forest, quiet and cool. Finally, Sofia was free to leave the farm behind her: the farm that demanded and imposed and took. The forest, she thought, the forest was her true home. She glanced at the man walking beside her. She was sure that he felt the same way. He was a man who thrived in woods and fields, it was plain to see. He walked slowly, attentively. Not like the farmers who had nothing in mind but the day's chores. No, he gazed up into the treetops at the sound of a bird's trill. He paused to crouch beside a cluster of flowers growing in a hollow. He inspected some animal droppings scattered on an old stump. Sometimes he pulled a piece of paper out of his round satchel and made notes or a quick sketch. Then Sofia waited quietly, so as not to disturb, and enjoyed the opportunity to admire his slender neck in peace, and his long fingers holding the pen shaft so delicately, his fair hair poking out from under his cap. She could have stood there like that forever.

He was a polite companion and tried to engage her in conversation, but she had no answer to most of his questions. She did not know how many barrels of rye the farm usually yielded. Or where the saltfish came from. She could provide simple facts on the cows, the quantity of milk produced and the calving, and a little about butter and cheese. Otherwise her response was mainly that he should ask Arne. She wanted to know about his life, not talk about her own—his life was the fascinating one, glittering and novel. Her own life was grey and tangled and wrong.

179

"What is Turku like?" she ventured, as they stepped over a clear rippling brook, which was a sign that they were nearing the marsh. Per looked at her with a soft smile.

"Bigger than your village, smaller than Stockholm," he replied.

"Is that where you're from?"

"No, I am from Vaasa. Which is probably why my professor sent me on this mission. He assumed I had some local expertise."

Sofia was not sure what that last word meant, but did not want to appear ignorant. "What is your home like in Vaasa?"

"My father is a printer and lives in a comfortable house near the District Court. My accommodation in Turku is much more humble, as is often the case for lowly scholars. I share a room with a friend." He looked at her with those deep grey eyes in a way that made her heart flutter. "It is much simpler than Nevabacka, that much is certain. I do miss the comforts of a proper home sometimes. I am very grateful for the hospitality you have shown me."

"Do you intend to stay in Turku?"

"No, when I finish my master's degree, I mean to travel. There are so many places with undiscovered flora. My professor has promised to write me a letter of recommendation to a colleague in America. I should very much like to go there."

"America! Is that not like 'east of the sun, west of the moon'? A fairy tale for children?"

He laughed. "No, I assure you, it is a real place. My professor has been there himself to study blackberries. There are people there just like you and me, with two legs and two arms and a head."

Sofia walked silently, lost in her own thoughts. The new life that had been gently sparkling on the horizon suddenly flared up so brightly it almost blinded her. Could there be a place for her in the sort of life that took a man to America? Though surely he would return at some point. And when he did, he would need a beautiful home, and someone to keep it for him. A safe place to rest his head after all his travels and travails. The dazzling flare faded back down to a rosy glow.

They arrived at the marsh.

"Well, here it is," said Sofia. "This part of the marsh is wet all over, and dangerous to walk on, but further on there should be a dry passage into the middle—see there?—where the mare-pines grow. There are the remains of a wood cabin there, which apparently belonged to a man of the church who hid there during the Great Wrath."

But Per was already walking along the edge of the marsh, hunched over and carefully studying all the plants, muttering words in some strange language. Sofia followed. It was an overcast, windless day. The forest was eerily quiet, as if everything, including her, was holding its breath. This is what happens before a new beginning, she thought. A pause. A stillness. And then, then...

She could not quite imagine what this "then" would be, what it would look like. Still, she clung to the knowledge that it must come soon.

*

They returned that evening unsuccessful in their mission. Per was disappointed but not discouraged.

"I think I found the young plants, but I cannot know for sure whether I have discovered a new species or not until she blooms." He bit into a hunk of bread, for which the guest of honour had been given butter as well. "It should only take another day or two. If you have time, Sofia, we can go back on Sunday. That way I shan't be taking you away from your work."

Sofia lay awake for most of the night, re-examining every look he had given her, every word he had uttered. His manner in showing her what he suspected to be the rare flower on the marsh, holding out his hand and pulling her down close to him and pointing: "Look, here among the rosettes of leaves, soon the flower's stem shall rise. See how the leaves..." And then he said something about leaves and growth but she was not really paying attention. She was too acutely aware of his hand next to hers, feeling the tickle of the light hairs on the back of his hand until she felt so weak that she needed support to get back on her feet. Oh, what a sweet moment *that* had been! The way he held her in a firm, warm grip, with those long, slender fingers against the delicate skin of her forearm! His scent, standing so close, his concerned gaze! No wonder her knees almost buckled again! She had thought he was going to kiss her then, he was leaning so close over her, looking down into her face. She had almost fainted. But instead of kissing her, he said only that they ought to head back because Sofia was looking a little unwell.

Then the silence as they walked back through the forest under the golden evening sun that broke through dispersing clouds to stream through the trees. This shared silence—was it not one of the most heavenly things imaginable? She sensed that they understood each other perfectly. He could see her as she really was—not a mere housewife on some old forgotten farm, but a shimmering being entering into a new life, by his side.

She continued to be a good mother to Karl, which kept him healthy and in good spirits. She knew that Sunday was the day. She and Per would be alone in the forest, and he would have an opportunity to speak to her, take her hands, look at her with those serious eyes, and then, then... well, she had not thought much beyond that. Sometimes it crossed her mind that she was in fact married; she was someone's wife. God had united her with Arne, and there was no way to break the vows they had made to each other. She had heard of something called divorce, but was not sure exactly what it was. On the other hand, she had heard many stories about men and women who "ran away from home", leaving their spouse and children behind. They were spoken of in the harshest, most damning terms. But that would not apply to her. All this, the farm and Arne and Karl— it was *wrong*. She had found herself in the wrong life, and she was simply going to rectify the error. Step into the life that had always been her true destiny.

She was willing to do anything Per asked of her. If he wanted to lay her down on the moss out there in the forest, if he wanted to claim her then and there, she would not deny him. There was nothing she would deny him.

A storm came on Friday, which kept Per and the women housebound all day. Sofia was glad to have him in the cottage, but worried that the weather would prevent them from going to the marsh on Sunday. Per sat at the table and wrote while curious little Karl tried to climb onto his lap. Sofia was kept busy trying to stop the boy from disturbing him.

"Is that about the flower?" Kajsa asked.

Per replied that he was writing letters to his professor and to a friend in Turku.

"Oh, yes, I can imagine what sort of *friend*," Kajsa said with a laugh. "Does the gentleman have a sweetheart, perhaps?"

An icy hand gripped Sofia's heart. The thought had never occurred to her. Was there another woman in his life? There was a bitter taste in her suddenly dry mouth, as if she had been eating bearberries. What if he was engaged to some young lady from Turku who wore silk skirts and calfskin shoes? How could she be so naive as to believe that someone like him would be unattached?

Per smiled politely without any sign of blushes or awkwardness at the question. "It is a friend, with whom I share accommodation. I am writing to let him know not to expect me back just yet."

Sofia's heart resumed its beating. She picked up Karl and buried her face in his fair curls to hide the smile of relief she could not suppress. Of course he was unattached! Otherwise he would never have looked at her with such wonderful earnestness. He was not the type of man to trifle with a girl's heart.

The storm brought some good fortune, in that Arne insisted that Per sleep in the house that night. Sofia lay awake, keenly aware of his presence in the main room, so nearby. She lay in bed listening to the storm rushing and tearing through the trees around the farm, thundering on the roof and around the walls. She no longer knew what she was hoping for—that the storm would die down, so that they could go out into the forest together, or that it would continue, so that Per would have to sleep under the same roof as her one more night.

The storm died down in the wee hours. The cloud cover dispersed, letting the full moon shine through. Sofia became so restless that she could no longer lie still. She crept out of bed, careful not to wake Arne and Karl, and tiptoed through the bedroom and out into the main room.

There, on a bench fixed to the wall, Per lay sleeping. She could simply walk across the room and sit down beside him and stroke his hair. Maybe he would wake up, gaze at her with that languid look in his eyes, and then... then... She pressed her fingers to her lips, imagining the searing hot kiss, his arms around her delicate waist, the heat of his body, how she would...

Her eyes fell on his round satchel, which he had left on the table next to a few sheets of paper. Moonlight filtered through the house's only glass window and the papers shone as white as snow in its glow. She walked silently to the table and leaned over to look at the paper. Back in her home town, the sexton had not been a drunken rascal and actually had taught her to read. Just barely, but she was literate all the same. Slowly and with effort, she spelled her way through the words that her beloved had written.

My dear brother,

It seems that Ostrobothnia is going to keep me in its clutches for a few more days. I have not yet stripped the mysterious marsh-orchid of all her secrets, for she has not yet deigned to bloom, but I am very close. As soon as I have fully explored her, I intend to head south on foot. If there is an as-yet-unclassified Nordic orchid here, what other treasures might be hiding in these vast forests? I have high hopes of making more rare discoveries. Perhaps I can hurry through my master's degree somewhat, if I manage to find a plant to astound old Wallenius.

It looks as though you should not expect me back before Whitsun.

These are long days of waiting. There is nothing to read here, of course, not even a Bible. The Ostrobothnian farmers are illiterate and completely ignorant of anything that happens beyond their fields and meadows. They are no doubt highly knowledgeable in matters of cattle and manure, but know nothing of the affairs of the kingdom. The delusions that are rampant here beggar belief! They suppose that cupping cures everything, as do snakes' venomous stings worn inside garments, and people throwing frogs' legs at each other, and what have you. The farmer who has invited me to stay is not

186

a stupid fellow. Yet on some topics he knows little more than a small child. Can you imagine how funny it would be to have him as a guest at one of Wallenius' soirées? We could talk about how a hunt is doomed to failure if one encounters a woman on the way! I have been warned and admonished many times about the dangers of the marsh, and the peasant woman who takes me there hardly dares go near the marsh herself. She becomes noticeably distressed when we approach, very quiet, hardly utters a word. Last time we were there, she became so frightened that she almost fainted. Apparently there is some sort of guardian of the marsh, who is not to be trifled with, and who can lure a man to drown in the shallow, stagnant water. The dead walk there too, those who have drowned, like the farmer's own father. I have been advised to always carry steel on my person, so that I may avoid the same fate. I think they also have suspicions about the golden flower I am searching for, and they have warned me that it may be one of the guardian's inventions, an illusion perhaps, to lure me into the marsh, or perhaps a bad luck charm of some sort. No good can come from the marsh, they say.

It is such a sin against common sense that these people have absolutely no education. The young housewife here is coarse and common like most Ostrobothnian women, but neat and pleasant in dress and manners. Most wholesome and healthy in a way that is rare among the young ladies of Turku. However, she has been fooled into believing that a child's fever is caused by his longing for his mother, and that she and no one else can cure his ailment by singing to him in Finnish. Naturally, I intend to relate all this to Johan, for a whole new perspective on his medical studies! With a little schooling, all of them, even the women, could have so many more opportunities to serve their motherland. It is not good to have a population that is ignorant and easily misled, that hardly know who their king is.

Otherwise, I am quite comfortable here, and am not looking forward to the upheaval of a southward trek. And yet—all in the name of science! Is that not your motto, dear brother? *Scientia potentia nostra*! I can put up with a little rain on my neck and a few nights under the open sky. Then from Vaasa I shall take some suitable ship down to Turku. My self-sacrifice for Lady Scientia need not extend beyond that!

In haste,

Per

She could picture them now. The friend Per wrote to, their acquaintance Johan, the medical student. She could picture them gathered of an evening on Per's return to Turku, perhaps in the little room where Per slept. How he would entertain his friends with amusing anecdotes about the rugged, ignorant peasants of Ostrobothnia and all their nonsensical beliefs. He had never imagined that anyone at the farm would be able to read, otherwise he would not have left his letter out so carelessly. She thought of the harsh words he would use to describe them, and how she would be painted as wholesome and pure and dumb as a goose. They would raise a glass and laugh at her, at honest,

188

hard-working Arne, at Kajsa and her superstitions. They would neglect to mention the fact that Kajsa worked from dawn to dusk and cared for the farm as though it were her own child. Not a word about the fact that the butter on the students' bread came from farms such as this one.

All those serious looks of his had not come from a place of love and tenderness, but pity, when she said something foolish or ignorant. This whole time, the only feeling she had aroused in his heart had been pity. Shame flooded over her so intensely that she had to steady herself on the table. In his mind, he had been laughing at her. She had made a mockery of herself for his sake.

She looked around the bare grey cottage. The only thing that was beautiful and shimmering was the moonlight. There was no other life waiting for her. She had been just as stupid as Per thought she was. Imagining glances and feelings that were never there at all. When she had been so overcome with emotion that she almost lost consciousness, Per had believed she was afraid of the marsh. She was nothing to him. Nothing at all.

There is no way out, she thought. No other life. This is all there is, all there shall ever be.

She stood still for a long time. Then she turned around, went into the bedroom and dressed quietly. Without waking anyone, she stepped out into the night and walked through the yard and into the woods without a hint of fear. The only one who saw her go was a woodpecker that flapped in fright at the edge of the forest. She was swallowed up immediately by the darkness.

Dear brother,

I have an addition to make to my original letter. I leave this part of Ostrobothnia deeply disappointed. I went out to the marsh yesterday, not with the farmer's wife as guide this time, for she said she was too afraid of the guardian of the marsh to go there again. The sexton, the drunkard I mentioned in my previous letter, was summoned, and together we found the stems of the orchid he claims grows there, and which I also saw on my last visit to the marsh. No flowers, however. There were signs that they had indeed grown, with a small stub left in some of the leaf rosettes. But it looked as though an animal or an insect had severed them just above the leaves, so it is impossible to say whether it really was a new species. The sexton ranted and raved so loudly that they must have heard him at least three villages away, but he too had to admit defeat in the end. Perhaps we can send someone to study them next year—but it shan't be me. I am too disillusioned.

Thus I head south. Perhaps I shall have better luck in a village where I have heard that there are blue wood anemones.

Wish me luck on my journey!

Yours,

Per

SHADOW SONG

MA HADN'T SPOKEN FOR THREE DAYS when the boy set out into the forest. He had done something to anger her. He wasn't sure what. He rarely knew. A joke she didn't appreciate? A tone of voice she considered impudent? A chore he performed poorly? Sometimes it was Pa who had upset her, but it didn't matter whose fault it was. They both suffered the same silence.

But Pa didn't have to stay at home in the cottage with her all day.

The boy knew that he risked angering Ma further with his disappearance. She didn't like the forest. She avoided it as much as possible. Perhaps this meant that her silence would continue even longer, as punishment. Or she might be back to normal by the time he returned. She never mentioned her days of silence afterwards. She always behaved as if nothing had happened. Neither did she ever reveal what had angered her in the first place. No one knew. They never knew anything.

The boy was eight years old. Ma had been this way ever since he could remember. Grandma said his mother had been different before. When he was very small. Grandma never said in what way she had been different, but he guessed it had to do with the silence.

He took the path between the little cottage and the hay barn, a barely perceptible dip in the weary, gritty spring-winter snow. The morning sun was pale yellow in a pale sky. Everything was pale. He longed for the warmth of summer, bright colours and fragrances. Even the smells were diluted now. At least winter was properly cold, properly dark, with glistening days and lightless days, and the type of cold that froze the hairs in his nostrils. Spring-winter was like porridge. Like Ma's silence.

He kicked a clump of snow and continued deeper into the forest. If only he could be a good boy in all ways, Ma would be kind all the time. He was sure of it. Her silence was all his fault. Pa hardly seemed to notice it. He came in from work with the farmhand, sat down at the table, ate the food that she provided. Pa never spoke much. But he did say a few words to his son, here and there. *Come along to the stables, you can help me shoe Grålle. Tomorrow we are digging ditches in the burnt field, come with us.* Without hearing these words from his father, the boy might have questioned whether he existed at all. He felt visible in Grandma's little cabin. But Grandma was old. She didn't always have the energy for visits.

Pa had gone to town. Then he was going to continue north and be gone for a long time. The boy didn't know why. He had overheard his parents talking one evening as he was lying in bed, with words like "tar" and "barrels" and "taxes". Ma sounded

192

concerned, Pa resigned. Something wasn't right. Pa had been gone for two days now, and Ma had been silent for most of that time. The farmhand only came in to shovel down food, then went straight back out to work. Without Pa's few daily words, a ringing had started in the boy's ears. His whole body felt loose and thin. As if a strong gust of wind might dissolve him completely.

He ventured deeper into the forest than usual. There was less snow here than out in the fields and meadows. Bare patches of ground beneath the firs. The lingonberry shrubs were a brilliant rich green, while the ferns and conifer needles were brown and dead. He found some lingonberries and popped them in his mouth. They were mushy and watery but there was still a little sweetness to them. He sucked on them as he walked. At the stream bed he saw otter tracks. He knew they often came and played here. He had seen them. He had told Pa. Otter skins were valuable. But Pa hadn't managed to catch any otters yet.

He realized that he was on the path to the marsh. He had never been there alone, only with Pa to pick cloudberries in late summer. Ma never wanted to go there. She disliked the forest, but absolutely loathed the marsh. He thought he could probably find it on his own. He was good at finding his way. There was the boulder that was bigger than Pa. There was the dead pine tree, full of woodpeckers' holes. He sniffed his runny nose and continued, over the ridge, past Mörktjärn Lake. There was the marsh, on the other side of the water. Vast and covered in snow. Cold and dead. He stopped at the edge and wiped his nose with his glove.

193

A sudden scream startled him. Then he heard a roar and another scream. He quickly crouched in the snow, his heart pounding. Could it be a bear? Had they woken up already? Did bears even scream like that? He forced himself to breathe calmly and quietly. He looked around.

Something was moving on the other side of the marsh, something with long legs and a snake-like neck. And not just one, but several. Grey and black shapes growing, rising, spreading their wings. Legs lifting and lowering.

They were cranes dancing on the marsh. They reached their wings out to one another, curled their necks and squawked. They started moving towards him. He sat completely still, breathing as quietly as he could. He had never seen anything so wondrous. He stared at their beaks and swaying tail feathers. Their necks moving up and down. The birds hopped about, as clumsy as newborn calves and yet the most elegant, graceful things he had ever seen.

As the sun rose higher, they stopped. They stood still and looked around. A raven screeched in the distance. The boy saw a fox running across the sparse snow on the marsh, its winter fur still thick. It was heading for the cranes, but then the nearest crane raised its wings menacingly and the fox changed direction and came running in a curve towards him instead. He sat completely still. The fox passed him by just a few paces away. His heart was racing with excitement.

He scurried home for the evening meal. They sat together at the table, he and Ma, and ate from the same bowl of porridge.

All that could be heard was the scraping of spoons, the wind whistling in the woods all around, and the cows starting to low from the barn as milking time approached. The boy counted the number of spoonfuls. When he got to fifteen, Ma put down her spoon, stood up, wiped her hands on her apron, tied a shawl around her head and shoulders and went out to the cows. He stayed at the table, alone in the growing gloom.

When the cows stopped lowing, the silence was complete.

He got up very early, while it was still dark. It was Sunday, a day of rest. He had brought the firewood and water in the night before, at Ma's request. Trying to anticipate what chores she might ask of him, he swept the floor and brought hay down for the cows.

He dressed up warm. Took a rye cake from the ceiling beam and stuck it under his wadmal jacket. He knew that would anger Ma. He tried to calculate how many more days of silence it would cost him. Ma never beat him. She very rarely scolded. She just stopped talking.

He knew the lake had thawed enough for him to poke a hole through the splintering ice. So off he went, with nothing but the pale spring-winter moon for company. The days were lightening now and the sun would soon rise. The sky was already brightening in the east.

The first thing he heard was a gurgling, bubbling sound. It rose and fell, undulating around him. How was it so loud? He had heard it before, on other spring mornings, but only from a distance. Now it was very close, and as loud as when everyone sang together in church.

A pair of swans flew over the pond, honking. He saw the cranes too, padding along the other side of the lake now. The sound wasn't coming from them.

The coarse late snow crunched under his boots as he carefully walked closer to the marsh. He found his little hiding place and crouched low. His grey cardigan and hat were barely visible against the grey forest, in the grey dawn. Then, as the sun peeked over the horizon, the first rays streamed through the trees and illuminated the marsh mists with golden light. The boy held his breath. How beautiful it was! Ma said the forest was a dark, cramped place. She had grown up by the sea and missed the open space and horizon. But the boy loved all the shifting colours and light of the forest. He felt safe among the trees, mossy boulders and dark waters. On several occasions, he had accompanied Pa into Kokkola and seen the sea. He didn't like it. It was too big, it went on forever. When he stood next to it, he felt naked and exposed. Visible to everyone. There was nowhere to hide from the wind's clutches.

Ma missed the sunsets at sea. She had once said that her life was over there, on the other side of the water. I travelled in the wrong direction, she said.

He thought of these words often. He didn't really know what they meant, but he knew they were important. He felt that once he understood them, he would understand Ma, and the silence

196

would end. She was quiet because he didn't understand what she was saying when she did speak.

A large black grouse came flapping down onto the marsh from the edge of the forest. It looked around, spread its wings and cooed. Then it turned its back to the boy and let him admire its snow-white tail and crimson crest, bright in the distant mist. The bird swung around, bobbing its head and cooing incessantly. When it opened its wings, sunlight filtered through the brown feathery edges. Its coos almost sounded like it was talking to itself. Another bird flew down and landed in front of the first. It raised its wings, hopped a few times and hissed loudly. The sky was growing lighter and brighter, and puddles of meltwater glistened among the snow. Now the boy also saw the female, dull-coloured and inconspicuous, pattering between the glossy black males, pecking at the cranberries or cloudberries she had found out on the marsh, keeping the males in her sights at all times.

Coos sounded from all over the forest. There must have been dozens, hundreds of grouse. It was like being at the big church in the town, where he had gone with Pa and Ma one Sunday, and the organ bellowed like a storm in the treetops. The music of the grouse around him lifted him just as the organ music had, up to Heaven, up to God. Could this be the birds' form of prayer? He must remember to ask, when he was old enough to be confirmed. He couldn't ask Ma; she would only say it was nonsense.

A little further away, he saw more blackcocks dancing, jumping and flapping in the receding mist. But the pair he was watching

197

were only a few paces away, and their battle was becoming more and more intense. They were completely focused on each other. The boy was hungry, but dared not move to get his bread. He thought that if he listened very carefully he might be able to understand what the blackcocks were saying to each other. Not because there were words in their clucking and chirping. No, it was more like he was one of them and could interpret the sounds themselves.

It was impossible for an outside observer to know what finally made one grouse admit defeat and retreat. But the boy knew which bird would emerge victorious.

When the sun was high above the crowns of the eastern forest and the grouse had long since quietened down, the boy ate his bread. He rose from his spot, stiff and cold, and began to walk. But not homeward yet. He took the path around the little lake. Studied the branches for signs of green spruce shoots and swelling birch buds. Would they sprout soon? Not yet, answered the spruce and birch. Soon but not yet.

Suddenly he became aware of something. He stopped. He had come to the opposite shore of the pond, where a summer stream flowed into the water. Some sturdy pines grew there, and up in the closest tree, at about man's height, he was taken by surprise by a pair of shiny dark eyes staring at him.

It was a wolverine. He could see the long claws on its powerful paws clinging to the trunk. A few large flakes of bark drifted down.

He stood completely still. The wolverine fixed him with its dark eyes. A wolverine could kill a forest reindeer. He was much smaller than a forest reindeer. And wolverines had cubs at this time of year.

He didn't know whether the animal in the tree was female. It stayed still and observed him, seemingly with neither fear nor aggression. He was struck by a sudden urge to take off his hat and bow. Instead, slowly, making no sudden movements, he began to walk in a wide circle around the tree. The wolverine followed him with its gaze for a while, then lost interest and looked out over the ice.

When he had come all the way around the pond and was about to head back into the forest, he turned. The wolverine was still there, a dark spot up in the tree, wrapped up in its own silence. A distant raven screeched. A red-capped woodpecker made a sociable trill in the next tree.

He turned back onto the homeward path. After a while he started humming to himself. Not a song or hymn, just a few random notes. Nothing like the cooing grouse or crying cranes. He was not singing for anyone else. Only himself.

He looked at his mother as she walked between hearth and table. Her long, curved neck. The grey shawl fluttering with every step she took. Her swaying, flapping skirt. Sharp eyes and pointed nose. Her head swung this way and that; she raised an arm to a shelf and lowered it again. There was something graceful about her, yet clumsy at the same time. He sat still, as he had done on the marsh. Silent and still. He didn't want to startle her or remind her of his presence. She seemed to forget he was there. After a while she started humming a song. He recognized it as an old Finnish folk song. She had sung it to him when he was very small. She hummed while kneading dough, and some of her sharpness softened. She had flour up to the elbows on her plump arms, and he realized that she was young. Much younger than Pa.

Ma had a language of her own, even when she didn't speak. She could be understood. If he studied her quietly and calmly, he might understand eventually. Like he had with the grouse.

The birds had such confidence in each movement, but at the same time everything they did was a test. The male grouse intimidating each other. The cranes courting each other. Here I am, here you are, what do I want, what do you want? Listen to me. Look at me.

Ma's silence was about excluding everyone else. She withdrew from the flock, into solitude. Like the wolverine. Ma was more like a wolverine than a bird. Wolverines live alone, except for when females have cubs. And eventually they push their cubs away too.

He and Pa were more like the cranes.

That was just the way it was.

BREAD AND STONE

BREAD

Jakob gave me a sweet braided bun the second time we met.

He had been to the market in town and bought a whole loaf just for me. That night I went out and buried it under the sacrificial stone on the pine ridge at Furustamsåsen. I feared he had laced the bread with something that would compel me to love him.

Not a single crumb passed my lips.

STONE

I could go up to the Skogsperä wetland, fill my pockets with stones, wade into the water, and it would all be over.

But I cannot bring myself to go.

Sometimes I think I must take the children with me and then I feel so tired, even more so. How could I carry them. And the weight. And where would I put all the necessary stones. I can manage Justus, but what do I do if Mina struggles, how do I explain to her that this is the only way, and should one of them survive then, then

I cannot bear it.

Sometimes I do not think of the children at all. One night I was already outside the door before turning back.

Why did I turn back?

BREAD

The second time we met, Jakob gave me a sweet braided bun from the market in town. I buried it for fear of losing my heart.

I was but seventeen. I did not want to love anyone. I saw that he loved me; it was clear in the way he looked at me and moved towards me and the way he breathed. It was obvious in everything he did.

He continued to pursue me. He came to the dances. Came to my door for the nocturnal courtship that is traditional in summer. Came for game afternoons in winter.

I brought other boys to my bedroom. Danced with others. Rode a sleigh with Matts from Nyjärv and accepted a hair band from Simon Ånäs.

It was as if Jakob did not see them. He displayed neither jealousy nor anger. He came to every dance, he sang his way in through my door time after time for nocturnal courtship, touched my hand in the jostle after church, helped me down from the cart at the midsummer party, managed to get me on his lap during some lively game.

Each time he touched me, he looked utterly incredulous, as if something inexplicable had just happened, something he had never experienced before and could never have expected.

STONE

I can still hear Jakob's wheezing breaths. The cottage is so quiet without them, and yet I hear. them and it is never quiet.

His head so heavy in my lap as he drew his final terrible breath.

And Justus who would not stop crying. It was hard to know whether Jakob was gone because I could not hear his breathing.

Justus is swollen and blue. I know what this means. This is how Isak looked when Hugo and Elna took Johanna Rebecka's children home to Nevabacka from the poorhouse after Johanna died. It is lack of food that turns the children blue. Then Isak wasted away. Eventually he looked like a skeleton, there was no flesh on his body. No one could understand how he survived.

And yet he did. For such a terribly long time. Until his large, pleading eyes were the only things that moved.

There is no mercy anywhere. No compassion. First all the poor harvests and starvation, and now the typhoid fever.

Hugo wants us to gather in the Old Cottage and pray under his guidance. We are poor sinners, he says, and this is God's punishment. We must humble ourselves even more, beg for mercy.

Elna no longer takes part in his group prayers. I know what she does instead. She goes into the forest and performs her offerings and prayers there. She believes the forest folk can be of help.

But there is no help. Not anywhere.

BREAD

The weight of the sweet loaf in my hands. Its aroma of butter and sugar. My hands shone with grease after holding it.

Not a crumb of the bread passed my lips.

205

STONE

Perhaps the harvest shall be good this year. Perhaps we shall have real bread to eat this winter. But what about the year after that?

I cannot farm the land alone. My children are too small to help. I refuse to go to the poorhouse. Everyone who goes there dies. I cannot possibly manage alone. We have no means to employ a farmhand. And I cannot turn to Hugo and his wife for help, they are barely managing as it is, and now have Johanna Rebecka's two children to look after as well.

BREAD

Jakob proposed in autumn. I turned him down and bade him to keep away. He said nothing, only nodded and took his cap, the blue one, and left. I watched his broad back disappear over the Dahl farmyard.

Then I did all I could to break the spell.

I asked my father to organize a dance at Dahl and danced with all the village boys.

When winter came I rode sleighs with many a lad. Went tobogganing on the river with them. Laughed and larked and let Samuel kiss me, hidden behind Steinbacka barn.

But it was too late. All was lost. None of it afforded me any joy. All I could think about was what Jakob might be doing. If he was dancing with Emma from Granby. If Hilda was laughing and pressing up against him in the sleigh.

When I came out of church on Christmas morning, I saw him standing there. He was talking to his brother Hugo and sister-in-law Elna. I pulled him aside, round the back of the church, caring not a button who saw us. Earnestly I whispered that he should reverse whatever witchery he had used against me, for I was but seventeen and far too young to bind myself to any man!

He removed his leather gloves and wiped away my tears with his broad thumbs and asked if he might talk to my father, and I wiped my nose on my church shawl and said that, well, he might.

207

Father told us to wait a year. Jakob gave me two gold earrings and said that I should wear them until the day I die.

Mother and Father gave us a mirror as a wedding gift. Sometimes when I am undressed I stand before it. Quite naked yet fully naked never more. The earrings are always there.

I was also given four gold finger rings, which I later discovered Jakob had bought on credit from Mrs Chorin. I no longer have the rings, having sold them when the grain was so expensive last winter and we had nothing to eat. Flour cost 48 marks a sack.

STONE

I have seen Mina lick the inside of the kneading trough in the hope of finding some remnants of dough.

Nothing tastes more bitter than famine bread.

BREAD

When Mina was born she was the most wonderful
weight in my arms. I never wanted to put her down.

STONE

My grandmother's grandmother, who lived past
ninety, had scars all over her body after what the
Cossacks did to her during the Great Wrath. In
the end they poked out her eyes with hot iron.

I think of her constantly.

Such scars are borne still. They do not go
anywhere.

I am not much older than twenty.

How many years must I continue to bear?

BREAD

Jakob bore every stone for the foundation of the
New Cottage himself during the year we were

betrothed. I could not stay away from Nevabacka. I often walked the whole way there in the evenings, once the day's tasks were complete. He was always working when I came, and did not stop when he saw me. I brought bread, sometimes a kringle or other treat. After a while he would remove his cap, wipe the sweat from his brow and come to sit beside me on a stone. I handed him what I had brought; he ate. A shyness came over us that had not been there before our betrothal. I glanced at his bare chest and tried to ignore the thought that soon this very body would be in my bed. This knowledge made me unable to find words to say.

Later Jakob told me he had felt the same. That he was so overwhelmed by the notion that I would soon be his that he could barely taste the food in his mouth.

STONE

When the typhoid fever returned, Elna and little Bror were the only ones unaffected in all of Nevabacka. They tended to the rest of us in our sickbeds. I remember Bror holding the scoop of water to my mouth in his child's hands.

I remember how quiet it was in our house when the children no longer had the energy to complain of their hunger.

BREAD

Jakob and I kept our two cows in the barn together with Hugo and Elna's seven. They were my responsibility, as were the five sheep. Jakob tended the land, and I the animals. Milking, churning, watering, sheering, carding, spinning. And the potatoes. It was my job to plant and dig.

Strange to think we once kept sheep. I can no longer even recall the taste of mutton.

We have one cow left. She is so thin after winter that I can hardly believe she is still alive. She has gone dry, of course.

STONE

The soil here at Nevabacka is not like the soil at Dahl. There the earth is thick and the stones are few. Here the stones are thick. Here every bushel

211

of grain requires enormous effort from the tiller of the soil. Nothing gives itself willingly. Each loaf of bread is a struggle.

I said to Jakob many times that we ought to leave. Buy some land closer to the village. Make our lives a little easier. But he laughed, took my words for jest. He loved the dark woods that whispered around us; he loved being able to walk through the forest and not meet another living soul. Whenever he was away from home for a night or more, in town on errands, or at the market in Kalajoki, or that one time he went all the way to Vaasa for medicine for Mina when she was sick, he always said it was a blessing to be able to live in such peace and serenity, here in nature's quiet haven.

But I have always missed the open landscape around Dahl. I miss the playful babble of the bubbling stream; I miss meeting another person to talk to as soon as I step beyond our fence. I miss the wide fields and pastures where the swallows can swoop unhindered for insects; I miss hearing distant human voices.

Now when I am alone, it is as if the forest is pressing up against the house. It is waiting. Waiting until

212

we are gone, all the humans, so it can reclaim what once belonged to it. With roots and seeds shall it edge closer, ever closer.

STONE

In our third year of marriage it snowed all the way until April. The newspaper said it was still as cold as minus 35 degrees in March. And even by May, there was no sign of summer. Well into June, the ice could still bear weight. It was the 20th of June before summer arrived, and then it came in full force. The leaves sprouted in haste and the cows could finally find something to eat in the outfields. There was a terrible lack of feed at the time, and the prices were sky-high. Most of the autumn rye had rotted, and the barley was planted very late. It was already past midsummer when the potatoes started to sprout.

There was a great deal of rain in July, which made haymaking difficult, but Jakob and I got some hay in at least. On the night of the 23rd of August came hoarfrost, which blackened the potato leaves in the lowest fields, mainly in the village. We were spared this at Nevabacka. Our fields are higher up and in the shelter of the forest. The daytimes were warm and summery. When Jakob and Hugo came to sow the autumn rye, they had no seeds of their own and had to borrow a barrel each from the crown's stores.

By the 3rd of September, everything was frozen. The barley plants, which had looked so promising, were completely ruined. As were the oats and potato greens.

Jakob turned away from me, at a loss for words. At a loss, once again.

STONE

Elna and I were already mixing various sorts of moss into the bread by October. No one could remember ever resorting to famine bread so early in the year. It is usually only ever made on the brink of spring, when the barley and rye have run out. In December, Elna and I took the children with us to Mörktjärn to pick wild calla before the first snow. Bror was so good, he looked after my little ones so that Elna, her girls and I could dig up lots and lots of roots. We mixed everything we could find into the bread: straw, grass-rush root, sorrel root, calla.

But this sort of bread does not sate hunger.

The winter was terribly cold. Minus 38 degrees, said Hugo, who kept up with the news. We were constantly making fires. We had firewood, at least. Jakob had put away a large store because the rowanberries had grown in abundance and he had guessed what was coming. Hugo had to dismiss all the farmhands and maids. But there were still so many mouths to feed, in the Old Cottage and New Cottage.

At times I could think of nothing but those mouths. Gaping black hungry holes.

BREAD

Once Jakob gave me a sweet braided bun from the market in town.

I have dreamed about that bread. His hands around it. The scent.

Hands, bread, scent.

If only I could give that bread to my children.

If only I could reach my hands back in time, and take that sweet loaf and break it into pieces and stuff them into these hungry mouths.

STONE

In January, the poorhouse opened in the village.

Jakob and I barely ate anything any more, so that the children might have as much of that miserable famine bread as possible. Still they moaned of constant hunger pains. It was the most horrifying sound I have ever heard.

In April, thirty-four people in the parish died. One of them was Elna's sister Johanna Rebecka at the poorhouse. That was when Hugo and Elna took her children in.

In May, the typhoid fever came for the first time.

216

BREAD

Bror and Jakob went hunting for birds together
in June. It was the first time we got a little meat
for our pot. Jakob was so weak after the typhoid
fever that he could barely walk; he had to lean on
a cane and could not help with the farm work at
all. But he put food on the table. Wood grouse,
black grouse. They knew where to set the traps.
They rarely came back without a catch. Bror said
he would travel to America as soon as he was big
enough. And earn so much money that no one
at Nevabacka would ever go hungry again. He
would have his own rifle, and dog, and two—no,
three!—horses.

Jakob laughed. He looked out across the fields.
I could never leave this, he said. This place. We
survived the winter. We never gave up. As soon as
I am strong enough, I shall see to it that we never
go hungry again. Never ever.

Bror and I did the sowing together as best we
could. He worked almost as well as a grown man,
despite his weakness following the hunger winter.
But our harvest shall not be great. Not even if it
turns out well.

217

STONE

In July, Jakob went to the parish meeting held in
the home of parish clerk Rask and when he came
back he was sick. He suffered terribly. He brought
the typhoid fever to Old Cottage as well; Hugo
fell ill and so did two of the girls. But not me, and
not my children.

Jakob was so weak. He had barely recovered from
the first fever. He had barely eaten a thing, for
the children's sake. He had barely he had barely

His body ached so much he did not know how
to lie in bed.

Finally he prayed for God to take him. And God
obliged.

I cradled his head in my lap when he died. A wonderful weight. I can still feel it. And its warmth.

BREAD

Jakob built this house for us at Nevabacka with his
own hands. This is where I laid my home-woven

rugs on the floor, and Jakob plastered the walls with clay water to make it brighter and cheerier indoors. He never knew how to show the extent of his love for me. He never realized that I already knew, that I had known ever since he handed me that braided bun from the market. I baked bread in the stone oven he built for me. Our own bread, from our own rye. We crawled into the bed he had built, between the sheets I had woven, and fed each other the bread. The scent of linen and bread and Jakob.

STONE

It is high summer now. Everything is growing as it should. It is set to be a good harvest.

If I sold my earrings, the ones I was supposed to wear until the day I die. Surely Hugo could give me something for the cow. Perhaps then I might get enough money together for tickets on a ship for me and the children.

Once my beloved gave me a braid of the finest, sweetest bread.

BIRD GIRL

My dear Miss Sarcelius,

I know we agreed to address one another as Alina and
Charlotte, but it felt rather ceremonial to begin my first ever
letter to you with "Miss". You do not mind, do you? I can hardly
believe that our wonderful spring and summer together is over
so soon and that we can no longer see each other almost every
day. I am profoundly happy that you have found a teacher there
in Helsinki, who can provide you with artistic training as well
as the discipline you have craved. Only do not tire yourself,
for you have your schooling to think of as well! Your friend up
here in the far north cannot help but miss her dear Charlotte.
I have never had a friend like you!

I remember the first time I saw you, when the good Pastor
Rannelius assembled his confirmation class for the first time.
I assumed I would know everyone there as former classmates
from public school and could not have predicted that I was to
meet anyone new in the rectory. Hence my surprise when I
encountered you in the rectory hall, next to the wall with the

220

beautiful golden wallpaper that I had always admired on the few occasions I had cause to be there. Perhaps this is why I still have such a vivid memory of your outfit that day: a sailor-inspired dress of white and blue, with leg-of-mutton sleeves bigger than any I had seen before, and a wide sash. You wore the most adorable little hat too, and your skin was creamy white with beautiful rosy cheeks. At first I was too intimidated by your elegance to approach you—there I was in my homespun striped skirt and Ma's best apron around my waist with a long girlish braid down my back. You were as exquisite as one of the fine vases in the rectory, as if you too were made of porcelain. It made me feel frumpy and awkward indeed. You were simply sitting there, reading a book. My schoolmates offered friendly greetings from the couch where they were sitting and chatting, and I curtsied to the pastor's wife, but kept glancing back at you. I was desperate to know what book you were reading! And when I saw that it was *Times of Gustaf Adolf*, I knew I could approach you. Because that is my absolute favourite book! But before I could open my mouth, you had lifted your eyes from the page and were looking at me with your clear, open gaze. Naturally, you addressed me first. That is how it will always be with us. I am the dreamy, hesitant one, while you are a decisive woman of action.

I am forever grateful that Pastor Rannelius and his wife are your godparents! Otherwise you never would have come to this corner of Finland to attend catechism school. And what marvellous fortune that they invited you to stay with them all summer long! I really do not know what I would have done if we had been forced to part already after Pentecost. How fortunate that we were able to spend the whole summer together—except for when I had chores to do at home, of course. My happiness would have been complete if only you could have stayed forever. Though perhaps such happiness would be more than my young heart could bear!

Did you know that there used to be an animal in these parts called the Finnish forest reindeer? They were so numerous that they were the most common local hunting game. We still have a gimlet with a shaft of reindeer horn at home. The very last forest reindeer was shot during one of the many famines a century ago, and it saved the lives of many people. Maybe it even saved my life by sacrificing its own. God truly works in mysterious ways.

I often think of that reindeer. I am not sure why. People rarely speak of it any more, because it is neither a dramatic nor interesting story. But I have a favourite spot down by the nearby Vittermåsa marsh, so called because people used to believe that *vitter* folk—trolls and elves and such—lived there. There is a particular hillock that I favour because it affords a magnificent vista over a large portion of the marsh, and some respite from the mosquitoes. I like to sit there, quite still, and simply breathe, enjoying the sweet fragrance rising from the marsh, especially on warm summer days. It is an intoxicating smell of herbs and spices. If I stay completely still, I can see animals: wood grouse and black grouse in spring, and the occasional fox in summer if I am there early enough, and late one evening I saw a badger trot past very close to where I was sitting. It looked so funny with its waddling gait! Whenever I sit there, beautiful though it may be, my thoughts turn to the forest reindeer and I am overwhelmed by a profound melancholy. How lonely it must have been! Imagine being the last of your kind, constantly searching for your herd. Walking and walking, calling and calling, with no response.

I have felt like that forest reindeer at times. Except I did get a response in the end. I got you. I am no longer alone.

Now I must attend to the milking. Write soon and tell me if you found the correct sort of easel! And I want to know everything about Mrs Såltin. Is she very old? Have you seen her altarpieces yet?

Your eternally faithful,

Alina

Dearest Charlotte,

How happy your letter has made me! I have been somewhat poorly and fatigued of late, with a persistent cold and subsequent cough that has kept me confined to my bed for the last few weeks, but Ma said that when I saw Pa had come back from the village with a letter from you, I was like a new girl. I whisked the letter away to my room and sat for a long time just *looking* at it. I imagined you writing it with your effortless, confident handwriting, and the letter travelling all those many kilometres here to me: by steamboat and courier. It almost felt as if I had travelled the whole way myself, and got to see all the parts of our beautiful country I have otherwise only ever read about in Topelius' *The Book of Our Country*.

How beautifully your Miss Jakobson describes the meetings between "different natures and intellects" that occur in school. And to think that now you get to tread on the same school floors as your role model Miss Thesleff! You wrote that you want to help shape the image we Finns have of our own country. That you want to learn about Finland, its nature and geography, so that you can paint it and arouse love for the motherland in all who see your paintings. I think this is a most honourable endeavour. There is so much wonder and beauty in this land, which I think its inhabitants often have a hard time seeing. We are so used to being under one yoke or another that we do not lift our eyes high enough to see the beauty that surrounds us.

You and I have different ways of looking up. You see mighty pine trees, majestic rocks and rapids. You see endless marshes where wood grouse play. I know that my parents' idea of beauty is a potato field still untouched by frost in September. For them, beauty is a golden field of dense rye, ready to be harvested. For them, this land is what gives us our daily bread, and for that they thank the Lord. I am not saying they are wrong, not at all! There was terrible famine throughout the country thirty years ago, as you know, when my parents were very young. They saw many friends and relatives go to their graves, and they themselves suffered greatly from want and hardship. As far as they are concerned, nothing but prayer is as important as a good

224

harvest. I am sure that this has influenced me as well, despite the fact that I have never experienced hunger as severe as the famine of 1868. I too pay close attention to the growth of rye and barley. I always feel gently concerned until we get the harvest safely under cover and know that we will survive another winter. I have decided to try to contribute what I can to our livelihood, and this year I cultivated a small plot of land where I am growing cabbage and cauliflower. I obtained plants from the village schoolteacher, who is very interested in such things.

Nevertheless, when I think of the motherland, my thoughts do not turn to grain and vegetable fields. Neither do images of mountains and rapids appear in my mind.

I think of the first forest leaves unfurling after a long, harsh winter. Green and bursting with life, they wait for the touch of spring's magic wand to sprout. I think about how it feels to walk in the meadows on a summer's morn when all is fragrant and the birds are singing; it is like a foretaste of God's heavenly kingdom. I think about the joy I feel in my breast when, on an early summer evening, mists sweep across the fields and meadows and I hear Maja-Stina call for the cows. She has such a beautiful, sonorous voice and a peculiar way of calling, which evokes a sense of melancholy in me. I feel both sad and uplifted at once. Have you ever felt that way? When I think of Finland, I think of these little things, which are difficult enough to put into words, let alone cram into a painting.

Every day, I miss our conversations. Spending time with you was something of an education in itself! You have seen so much, travelled to so many places, experienced so many things—when you told me about Imatra and Turku, about the herring market in Helsinki and Stockholm's reflection in the sea, it was almost as if I got to experience it all myself. Oh, the evenings we spent together, in the rectory and here in our humble home! I vividly remember sitting together here in my room, discussing something we had just read aloud, and Ma coming in to ask why we were arguing so! But we were not arguing at all, we were simply excited about what we were reading and wanted to explore the novel ideas we had encountered in some book or gazette. Ma could only shake her head and say that she did not understand half of what we talked about, and where on earth did we learn it all? It was from books, and gazettes, and our conversations. Why should we not be able to use our minds just as well as Pa, or Sven, or any man?

Yes, that reminds me: thank you for the book you sent. I have already had to promise Elsa that she can read it once I have finished, which I just have. Miss Westermarck writes so captivatingly on topics I have rarely read about before: how young girls and women see their own lives. As much as I love *Times of Gustaf Adolf*, one certainly could not credit it with a great understanding of the dreams of young girls!

I especially liked the story "In Youth". I recognize in Westermarck's writing much that I have often felt myself, but never understood. I would never have been able to put the roots of these feelings into words.

"Her deepest desire was to find her life's purpose," writes

Miss Westermarck. I have often felt this too. We even talked about it last summer, remember? You were helping me hang laundry on a hot day, and you were telling me about your artistic ambitions. Your cheeks flushed pink with excitement, and you were so pretty that I wanted to eat you up. Yet I was also aching with envy, wishing that I too could have a similar sense of purpose, a calling, something to accomplish on this, our Earth. I almost envy Högh in the story, who, despite humble beginnings, manages through hard work to get an education and make his way in the world. But he is a man! This is not the reality of women's lives.

There was one line that made me look up from the book to see if Miss Westermarck was not right there in my chamber speaking directly to me:

> "If you only knew, how trapped I am, and how unlearned and useless I feel."

How can Miss Westermarck so accurately express what I myself have felt all summer, ever since I became acquainted with you and the world opened up to me in all its glory? Of course Alice, who utters the statement in the story, has a completely different life from mine, and she may mean something different when she says this. But the words still resounded inside me like church bells.

How glad I am to know you, dearest Charlotte. Our friendship means more to me than it does to you, I am sure, surrounded as you are by other schoolgirls and all the pleasures and temptations of the capital. You are my window to everything out there. You are also the one who has shown me the walls within which I live.

Your forever faithful,
Alina

Dear Charlotte,

I must begin by thanking you so much for your generous invitation. Of course it would have been delightful to come and spend Christmas with you and your mother. No, "delightful" is not a grand enough word to describe it! I felt utter bliss and joy on reading the lines you had written, and the lines your mother so kindly added. I was filled with thoughts of the exciting journey, of boarding a steamship, of you and your mother meeting me at the harbour in snowy, sunny Helsinki, and finally seeing with my own eyes the white and yellow houses and churches of the capital! Everything you wrote about—the theatres, soirées, dancing, concerts and lectures—was beyond the limits of my imagination, for I have only ever read of such things. Instead I imagined how pleasant and cosy it would be to sit with you and your mother by a blazing fire and sing carols while your sister accompanied us on the pianoforte.

Then I came to my senses and put all these visions and fantasies where they belong: in the dresser drawer where I keep my most treasured possessions (including letters from you). I know that you invited me with the best of intentions. You have a warm and generous heart, which is one of the reasons I love you so. How can I make you understand the utter impossibility of what you propose, without causing offence or hurting my own pride? Because yes, I am proud, dear Charlotte, it is one of my great faults, may God forgive me!

You see, Charlotte: a farmer's daughter from a small village has neither the money, clothes nor time to undertake such a journey and participate in all the pleasures you describe. It is quite impossible. Sometimes I struggle against this fact but I must surrender. As much as I long to see you, my dear, beloved friend, if we had a coin to spare, I would spend it on an education, though I do not know whether such a thing could ever be available to me. For though my vain heart is tempted by pleasures and fancy, there is a part of me—and I believe it is the purest, highest part of my soul, to which I should listen as much as I can—that yearns even more for knowledge, education and learning. If I could only have that, I would be more than satisfied with my lot in life, with my home-woven skirt and my striped cotton cloth that Pa was so proud to bring home from the Nykarleby market last spring.

So you see, I did not write those lines about feeling trapped and useless with the intention of eliciting an invitation to the pleasures of the capital. It was because you are the only one to whom I can air these thoughts and musings. Nobody at home understands such things at all. Pa would pat me on the back and say that he never would have managed the haymaking without my help this summer. And maybe add that he knows how much Ma appreciates my help in her work. And if I said I felt useless, Ma, God bless her, would tell me that there were any number of chores waiting to be done.

You are the only one who speaks the same language as I do. It is the language of longing: the longing to accomplish something great, to help our burdened motherland, to do something *meaningful*. You have art, whereas I, I have cows.

No, I refuse to fall into melancholy and ingratitude. You and your mother are terribly sweet to have thought up such wonderful pleasures for me. Tonight before bed I shall say a prayer of gratitude that the good Lord brought you my way. May you and your mother know health and vitality.

Your Alina

My sweet Charlotte,

I am sitting in my bedroom as darkness falls outside, and I can hear my mother walking around in the adjacent room, humming a hymn. I have been in good health for some time now, and have therefore been very active in village community life. I went to the temperance society meeting today, and we rehearsed a play called *The Emigrant*. It always makes me think of Sven. We received a letter from him in Africa last summer, but have heard nothing since. May God protect him over there! Before he left, he told me that he wanted to do what Pa never had the courage to do: travel to some faraway land and earn lots of money to enable the farm to truly flourish. I disagree with Sven, however: it was not cowardice or fear that prevented Pa from doing so. He was his parents' only son, and had he left, it would have broken Grandma's heart, I am sure. Grandpa died when Pa was very young, and had he not taken care of the farm and his mother and sisters, they would have ended up destitute. Things are different for Sven. Mother and Father are still young and able to work, and he knows that I am here to help.

Last summer, Sven wrote about lions and people with black skin. He had found work as a miner and believed he would make his fortune. He has so many plans for what to do with the money when he gets home. Tiled stoves and agricultural machinery and livestock. He plans to drain Vittermåsa marsh and buy more forest land to provide timber and various other resources. He has never been satisfied with what he has. Even as a child, he always coveted someone else's horse, someone else's fine sleigh or elegant hat. I pray every night that God will teach him about gratitude and contentment.

You must miss our beloved youth association sometimes, surely? I often think that we would never have got it off the ground without your drive and ability to rally people. The idea was mine, that I will admit, but one cannot get very far with ideas alone. Oh, how I miss your presence at our socials and meetings! Kurt Mjölnars founded a gymnastics association for the boys last winter, and this autumn I would like to start a study circle in which we could support each other in private study and edifying reading. I know that Moa Andersson and Uncle Ingmar's Tilda would be interested, at least.

I will have to content myself with this, for lack of better options.

The harvest is done now. We have a moderate amount of rye. The cattle will not starve during the winter, at least, and for that we thank God!

Oh, Charlotte, do you remember Matilda Wennberg's little brother Hans Anders? The one who was so helpful that time when we overturned Pa's cart in a ditch, and Prince was so spooked and wild that I dared not approach near enough to untie him and get him out of the ditch? Hans Anders calmed him down and freed him, young though he was, only eleven going on twelve. He would often meet Matilda after confirmation class and walk her home. They were very close, the two of them, ever since their mother died of tuberculosis a few years ago. He died last Sunday, hit by a hunter's stray bullet. It is so terribly sad, but it must have been God's will. The funeral is on Wednesday, and Ma and I plan to attend.

It has made me think a great deal about death. It does not frighten me all that much, Charlotte. I know that I shall meet our Lord God, and that thought fills me with more joy than sorrow. Today, when I was out looking for the three heifers let out to pasture—which were doing such a good job of hiding that one might have thought they had been stolen—I looked around the forest. The tall, mysterious firs rising out of brilliant green moss. The friendly red lingonberries, shining out from among dark, waxy leaves. The fresh, sweet scent of the forest, the yearning calls of migratory birds, the light filtering through the trees, the dew adorning the spiders' webs and making them sparkle like crystals between the dark spruce branches. I was so overcome with all this beauty that even death would seem a happy thing if all I had to do was lie down and rest my head on a mossy stone under rustling firs to draw my final breath! The beauty that nature exhibits here on Earth takes my breath away. How beautiful then must the Kingdom of Heaven be? Hence, death here in God's creation and transcendence to His eternal paradise would be a blessing and nothing to fear at all.

But first I want to fulfil the task the Lord put me on Earth to accomplish, except I do not know what that might be. I do so wish I had a goal to work towards, as you do. Something better, more worthwhile than simply marrying someone from the parish and having children and toiling in the fields. Not that I am afraid of hard work! No, in fact I long for it, but it has to be my own. My own mission in life. I ask God every night to help me find my path. I also pray that He watch over you and keep you in good health.

Yours,
Alina

Beloved Charlotte,

It is a beautiful, glistening winter's day here on the plains of Ostrobothnia. Topelius described just such a day: "It was winter, the morning's blush coloured the clouds in the south-east; a pale, panting shimmer flew over the waves of the Baltic Sea. The snow on the mountains crimsoned by its light, the dark tops of the pines brightened." I believe it must have been recollections of mornings such as these that inspired you to write such lofty, romantic lines about how being in nature and the forest is really, truly living.

When I read your lines, I too am filled with the same feeling: that everyone should get out into hearty farmland to learn what life is really all about! Then I am reminded by my cold aching hands that I live and work on "hearty farmland" already. And there has been plenty of work here at Nevabacka this autumn, but we also had a wonderful Christmas celebration!

The festivities begin in earnest when Aunt Anna-Lisa and Uncle Elis arrive from town on a sleigh. Anna-Lisa is Pa's sister, and Elis is a telegraph operator in town, which is a good job, and they have three daughters and a splendid home. Their eldest, Emmy Susanna, is the same age as me. They always have such nice clothes, my cousins! I used to have to wrestle with the demon of envy whenever I saw them, but my mind was not plagued by comparisons this year. Perhaps God has heard my prayer and helped me eradicate envy from my heart! But I have reason to believe that your friendship is partially to thank. Perhaps I am above such petty feelings now that I have found a true best friend in you.

Aunt Anna-Lisa had brought a letter from America, where Grandpa Hugo's brother Jakob's widow Magdalena lived for over twenty years. She emigrated with her two children after the great famine of the 1860s. She has done well over there and does not plan to return. Her daughter Mina is married to a millworker, and her son Justus is also married and works at a stone quarry, or what was it called? A *factory*, according to Magdalena, where they work with granite. It is in Washington.

This time, however, Magdalena's letter came with sad news. My grandmother had a sister, who was married to a man named Wilhelm Korp and had three small children. During the famine, Wilhelm travelled south in search of work, and after his wife died in the poorhouse in town, Grandpa and Grandma took their children in and raised them. The youngest died of starvation. Albert travelled to America three years ago and found employment at a sawmill there, with the help of our relative Justus. Now Magdalena writes that there was a terrible accident, in which "a large mass of earth containing great rocks and stumps came crashing down from the mountains and buried almost half of the workers. Some were buried and some were carried down to the rapids, where they drowned. Albert is no more."

Grandma had come to the house to greet our guests. She lives in New Cottage, but of course we celebrate Christmas together here in Old Cottage, so she heard the news at the same time as us. She took it very hard. I was genuinely afraid that her heart might fail.

Imagine dying so far away, surrounded by strangers! I am terribly worried that the same fate might befall Sven. How I wish we could afford to send him to school, so that he could find a safer job than mining!

My favourite part of Christmas is when we all gather for dinner. There are so many of us around the table and the atmosphere is warm and heartfelt. The candles in the Christmas tree are burning, a fire is crackling in the hearth, and it is warm and cosy and lovely. I can think of no better Christmas Eve celebration—not even in the King's palace!

After the evening meal, the Yule Goat comes in his hideous mask! When we were little, we were terribly afraid of him, and I saw that Malin was indeed still somewhat frightened. I was given a skirt made of fabric which Pa had ordered from town and which Aunt Anna-Lisa had brought with her. She had helped Pa choose it, so it was both beautiful and fit me well.

Then Christmas morning is even more wonderful than Christmas Eve. You see, I am the one who sneaks out in the wee hours to milk the cows so that Ma can sleep. I light a lantern and walk out into the serene, holy beauty of Christmas morning. The night is black and bitterly cold. If I am lucky, thousands and thousands of stars sparkle in the sky above. I was lucky this year. The forest was silent beneath its white blanket, slumbering, dreaming. It felt as though I were the only one awake in the whole world.

It is warm inside the cow barn and smells of cattle and hay; it is a reassuring smell for me. I milk the cows and talk to them. When I have finished milking, I pour some milk into a saucer and put it in a dark corner for the Christmas elf. Grandma has told me all about him. You will probably laugh at such superstition over there in the big city, but you must understand that out here in the woods, with very few human neighbours, one must take good care of our non-human neighbours! We depend on their favour and goodwill. And I cannot imagine God would disapprove of one innocent little dish of milk.

By the time I emerge from the barn, Grandma has come into our cottage and lit candles in every window, to welcome our Saviour. And that sight, Charlotte—our humble home, nestled deep in snowdrifts sparkling in the starlight, with twinkling lights in every little window—is among the most beautiful things I know on Earth. I like to stand outside and enjoy the view for as long as I can, until the cold chases me inside, and then Grandma and I enjoy a cup of coffee, some sweet buns and a chat until the others wake up and it is time to get Prince and the sleigh ready to go to church for the Christmas sermon.

Yes, that was our cosy Christmas at Nevabacka. I hope that you were similarly surrounded by love and warmth and holy peace. You wrote that you were suffering from a cold before Christmas, and I do so hope that you are recovered and back to full health!

Yours,

Alina

My dearest Charlotte,

I must tell you about something utterly incredible that happened to me last month. Our little school—which is located near Nevabacka here in Österby, not the one in the church village—hired a new teacher at the beginning of the year. But just as she was about to arrive to take up her post, her mother fell terribly ill and she was unable to leave home. So the village council asked if *I* would agree to teach until she is able to come! I asked my parents for advice, and they both agreed that I was very well suited for it. And I get paid! Albeit not as much as a real, trained teacher. I was almost sick with nerves as I skied to the schoolhouse, which was built last year, in the middle of January. After all, I only have an elementary education, and I was rather nervous as to how it would all turn out.

However, when I stood there in front of my eleven little students, with the fire crackling in the stove and their eager eyes fixed on me, a feeling washed over me with such intensity that it almost took my breath away. It was a feeling of coming home. Even though I had never taught before, I was not the least bit nervous or at a loss once I began. I would not say it was easy, but even when I encountered setbacks or problems, it was not too difficult or unpleasant to find ways out and solutions. The children were all familiar to me already, including my own youngest sister Malin, so we were not strangers to each other. This had its downsides, as some of the boys thought that it was their playmate Alina standing in front of them, who could be subject to pranks and trickery. But no, I immediately stepped into my role, and it was the role of teacher. And, sure enough, they quickly understood that there was a difference between the Alina who drilled them on religious history and multiplication, and the Alina who used to throw balls and discs with them in springtime.

What a fantastic feeling, to have the opportunity to do something I am good at! Now I finally understand how you must feel when you paint and draw. God has heard my prayer, and now I know what it is He has put me on Earth to accomplish. I am going to be a schoolteacher, Charlotte. Is that not a wonderful idea? I have not told anyone else. I think this dream began to germinate last summer when you told me what it is like there in the girls' school and all the things you learn about. It made me think about how precious learning and knowledge are, which is something I have pondered a lot during the autumn and winter. I have also thought a lot about how many children there are in our country who still have access to only the most basic education. There is work to be done! If I could continue down this path, I would consider myself the luckiest girl in the world. What a privilege, to be able to lead Finland's children along the path of knowledge, to contribute to the eradication of ignorance and the state of helplessness that it inevitably creates. But *how* this can be accomplished remains unclear. We have no money whatsoever for me to attend the seminary. If only I could find some way to earn the money myself! It would take years, but I can be patient. I save all I can from the small salary I get now. This autumn, I intend to pick a lot of lingonberries to sell, which certainly will not go far, but it is a start. With God's help, I might succeed!

Yours faithfully,

Alina

Beloved Charlotte,

What a hateful month is March! Daylight returns and lures you into thoughts of spring, when in reality spring is infinitely far away. Of course, bright sun on hard snow crust is beautiful, and it is wonderful to see willow buds budding and meltwater dripping from the roof on the warmer days. But the road is a great big muddy puddle, untraversable by cart and perilous by sleigh, and Prince becomes so flighty in bad road conditions that he is completely impossible to handle. We can still ski, thank goodness, so I can get to the schoolhouse without too much trouble. I have heard that the schoolmistress' mother is on the mend, and we should expect her after Easter. I will be sorry to have to give up my post, which has already become so dear to me in this short time.

It was wonderful to receive your letter and read about all the grandiose plans you are making on my behalf! You are absolutely right: I simply must attend the seminary in Ekenäs if I want to become a teacher. There, I could learn everything I want and need in order to help nurture the nation's youth.

I have cautiously mentioned my dreams—I cannot yet consider them worthy of the title of "plans"—to Ma and Pa, and they were not as averse to the idea as I had feared. *How* it might be done is a completely different matter. They cannot spare me here at home, as Sven is still in Africa. No funds are available for my education either. Not yet.

Enough now about me and my life—there were details in your letter that worried me. I hope you did not catch a cold

240

during that long sleigh ride in February, did you? My own chest cold stubbornly persists. Sometimes I feel better, but then my cough will flare up and I feel weak again. I have also thought a lot about how much you write about sleigh rides, dances and various soirées and parties you attend. It is not that I begrudge you your pleasures and diversions but—and now I know I am going to come across as an old biddy, but it cannot be helped, for who will tell you this if not your own friend?—it is obvious to me what is *missing* from your letters. You write almost nothing about your studies and schooling, and nothing at all about your art and lessons. In the past your letters were so full of sketches and easels, still life and colour study, and it always made me happy to know how seriously you were taking your studies. It is your ambition and vision that pushed me to find my own equally valuable calling to strive for. Tell me you have not forgotten all your old plans, Charlotte? I realize that you are being courted by a number of amusing and attentive gentlemen there in Helsinki, and that it is a pleasure to be admired and wooed. But surely there must be a balance, Charlotte. It cannot be all that hard to achieve a balance, can it? What does your mother say about all this? I am almost tempted to write to her directly. No, that is not a threat, dear friend, do not frown at me in that way you do. It was just a thought.

Oh, now I fear I have vexed you, and am filled with anxiety and anguish. But not with a guilty conscience! For I know that I am correct in this matter, though I know it is bound to displease you. Do not be angry with your Alina, but please think about what I have written and answer me as honestly as you can.

Your forever faithful,

Alina

Dearest Charlotte,

April has come, bringing sun, warmth and your letter! You cannot imagine how anxious and tormented I was while waiting. I think you must have delayed your reply a little, just to keep your poor friend in suspense! But your letter brought solace and relief.

It is precisely this aspect of your nature that first drew me to you, I think. The casual observer might find you too flippant or frivolous: you laugh heartily and often; you love to joke and are always open to games, fun and pranks. But your jokes and antics never come from a place of cruelty, and there is always a serious undertone to your laughter. If I have helped you see that you were losing your way and forgetting your calling, as you say, I am quite sure that you would have realized it for yourself sooner or later. I just helped you see it a little earlier, that is all.

The portrait of me you sent was really quite stunning. I had it framed and it now sits on my little table next to my bed, where it is the first thing I see when I wake up and the last thing I see before I close my eyes at night. It is almost like having you here with me—almost. What would I give to hear your bubbly laughter again, to hold my arm around your waist, to kiss your rosy cheek!

I do not quite know how to respond to your mother's suggestion. It is so wonderful that it feels like a dream—a dream from which I never want to wake. I took your letter with me out to the stream, which has discarded its icy cover and is now flowing high and strong like a little river. There is a special rock where I sit sometimes to listen to the murmur of the water. There I sat, your letter in hand, letting the trickling flow envelop me and the spring sunshine warm my back, and I felt like anything was possible. Tonight I will tell Ma and Pa about your mother's proposal, and if they are amenable, then yes, I will write to the headmistress of the seminary school, Miss Sohlberg, and enquire as to the opportunities for autumn. You must express my deepest thanks to your mother. I intend to write to her myself as well, of course, but please take her face in your hands and kiss her on both cheeks from me. She must be exactly as I imagined from your descriptions: good to the depths of her soul. I promise that I will repay her the debt in exactly the way she describes, and I promise her a high interest besides: I intend to work as hard as any girl in the seminary before me and educate all the children who ever come into my care to be God-fearing, loyal citizens of our nation.

Your letter is not the only thing that has brightened my life of late. At the end of March, a letter arrived from Sven! He is working hard down there and says that his job is certainly not for the weak or lazy. He seems to have found some pleasant fellows from Vaasa and Korsholm to socialize with, and there is even a young man from Kokkola in his work team. He writes that these are bad times for labourers and that many roam from place to place without finding work. The ones who have a job, like Sven, get a good daily wage, but food costs dearly. When Sven went to the Christmas service, the church was decorated as though for midsummer, he wrote. He almost expected the pastor to talk about John the Baptist instead of the birth of baby Jesus! The pastor urged them to be guided by the Star of Bethlehem, so that they do not lose their way in that foreign land. Beautiful words, and I hope Sven takes them to heart. Though I am not altogether sure he has, for he wrote that as he and his acquaintances were walking home that evening, they saw the great lamp shining above the opening of the gold mine. His companion said: "There is our Star of Bethlehem," to which Sven replied: "Yes, but it lights the way down."

I often wonder how it would feel to be so utterly detached from one's homeland and flung far out into the world, where nothing is familiar. Not even the starry sky is the same. I know that there are people who grow tired of seeing the same old stars year after year, but to me they are like dear friends, benevolently shining down on me from their familiar places. I could never leave them behind.

Your eternally faithful,
Alina

Beloved Charlotte,

It is raining today. A lovely, bountiful spring rain that is washing away the last of the snow. Now the forest, fields and meadows are preparing for spring, for life! And I too am preparing for life, dear Charlotte! You will never believe it, but Pa is letting me attend Ekenäs! All your and your mother's care and effort have not been in vain! I do not know if you could ever understand the depths of my gratitude. And, if this happy news were not enough, you also wrote in your letter that you are going to spend the summer at the rectory! Oh, Charlotte, it is simply too wonderful for words! How I will kiss your sweet face when you are here! You will hardly have the time to settle in with your aunt and uncle before I am there, drawn to you like an ant to sugar. A whole summer with you, and then autumn at the seminary in Ekenäs—it is too much joy to bear! This is when my life begins, I can feel it.

Now that Ekenäs is truly on the horizon, I have been struck by a completely unexpected feeling: homesickness, Charlotte! Yes, truly—I am homesick before ever having left home! The mere *thought* of leaving behind these dear daily sights brings tears to my eyes. Will I not bid farewell to the migratory birds from Furustamsåsen as I do every autumn? Will I not ride to church with my family in the sleigh through cold, silent, star-sparkling forests, with the horse bells ringing in my ears and a shawl wrapped around my head? Will I not greet the happy face of the first coltsfoot growing up the wall of our dear cottage?

How can I feel this way, pray tell, when I am about to realize my dreams? You must think me very ungrateful, dear

Charlotte! Do not think I do not want to go. Because I do, terribly! It is only that this land is such a big part of who I am that I wonder if I will recognize myself without these hills, rocks and lakes around me. I imagine myself as a dug-up plant with bare roots. I hope that my root threads can reattach to Ekenäs soil.

Yesterday I went to sleep on my bedroom floor, fully clothed. I wanted to be woken by the sun! I woke up very early this morning, when the eastern horizon was just beginning to pale from black to indigo blue, and hurried up and out without waking anyone. In my sturdiest old boots and with a thick shawl around my head and shoulders, warm enough despite the cold morning. There had not been a night frost, but it was probably close to freezing. The buds on the birches are swelling but are yet to burst. Soon though, so very soon! I can hear the sap rising and bubbling in the tree trunks.

I did not hurry as I walked along the paths, for it was still dark and I wanted to be careful not to stumble or take a wrong path. There were glorious perfumes in the air—and not of sunshine and flowers and grass like in summer—but of the last meltwater, the rich sweetness of the soil, of promises and possibilities! I came upon a little valley of bluebells in full bloom, a whole sea of them, and their fragrance was sweet and strong. I sat down and bathed in their intense blue colour, so bright amongst all the dry, dead things that had not yet come to life. But soon the dawn chased me onward, until finally I came out of the forest to Mörktjärn Lake that lay, mirror-like, under the bright blue sky. A swan honked its warning when I arrived, but did not fly away. I walked past the devil's fields to the edge of the marsh and positioned myself in the exact right place to watch the sun rise over the marsh. Then I sat down on a fallen tree trunk and simply—simply existed, Charlotte. First the sky turned red, almost scarlet, with streaks of pink and gold. And then the sun rose above the horizon and shone through the forest, slashing golden streaks across the trees' shadows. I have never written any poetry or verse, but in that moment, my dearest, my whole soul was a poem.

Thin veils of mist floated over the marsh, and the birds greeted the sun with their most exquisite song. No church choir could sound as uplifting, as cleansing and healing as their winged choir! I believe that birdsong is God's way of giving us a foretaste of His heavenly choir. Do you not agree?

When the sun had risen above the treetops, I decided it was time to go home, stood up and stomped some warmth into my frozen toes. Then I caught sight of an inconspicuous little yellow flower at my feet. I have seen it before on the marsh in early summer, but I have never seen it bloom so early. I do not know its name. Its sisters had not yet unfolded their petals, but it was as if this one particular flower could not wait; it was keen to greet the spring and sunshine with its own golden splendour. I think it is the same colour as the marsh cloudberry. I picked it and have pressed it with the intention of sending it in the envelope with this letter. So you get a little greeting from Ostrobothnia, from spring and your friend!

Write soon and tell me exactly when I might expect you! There is so much we have to do this summer, there is no time to lose!

Yours impatiently,
Alina

My dearest, sweetest friend,

Do you remember when I showed you the marsh teeming with cloudberries at the end of summer? The entire marsh appeared as though covered in most precious gold silk. We had taken a blanket with us to sit up on the small stone stack between Vittermåsa and Mörkvattnet, and you gazed in delight at the view spanning before us. "Someone should paint this," you said. "This landscape deserves to be immortalized just as much as Gallen-Kallela's dramatic eastern landscapes! This, too, is true Finland, the motherland that we all hold so dear!" And you took out your sketch pad and began to draw with quick, sure strokes.

I sat next to you and tried to see through your eyes. Tried to see the drama of it, as you said, but I am still not sure what that means. I wish I could see all the works of art you talk and write so much about; maybe I would understand better then. But even then, I suspect it might not help. All I saw was the marsh where I have picked cloudberries and cranberries ever since I was a child, near my and my mother's blueberry spots. On the other side of the lake is the place where we pick lingonberries, and I have earned a coin or two from picking and selling berries from these forests. I saw the place where Pa killed an elk, and I saw the site of a hidden old hut, inhabited by priests and robbers of the past, apparently. Even though I could not see it from where we sat, I know where the cross is that marks the spot where one of my ancestors drowned. I know where the tar pit is, where we burn pine into dark liquid tar, which fetches a good price.

That is what I saw when I looked out across the marsh and water: God's good gifts to us poor lowly mortals. I cannot agree with Snellman, however learned and righteous he may be, when he says that "where the forest reigns, there also reigns misery, ignorance and brutality". We are not brutes, are we, Charlotte? We who cultivate the land, who toil so that all of Finland may have bread on their table and butter on their bread. Are we brutes for not being literate in the same way as Mr Snellman?

Ah, I am vexed, as you can tell! I happened to read this quote in the newspaper the other day, and I get angry every time I think about it. Now, how did I get from the golden cloudberry marsh to anger at Snellman? You know I have a hard time sticking to the subject.

I have been bedridden with a cough and fever for a while now since you left, but have not suffered too badly. I have all the memories from our summer together to recall and enjoy! And Pa has been unusually kind and caring towards me. Whenever he has a moment to spare, he sits with me in my chamber and talks to me, and if I am too tired to talk or read, he entertains me by reading aloud from the newspaper. One evening he came in just as it was getting dark. He did not light a lamp but simply sat down with his legs stretched out in front and his feet on the rag rug, gazing out of the window. We were both silent, watching the slowly fading light and listening to the sounds of the night take over. August evenings are so gentle and beautiful, do you not think? I am always a little more romantic than usual on August evenings. I lay thinking about that bright, wonderful evening before midsummer when we swung in the garden swing by the rectory, looking out over the river, the scent of lilacs in the air, and everything was like a dream. How we chattered during those first weeks together! It was as if we were afraid the words would run out. Eventually, one evening we calmed down and were able to sit together quietly. A late cuckoo called and the river murmured and whispered. I heard you breathe, and took your hand, and thought that no moment on Earth could be sweeter than this.

My mind was back there, in the garden swing, when Pa suddenly spoke. He was not looking at me, but out the window at the sky, which was now completely dark and slowly filling with stars. I could not see them from where I lay, but I knew they were there. My dear friends, the stars.

"When you were very little you imitated all the birds you heard," said Pa. "You couldn't say any real words yet, but if you heard a bird chirping, you would always call out to it in the same way. If it was a screeching seagull, you let out a loud and joyful screech. If it was a cuckoo, you repeated its cuckoo call and often got an answer, much to your delight. You echoed the chirping of the littlest birds with a shrill 'ee-ee'. You imitated human speech in the same way. Like you didn't know whether you were human or bird, didn't know which language you needed to learn. Or maybe you saw no difference. You were equally eager to learn both."

Then he stopped talking because I began coughing terribly. Once my breathing had calmed down, he continued. "Your mother thought it was very funny, but it always frightened me. It was as if you weren't sure you belonged with us, and might as well be a changeling, a wild creature of the forest that we only had on loan. I started throwing stones at the birds that came into the yard. When you imitated a thrush or scuttled across the yard on your chubby little legs, aping a waddling white wagtail, I felt a cold hand grip around my heart. I'm afraid I often berated you sternly on those occasions."

"I don't remember that, Pa," I told him. "But it amuses me to hear that I wanted to sound like the birds. I have always felt as though they were my brothers and sisters."

He shivered. "That's just as I feared. That you were more bird than girl, and would fly away from us."

"I'll be well again soon, Pa," I said. "By harvest I'll be back on my feet and out with the rake, I assure you."

He was silent for a long time, as if he wanted to say something more but could not bring himself to. Finally he got up, leaned forward and kissed the top of my head. Then he walked out of my chamber without another word. Later that evening, when Elsa came to help me with the evening chores, she told me that there had been a big eagle-owl sitting in the yard that

251

morning when Ma came out to milk the cows. It had just sat there in silence, staring at Ma with its strange yellow-brown eyes. When Pa saw it, he turned pale with rage. He fetched his gun, but by the time he came back out onto the steps, the bird had taken off and swooped soundlessly away over the treetops, and his shot missed. I must have been sleeping very deeply, because I heard no shot.

I am telling you all this because last summer you said that I was so good at imitating the sounds of different birds! And it is true—it has always been a skill of mine. Once I even coaxed a little blue tit to land on my outstretched hand by whistling just like it. I have always envied the birds their wings. Not because, like so many bards and poets, I dream of leaving home and wish I could fly away. No, I envy their flight because of the views it affords them of our homeland! Imagine seeing a blooming summer meadow, a sparkling blue lake or a river shivering off its icy crust from above, from the sky! How glorious would that be? If I were a bird, I would be a sedentary bird, and never migrate away from these woods and fields—I would simply enjoy them all the more. I would open up my eyes each morning in my nest, jubilantly dive into the cool morning air and sail over the treetops!

Now that I have recovered from my illness, it really feels like I could do it. If only I regain the strength in my limbs, I might climb some really tall tree and hoot like an eagle-owl! What do you say about that?! As you can tell, I am much better now, and even managed to write this letter all in one sitting.

By the way, what kind of hat do you think I need for the seminary? I have all my other attire ready, but I am concerned about my hat. Nobody has better taste than you. Please advise, dearest!

Yours,
Alina

Beloved Charlotte,

As you know, I have been frail and sickly for quite some time now. I have suffered recurring bouts of fever, accompanied by a cough, and have lost so much weight since last spring that Ma has had to take my skirts in twice. I remember you pointing out how pale and quick to tire I was last summer. This has worsened since you left. My last letter may have come across as optimistic, but that was because I was in the midst of a good spell at the time. During the autumn, I have hardly been able to help with any of the work, and I know that Ma even wrote to Sven and asked him to come home again, as they do not know whether they can manage here on the farm without my help. The boy we hired last autumn left for the town, and we were never able to find another. I have felt so miserable, knowing how hard Ma and Pa had to toil while I lay idle in bed. Elsa has helped them to the best of her ability, but she is not yet fully grown and not as strong as I am. Or as strong as I was, before. Now that I think about it, it has been rather a while since I was at full health and strength. I think the last time must have been our first summer together. I was still my normal healthy self then.

253

Because of this, I will have to postpone my admission to the seminary by one semester. I have already written to headmistress Sohlberg and she replied that it is perfectly all right for me to start a little later. I am frustrated, but it cannot be helped. If it be God's will, I must surrender to it.

I hope that you and your mother will not be too terribly disappointed by this news. I know that you were both looking forward to having me there in Helsinki. And so you shall, as long as I can come after Christmas instead!

I am not as disappointed about not getting to travel as I thought I would be. As weak and unwell as I have been for the past month, it has mostly felt like a dream to stay in my dear home, surrounded by my family and my beloved forest. The September light is magical. Even when it is cloudy, the air shines as though with an invisible energy. The rowan trees bend their berry-laden branches, and the birch and aspen have acquired new colours; a gentle haze beside the heavy greenery of the firs. I just know that you would want to paint them! If you could see them, you would start talking about colours and composition, and all sorts of other things I will never understand. All I know is the feelings it evokes in me to see the colours change, first slowly, then faster and faster. Autumn is here. I miss summer, but I love autumn too, with its intense hues, all the delicious things you can find in the forest, and the all-consuming harvest.

It is still warm, strangely warm, but the nights are getting cool. It is humid and the evening air is alive with mosquitoes.

Harebells and yarrow bloom here and there, in forgotten patches of summer. In some places, the forest smells almost overwhelmingly of rotten mushrooms. Flocks of great tits chatter in the trees while the jackdaws shriek and a silent raven sails over the as-yet-unharvested fields. Soon. As soon as drier weather comes. Right now, rain is always looming. It comes in short, violent downpours, often while the sun is shining too. I have never seen so many rainbows. Sitting in the warm direct sunlight, one might mistake it for late summer.

I have felt a little stronger in the last few days and have started helping out a little here and there. I was cleaning the granary today before the harvesting and had a little chat with the barn elf while I did so. Yes, laugh if you must! But we are good friends, he and I, and I have spoken to him ever since I was a little girl. My little sisters are terribly afraid of him, and perhaps rightly so—he is not so keen on noisy little children. But I have always approached the granary with respect. Usually bringing a little gift for the elf. Yes, we know each other well, Papa Elf and I, and he likes me to help him clean.

As I was working, I contemplated the grey weathered walls. All the huddled little grey barns alongside every little field! Some with sagging old roofs, some new, proud and imposing despite their small size. How many hours have been spent in total building barns in Ostrobothnia? Thousands? Millions? They have seen generation after generation cultivate this land. They have received hay and grain. They have provided shelter during storms, privacy for lovers and play areas for children.

Animals, too, have sheltered in the barns. Do you remember when we sought shelter from that sudden downpour? We were walking home from the dance at the temperance society's summer party. Ma would have said it was much too far to walk in the early hours of the morning, but you and I refused to ask anyone for a ride. We were so content with each other and with life; we did not want the night to end. We spoke very little as we walked, if I remember rightly, but every step felt magical, gilded by the pale light of the midnight sun, accompanied by the fragrant roadside flowers, by the calls of the cuckoo and hypnotic birdsong. When we reached Shaving Stone Hill, you took my hand, and we stood for a long time in silence, gazing out over the brilliant green birches and dark green firs.

Then came the rain, as if out of nowhere—there had been hardly a cloud in the pale blue sky—and you pulled me along with you, laughing, we ran side by side down the road, watching the sand and stones slowly darken with wetness. We came to Jansson's barn and I pulled you under the roof where it smelled sweetly of last year's hay. You had raindrops on your eyelashes and on your freckled nose.

You recall the words we spoke to each other then. You remember what happened.

I often bring that memory to mind and it makes me happy whenever ordinary life feels grey; when it has been raining for three weeks straight and there is mud everywhere and we cannot even take the cart to church; when my cold refuses to shift; when Ma is exhausted and snaps at me or my sisters.

256

That memory is one of my dearest treasures, and the best part is that nothing and no one can ever take it away from me. It is mine forever.

Your faithful friend,

Alina

My beloved Charlotte,

I am not sure how to tell you what I must tell you now. I think it will be best to state it plainly.

I have been to the doctor and our fears have been confirmed. I have tubercles in my lungs. At present, I feel healthy and well, so there is no need to worry. I intend to live a long time! My principal fear is infecting my loved ones. I also fear I may have infected you during the summer. It is all in the Lord's hands. I try to follow the doctor's advice and take a lot of fresh air, and Ma and Pa take care of me in every possible way. I am given the best food at the dinner table. Pa eats less than he should, I can see that, but if I refuse to eat the extra pieces he puts on my plate, I see worry in his eyes that almost rips my heart out of my chest, so I do as he wishes and eat. Though it seems that nothing can convince my body to put on weight.

We have received a letter from Sven; he is on his way home. He never received Ma's letter, but the country where he has been working is at war and has become too dangerous for him to stay. We fervently hope that he will find safe passage out of the country and a ship that can return him to the north. It will not be easy, but God will help him on his way.

I heard the last cranes heading south today. Their cries sounded so inviting, and I felt what I must have felt as a very small child: the urge to call out to them in their own language. I am sure they would have answered me! "Take me with you," I wanted to shout. "Take me with you." For the first time, I feel a longing to fly away with the migratory birds. It is not this place that I long to leave, but this, my fragile body. Perhaps it is a sin to even think such things—yes, certainly a sin. God has given me this body, this earthly tabernacle. I ought to be grateful. But now, in this intimate moment with you, I can allow myself a brief moment of sin. Please pray for my soul. But imagine—just imagine—having a body of feathers, to be able to soar on the winds, to follow your beak and move with the thrust of beating wings! This is what I intend to focus my thoughts on now, as I lay down my pen to rest.

Yours, forever yours,
Alina

Sweetest friend,

Did you ring in the new year with a hearty celebration? To think, a new century has dawned! May it be filled with enlightenment and progress for mankind! And for you, my beloved little painter. May you find your voice and expression in your art, may you offer the world your unique gift with both hands, and may the world receive this invaluable gift with open arms.

My greatest joy in this dark, difficult winter is the knowledge that I have not infected you with my lung bacilli. You come across as healthy and happy there in the capital. I hope your mind is as healthy as your body. And that you are in the company of like-minded young people? People who care about more than frivolity and frolics and dancing. People like you and me, who want something more from our existence on Earth.

Though it looks as though my time on Earth grows short. I may not even live to Pentecost, the doctor said. There have been complications and nothing can be done.

I remember telling you that I do not fear death because I know that all the beauty I get to experience here on Earth is but a fraction of the glory of God's heavenly kingdom. This is still true, nevertheless—oh, Charlotte, it is difficult for a girl of eighteen to accept that her life has added up to so little. All my dreams, everything I wished to accomplish, it has all been for nothing. This is what I mourn, though I try to be humble and submit to God's will. I have wondered what God's purpose might have been in allowing me to be born only to inhabit His Earth for such a brief time. Still, I have lived longer than many others, I know that. I have seen the grave of several of the parish children. Ma and Pa have buried two of my siblings born before me who only lived a few years each. I know that I am being ungrateful. I pray constantly that God will help me find contentment and peace in my soul, but in the never-ending winter darkness, both are in short supply. It is strange—in the summer I can happily imagine dying, in

259

the midst of God's glorious creation. In winter, the prospect is bleak and cold.

Sven is home from Africa now. He has changed a great deal. Do you remember me questioning what happens to a person's soul when they leave the land of their upbringing? Now I have an answer to that question: they lose all civility. It is as if Sven's soul has been leached out, piece by piece, leaving a void to be filled with the darkness of the mines. I do not mean to say he has become cruel—he shows me brotherly love and concern—but I am afraid he has lost his faith. He has no interest in any higher purpose, in a life filled with the Lord's love and grace. All he cares about now is money, profit and material things. He makes merry with other young men in the church village on Saturdays, and they are not companions of whom Ma or I approve. He laughs at vows of sobriety. His language and manner have become coarse and boorish, and I see the pain that his comportment causes our mother. Elsa said that he was secretly engaged to Sara Katarina, but that she broke off the engagement as soon as they saw each other again on his return. However he behaved then, it made her come home in tears. When she tearfully returned his engagement rings, he sneered and said she could keep those cheap trinkets, for the next girl he proposed to would have real gold and diamonds. He intends to return to Africa as soon as the war down there is over, and says he will come back home a wealthy man. He already has so much pocket money that even after giving Pa and Ma a substantial sum, he can buy whatever he wants. And since he has his own funds, Pa has no say in the matter. I think he gambles. When Pa asks him to accompany him in the forest or do some chore, he laughs in his face and says that he has paid enough for his keep, and when Ma tearfully entreats him to stop associating with those unpleasant friends of his, such obscene words come out of his mouth that—well, Charlotte, I would not like to even put them on paper. When I ask him about the people of Africa, he describes them in terribly condescending terms, as though he sees them as lower than animals. But we are all God's children, Charlotte!

I am afraid I must be distressing you with this letter. I ought to rewrite it, but I do not have the strength. Please know that the thought of you lightens my heart from all its heavy burdens, and that is as good a medicine as any.

Yours faithfully,

Alina

Dear Miss Sarcelius,

I'm writing on behalf of my sister Alina, because she is now too weak to hold a pen. She asks me to tell you how much joy your letter and pictures brought her. The portrait of Alina is very like her. She asked me to hang the watercolour of the marsh above her bed, and she looks at it often. She says that she can almost smell the wild rosemary and moss. Her face lit up when I held it up to her for the first time. She said that she knows you see the beauty in nature's small wonders, not just the grand landscapes. I don't really understand what she means by that, but Alina often says things that I don't understand. I think the picture is very beautiful, but don't know why there is a figure with golden hair in the middle of the marsh. People can't walk there, it is much too waterlogged.

Since December, Alina has mostly been bedridden. Her cough is very bad, and she is usually too weak to eat anything, try as we might. But she often asks me to take out your letters and read them aloud to her, or simply lies with them pressed to her chest. As if their presence is enough to bring her relief.

Ma and Pa say that Alina will die soon. Alina thinks so too. She has arranged her possessions, told me which of us sisters will inherit which of her headbands and dresses.

But, Miss Sarcelius, can God really be so cruel as to take away my best friend? He cannot rob such a good, beautiful girl of her entire future, can He? Alina has always been by my side, she has been my companion and my confidante through everything. There are four years between us, but I have rarely felt the difference. We are more like peers. When Alina was happy to study at the seminary, I was happy for her, even when it felt like my heart was going to be ripped out of my body. I am ashamed to admit this—now, when everyone is saying that she will be taken from us forever.

I must now also confess another sin. Alina doesn't know that I am telling you this. She thinks I am writing about how she is, and replying to your letter, about how you plan to travel to Paris for further art studies, and that you and your mother will then continue to the south of France and Italy. Alina says that you are like a migratory bird. She says that you will understand what she means by that. My sin is that I have been so terribly jealous of your friendship with my sister. Since meeting you, she has had another girl to turn to, another to shower with love and kisses, and another to whom she can confide the secrets of her heart. It has left me feeling lonely, on the outside, and I have secretly blamed you for this. Perhaps you noticed my hostility last summer, and if so I beg your forgiveness. Now I see how foolish and stupid I was. What you and Alina share is something completely different from the sisterly love that exists between her and me. I never lost her at all, then. Now I am facing the prospect of losing her entirely, and don't know how I will be able to live on if she is taken from me.

She has begun to fear death, Miss Sarcelius. If you can think of something to say in your next letter, some words of solace and comfort, please do so without delay. I promise to read everything you write out loud to Alina.

Respectfully,
Elsa Nevabacka

THE 20TH CENTURY

If a myth no longer works for you,
find yourself a new one.

LARS LERIN

PESTS

O TTILIA HAD FALLEN ASLEEP in bed with her cousins, but was woken up by something eclipsing the moonlight flooding into the room. She opened her eyes and saw Mama sitting on the edge of her bed. Mama held a finger to her lips and Ottilia said nothing. Mama stroked her hair fleetingly.

"You're a good, well-behaved little girl, now, aren't you? You're not going to cause any trouble for your uncle and auntie?"

Ottilia didn't know whether to nod or shake her head. She tried to adjust her eyes to see Mama's face clearly, but the darkness wouldn't let her. The moon shone behind Mama's back and transformed her short curls into a shining crown around her head. Ottilia thought it looked like feathers. Soft, smooth feathers. She wanted to reach out and stroke them, but Mama didn't like Ottilia touching her hair.

Mama gave the bedsheets one final little pat. Then she stood up. Ottilia saw that she was fully dressed and had her coat on. She picked up her little suitcase and leaned towards the window. Ottilia knew what was going to happen next. Mama would open the window and crawl out through it. She had seen her do this several times before. At Miss Edith's house, and the Sundberg sisters' house, and once at someone's party, but Ottilia couldn't remember whose. That time Mama came and fetched Ottilia after only three days. At Miss Edith's she was gone for the whole summer. The Sundberg sisters had taken her to an orphanage, and Ottilia wasn't sure how long that was, but it was a very long time. Mama had promised to bring her a tasty treat when she came back, but of course she forgot. All she came back with was a short haircut and red cheeks. Now it was nearly summer, and Ottilia and Mama had been together since as far back as Christmas.

This time Mama didn't promise anything.

Ottilia turned her back to the window so she didn't have to see her mother disappearing from her life one last time.

Ottilia sat in Uncle Sven's lap and held on tightly to her spoon. If someone would just push the milk pot a little closer, she could reach her spoon in and get the skin off the top. She had been given a taste of milk skin the day before, when she and Mama arrived, and it was one of the yummiest things she had ever eaten.

The grown-ups' words whizzed over her head like swallows—quick, sharp and hungry. Uncle's wife Lovisa fluttered with a jittery "shame" and "scandal" and "our children". Uncle Sven's words were heavy with "money" and "cost" and "who will pay". Ottilia was used to hearing these words, though she didn't know what most of them meant.

Then Uncle Sven absent-mindedly pulled the milk pot closer. He was holding a spoon as well, but was waving it around and using it to gesticulate. Quick as a squirrel, Ottilia stuck out her spoon and cut into the skin.

Across the table, two of her three boy cousins sat watching her every movement. Hannes was the eldest, already seven years old. Erik Mikael was only a little older than her. Otto was little enough to be sucking his thumb on Auntie Lovisa's hip. Ottilia saw Erik Mikael's mouth open in angry protest. She quickly got the last of the skin onto her spoon—it was almost too much to fit in her mouth. By the time he let out a howl she had already swallowed half of it. She shut her eyes, ignored the sound, chewed, chewed and swallowed.

"Cuckoo in the nest," said Uncle Sven, giving her a shake, but not very hard. Miss Edith would have grabbed her much harder if she had seen Ottilia being greedy. Or selfish. Or stubborn. Or dishonest.

Ottilia let go of the spoon and wriggled her way off her uncle's lap, down to the floor and under the table. The big clock on the wall chimed and a little wooden bird stuck its head out with a hoarse *cuckoo*.

"Cuckoo!" whispered Ottilia under the table. "I'm a cuckoo in the nest. Cuckoo!" She crept out between the bench legs and human legs and ran out the back door and into the garden.

It was a clear spring morning and the dead grass rustled under the soles of her shoes. Ottilia was in her calico dress and buckle shoes, with one of Hannes' old jumpers on top, which Auntie

Lovisa had put on her. It was too big and the sleeves dangled far below Ottilia's hands. She lifted her arms and flapped. "Cuckoo!" she called, and heard cackling from the henhouse in response.

Someone was standing by the well and cranking up a bucket with a squeaking sound. Ottilia ran towards them, flapping her arms and sleeves. When she came closer she saw it was the man her mother had called Pa yesterday. Not having had a chance to look at him properly before, Ottilia did so now. He was dressed in trousers, shirt and waistcoat, and wore a cap on his head. He was barefoot and didn't seem bothered by the hoarfrost here and there. She walked towards him.

"Cuckoo," she said. He turned around and looked at her. He had brown eyes and clean-shaven cheeks. He must have been frightfully old, about the same age as Miss Edith. Now that she was standing right up close to him, she noticed there was a strong smell about him. Not like people smelled at the children's home, but not nice either, like Mama. It was a sharp, rank smell.

"You should say: 'Good morning, Grandpa'," said the man.

"Good morning, Grandpa," said Ottilia. "I'm a cuckoo."

"Is that so? Well, that means it must be spring, if the cuckoos are calling."

He lifted the bucket from its hook and carried it across the yard to a low building that stood at an angle to Uncle Sven's house. It had two windows either side of a narrow porch, through which Grandpa entered the house. Ottilia followed him. He took the bucket into the little kitchen and she padded after him.

Inside, that same sharp smell was very strong. Ottilia stopped in the doorway and stared. Dozens of pairs of eyes stared back. It was a room the likes of which she had seen many times, with wide floorboards, rag rugs and a large hearth in one corner. Yellowed lace curtains in the windows and a few paintings on the walls. But at the same time, it was completely different from any place she had ever seen.

In the middle of the room was a large table with a bench underneath and a number of peculiar contraptions on top. In the middle of said contraptions was a skeleton. Not a large skeleton, but one with thin, delicate bones. On three of the room's four walls were several rows of shelves, and on the shelves were birds of all sorts and sizes, staring into space with empty eyes.

"Cuckoo," Ottilia greeted them warily. None of them answered or turned to look at her.

"Are these your birds, Grandpa?" she asked. Grandpa was standing over by the hearth, pouring water into a coffee pot with a scoop.

"These are my birds. I made them, every single one."

Ottilia had never heard of people making birds before. She ran across the rag rugs, because Grandpa had taken a sugar loaf down from a shelf. He shaved off a little sugar and gave it to her without a word.

"Cuckoo! Cuckoo!" Ottilia shouted, grabbing the sugar and running several laps around the table. Grandpa sat down and waited for his coffee to boil.

271

"Well then, is your mother still asleep?" he asked. "She always had a problem with sleeping late in the mornings."

"Mama went away last night," Ottilia answered. She popped the sugar in her mouth. Grandpa leaned back, stuck his hand under his cap and scratched his hair. He had rather a lot of hair for one so old.

"Did she? When is she coming back?"

"You never know." It wasn't easy to talk with a chunk of sugar in her mouth. "I was at the children's home for a very long time."

"You've been in a children's home?" Grandpa furrowed his brow and Ottilia got the feeling she had said something wrong. She crawled under the table and sat on her haunches. On the rag rug there lay a shiny black feather. She picked it up. She moved it through a ray of sunlight that fell across the rug and saw that it wasn't black at all but shimmering green. She moved it in and out of the light.

"Cuckoo," she whispered. "Cuckoo."

Ottilia was given a bed in Grandpa's room. He said he had space for a little cuckoo amongst all his other birds.

"But I need food, Grandpa," Ottilia said sternly. "The other birds don't."

"Little cuckoos don't eat much," said Grandpa. "It'll be all right."

"Uncle said I'm going to eat them out of house and home." Ottilia looked around the room. How nice to have a bed of her own. In the children's home they had slept two to a bed, and all the while she was at her uncle's house, she'd had to share with her cousins. Erik Mikael kicked.

"But my name is Ottilia," she said, pointing at the beautifully monogrammed sheet on her bed. "Not A.N. Miss Edith taught me letters, you know."

"That sheet belonged to your Auntie Alina. She embroidered them herself. N stands for Nevabacka, which is your surname too."

"Like Mama!"

"Yes, like your mother."

"Where's Auntie Alina now?"

Grandpa stroked her head.

"She went away long ago."

"Like Mama, out the window!"

"But your mother is coming back. Alina isn't."

"Are you Mama's father?" Ottilia looked up at him. It was strange to think that Mama had a father. Grandpa nodded. "I don't have a father of my own. But Mama says we don't need anyone else."

"Mm. But it might be good to have a grandpa around?"

"Can I eat the skin off the milk?"

"I don't usually boil milk. I live on coffee and porridge, mainly. Sometimes I eat in the house with Sven and Lovisa."

"There'll have to be changes now, Grandpa. I need milk and good food, that's what Mama says. That's why she came and got me from the children's home. It was a home for kids with no fathers after the sizzle war."

"Civil war," said Grandpa.

"Yup. I got very sick there, you see, and weak like this!" She collapsed on the bed to show how feeble she had been. "I couldn't even walk! Mama was ever so angry at all the ladies in the children's home when she came to get me. But she didn't know I was there, you see, she thought I was with the Sundberg sisters."

"Is that so?"

"But I wasn't because I was at the children's home and all we got there was cabbage soup."

"I don't grow cabbages. So you'll be safe from cabbage soup here."

"Good. But I'm really very fond of milk, Grandpa."

"I'll see what I can do." Grandpa held out his hand. "Come on, I need your help to chop some wood."

Ottilia was given her own little axe and her own little knife, and Grandpa taught her how to chop wood and split out shingles. She liked the smell of the wood, and was happy to spend all day with Grandpa in the woodshed, splitting shingles.

"It smells better here than in your house," she said, surrounded by showers of wood shavings.

She liked the animals most of all. Grandpa had a horse called Putte that was very gentle. Ottilia liked greeting Grandpa and Putte when they came back from the woods, and helping to unharness Putte and leading him to the well to give him a drink. The horse's lips looked so funny slurping around in the bucket as he drank. Sometimes Grandpa would lift her onto Putte's back and then it felt like she was as high as the sky where the birds flew. She would shut her eyes, hold out her arms and make a sound like a cuckoo.

When Grandpa was out in the forest or busy with work, she had to stay with her aunt and cousins in the big house. Then Ottilia had to help to water the sheep and feed the hens. Her hands were too little and weak to milk the cows, but she could help to wave away flies, which she was happy to do.

"In town there's only dogs. And horses that pull the night soil carts. But I'm not allowed to pat them," she said, stroking Lilja's side as her milk squirted into the bucket with a hiss in between Auntie's strong fingers.

Auntie rarely said much to Ottilia, but it didn't matter. Ottilia enjoyed chattering away. She had learned not to talk too much about Mama, because then her aunt tended to get a bit more aggressive in her movements and give Ottilia less food on the occasions that she ate in Uncle's house. That was the way it had been at Miss Edith's house as well, so Ottilia was used to it. But it was much better at Nevabacka than with Miss Edith, she told Grandpa. "Because I can talk to you about Mama and you don't get angry."

"No, how could I? Elsa is my little girl. Even if I don't always approve of the things she does."

"What was Mama like when she was little?"

This was Ottilia's favourite topic of conversation. If Grandpa had some free time, like if he was splitting shingles or fixing something at his big table, he could talk about her for a long time. He told Ottilia about Alina and Elsa and how they used to be inseparable, and how terribly sad Elsa had been after Alina died. She had a younger sister Malin, but they were never as close as Alina and Elsa had been. Malin was married now and lived in town, not Ottilia's town but a different one.

"Elsa loved to swim," said Grandpa. "I used to take her and Alina in the cart to Storträsk sometimes, where children swim in summer."

Ottilia tried to imagine Mama with wet hair and mud between her toes. But all she could see was her short curly hair and white coat with a fur collar.

When Uncle Sven delivered milk to the dairy, only Ottilia's cousins were allowed to accompany him. Ottilia understood that Auntie and Uncle didn't want people in the village to see her. There was that word that always hovered around her: shame. But it didn't bother Ottilia. She was used to it. And as long as she remembered never to mention Mama, gradually Auntie started being very kind to her. One time she even called her "poor child". Ottilia understood that they were making progress when she was given extra butter on her bread at supper one night.

But she still preferred to eat in New Cottage with Grandpa. He would put his peculiar utensils and half-finished animals aside and serve a dish of porridge with a big dollop of butter in it, and they would eat from the same dish with a spoon each. "Like we did when I was a child," he said and winked at her with his brown eyes. If it was hard to imagine Mama as a child, it was even harder with Grandpa!

276

"Did you live here when you were little?" Ottilia wanted to know as she licked the last grains from the porridge spoon. It was late spring, and still light enough in the evening that Grandpa hadn't even bothered with a lamp. It was light in the middle of the room, but up on the shelves, shadows gathered around the lifeless birds. Ottilia wasn't scared of them any more. Or not usually anyway. Now she mainly felt sorry for them because they weren't allowed to fly around. Grandpa had decided that they were to stay put.

"In Old Cottage, yes. With my parents and sisters. My little cottage had just been built. My Uncle Jakob built it."

"Then did he die?"

Grandpa nodded. "Yes, of typhoid fever. His widow took the children with her to America. She's dead now, but last I heard her children and their children are still living over there."

"I like your house better than the big house. It's so full of people all the time. Here there's only the birds, and I'm not frightened of them any more."

"Were you frightened of them to begin with?"

"Yes, but now I've spoken to them, so I'm not any more."

"Well, good." Grandpa bent down to pick Ottilia up and put her on his lap. He started to bounce her on his knee and sang in time with the movement.

"Mother is weary
Sleep now my dearie

Lovely goose flies
Through twilit skies
Where shall we go?
To the land of milk and honey
Where all things are funny
With succulent meat
And sugar so sweet
Pies on the windowsill
Angels climbing the hill
Carrying pails as they go"

"I know that one!" Ottilia was excited. "Mama sang it to me! When I had to go to sleep so she could go out. But it didn't make me sleepy at all, it made me hungry! And then she'd have to go and fetch me some bread and butter."

"Where did you and Mama live?" Grandpa was sitting perfectly still now. Ottilia's legs dangled down from his lap.

"All sorts of places. When I was very little we lived by the sea, but I don't remember that. Then we lived in a house with lots of people in. It was very crowded there and I had a friend called Mari. Then I lived with Miss Edith. And then we lived with Mama's friend Mr Lundberg for a while. But then Mr Lundberg's wife came and we had to leave, and I lived with the Sundberg sisters who took me to the children's home, though Mama didn't know."

Grandpa held Ottilia tight. She let herself be enveloped in his arms and leaned her head against his shirt. Underneath

278

that pungent smell, which she now knew came from his birds, there was another smell that was maybe the tiniest bit similar to Mama's.

Every evening from then on, Ottilia wanted to hear "Lovely Goose" before she went to sleep. She shut her eyes and listened to Grandpa's booming voice and almost felt as though she were Mama when she was little, sleeping in the very bed Mama used to share with her sister Alina.

Other than that, Ottilia thought about her mother less and less. This was what usually happened. At first, when Mama had recently left, she would think about her constantly. Then less often. And eventually, when Ottilia had stopped thinking about her at all, that was usually when she would show up again.

But not this time.

One night Ottilia was woken up by a loud call outside the house. She sat up. Grandpa was snoring softly in his bed. She heard something that sounded like light, rhythmic footsteps across the roof. Her bed was directly beneath the window, and she kneeled up to peek outside.

It was snowing. Fat snowflakes, as big as her thumb, floated slowly down to the ground. That was the sound she could hear. Snowflakes tumbling on the roof. Ottilia frowned. It was beautiful, but she remembered Grandpa saying it was important that the fields dried up so that he and Sven could start to plough. It was late April and there hadn't been any snow on the ground for several weeks already.

She heard the calling sound again. *HOo. HOo.* It didn't sound like a ghost. Ghosts barely made any sound at all. Carefully, Ottilia crept out of bed, pulled on her cardigan and a pair of woolly socks and sneaked out of the bedroom. All around the cottage she could see the birds' eyes glinting in the pale light from the falling snow outside. She could sense that they wanted to follow her outside.

"It's cold," she whispered. "Your feathers would get wet, and then Grandpa would get angry."

She found her boots, hand-me-downs from her cousins, and opened the door.

The falling snow made a sound like whispers. Everyone was asleep. Even the animals in the barn and the henhouse. A thin layer of snow lay over the farmyard, and Ottilia's steps became dark imprints on the ground as she walked across the yard.

HOo.

The sound was coming from the forest, but nearby. She walked towards the fence that separated the homestead from the dark woods and saw something sitting on the fence post. Ottilia stopped and stood completely still. It was one of Grandpa's birds. A large owl with feathery tufts above its ears and huge yellow-brown eyes. She could see their colours in the darkness. As though they were shining.

"How did you get out here?" she whispered. "Grandpa will be ever so angry when he finds out."

The owl turned its head slowly to look at her. How would she get the bird inside again? Cautiously, she stepped closer.

HOo.

It sounded like a warning. Ottilia swallowed and went even closer. The owl flapped its wings—they were enormous. Snowflakes swirled all around. Ottilia stopped.

"Well, on your head be it," she whispered. "Trying to escape like this. I don't know what Grandpa will do with you."

In response, the bird took off from the post it had been sitting on. It flew up, up among the swirling snowflakes, and very quickly disappeared into the dark wall of pines and firs.

She wrapped her jumper tighter around her and ran almost silently back to New Cottage.

Next morning, when he and Grandpa were sitting at the table with a crackling fire in the hearth and a dish of barley porridge between them, Ottilia inspected all the birds on the shelves around the room.

"Grandpa, do you have a big bird with tufty ears that says *HOo*?"

"An eagle-owl, you mean? No." Grandpa sort of snapped his answer, and Ottilia didn't dare ask anything else. But after a few spoonfuls of porridge, Grandpa looked up and out the window, where snow was still falling.

"Eagle-owls are bad luck. I'd never have one indoors like these ones. I've shot plenty of them though. The council pays five marks for an adult and two for a baby. Pests, that's what they are. Vermin. All predatory birds are. But it's been years since I last got an eagle-owl. They're gone now, and good riddance." He turned to look at his shelves and unconsciously sat up straighter as he did so. "I've shot many a bird in my time. Each bird shot is one less pest."

Ottilia wasn't sure what Grandpa's birds had to do with pests in the forest. "How do you make your birds, Grandpa?"

Now Grandpa got excited. He stood up from the bench, searched through the objects on the table, found a little box and held it out to Ottilia. She let out a terrified yelp. Inside the box were lots and lots of eyes in different sizes and colours, all staring up at her. Grandpa chuckled, picked up an eye and held it out to show her. She hid her face in her hands.

"They're made of glass, Ottilia. I order them from Germany… I took a correspondence course in German so I could read the brochures and write to them and order what I want. I'm employed by the whole parish, you know. The district judge himself has an osprey that I made. In his courtroom in town."

Ottilia slowly removed her hands from over her eyes and studied the little glass beads. "They're looking at me!"

"I only use the very best," Grandpa said proudly. "It costs a few coins, but the people who buy my birds pay well. I've got more orders from schools around Ostrobothnia than I can manage." He set aside the box and held up a clay figure, a little smaller than the owl Ottilia had seen the night before. "This falcon is going to a school in Vaasa. But you can think of it as fabric for a dress. You shall have a fine summer frock with the money I make!"

For the rest of the day, Grandpa showed Ottilia his work with the birds. He was more talkative than ever before, and Ottilia listened and asked questions. She thought the box of eyes was the most exciting thing of all—both horrifying and beautiful at the same time. Just like when they chopped the shingles and firewood, she soon had a tool in her hand and got to try out various steps of the process—not on any of the birds Grandpa was going to sell, but on leftover scraps of skin, wood shavings and cracked glass eyes. In the evening, when all the chores were done, Grandpa took out a bag of bird feathers. There were white, black, brown and speckled feathers. Ottilia got a whole bag for herself, and sat making herself a feather necklace, happy and content. Grandpa watched her with glittering eyes.

"Rich ladies in town would pay a lot of money to have feathers like those in their hats," he chuckled. "You're donned up like a pastor's wife!"

That night Ottilia lay awake for a long time after Grandpa had sung her "Lovely Goose" and tucked her in with the sheets that said A.N. She wanted to listen out in case the eagle-owl came back. She hadn't said anything about it to Grandpa. He can make his own birds. This one is mine, thought Ottilia. My bird, that I saw.

But no *HOo* call came.

Two pictures hung above the chest of drawers: a portrait of a young girl, drawn in heavy black strokes, and a watercolour of marshland with a golden-haired figure hovering above its sedge grass and moss. Just as Ottilia was dropping off to sleep, she was sure she saw the figure wave to her with a softly glowing hand.

*

Summer came and the grown-ups became terribly busy. Auntie was only indoors to put food on the table, and Uncle and Grandpa only ever came inside to gobble something down before going back out into the fields. In the evenings Grandpa was much too tired to work on his birds, and he barely even had the energy to sing "Lovely Goose" to Ottilia. The cousins had to take care of themselves and each other, along with the children from the neighbouring farms. They were outdoors nearly all day too, whatever the weather, because what would they do inside?

The first time Ottilia met Susanna from Storbäck, the older girl, two years older to be precise, looked at her critically.

"Is it true that you're eating your grandpa out of house and home?"

"I can eat just as much as Hannes," Ottilia answered proudly. "And sometimes more. But I can't eat as much as Uncle Sven," she added truthfully.

Susanna shook her head. "No one can. My mama says he's the tallest man in all the parish."

"Auntie Lovisa says that Hannes is likely to grow just as tall," Ottilia boasted. "I can spit on target, want to see?"

Susanna did indeed, and from that moment on Ottilia and Susanna were inseparable, even though they fell out and made up again at least three times a day. Sometimes they ate dinner at Storbäck and sometimes at Nevabacka. At Storbäck they usually had soup: cabbage soup, pea soup or meat soup. Sometimes Auntie Lovisa served hot milk dumplings—something Ottilia had never tasted before—much to the delight of Susanna and the cousins. It was a dish made from milk, wheat flour and egg, beloved by all the children. Otherwise Auntie mainly cooked potatoes in white or brown sauce with either meat or saltfish. On Sundays they had rice pudding. Grandpa and Ottilia ate lunch at Uncle's house, but usually had supper at home. Then Ottilia would tell Grandpa everything that had happened throughout the day, to which he would respond with an "Mm" and eat his porridge or gruel in silence. They always went to bed early, and Ottilia was too tired to check if the lady in the painting might wave at her again.

The long summer months were filled with playing, running, swimming in the river, songs and games, and the occasional trip to the village, but Ottilia wasn't allowed to go there. The cousins took Ottilia out into the forest to pick blueberries and near the marsh to pick cloudberries. But she got a sharp telling-off from Hannes for almost walking straight into the marsh. He grabbed her firmly by the arm—if he had hesitated for a second it would have been too late.

"What do you think you're doing? Can't you see that cross over there? A Nevabacka man drowned here once."

"I wanted to see if I could find the lady in the painting," she said crossly, rubbing her arm. "You hurt me!"

"And I'll do worse if you don't keep to the edge of the marsh. I'll show you where it's safe to walk and you can stick to that or else go home."

Ottilia crouched glumly among the wild rosemary. If she were a bird she could fly across the whole marsh and find the lady easy-peasy. It wasn't fair that some could fly while others couldn't.

That evening Ottilia did manage to stay awake until the figure in the painting waved at her. She would have liked to imagine it was Mama, but Mama had different colour hair. Though perhaps it could be Alina? She had fair hair, though not quite as golden as the being in the watercolour. Ottilia liked sleeping under that picture. It felt like it was watching over her.

By autumn it was clear that Ottilia's mother was not coming back for her, so Grandpa sent her to school. She was a bit too young perhaps, but she could go with her cousins and be out of the way during the day. That was hunting time.

The first time Ottilia came home from school to find Grandpa and King, the dog, with two black grouse in the farmyard, she stopped and looked curiously at the birds and the red blood on their black feathers.

"Are they for eating?"

"No, these are for two schools in Oulu," answered Grandpa. "If they come out well, that is. But why shouldn't they?"

Ottilia followed Grandpa to the woodshed, where he carefully skinned the birds with King by his feet. While he worked he explained everything he was doing to Ottilia, and how to prepare the skin in such a way that the feathers would stay on. Then he went inside and showed her how he shaped the body that would wear the bird skin.

Ottilia slowly began to understand the connection between these birds that had been shot dead and Grandpa's glass-eyed birds in the cottage. She wrinkled her forehead and stared at Grandpa.

"I thought you made them," Ottilia said reproachfully. "But you don't."

"I preserve them. I take their bodies and make them all nice and clean inside, then stuff them and give them eyes that never decay. So they can sit on the shelves forever."

"Did you do that to Alina as well?"

Grandpa looked down at her where she stood leaning over the table and made a movement that almost looked as though he might smack her, but of course she was wrong because Grandpa never smacked. His eyes were filled with anger. He took a deep breath and leaned back.

"That doesn't happen with people."

"Pity. Otherwise people could be kept forever as well."

"It wouldn't be the same. They wouldn't be able to think or talk like you and me."

"No, and the birds can't sing or fly any more either. It's a pity."

"Birds are pests, I told you." Grandpa turned away. "The fewer there are, the better."

Ottilia gazed awhile at Grandpa's tanned, callous hands working with quick, expert movements. She was a cuckoo in the nest. Who was eating Grandpa out of house and home, and Uncle and Auntie too. She wasn't their child. She knew that.

287

Was she a pest too? Ottilia swallowed. Was Grandpa going to shoot her also, and give her glass eyes?

Ottilia lay awake long after Grandpa had sung her "Lovely Goose". She counted and realized Christmas was still very far away. Would Mama come for her then? She hadn't thought about her in a long time, but now she shut her eyes tight and tried to picture her face. But she couldn't. She saw Mama backlit by moonlight but her face was in darkness. Then Mama leaned forward and the moon lit up two enormous brown owl eyes over a hooked, pricker-sharp beak. Owl-mother reached out her hand, except it was a claw, and she wanted to scratch Ottilia's eyes out, and Ottilia screamed with all her might.

"It's just a dream," came a sleepy mumble from Grandpa's bed. "Go to sleep."

"Grandpa, is it long till Christmas? Do you think Mama will come to get me then?"

Grandpa was quiet for a while. At first Ottilia thought he had fallen back to sleep. "I don't know, little one. We've written to her, Sven and I, but no one seems to know where she is. We wonder... She might have travelled far away. Did she ever talk to you about America, Ottilia?"

Ottilia pulled the covers over her head. She wanted Mama to come and get her so she wouldn't end up on Grandpa's shelf, but now she was afraid of the Mama with the owl eyes. She could no longer recall her real face.

*

Ottilia took as small portions as she could. If she and Grandpa ate at Uncle and Auntie's house she ate almost nothing. At first her tummy rumbled terribly. It had got used to getting good food at Nevabacka, nothing like the watery cabbage soup at the children's home. "Pretend we're at the children's home," Ottilia whispered to her stomach. "You didn't even want soup then."

After a while her tummy stopped rumbling. And there were still lingonberries in the forest, and crowberries and a few tasteless blueberries. She ate them up as soon as she got a chance. She didn't dare sneak food from Grandpa's little cupboard or Auntie Lovisa's cellar and larder. That was exactly what pests did. Mice and rats. Squirrels and foxes. All those things that Grandpa and Uncle Sven shot on sight. The cats, Tossan and Big Tom, chased the rodents and caught crows and jackdaws, especially if they were old or weak, and the swallow babies under the barn roof. Just to be on the safe side, Ottilia started avoiding the cats as well, even though they used to be her friends. She could probably fight them off if she had to, she thought, but she would rather not. Their teeth and claws were so very sharp.

"Are you feeling poorly?" Auntie Lovisa furrowed her brow, as Ottilia pushed away the potato dish after only taking one very small potato. "Or don't you like my food?"

Ottilia looked around the table, frightened. What could she say that wouldn't make them get angry and shoot her?

Grandpa, who was sitting next to her on the bench, turned and peered at her thoughtfully.

"Now that you mention it, she's been eating next to nothing of late."

"Not at the Storbäck house! There she ate four potatoes with meat and gravy." Hannes was going to ruin everything. She had been so hungry the last time she and the cousins were at Susanna's for dinner. She didn't think she could eat the Storbäcks out of house and home since she was so seldom there.

"So my food isn't good enough for you?" Auntie slammed the pot of boiled meat down on the table. "Well, you can go without then!"

Ottilia got up at once and ran blindly out the back door. She heard Grandpa call after her, but he might have his rifle with him, and she was too scared to stop and check. She ran and ran, bare-headed through the dark-wet autumn forest that shook raindrops down her neck. She didn't look where she was going, she really didn't care, she had to hide so she wouldn't become one of the birds on Grandpa's shelves. There was nowhere she could go, no one wanted her. She held out her arms and beat them through the air as she ran—if only she could flap hard enough perhaps she could take off and fly far far away from them all! She could fly across the ocean, all the way to America.

Suddenly she stepped into knee-deep ice-cold water. She sniffed runny snot back up her nose and looked around.

She was out in the marshland. There was fog all around her, and the sun had set but it was still dusk and not completely dark. She could see where she was. Exactly where Hannes had warned her not to go. She pulled up her leg and her boot came with it, which was lucky. Otherwise she would have to ask for new boots on top of everything else.

Actually no, she wasn't going back there. She would fly like a bird far far away.

She crawled up to kneel on a tuft of grass, but all around her was boggy moss and pools of water. How had she got here? Her feet were soaking wet, and her stockings too. All she had was her cardigan, and now the fog was growing thicker. She took one tentative step but her foot sank straight down into the moss so she snatched it back at once.

She started to cry. Very quietly, just like she had learned to at Miss Edith's house. Miss Edith had no time for crying children. The first time Ottilia cried for her mother she had got such a slap that her ear kept ringing for a good while afterwards. She learned how to cry quietly.

Pests are supposed to die, she thought. Now I'll probably die. And no one will miss me.

And then she cried even more, and this time it was harder to do so quietly.

But there was a series of grass tufts, and Ottilia didn't weigh much, so she found a patch of ground that held, and then another. She couldn't stop crying, but slowly she got closer and closer to the solid rocky ground of the forest edge.

She heard a snorting and grunting sound coming from right in front of her, and Ottilia became so frightened that she stopped crying at once with a hiccup. What was that? Could it be the ghost of Old Man Nevabacka, come to drag her down into the marsh? Like the ghost of the dead Cossack that Susanna said haunted Ryssträsk near Storbäck. He had been killed and thrown into the swamp when Russia took over Finland more than a hundred years ago. Now it was very dangerous to swim there because he wanted revenge on every Finn he came across.

Ottilia wasn't afraid of ghosts. Not usually. She was pretty sure she had seen her great-uncle Jakob once, and he hadn't felt scary. He just gave her a melancholy nod. And she had seen Alina many times, but never said anything to Grandpa because he got such a sad look in his eyes when he talked about her. But Hannes had told her that Old Man Nevabacka was a real nasty piece of work. Cruel and stingy and very badly behaved when he was drunk. Maybe he wanted to drown her to keep him company.

Then she saw something through the mist. Large and dark in the fading light, it moved along the edge of the marsh. Sniffing, smelling. A small head and a huge furry body.

"Teddy," whispered Ottilia, and a warm stream trickled down the inside of her thighs. The bear was following her scent but couldn't see her in the mist. It stood on its hind legs and looked straight at her, and she stood frozen on the spot. Could it walk on the marsh? Did it mind getting its paws wet?

She couldn't go back. And the path of grass patches led straight towards the bear.

It landed back on all fours with a grunt. She thought she saw its small eyes shine through the mist.

Just like Big Tom when he caught sight of his prey, the bear swung its head from side to side and started charging forwards. Straight at her.

"No, no," she whispered. "No, no."

But the bear paid no attention to her words. It hurtled towards her through the mist, maybe it had its own bear footpath. Maybe it didn't want to eat her at all, maybe it was just curious. But she wouldn't know until it was too late.

A shadow came gliding over her head. A large black bird flew low over the swamp and landed right between her and the bear. It turned around and glanced over its shoulder at her, then strutted towards the bear, unafraid.

The bear snorted.

The bird flapped into the air and landed even closer to the bear.

She quickly stepped from one grass patch to the next. The bird flapped its wings and let out a loud, sonorous caw. When the bear took a step forward, the bird flew at its head. Annoyed, the large animal shook its head from side to side.

Ottilia took one quick step closer to the edge of the forest. And another. She was nearly there. She could see the great moss-covered rocks, the tall straight pines. She was very close to the bear. She was so frightened that her legs could barely carry her, but still she carried on.

Suddenly the bear turned straight towards her and reared up on its hind legs. It was so close. So big. Twice the size of Uncle Sven. It sniffed at the air, and Ottilia turned away and ran, straight into the trees, straight into Grandpa's arms.

"My little one, you're all wet!" Grandpa lifted her up and held her close.

"The bear, Grandpa, the bear!" She could barely get the words out, her teeth were chattering so. Grandpa froze and looked out over the marsh.

"Damn. My rifle is at home," he whispered. Then he hugged her hard. "He's going away. Look."

Ottilia peeked out from behind Grandpa's arm. She saw something big and dark lumber off through the dusky mist. And something else was flying around it, something smaller, flapping and gleaming black.

Grandpa lifted her up properly and walked home through the woods.

Once Ottilia had put on some dry clothes and eaten a whole bowl of porridge all by herself and crawled into bed under double blankets, Grandpa sat on the edge of her bed and held her hands between his.

"Now you must tell me why you ran away, Tilia."

Tilia. She liked it. Better than cuckoo in the nest.

"I thought you were going to shoot me, like one of your birds, if I was a pest and ate you out of house and home. So I tried not to eat. And I don't remember what Mama looks like any more. What if she never comes back?"

Grandpa sat in silence for a few moments, patting and stroking her hands. It made her feel nice. Then he got up, opened a drawer in his dresser and rummaged around. He found a framed photograph and picked up the oil lamp from the dresser and carried both over to her.

"Here are all three girls. We had the photo taken when Alina was confirmed." He held up the lamp so she could see better.

Three young girls stood in a row with serious expressions and dark skirts. The tallest and oldest was Alina—Tilia recognized her face from the portrait on the wall. In the middle stood a young girl, who looked a little bit like her.

"That's Mama, Grandpa!" She looked up and into his kind face. "I remember her now! She has the same eyes!"

Grandpa put down the lamp and sat down on the edge of the bed again.

"You can stay here as long as you want. I might be old, but I'm not so old that I can't take care of a little girl. And you have no idea how much happiness you bring to this old man. It's been lonely here since all my girls flew the nest. Very lonely." He leaned forward. "And you can stay here even if she does come back, Tilia. Remember that. You don't have to leave again. This can be your home, if you want. Forever."

"Even though I'm a cuckoo?"

"You're not a cuckoo. You're my grandchild."

He blew out the lamp and Tilia snuggled down under the covers. He left the bedroom door ajar and the smell of pipe tobacco soon spread throughout the cottage.

I'll sew him a new tobacco pouch as a Christmas present, thought Tilia. I'm sure Auntie can show me how.

She didn't fall asleep straight away. Once her eyes had adjusted to the dark, she looked up at the watercolour picture of the marsh, to see if the figure would wave at her. Instead she saw something she hadn't noticed before. She had to sit up to look more closely but yes, it was true—above the golden-haired figure, high up in the storm cloud-filled sky, there flew a black, sharp-winged bird.

MAPS

THERE ARE SO MANY PATHS THROUGH a landscape. Ant wanted to draw a map of them all on one piece of paper, but it was impossible. It came out as an indecipherable mess. Instead, he drew a map of each road network on the thinnest paper he could find and layered them on top of each other. Then he could see them all at once.

Individually, none of them felt real. Separately, each road was isolated, lonely, nothing. The landscape was made up of all of them combined.

He had never actually left the parish. This was his choice. Every time he had been offered an opportunity to leave—to go to the market in town or attend a meeting at the youth centre in the neighbouring parish—he had turned it down. The Forskant parish was his whole world and he liked it that way. How could he feel safe otherwise? He needed to be surrounded by familiarity. His feet had only trodden the paths of his own parish, but he took pride in exploring all the roads in the area, one by one.

When he was sixteen, he decided to draw a map of his own paths. He wasn't very good with letters and words and all that, having only attended public school for four years before his mother died and he was forced to enter service. By the age of sixteen, he had been working for four years, and had drawn as many maps. On the map of his own paths, he drew the croft where he was born, and all the places that had been important to him before he moved away: the outhouse; the sauna; the shed where father used to beat him; Jerusalem, where he did his first ever day's work; the fishing rock in the river; the place where Johanna had fallen through the ice and drowned; the church and the road that led to it; the cemetery; Sugar-Stina's house; the kiosk at the Karlas crossroads where you could buy playing cards and coffee; New Cottage at Nevabacka, home to Tilia with the curly hair, the object of his childhood infatuation. He didn't write the names of the places—there was no need. He knew them by heart, and if he closed his eyes he could walk all the roads and paths between them, at any time of year.

He drew a little rowan tree in the cemetery to mark his parents' graves. He was very skilled at drawing. It didn't require any schooling, and he could draw any animal or tree or berry or bush, and it was plain for all to see what it represented. His mother once said it was because he always had his eyes open. Some only have eyes for what they hold in their hands, while others only have eyes for skies and clouds and daydreams, but Ant's eyes were open to everything around him.

The strangest of Ant's maps was probably the one of winter's paths. Not the roads that the villagers used in winter, but the pathways that winter travelled when he came and went. The places first touched by cold and bitten by frost. Where the snow lasted longest, sometimes into May or June, in bad years. After the winter map, he made a map each for spring, summer and autumn. He studied where the different maps overlapped, where it might be spring in one place and still winter elsewhere. At Raino's barn in Ormberget, for example. Sometimes spring arrived there as early as March, along the south wall. Cowslip primroses and violets grew there while there was still snow at Steinbacka and Smalabacka and Länsman's ditch. He drew in where the ice first melted, where the first swallow was heard, and where the wood anemones first bloomed.

On the summer map he drew the best lake shores for swimming and the high-diving platform and where dances were held. Where they used to take midsummer birches to Nevabacka, where the most magnificent rowan trees bloomed and the exact spot under the barn roof where the swallows built their nests. He drew in the place where lightning had struck during a July storm, and where the hay would first ripen and the first rye be threshed.

Autumn's map showed where the first aspens turned golden and where the migratory birds came to rest on their journey south. He marked the spot where he first caught that distinctive autumn scent that cannot be described in words, and where the evening mists were most beautiful in September.

The berry map was one of his favourites. He drew in all the places where wild strawberries grew, and Arctic raspberry ditches, and bogs and marshes full of cloudberries and cranberries, and raspberry thickets and crowberry carpets, and the best spots for blueberries and lingonberries. He was sure that there must be secret berries he didn't know about as well; on several occasions he had caught Affe's wife Marita with a basket brimming with cloudberries but she refused to tell him where she had picked them. He would find out sooner or later. It must be somewhere in Granby, because he met her on the Stackovägen road.

It didn't matter that he didn't have all the berry locations on his map yet; no map was ever truly finished. He was adding new things all the time, working on the little table he had built himself in his attic room at Nevabacka. In summer he could sit by the window and tinker with them long into the night, because at that time of year he didn't need to light the lamp and waste electricity. Winter was harder, and he filled the limited hours of daylight with work. He worked more than farmer Sven and at least as much as Erik Mikael and Otto. But Hannes, he was a good worker, and Ant was no match for him. It might have been considered strange that they had taken on a farmhand at Nevabacka at all, and though they had mainly hired Ant to help with the forest work in winter, there was an element of compassion to it too. Ant showed his appreciation for this, in his quiet way, by working hard and rarely taking a day off, even on Sunday. Not many people would hire a twelve-year-old farm boy; indeed, not many people had farmhands at all these days. But Nevabacka was the largest farmstead in the parish and had a lot of woodland that Sven had purchased with all that money he was rumoured to have made in America. If this were true, all the wealth must be in the woodland, because Ant saw no evidence of it otherwise. At Nevabacka they lived just as they did on other farms, ate the same food and wore the same clothes. Admittedly, they had their own harvester, and three horses and a lot of cows, sheep and pigs. And they had electricity because Sven was chairman of the electricity cooperative, and they had their own telephone installed. Nevabacka didn't suffer from a shortage of anything, and Ant never went hungry. He had known hunger at times back home in the croft with his mother after his father had died.

And there was plenty for him to do, even though the farm had three capable sons and a master who could still work, as well as a little daughter who helped her mother with the cows and other livestock. And the elderly Bird Man lived over in New Cottage, so called because his main activity for many years had been hunting and stuffing birds.

He must have had a whole collection of them in his cabin, but Ant had never seen them. All he saw were Tilia's beautiful bird paintings on the walls in the entrance to New Cottage. Ant had seen them when Sven had sent him on some errand or other for the Bird Man, who was Sven's father and needed help sometimes. Tilia had gone off to Helsinki and only came back to visit occasionally. She was a student, and Ant had heard the word "forestry" mentioned. He wasn't sure what that meant, but it was something involving the forest, and he liked the forest. He didn't clench his jaw quite as hard in Tilia's presence any more, and had even managed to say a proper goodbye when she left. The Bird Man had looked deflated in the cart, while Tilia sat up tall with her dark curly head held high as the Bird Man took her to the station in town.

Ant's days were filled with transporting milk to the dairy, driving Rölle, the colt, harrowing and ploughing, sowing and scything, harvesting and threshing. In addition, there were all the other small jobs that always had to be done: preparing feed for the horses, digging and repairing roads, loading up the work cart and spreading manure, putting a new blade on the plough, a new blade on the bandsaw, repairing enclosures and fences, soling shoes and moving barns. The work was never-ending, but this didn't bother Ant. As long as there was work, he could stay at Nevabacka, and that was all he wanted. He had no other home in the world, and after six years on the farm he knew all of its roads and ways.

Naturally, he kept a map of animal trails: both wild and tame. He didn't know the animals of other farms very well, but Nevabacka's livestock got their own little map, with the cow pens and pastures, and where Lilja had succumbed to the swamp, and Silver White was found when she ran away (it was on the other side of Björkas, next to an alder thicket, and he drew a small flourish to represent Hannes running several laps around the thicket). He drew in the sheep paddocks and trails, and the place where seven sheep had been badly ravaged by unknown dogs in his second year at Nevabacka, rendering them worthless. He also drew in where they had found the three heifers that died after straying too far one summer. They had been dead for a long time when they were found, and Sven had cursed terribly.

He desperately wished he could draw a little map of Little Tom's nocturnal wanderings and adventures, but cats keep such secrets to themselves.

He drew the moose trails, and all the foxholes he knew, and where he had heard a tawny owl and a Tengmalm's owl and where the woodpecker had its nesting tree. He drew where the Arctic loon brooded, where the ravens nested, where he had once scared a wood grouse away from her eggs, where the cranes danced at Mörktjärn Lake, and where the finest birdsong could be heard. He marked the best places to trap hares. He drew in where the Bird Man had saved Tilia from a bear one October evening, and where Doris had been bitten by a snake. He drew the paths the hedgehogs walked across the farm on summer evenings.

He drew a map of the devastating forest fire that had claimed all of Dahlsgården including seven granaries and barns one hot July after seven weeks of drought. He marked where the first vegetation began to grow back after the fire, and where fat, sweet raspberries could be found among the scorched trees the following year.

One winter, he drew a map on which he marked every tree he had felled, and the paths he and Pricke had taken to haul the logs home, and where he sawed and chopped them up for firewood. On a good day, he could chop four cubic metres of wood. He drew the trees he had sawn. He put a small cross at each stump. It was a sad map. He didn't like it and hid it at the bottom of the pile.

The paths of the wind were one of the biggest challenges. He knew how an easterly wind could come and cool him in the hay, but next time the wind might be southerly. Winter came with easterly winds often but not always. The summer's southerly winds could usually best be felt by the river, but at other times blew strongest at Tallsjön. At Brantsvängen it was *always* windy. Even Drinkwater-Minna said so. And he drew the paths the storm had cut through the forest east of Mörktjärn one winter.

One of his favourite maps represented events from the past. Where there were rumours of hauntings. Where Cossacks and parishioners were killed during the Great Wrath. He drew the Russian stone where, in 1808, a company of Russians were taken by surprise while eating, killed by locals and buried beneath the stone. He drew crosses where people had drowned and been killed or died in some accident with horses or cattle. He was especially pleased with his drawing of the rock that fell onto Matti Antinpoika as he was trying to clear it from a field. At Stormossen marsh a little boy had got lost in the forest and was found frozen to death in 1822. He drew the supposed location of the robber's hut on Vittermåsa, where some said there were still sightings of the marsh spirit. Only ten years ago, Helge Sten had got lost in Korpmyren and was found there dead. Ant also drew in where people used to burn tar, and the winter road along which the tar was transported out of the forest and to the city. He drew in old wolf dens and foundations of crofts that no longer stood, such as Skogsperä at Nevabacka.

One Sunday in November, Ant went up to his attic room after dinner, sat down at the table by the window where he had a view of New Cottage, part of the brook and the road into the village. He pushed aside the half-finished boot he was working on for Doris and took out a fresh sheet of paper. He had bought a new bundle the last time he was at the cooperative store in the church village, which carried no fewer than three different kinds of paper. The cooperative was a blessing, everyone said so.

He drew all the usual points of reference: the church, bridge, rectory, cooperative store, the road to the neighbouring parish, the three larger lakes, schools, the largest villages.

Then he drew a small feather to mark the place he had first laid eyes on Anni. It was at Nyjärv. She had been standing by the cattle trail, looking out at the cow paddock, and her braid lay over her left shoulder, shining like polished wood in the evening sun. Her mouth was small and her lips pale, but a little smile seemed to be hiding at the corners of her mouth. Her nose was covered with freckles, and she had pushed her headscarf back all the way as if to get a clearer view.

He knew who she was: the new milkmaid at Nyjärv, hired as summer help. Emma of Nyjärv hadn't recovered from childbirth and couldn't cope with outdoor work. He had never run into her before, and it was a coincidence that he did so now. It was a

305

Saturday evening in May, and he was on his way to Kobacka to play a hand of cards with Simon. Maybe he would stay the night, at least if Simon had something strong to offer. Ant didn't say no to such things, though he never partook in them on his own.

Ant wasn't a shy man. He had many friends in the village, though he was considered a bit odd and different. It was because he wasn't very good with words. But neither were a lot of people in these parts—despite the parish's reputation for sharp-minded, wise-cracking residents—and Ant didn't mind much. Simon, Tore and Gobbas-Anders were his closest friends.

With girls, it was a different story. Words became even knottier in their company, and they always seemed quick to laugh at him or became impatient while he searched for the right expression or when syllables got tangled in his throat. He could talk to Doris—they lived under the same roof, after all—but she was very young, just a child, really. He was very shy with Tilia. He couldn't relax in the company of someone so pretty. She was a few years older than him and attended the school in town during winter.

Ant mostly avoided all females except Doris and Lovisa, although he did sometimes attend dances. He didn't often dance but enjoyed the music, and the sight of the well-groomed couples dancing, and maybe the odd swig from someone's pocket flask.

And so he walked straight past Anni, doffing his cap but saying nothing, and she nodded and said something that he didn't understand in a soft, chirpy voice. She was speaking Finnish, of course, and Ant had never fully grasped the language, so he cleared his throat and hurried on with his eyes fixed on the ground. When he looked back after passing the big fir and the shaving stone, she was still standing there, gazing at the meadow. She wasn't looking at him. She wore a striped apron and stood with as straight a posture as anyone he had ever seen.

When he went home late that May night (he hadn't felt like staying over at Simon's, after all), he found a small white feather in the spot where she had been standing. He picked it up and took to carrying it in his shirt pocket wherever he went. Hence the little feather to mark the spot where he had first laid eyes on Anni.

He saw her at church the following day. Then twice more near Nyjärv, once from a distance, when she was herding the sheep, and once when he went to the farm to ask Janne for help fixing the sleigh that had broken last winter and no one at Nevabacka knew how to repair. Anni was sitting in the yard with the youngest little girl of Nyjärv on her lap, playing with a kitten. Ant thought that the sound of Anni's and the little lass' laughter was more beautiful than the finest violin music. He kept glancing at her while he spoke to Janne. Eventually, Janne burst out laughing.

"She doesn't have any suitors yet, so why not talk to her? If the cat ever returns your tongue," he said.

But this only rendered Ant completely speechless and made him scurry back home to Nevabacka, leaving Janne to follow behind with his work tools. After that, Janne teased Ant every time Anni was in sight, but he didn't mind. All he could think about was her.

What would he say to her? He lay awake at night and tried to draw maps of his thoughts, maps of the right words, how they might come to him and build a bridge to her. There were two bridges over the river in the church village: one by the rectory and a suspension bridge a little further north. Now he had to build a bridge of words, but he knew nothing of bridge-building.

This was unknown territory, as unknown as if he had left his own parish for the great world beyond.

Every summer, the youth centre threw a midsummer dance. The courtyard was filled with green leaves and decorations, and the band played the merriest, prettiest tunes. Ant had always been very fond of music. The notes flowed over and around him in streaks that he could almost see in the air. Maybe someday he would understand music well enough to draw a map of it. But this evening, his mind was fixed on Anni's movements. Where she went. The way she raised a hand and held it over her mouth while laughing at something Greta said. Then she danced with Karl-Oskar all around the space. Every step she took carved glowing lines inside Ant's mind, and he knew he would carry them with him for the rest of his life. He stood by the lilacs that still bore scented bunches, sipping from pocket flasks offered to him, watching the dancing couples, knowing exactly where Anni was at all times. It felt like a fire, warming him, burning him. Now she was sitting by the river, taking an opportunity to cool down with a few of the other girls. Now she was helping to light the bonfire and cheering as the sparks rose up into the bright summer night sky.

Now she was in his arms. He didn't know how it had happened. His whole soul had been directed at her all evening and he had quite forgotten himself. The band had started up again for a few last dances after the bonfire burned low. Soon everyone would have a coffee and go home. And somehow Ant had managed to ask Anni to dance, though he couldn't for the life of him remember how this had happened. He remembered her curtsying to him, and smiling up at him with her freckles dancing in the light of the coming dawn. His hands around her waist. Her hands warming his shoulders through the fabric of his shirt. Together, they danced and twirled, and he kept a firm but not-too-tight hold on her, and he knew exactly how they should dance—he had maps of all the steps in his head—and led her through fox trails and summer paths, along moose routes and stream courses. There was no need to speak, because he could show himself to her through the steps and notes and their two bodies together.

Then the music was over. The dance was over. The night was over. But Anni's hand was still in his. They walked together all the way to Nyjärv, just the two of them. They could have got a ride in one of the cars or carts that overtook them, but neither made an effort to stop anyone. The beauty of the midsummer night spoke for itself; there was no need for words. He ran his thumb along the contours of her hand, as he learned its geography and he would remember every dip, every soft valley forever. When they reached Nyjärv, they stopped by the barn, and Anni looked up at him with a broad smile and pointed. He turned to see the sun rising over the birch forest in a haze of pink and gold, and he pulled Anni close to him, and together they watched the morning dawn and a new day begin.

He desperately wanted to kiss her, but he didn't know how. She yawned and leaned her head against his chest. He never wanted to move, he wanted to stay like this forever and just hold her close to him, feel her body against his, her warmth, the scent of her hair and the withered summer flowers she had tied into a wreath, a crown.

Eventually, she withdrew from him.

"*Hyvää yötä*, Ant," she said. He couldn't squeeze out a single word in reply. He couldn't remember saying a single word to her all evening, but he had to say something now, say goodnight, ask if he could accompany her to church one Sunday—something, anything.

She turned and walked along the stone wall to Nyjärv farm. The sun shone on his neck, and though he tried to move his jaw, he couldn't make a sound.

He went home and tried to draw a map of their dancing, but it refused to be captured on paper. Everything he had felt, the paths of her movements—how could they be shown in points and lines?

He saw her again, of course. A couple of times, from a distance. But there was so much work to be done, with the scything and haymaking and everything, and he didn't have time to stop by Nyjärv. There were dances at Lågsveden and plays at the youth centre, but he didn't go. He didn't know why. It wasn't that he was afraid of getting tongue-tied, or that Anni would look at him reproachfully. Maybe it was because nothing could ever match that midsummer's night.

He was having trouble drawing new maps. He tried to make one of music, and one of all the places Pricke had misbehaved or injured himself or been especially good, but abandoned them before long. It was autumn, and there was much urgent work on the farm. In the evenings he fell into bed and was asleep before he knew it.

In October he heard word that Anni no longer worked at Nyjärv.

The first reservists left the village in November. There was unrest in the east. Cold weather and bad news came creeping in at the same time. Ant didn't pay it much heed. He was busy burning thickets with Otto. He was driving to the dairy and taking part in the march of the White Guards. Sven repaired the well pump. Ant cut back vines and dug trenches. He carved a toy sledge for Janne's youngest brother and did building work on Rectory Road. He ploughed at Korpmyren and transported carts of hay with Pricke. He brought grain to the mill and drove fodder carrots home to the farm. He repaired roofs and threshed with Hannes and Erik Mikael.

Then the first horses were selected for the army. Polle was among them but Pricke was not, and Ant was grateful. He had

311

spent so much time working with Pricke. They were friends, he and the horse.

In December, the conscriptions began. Hannes and Simon were among the first. Ant drew a map of where the men had been called up from and where the first air raid was heard. He marked where the security guards gathered and where sugar and coffee could be obtained. He had to do it behind blackout curtains. There were some in the parish who weren't so careful about the blackout, but the farm mistress made sure that all the cottage windows had blackout curtains. She and Doris sewed snow camouflage for the soldiers.

Ant was still quite young and probably wouldn't be drafted. He hadn't completed his military service yet. Erik Mikael joined the army after Christmas.

Ant didn't want to go away to war. It was the word "away" that scared him more than "war". Of course he was willing to fight to defend his homeland. There was no question about that. If the Russians came here, he would be at the forefront, defending every inch of his home parish. Every farm, every cairn, every tree was more precious to him than gold. What if the Russians came here, trampled the blueberry bushes and wild strawberry patches, burned down the church or made the youth centre their own headquarters, cut down forests or otherwise desecrated and destroyed? Ant would be the first and the last to fight them by any means possible. He talked about it with Sven and Lovisa and Otto in the evenings, saying how he would shoot them with the hunting rifle if necessary. As long as Ant lived and breathed, they would be safe from the Russians here. And his master and mistress didn't laugh at him or at the way he garbled his speech when he got worked up. Sven patted him on the shoulder and said he was a good man. And his mistress gave him extra butter on his bread. Otto didn't seem to fully understand. He was brave and said that he would enlist as soon as he turned sixteen. But then the farmer's eyes turned dark and he said that he intended to keep at least one son on the farm, no matter what. He had already sent two to the front, wasn't that enough?

But the thing that kept Ant up at night, that filled him with the deepest dread, was being buried somewhere far away. Being denied eternal rest in his home soil. It didn't have to be in the cemetery. For Ant, every inch of the parish was sacred. Anywhere would do just fine. If he were to fall here, with his feet firmly on the slopes and stones he had known and loved since childhood—well, that would be all right with him. It would be a good way to end his time on Earth. But the idea of dying far away, under trees that didn't know him, on some nameless hill, filled him with unspeakable horror. To be laid in a foreign grave with other anonymous soldiers. Not being allowed to come home for his final rest.

Before the turn of the year, Hannes was reported missing. He might be dead. Ant thought so. He knew that Sven and Lovisa were hoping that he had been captured and might be released.

In January, the same news came about Erik Mikael. Sven suffered what seemed to be a small stroke and became bedridden. His wife took care of him, grey and silent. Little Doris was busy helping out at New Cottage, because the Bird Man was also unwell.

In February, the summons came. Ant would receive rapid training and be sent straight to the front.

It was a sparkling cold day when Otto had to drive Ant to the church village, where he and the other recruits would be picked up in a truck and taken to town and then southward by train. Lovisa and Doris provided Ant with warm clothes: woollen underpants and socks and some snow camouflage. He was also given skis to take with him. Hannes hadn't been as well equipped. Ant wondered if he had been very cold; it had been a dastardly cold winter. Maybe Hannes had been allotted some socks.

Ant went to see the farmer in his bedroom to say goodbye. Sven suddenly looked terribly old. His skin was pale and half his face was hanging loosely and strangely.

"Thank you for everything."

"You will write if you hear anything about the boys?"

"I will." He fiddled with his woollen cap. He would have to ask someone else to write for him. But that was okay.

"Take care of yourself, Ant. You are a good man."

"Thank you. This…" The words got stuck. He tried new ones. "Here at Nevabacka…" No, he couldn't make bridges of words there either.

Otto was waiting in the sleigh out in the yard. He had hitched up Pricke. Ant hadn't had to do it this time. He was glad that Pricke would take him on this journey. His first away from home. He thought that it would probably be his last as well.

Doris and Lovisa followed him out onto the hill. Lovisa handed him a package of sandwiches. He tossed his sack into the sleigh, took off his hat and bowed.

Lovisa's nose was red and sniffing. She embraced him, which was odd. She had never done that before.

Suddenly a thought occurred to Ant. He had heard a few rumours about the women of Nevabacka. About special wisdom and abilities they had possessed, once upon a time. He had heard some of it from Doris.

"Will I come home again?" He looked down at her pale little face. She had wrapped her shawl so tightly around her head that none of her dark hair showed. She looked him straight in the eye.

"You will come home from this war," she said. And she pressed something into his hand. He nodded silently. All words seemed to have completely disappeared.

"God bless you," said Lovisa, stepping forward to give Pricke a clap on the neck. The horse's breath formed a cloud around his muzzle, and Otto was sitting huddled in the sleigh in his father's old American fur.

Ant climbed up and Pricke set off. Ant turned to watch the two figures, dressed in grey, go back inside the white-painted house and close the door behind them. There was smoke coming from both the old house and New Cottage.

A pale yellow sun hung above the treetops. A soot-black raven swooped across the clear blue sky.

As they drove off, Ant looked around with hungry eyes. There was the forked fir tree. There was the potato field and the Great

Field. They drove past Mustalampi. There was the section of road that caused such a hassle every year at the annual road inspection. They passed by the grey and white houses of the neighbouring village. They had reached Nyjärv already—how could this be happening so quickly? He saw the gate and for a moment he thought he saw Anni standing there, but it was Maja of Nyjärv who had come to wave them off.

"You're lucky to go," Otto said through his scarf. "I don't care what Ma and Pa say. It's shameful to stay behind and not fight for the motherland. The war will be over by the time I'm old enough to fight."

Ant looked out over the sparkling white fields. They were approaching the church village now. Everything was going so very quickly.

In Forskant they stopped at the youth centre where they had coffee with some bread but no sugar, and then Otto said goodbye.

"Good luck at the front," he said and shook Ant by the hand.

Ant went out and stroked Pricke's muzzle one last time. Then Otto drove off, sending snow flying around the runners. Ant and Janne had fixed the sleigh. It would last a good while.

That morning, everyone from the parish who was heading for training gathered at the youth centre. They were all young men. The older ones, who had already done their military service, had been taken in December. A truck drove up, it belonged to Lovisa's father, the merchant. The young men chatted as they jumped onto the cargo bed. Ant was one of the last. As they waited for the truck to start, Ant remembered Doris' gift. He dug into his pockets and picked it out.

It was a little lock of rough horse hair, tied up with red wool. Ant recognized it straight away as Pricke's mane. He had brushed it so many times, and braided it neatly at Christmas. He held it up to his nose and inhaled the safe equine smell.

The truck started and they were waved off by sisters and fiancées and mothers and fathers. Then there was silence among the passengers.

There was the cafe. He could see the yellow church tower. Then they left the river behind. They arrived at the big cross-roads. And then...

Ant closed his eyes. They were going outside the borders of the map, beyond which there were only monsters and beasts: a vast white field that surrounded his small, carefully drawn world. He didn't know if the land beyond the edge of the map looked anything like home. If the people looked the same. If they spoke the same. If they could understand him at all. Ant pulled his hands into his coat sleeves and huddled down. He felt the truck swerve and now they were on the main road. The engine accelerated.

They drove north. Ant was leaning back on the cargo bed and the sun was shining directly in his face. It was warm, like a summer evening. It burned through his closed eyelids. He was standing at the gate of Nyjärv with Anni in his arms, in silence and mutual understanding, watching the sun rise over the treetops.

Ant opened his eyes.

SLEIGH RIDE

I N THE MOONLIGHT, the trees cast long blue shadows on
the snow. It was a windless, starry night and the temperature was dropping steadily. His hands were stiff with cold on
the reins, but Pricke knew the way to town. Sven was dressed
in his old greatcoat with a thick sweater underneath and had
his leather cap pulled down over his ears. But he was sitting
motionless and therefore still cold. He knew he should get off
and move around a bit, but he was too tired. Despite the cold,
he nodded off a few times and woke up surrounded by forest
that looked exactly the same. He knew where he was anyway.
No matter how dark it was. He didn't need light to know his
own village. He had been walking and riding these roads for
seventy years.

There had been a different kind of darkness in Africa. There
was no snow to catch the light and darkness fell like an axe
chop in the evenings. Everything went black and he had no
idea what might be hiding in that blackness. He heard strange
and terrifying sounds. Once a dead lion was found lying outside

his house in the morning. No one knew how it had died. It was just lying there.

And the mine. When he was alone and all the lights went out. Damn, that was scary. The walls of the mountain pressed down on him, wanting to crush him with their weight. He would lose his orientation straight away and barely knew which was up or down. The darkness compressed his lungs. As if all the oxygen had disappeared.

Sven shuddered on the seat. Gasped for air. Cleared his throat and spat over the edge of the sleigh. Pricke flicked his ears and trotted on. The conditions were good for driving. Which was a good job, seeing as he had to waste an entire evening driving to and from town.

What the hell was she even doing here?

He huddled inside his multiple layers of clothing. He thought back to those warm Rhodesian nights when he never felt cold. The taste of banana and sugar plum. The taste of Hope's kisses. The scent of roses and geraniums at Christmas time.

He was far away from midwinter and snow when the train whistle woke him up. Pricke had reached the station just as the train arrived, so they didn't have long to wait. Sven saw a few familiar faces and raised a hand in greeting, but it was too cold for conversation.

The Cuckoo Girl appeared next to the sleigh and tossed her bag in.

"Hello, Uncle Sven! Have you been waiting long?"

Sven grunted something inaudible, and as soon as the Cuckoo Girl sat down next to him, he urged Pricke to set off. The runners creaked as the horse swung the sleigh around and began the journey home. Out of the corner of his eye he saw that she was wearing fur. And trousers.

The sleigh glided through the outskirts of the town. The Cuckoo Girl looked all around with eager eyes, waving to people she recognized. She noticed and mentioned various changes from the last time she had been there—fences removed, new houses built. Sven was barely listening.

"My mother is dead."

Sven jerked awake. He had dropped off again.

"How do you know that?"

"I got a letter. From America. It was from the nurse who was caring for her in her last days. Apparently she had found my name among Elsa's papers. Afterwards."

"When?"

"Last spring. It took a while for the letter to find me because they didn't have my exact address. Lucky that it happened now, while Nevabacka is still my surname."

"So, Elsa is dead." Sven barely remembered his little sister. He was away a lot when she was growing up. First it was Africa, then America. Two stints in Wisconsin. Six years away from his homeland, during which time Elsa grew up and flew the nest. And then she flew away entirely and was never heard of again.

The last time he had seen her, she stank of perfume and dumped the Cuckoo Girl on him and Lovisa.

"She was married with children. Over in America."

"Oh? Many?"

"I don't know." The Cuckoo Girl made a movement inside her fur that might have been a shrug. "The nurse didn't say. Her husband had already died, he did something in shipping, but there wasn't much inheritance. It all went to them." She sat quietly for a while. "You did well in America, didn't you? Maybe that's why Mum went there. After seeing how well you did?"

There was hope in the Cuckoo Girl's voice. She sounded like she used to twenty years ago, when she would ask if her mother was coming home to collect her soon. He cleared his throat.

"Maybe."

She could have written, he thought. How hard was it to write and say where she was? Say that she wasn't coming home again. To her daughter.

"Did you ever consider staying? In America?"

"Yes, that was the plan at first. But it wasn't to be."

"Why not?"

"Who knows." He could feel himself getting irritable. What business was it of hers? Digging and prying. He refused to elaborate.

Clouds of vapour were steaming out of their mouths and around the horse's muzzle. They had left the town and were already out on the wintry road. The sounds of a harness and bells warned them of an oncoming vehicle, and Sven steered Pricke to the side to allow them to pass. It was Anders of Nyjärv on his double sledge, packed full of firewood, on his way home from a day's work in the forest.

"Sven." Anders nodded and lifted a hand in greeting. He reined in his brown mare. "And who's that you've got with you?"

"Hello, Anders," said the Cuckoo Girl.

"Ah, it's Tilia! Are you staying long?"

"No, just a few a days. Aunt Lovisa wrote and invited me for a visit."

"Long time since you've been home. How did it go over in Hyytiälä? Were the boys nice to you?"

"It was good. It was tough to begin with but they came round."

"I'll bet you were just as good as any of the boys."

"We were supposed to work in pairs and collect a stere of firewood the first summer. After the first day, all of the boys refused to pair with me. I never took a break. They couldn't keep up."

She said it quietly, without bragging. Sven glanced at her.

Anders laughed softly. "I can imagine. Well, I'm off home. Maja is waiting with dinner." He set his horse in motion and was soon gone. Pricke started moving without Sven having to do anything.

"It was my father who taught you to chop wood." Sven wiped his nose with his gloved hand.

"Yes. We had our own wood-cutting campaign, he and I, long before everyone else started doing it for the war effort. He was the one who inspired me to become a forester."

"My father? He probably didn't know such a job existed."

322

"No. But he showed me the forest. He taught me about all the birds, animal tracks, trees and types of wood. One Christmas he gave me those children's books about the forest by Martti Hertz, remember? And then I read all the boys' books about woods and wildlife, Curwood and Zane Grey and Jack London and whatever I could find."

Sven imagined Otto's flaxen hair as he lay on the sofa, reading adventure books. Otto perched in the yard, reading, with his bare legs hooked around a branch. Lovisa standing under the tree and calling him in for dinner without noticing the boy in the foliage above her.

But he could no longer envision Otto's boyish face. Just the photograph of Otto in uniform, serious, ready.

He shook himself.

Ottilia looked up at the starry sky. "The work of a forester is not quite how I dreamed it would be. It's more paperwork than dealing with land and forest. But that summer in Lesti, when I was an overseer, and we gathered around the fire in the evenings. There was good camaraderie there. That was probably closer to what I had dreamed of: life in the wilderness, the smell of resin and needles and all that." She fell silent. As though she expected him to respond, but what was he supposed to say? She sighed softly and continued. "It can be rather difficult sometimes. Many places make it quite clear that they don't want female employees, except as secretaries and clerks at most."

"Yes, well. Never understood what you were hoping to find out there. Plenty of work to be done at home on the farm."

"But the farm isn't mine. And it never will be. Doris will inherit it. But the forest—that was always mine."

"Pa left you a fair bit." This had always been a thorn in Sven's side. That Elsa's cuckoo in the nest would own some of the forest. He should have inherited everything. His sisters and their children could have a little money, or a cow if they moved to a farm when they married.

"That's not what I meant." Ottilia spoke cautiously. Sven knew it was because she was contradicting him and didn't want to anger him again. He was annoyed, but didn't know whether it was at her or himself. "I meant that the forest was always my home. Grandpa and I were out in the forest more than we were home in New Cottage. And I knew I had to find a job. So why not forester? Then I get to be outside, I thought. In the forest."

"Mm-hmm." He was rigid with irritation and didn't know where to direct it.

"The most time I got to spend in the forest was at the district office in Oulu. I enjoyed myself very much there."

"Before the war?"

"Yes. Then there was the office in Helsinki." She said this as if it were something he should have known. Lovisa might have mentioned something about it. But that was when Erik and Hannes were at the front. What would he have cared about Tilia in Helsinki? But then he remembered something he had heard, a place name that he committed to memory because it had to do with the front and the war.

"I thought you were at Äänislinna."

"It was during the Continuation War. I supervised the resin collection. I was afraid a lot of the time. Many of the Lotta Svärd volunteers were shot by the Russians there. I had a gun but don't think I could have used it if anything had happened. They said the place was teeming with Soviet paratroopers in 1943, but I never saw any."

"What about when you get married? Surely you'll stop working then?"

"Well, not at first. Maybe later if I have children."

"What does Bengt say about that?"

"Not much. He thinks it would be good to have two salaries, at least to begin with."

"And you've never considered living in New Cottage?"

"No." Ottilia looked at him in surprise. "No, our work is in Helsinki. Is that what you would want?"

"Bah. The house is falling into disrepair. You would have to see to that."

"Maybe one day, when we're not so tight on money. Accommodation and everything is so expensive in Helsinki."

Tight on money, she says, in her fur coat. If they weren't planning on living at Nevabacka, what business did she have there at all?

They passed a high, smooth wall of logs that followed the curve of the road for a good distance. Ottilia's gaze followed the logs approvingly.

"Few people stack wood more neatly than Forskant residents.

In most places, people pile logs haphazardly. Have you been in the forest a lot this winter?"

"Sledging has only been possible for the past week or so, so there's not been much time. But this month I have men coming to fell a few more trees. I'm only taking firewood now."

"This summer I oversaw a large clearing in northern Ostrobothnia. 21,000 hectares!"

Sven tried to imagine such a vast area felled of all trees. Cold. Dead.

"What would Pa have said about that?"

Ottilia turned to Sven in surprise. "What do you mean?"

"That's not how Pa taught us to manage the forest."

Ottilia looked around and assessed the snow-laden firs along the road.

"Selective felling weakens the forest. In the state-owned forests, we are now making large uniform clearings. The stock is then renewed by sowing seeds or saplings. That makes it easier to get a uniform harvest in the future."

"We never used to have to do that. Plant seeds and whatnot. Back before people cut everything down. The forest renewed itself."

Ottilia turned to him eagerly. "The forest is kept healthy and viable with efficient modern methods. Think of Vittermåsa, for example! You could grow almost a hundred hectares of forest there if only the marsh were properly drained."

"Vittermåsa is part of my land. You take care of yours as you wish, and I'll take care of mine."

But he couldn't manage the forest as he wanted. He knew that. The world had its laws and regulations. How much the forest must yield and how it should be felled. The war reparations had to be paid with Finland's green gold.

First the war took their sons, then it took their forest. That was how Sven saw it.

Ottilia hesitated. She could see that he was vexed, but it was a subject she wanted to pursue.

"Aunt Lovisa wrote to me and said that you're having difficulty managing. It's hard to meet the felling requirements. She asked me to come and talk to you about taking over the work. I know all about it, after all, and it would save you the trouble."

"I'm not dead yet!"

So that's what these meddlesome bitches were planning. To steal his forest, his work. Sven's heart was pounding with fury. He had to press his hand to his chest.

"Now don't get angry. Lovisa was only thinking of what's best for you. You've suffered two strokes now. And when you started thinking about selling the sawmill, she thought that..."

"Are you going to tell me what to do with my saw as well?"

The industrial saw was his pride and joy. He had built it after he returned from America. He had learned a lot about sawmills there. Had worked his way up at the sawmill in Wisconsin and eventually become foreman. But after his second stroke, he could no longer manage. And it was too hard for a small sawmill to survive these days.

The saw was what made him stand out from the other farmers. Raised him above them. He had a bandsaw. A small industry. He didn't want to sell. But he had no one to take over either.

He wrapped himself up in furious silence, and Ottilia huddled in her fur and decided to keep her mouth shut. The temperature dropped steadily; Sven could feel it in every breath. He had been young when he worked in Wisconsin, and young people don't feel the cold in the same way. Now it nipped at his legs. He was damned if he was going to get frostbite for the sake of the Cuckoo Girl. He used to have a rabbit fur coat. American fur. He had given it to Otto to take to the front. Sven had bought the coat when he became foreman. It was expensive and he was usually very careful to save most of his earnings, but had thought it appropriate for a foreman to dress according to his position.

And he had also bought it with Nelly in mind. So that she wouldn't be embarrassed to be seen with him on their walks together.

Of course, a fur wasn't enough to make a gentleman out of him. To the boss' daughter, he was still just an immigrant worker, foreman, in a rabbit fur or not. No matter how hard he worked, no matter how honest and trustworthy he proved himself to be. He was good enough to escort her to dances and parties, but not to marry her.

He could still hear her hoarse, nervous laughter when he proposed.

Over there, he could never become someone important. But at home, with money in his pocket, he could. Money for a sawmill, to elevate the farm. Here he was a person with a history and context, whether he liked it or not. Bror Nevabacka's only son.

A raven flew across the road and let out a low, lonely cry. Pricke flinched but soon calmed.

Otto used to have a tame raven when he was a boy. He found it as a chick. It had fallen out of its nest, so he took it home. This angered Sven. Crows bring bad luck. Lovisa refused to let it into the house. Otto named it Kalle and kept it in the stable.

Wherever Otto was, he could call out to Kalle, and Kalle would come flying and land on his shoulder. The flaxen-haired boy and the night-black bird were inseparable that summer. The bird liked to peck at Otto's ear with its pointed beak. Sometimes it rode their horse Jänta, and once Lovisa caught it in the pantry with its beak in the butter.

Kalle stayed at Nevabacka for over a year. In the winter, Otto and Kalle went sledding together, Kalle perched on the front of the sledge or on Otto's shoulder. When they got down to the bottom of the hill, the bird flew up and waited for Otto at the top. The raven was also good friends with the farm dog King. They would chase each other for hours. King could never catch the bird.

When spring came, Kalle disappeared. He must have found himself a mate. Otto was devastated. Sven remembered how the boy called for the bird all spring. Sven tried to explain that this was the way of animals. They found a mate and left their parents. That was the way it was supposed to be. But Otto was inconsolable.

"Uncle Sven?" Ottilia shook his arm gently and woke him up. He let go of the reins briefly to rub his hands together. He barely had any feeling left in his fingers, and his feet felt like dead lumps.

"Let me," said Ottilia, taking the reins from him without waiting for an answer. "You need to move."

Sven muttered something under his breath and hopped down from the sleigh. His feet refused to obey and he stumbled as if he had no feet at all. Ottilia held Pricke at a steady plod, and Sven stumbled forward in the snow alongside them. Every step hurt. He was getting snow in his boots, and it was so damn dark. Without the sleigh to hold on to, he would have lost his way very soon.

Sven remembered Otto's last leave. He had been allowed to come home for three days. Doris and Lovisa had prepared food, and all the neighbours promptly came to visit. Otto took it all with equanimity, but when Sven went out into the forest with him on the last day, he seemed relieved. They brought the guns with them. It was spring-winter, as snowy as now but with longer days and not nearly as cold. Birds were already singing and sometimes meltwater rippled in the day only to refreeze at night. The ice crust still held and they had easy access to the deep forest.

The next large offensive of the Continuation War was only a few months away, but they didn't know it at the time.

Sven couldn't remember if they had shot anything. He didn't really care about the hunt. He got time alone with his youngest son. Otto pointed out the stream where Sven had taught him to fish. Sven thought about all the things he had never had time to teach Otto. He hoped there would be time. Otto had grown up so much since going to the front. Calmer. Quieter. He had been a talkative child, but now he was mostly silent. Sven wondered what he had seen over there. What he had done.

His thoughts turned to Africa. What he had seen there. What he had done. Things he never spoke of.

Otto did shoot something—he remembered now. There was blood on the snow. Otto sat crouched over the kill, and the snow was red around him. Sven suddenly felt horrified at the sight of the blood. Though he had never in his life been squeamish. He regretted suggesting hunting. What was he thinking? Putting a gun in the boy's hand. As if he hadn't had enough of weapons. Even now, next to the sleigh in the midwinter cold, Sven's stomach turned at the thought of it. It was as if he was tempting fate. On purpose.

The blood attracted two ravens. They came flying over the forest. Sven felt unease creeping in, after everything his father had said about ravens as harbingers of doom and other birds of misfortune. The eagle-owl that Pa said had warned of Alina's death. But Otto stood up straight and shouted: "Kalle!" and one of the birds immediately turned around and flew straight to him. It landed in the snow a few metres away and looked at him with its head tilted.

331

"Hello, Kalle," said Otto. His voice was high-pitched, the happiest it had been for days. A boyish voice. The raven hopped a little closer but didn't come all the way. Otto held a hand out towards it. Then the other raven cawed hoarsely, and Kalle flew up, and together the two birds circled above them once before disappearing over the treetops to the north. Otto looked for them for a long, long time after they had gone.

When he finally turned back to look at his father, he was beaming. Sven remembered his face now. The smile, the light in his eyes. He remembered it quite clearly. The hair sticking out from under his cap, cheeks ruddy from cold, stubble.

His Otto.

Ottilia reined in the horse, and he laboriously climbed back onto the sleigh. His feet and hands stung and burned, and he was hot around the collar. He sniffled, which he blamed on the cold. An old man's eyes often watered in the cold too.

They had reached the crest of Steinbacka hill, and below them lay the potato field on the left and the great field and small field on the right. The road descended between them and then rose up towards Nevabacka Farm, against its background of snow-covered pines and firs. The grey outbuildings were crouched beneath thick blankets of snow, and the fence posts wore small snowy caps. But the white farmhouse stood out proudly in the snow, and friendly lights shone from all the downstairs windows.

"We'll be home soon." Ottilia clapped the reins on Pricke's back, and the horse was not difficult to persuade. He trotted briskly down the hill and towards the awaiting warmth.

SUMMER WITH DORIS

3 JUNE

The train journey here took forever. I only had two Lotta books with me, and I read them both before we got to Tampere. Then I had nothing to do, but Mum didn't care because she was reading her research reports. And all we had packed for lunch was crispbread with salami. I hate eating crispbread on trains! Everyone in the compartment was *staring* at me and Mum while we were eating, and I was mortified. Then, when we got there, we weren't actually there at all. First we took a bus to Forskant, and from there one of Auntie Doris' and Great-auntie Lovisa's neighbours picked us up by car, because the weather was bad and Auntie Lovisa didn't want to bring the horse. The car smelled terrible, and I was so tired and hungry and annoyed I almost cried. I could barely bring myself to say hello to Auntie Doris and Auntie Lovisa, and I could tell that Mum was getting angry because I wasn't being polite enough. Serves her right!

Dinner was surprisingly tasty. At least I won't starve to death here. There was freshly baked bread and home-made butter, two different kinds of jam, and boiled eggs and porridge. The only thing that was disgusting was the milk—it was *warm*. They don't have a fridge here! How am I supposed to drink horrible warm milk all summer? Me and Mum were given a small room to sleep in, where she used to sleep when she was little and shared a bed with Auntie Doris' brothers. It's Doris' room now so she's bunking with her mother. Her brothers are all dead, because of the war, of course. I was lucky that my dad was too young to go to war. Mum only spent one night here and is taking the train back today. We got up very early because it was impossible to sleep with the cows in the barn mooing so loudly. Mum said it's because they want to be milked. Is it going to be like this every morning? I asked. She just laughed. Then I got so angry that I almost cried again. All very well for you to laugh, I said, you don't have to spend all summer with these old women, you can go off on your travels and enjoy yourself without me, pretend I don't exist for all I care! I won't remind you of my existence by writing letters!

Then Mum suddenly turned very pale, sat on the edge of my bed and took my hand. She explained that it is only for one summer while she is on her research trip in northern Finland. She and Dad will come to collect me in August, and she would never ever abandon me.

I know that. But it *feels* like being abandoned. I wanted to stay with Dad in the city while she went on her trip. I'm almost thirteen, I can be left alone during the day while he's at work. But no, they think I'm too young.

Mum wouldn't let up and kept holding my hand and reminded me that my friends will all be away for the summer and I would have been very lonely in the city, and maybe she's right. But still. They don't even have a TV here!

Mum left me alone and went to have breakfast. After a while I decided to get up and dressed and get some food too. Auntie Lovisa was doing the dishes, and Auntie Doris and Mum were sitting and talking. Mum is older than Doris, I know that, but I suddenly thought that Mum looked younger. Mum looked so cool in her trousers and chequered shirt. Doris was wearing this ugly brown polyester housecoat and even uglier slippers. She looked at least ten years older than Mum. Auntie Lovisa looked really old-fashioned in a long skirt and blouse and apron. It's hot now, so I had my miniskirt on, and I *saw* the look Lovisa gave me. But she didn't say anything.

Mum and Auntie Doris were talking loads about a house. It's here on the farm and Mum owns it apparently, and Doris had all sorts of opinions about what Mum should do with it. I wasn't really listening. There was porridge with butter to eat—but I didn't drink the warm milk. They can keep it!

Then a car horn honked from the road, it was their neighbour Uno who had come to drive Mum back to the bus in the village. Mum took her hat and her bag full of books, and then she kissed me and hugged me tightly and suddenly I didn't feel angry at all, just very sad. I promised to write to her, and she promised to write to me and told me that Auntie Lovisa said I can call Dad whenever I want. I hugged her and cried and she cried and then Uno honked again. Mum went outside and I heard the car speed away. It was just me and the old women.

5 JUNE

Bored already. Auntie Doris has a bookshelf full of books in her bedroom. Most of it looks pretty dull, but there are some by Jack London that I haven't read, and *The Pickwick Papers* is always a fun read. And she has everything L.M. Alcott has ever written, when I've only ever read *Little Women*. I'll have to ask if I can borrow some books—else I might die of boredom. I've already read my Lotta books four times each. I'm worried that Auntie Doris doesn't like me much. She noticed me turn my nose up at the milk, and I tried to follow her into the barn last night but it just smelled *too* disgusting. She seemed to take offence when I said that.

Last night I went to the house Mum owns, which they call New Cottage. It's across the yard from Great-auntie Lovisa's house and looks quite dilapidated. The door was locked, but after a bit of snooping I found the key under the front step. I went in, because if it's Mum's house, then it's pretty much mine too. It had a cold, gloomy smell—not musty, just *gloomy*. Like the smell of darkness itself. In the boot room in the front porch there are a lot of life-sized painted birds, and I could tell straight away that they were Mum's. She hasn't painted in a long time, but when I was little she used to paint and draw birds all the time on various cards and letters she sent. And she made a book for me when I was three or four, with pages that she sewed together, where she painted all the types of owl found in Finland in watercolours. I still have it.

Other than that, there's not much of interest in the house. It's one big room with an old-fashioned long table and benches on dirty, faded old rag rugs. The wallpaper is dark around the stove, I think the rain must have leaked in there. Then there's one bedroom with two beds, a chest of drawers and some paintings on the walls. One is of some marshland with a black bird flying high above a pale birch tree or something. It's hard to see exactly, but I like it.

Auntie Doris saw me coming out but she didn't get angry. She just said that I should be careful because the floor in New Cottage might be rotten. Later that evening, she told me that Mum lived in that house with her grandfather when she was little. I asked why she didn't live with her parents, and Auntie Doris looked at me for a long time and finally asked me what I know about Mum's parents.

I admitted that I don't know much. Then she told me that my grandmother left Mum here with my great-grandfather, then went to America and never came back!

Mum never talks about her family. Now I think I understand why. She must have been very little when her mother left. How could a mother do such a thing?

6 JUNE

The birds are awful here! They sing so enthusiastically I'm surprised they don't fall off their branches. And there are at least as many mosquitoes, gnats and flies. They're driving me crazy! My legs are all red and scratched bloody. And they don't have any Infrasol anti-itching spray. The aunties spray fly poison indoors so there aren't too many flying bugs in the house, at least. There was an invasion of ants in the bedrooms the other day, so I, being the small and bendy one, had to crawl under the beds and spray DDT. That got rid of them. Mum won't let us use DDT in the cabin that Dad inherited, because she says the birds need their food. But there are plenty of insects for them anyway, I think. They don't have to come inside!

But there are nice creatures on the farm too: the cat and her kittens. They are so cute, I could sit and watch them all day! They live up in the hayloft, and it's really cosy sitting up there in the rustling hay and watching them scamper about. My favourite one is all grey but for a white chin and paws, and she likes to crawl up on my lap and play with my fingers or the tassels on my blouse. She's fallen asleep in my lap a few times and I couldn't move until she woke up! I call her Cordelia, from *Anne of Green Gables*, but I haven't told the aunties that. I wish I could take her home with me, but when I phoned Dad yesterday, his answer was a firm no. Then I told him that he could at least spare a thought for his only daughter, neglected in the north for his convenience. He laughed at me!

7 JUNE

It's been raining and thundering for a couple of days now. I've been reading Jack London and listening to Auntie Doris' transistor radio. She said that we can cycle to the library in the village one day when the weather is better. It's really hot all the time! I'm dying for some ice cream, but we can't have any here because they don't have a fridge-freezer.

There was a clear sky this morning and I thought Auntie Doris was going to suggest we cycle to the village, but instead she suggested we cycle to the lake for a swim! There are a few little lakes near here, but she thought we should go to Storsjön where there is a campsite and dance floor and a nice sandy beach. It's quite a long way, she warned. But I told her I have strong legs!

And they were put to good use because there were some nasty hills to climb, and the road was a mostly lumpy, bumpy forest path. But we got there in the end, and I was surprised to see a really nice swimming beach full of people in the middle of the forest!

There was music playing from a few different radios, a badminton net where some boys were playing—and a kiosk with ice cream! Dad gave me some pocket money, so I splashed out on ice cream for me and Doris.

We had our swimming costumes on under our clothes, so all we had to do was jump out of our shorts and into the lake. Doris only swam for a little while, then she lay down on a towel with a magazine. But I swam a long way out, even though the water was quite cold. I am a good swimmer. Then I lay on my back and looked at the sky and the few white clouds that came gliding by.

It is true, of course, that if I'd been in the city with Dad, I'd have mostly been at home inside. My friends are all at their summer cottages, except Britta, and she never wants to do anything outside. She just wants to watch TV and paint her nails. Which is fun for a while, but I'd probably get bored and want to go swimming or to a forest or somewhere I can move around a bit.

When I swam back to shore, Doris was sitting and talking to two boys who were about fourteen or fifteen years old. She waved at me and I wrung the water out of my hair and walked over to them. One was blond and freckled and had big, sticky-out ears. Doris introduced him as my cousin Gustaf. The other was Gustaf's friend Jan. He was tall and thin with curly dark hair and big brown eyes. He looked a bit like Robertino Loretti. Especially if I squinted.

We shook hands. I thought it would be really fun to have some kids my age to hang out with. Especially one as handsome as Jan. Gustaf said that they come to Storsjön most days, because it's the best beach in the area and the only one with a diving platform. Jan smiled at me and I realized that now I will *also* have to come here almost every day. Unfortunately, I couldn't think of anything to say in that moment and just stood there speechless like a dope.

As if she could read my mind, Doris said now that I knew the way, I could cycle here whenever I wanted. I definitely will!

Dinner is ready now, meat soup with dumplings. I didn't think I'd like it, but it's actually really good!

10 JUNE

The lilacs have come out now, and the whole of Nevabacka is covered in purple and white flowers that smell so good that I can hardly fall asleep at night. I want to bottle this scent to take it home to Helsinki and live on it all winter! And perfume is *not* the same thing. The rowans are blooming too, and they don't smell that great, but the trees are buzzing with all the bees dancing around the flowers. It's a really nice, homey sound, I think.

I cycled to Storsjön again, but I didn't find Gustaf and Jan, even though the beach was full of people. I swam anyway, and ate an ice cream, and it was quite fun to watch people all by myself. Storsjön is such a funny place—right in the middle of the forest, so far away from everything, where all these people gather and swim and dance and eat, surrounded by kilometre after kilometre of deep forest.

It was different cycling there all alone. The forest didn't feel as friendly as it did when I had Doris with me. It rustled and creaked and made all sorts of strange noises. As I was cycling home, a big brown bird flew up with a terrible squawk, and I thought my heart was going to burst out of my chest! After that I cycled as fast as I could.

Nevabacka is really in the middle of nowhere. I don't think I could handle living this far from everything. There are no buses, and I think they use the milk truck to get to the village. But Doris and Lovisa don't seem to mind in the slightest. So far I haven't seen them leave the farm other than to visit the neighbours and when Doris cycled with me to Storsjön. They are busy with their work, I guess. And if you have cows, you can't leave them, I remember Mum saying.

In the evening I took Doris' transistor radio up to the hay-loft and played music for Cordelia and the other kittens. In the middle of it all, they played "O Sole Mio" by Robertino Loretti! I told Cordelia about Jan who looks like Robertino if you squint.

13 JUNE

There was a terrible storm last night. I was woken up by a bang that shook the whole house. There was a cascade of lightning and thunder, so it was impossible to sleep. Maybe I was a bit scared too. There are so many trees for lightning to strike. What if they fell onto the roof of the house? Or caught fire? It would take ages for the firefighters to get here. Finally I got up and peeked into Doris and Lovisa's room, but Doris wasn't in her bed! I didn't want to wake Aunt Lovisa: she would just send me straight back to bed. When I got back to my room there was an extra bright flash that sounded like it had struck somewhere nearby and it made me jump. I ran to the window to see. Then I saw something moving inside the window in New Cottage.

I don't know how I summoned the courage to go outside—I did it without even thinking. I was already so scared from all the thunder and lightning that there was no room for more fear. I jumped into my clogs and ran out without even putting a sweater on over my nightie.

The door to New Cottage was unlocked, so I opened it and tiptoed in. Doris was in there with her transistor radio on the table in the middle of the room, blasting out pop music—The Brothers Four, I think they're called. It was a sad song about summer and green fields. Doris had a cigarette in one hand and was dancing slowly and dreamily on her own, while the cigarette smoke drew loops and patterns in the gloom around her. She was lit up by a sudden flash, and then I saw that her eyes were closed and her mouth was half open. Her dark hair tumbled over her shoulders, and I thought she sort of looked like a dark, dramatic version of Monica Zetterlund.

I stood there in silence, watching her dance until the music changed to "Little Devil" by Neil Sedaka. Her face lit up, she threw her arms in the air and opened her eyes. Without stopping dancing, she motioned for me to come in.

While thunder rumbled and lightning flashed, we kicked the rag rugs aside and danced.

I don't think I can call Doris an old woman any more!

17 JUNE

Everything is growing like the dickens this summer, Auntie Lovisa says. The flowers rarely bloom this early, and apparently the rye and barley are early too. But then it has been incredibly hot and there has also been a lot of rain. Dad said on the phone yesterday that the heat is unbearable in Helsinki! Maybe it's lucky that I'm here after all.

We were invited for coffee with the neighbours, Astrid and Uno. It was Uno who drove me and Mum here when I arrived. They have a farm just a bit further up towards town, a few minutes' walk from Nevabacka. Astrid is Doris' best friend, I think. They are the same age. I thought Uno was an old man but he's the same age as them—he's just really old-mannish. He doesn't say much and mostly just sits there patting his hound on the head. But he seems kind. Astrid talks an awful lot, which made me go quiet—I often get like that around talkative types. Some people are clearly more interested in talking than listening, so you might as well not say anything, I think. Astrid has a perm and a very shrill voice—I don't understand what Doris sees in her!

I said so as we were walking home. Doris said that Astrid was unhappy, that she never should have married Uno. That's why she talks so much. So she doesn't have to stop and think about how her life turned out.

I asked if she had been in love with someone else, and then Doris went silent for a while and said, yes, she had, but it was someone she couldn't be with. Then she married Uno so she wouldn't have to be alone. I think Doris is wise not to get married at all, and I told her so. We were almost back at Nevabacka by then.

Doris stopped and stood limply, looking up at the hill where the farm was nestled among inviting lilacs and rowan flowers, with Aunt Lovisa's bright geraniums poking out from between the light curtains. The hens were clucking in the henhouse, and Cordelia's mother was sitting on the stairs licking her paws. Everything looked so homey and idyllic that it gave me butterflies in my stomach.

"Sometimes I think I am married after all," Doris said softly, her eyes fixed on Nevabacka, and something in her voice surprised me. I turned to look at her, but I couldn't see her face.

She sounded almost bitter when she said it. I didn't dare ask what she meant.

23 JUNE

It's the morning of Midsummer Eve, and the weather is absolutely perfect! Not a cloud in the sky, how lucky! But it has cooled down quite a lot. There's going to be a dance at Storsjön Lake tonight, and Doris and I are going to cycle there. Yesterday Doris said that all the young people from the village usually go, so I hope that Jan and Gustaf will be there.

Now I'm glad Mum packed me a dress, even though I thought she was being silly at the time. You can't go to a dance in shorts, at least not out here in the countryside! Really, I'm too young to go, but Doris doesn't care about that sort of thing. Auntie Lovisa does though, and I've started to notice that she is quite controlling of her daughter. Doris has been saving up all winter and has bought herself a Marimekko dress in pink and orange, it's really groovy. But Lovisa raised her eyebrows and said: "Is

345

that what you're going to wear?" as if Doris were standing there in a sheer curtain. It's not even that short! Doris looked down at the floor, deflated. Imagine still caring about what your mother thinks when you're over thirty! I thought Doris was a knockout, and said so too.

She's going to wear the dress to the dance tonight.

We have been practising dancing in New Cottage. When Lovisa has gone to bed, we wait for a bit, then sneak over with the transistor radio and a bottle of Pommac, and Doris smokes her Kents. We share the Pommac, but I'm not allowed to even try smoking. Then we turn on the radio and practise together. Often we end up laughing so hard we can barely breathe. Then we sit and rest and listen to the music and talk a little. Doris asks what Helsinki is like, and I ask her about Mum's family and stuff. We have a blast.

I really hope that Gustaf and Jan will be there! I think I could pass for fifteen, at least, when I put my hair up and sneak a bit of Doris' mascara. I just wish I was a bit more developed! I have the body of an eleven-year-old, not a thirteen-year-old. This is My Great Sorrow.

24 JUNE

What an incredible Midsummer that was! I don't really know *what* to think. At first I was in a bad mood.

Doris and I cycled to Storsjön early in the evening. It was cold, and there were mosquitoes everywhere. We stood there for a while listening to the music floating out over the lake and eating hot dogs with our sweaters wrapped tightly around us, because it was really chilly. I looked for Gustaf and Jan, but couldn't see them anywhere. In the middle of it all, we became aware of a tall, dark-haired man with sideburns like Elvis, looking at us. Or at *Doris*, to be precise. He came over to us and asked Doris to dance, in Finnish.

I felt abandoned and forgotten. I spent a good hour just wandering around the children playing, couples dancing and clusters of people sitting around talking and laughing, dressed in their best summer clothes. Everyone seemed to be having a gas except me. I couldn't bring myself to be angry with Doris, though part of me wanted to be. When I saw her in that dark-haired man's arms, she had the same expression on her face as when I first saw her dancing alone in New Cottage. Dreamy and happy.

At around nine o'clock I saw Jan and Gustaf among a large group of boys. They were sitting out on the pier and passing around a bottle. Judging by the amount of noise they were making, I doubt it was a bottle of Pommac. I didn't feel like approaching them.

Luckily, Rut showed up, otherwise I probably would have cycled home alone. She is Gustaf's younger sister. She stood next to me and crossed her arms over her chest, glaring at the gang of boys. One of them had just been pushed into the lake and a roar of laughter drowned out the music from the dance floor. "Gustaf is an idiot," she said. Their dad would obviously notice that the whole car stank of booze on the drive home! Then she took me by the hand and pulled me to the dance floor, and we boogied until we were all sweaty. I saw Doris standing on the dance floor in the dark-haired man's arms, with eyes only for him. She looked very snazzy in her Marimekko dress.

Rut whispered that it was good that Doris was taking advantage of her freedom while Auntie Lovisa wasn't there. Rut's mother Auntie Maja said she keeps men away from Doris. Lovisa is terrified of being left alone, ever since her sons died in the war and then she lost her husband not long after. Doris had a suitor once, but Lovisa chased him away, according to Auntie Maja.

Then the dark-haired man kissed Doris. Rut stared, but I looked away. We agreed that we both plan to wait until we are confirmed before we get involved with boys and kisses.

Then Rut said we should do the Midsummer ritual of picking seven kinds of flowers to put under our pillows so that we would dream of our future loves, but there weren't enough flowers around Storsjön, because it's in the middle of the forest, and lots of flowers had already been picked for the Midsummer pole. We searched and searched but all we could find was rosebay willowherb, buttercups and bellflowers. Rut suggested that we cycle to Nevabacka where there are plenty of wildflowers, and then she could stay overnight. I agreed, so she went off to find her parents to ask permission, and I went to look for Doris. First I went to the beach, where they were just about to light the bonfire. I saw Gustaf and the other boys, dragging over branches for the fire. But neither Doris nor the dark-haired man was anywhere to be seen. I walked around the dance floor, restaurant and camping cabins, but they were nowhere to be found.

At the edge of the forest on the other side of the cabins, I found Doris' sandals. They are white with lots of narrow straps, I'm pretty sure they were hers. And then I saw movement coming from the bushes. And heard noises. Then I backed away as fast as I could.

I met Rut by my bike, her parents had given her the okay. She sat on the back of my bike holding the flowers, and we had a bumpy ride along the uneven forest track back towards Nevabacka. The sun was still high above the treetops, it wasn't even midnight yet. I thought this Midsummer was going to feel like a washout, but it ended up being pretty cool.

In the meadow by Nevabacka, we gathered seven kinds of flowers in complete silence, as is traditional, because speaking breaks the magic. But then, lying in my room with the flowers under our pillows, we couldn't help but talk until the sun began to rise again over the edge of the forest, and we couldn't keep our eyes open any longer.

I was asleep when Doris came home.

25 JUNE

Rut stayed here all Midsummer's Day. She is exactly the kind of person I like to have as a friend, not pretentious like Britta or judgemental like Anne-Maj and Elin. She likes to read, and we talked for hours about books we've read and liked. Then we took Doris' transistor radio and lay down in the lilac arbour and listened to music and did crossword puzzles in old newspapers that we found in a stack in the hall. Lovisa was really kind, she brought us out some strawberry cordial and buns, and I didn't have to help with any chores all day.

Doris didn't say anything about me leaving her at Storsjön, and I didn't say anything about… you know. At first I found it hard to look at her, because I kept thinking about finding those sandals at the edge the forest. But I got over it. I think I've matured a lot lately. In the evening, the dark-haired man, whose name is Ilmari, came to pick her up in a nifty new car. Doris came out in her Marimekko dress with lipstick on and her hair loose with a dazzling white tiara in it. Rut and I thought she looked like a movie star. I remembered what Rut had told me about Auntie Lovisa, and when I glanced at her I saw that she was pursing her lips so tightly that they had turned white.

"You guys look really groovy!" I called from the stairs.

Doris laughed and looked like a teenager as she jumped in next to Ilmari. He winked at me before they drove off. I hope she has fun. She is always working here on the farm, I rarely see her relaxing or doing anything for herself. It's only at night when she dances in New Cottage that she really seems like *Doris*. I can't explain it better than that.

Rut called her mother and was allowed to stay one more night. I lent her clothes and she borrowed Doris' bike, and we cycled to Storsjön in the evening. There were only a few campers there now, and the charred remains of the bonfire. It was still quite cool, and there was a shower while we were swimming, but we didn't mind. Rut knows the names of all the birds, and as we floated on our backs and drifted a fair distance from the shore, we listened to the sounds of the forest and she listed all the bird calls we heard: woodcock, pied flycatcher, bullfinch, redwing, curlew, blackbird.

Doris came home late, and Lovisa hasn't spoken to her all day today. Not that Doris seems to even notice, she is wandering around with a dreamy smile on her face, humming snippets of various songs, in her own little world.

Tomorrow I'm going to cycle into the church village and pop in on Rut. She has chickens and rabbits, which I would very much like to see, and then we'll take a boat out on the river and do some fishing.

Oh, and I didn't dream of my future love—what a disappointment! I dreamed about the marsh in the painting in New Cottage, and someone with golden hair singing to me in a language I couldn't understand but that also felt familiar somehow, as if I might start understanding it at any moment.

7 JULY

I can't believe I've already been here for over a month! I feel like I've been here forever but at the same time it has gone by in a flash. Just one more month until Mum and Dad come to pick me up! They're planning on driving, so we don't have to do the car–bus–train combo. Hooray!

I haven't had time to write much lately. I've been hanging out with Rut every day, either here at Nevabacka or in the church village. We play cards, badminton, croquet and Yatzy. We play with Cordelia and her siblings, who have finally started venturing out of the hayloft. Rut is going to get to keep one of the kittens, one with grey stripes that's so cute! She has named it Geraldine. Sometimes we draw pictures and write letters to our friends, and swim in the river and at Storsjön. We went fishing and caught some whitefish, which her father smoked, and it was some of the best fish I've ever eaten! One day her parents drove to Kokkola to go shopping, and they took us along and we went to the flicks while they went shopping. Afterwards we ate ice cream in the town square. I really like Rut's parents, Auntie Maja and Uncle Hasse. Uncle Hasse is Mum's cousin. Jan has gone home, which Rut is pleased about, because she says he tried to peek at her in the sauna. I thought he looked creepy!

When Rut was here, we slept in New Cottage. It feels a bit like sleeping in a tent, but less scary. We don't disturb Auntie Lovisa with our giggles out there, and we can listen to as much music as we want. Doris is very kind and lends us her transistor radio. She is out a lot, Ilmari picks her up in the car almost every evening. Lovisa is furious, but Doris doesn't seem to care. She doesn't seem as scared of her mother any more.

Mum's letter was a harsh reminder of my herbarium project for school. Doris is busy with the haymaking and said that I don't have to help if I still have lots to do on my herbarium, which made me realize how much there is to do. I called Rut to ask if she wanted to help me, but she was busy haymaking too! So annoying. I've picked some of the more common plants that grow along the side of the road, but I know I have to come up with something other than rosebay willowherb and cow parsley to appease Miss Sunnan. She hasn't been impressed with my performance in biology this past year, to put it mildly. After gathering a small bunch of flowers, I was drenched in sweat and had to go inside and drink two glasses of cold water. I saw Doris and Lovisa out in the meadow with their scythes and rakes or whatever. I felt drawn to New Cottage. It's always quiet and kind of cool there, no matter how hot it is outside. I sat down on the bed where Mum used to sleep and where I've slept for a few nights, with Rut in the other bed that must have belonged to Mum's grandpa. I tried to imagine her—Mum, that is, not Rut—as a little girl. I wonder what it was like growing up with a grandpa? Was he kind? He let her go to Helsinki to study forestry, so he must have been quite kind. I don't think it was common for women to study back then.

In the dresser with all the drawers I found old letters, sewing things, a pipe, some old newspapers and—a herbarium! I wonder if it used to belong to Mum? Although it looks even older than

353

that. Everything is very carefully pressed with labels written in tiny handwriting. There is one flower, a yellow one, that has no label, and I tried to find it in Lovisa's botany book, but I couldn't. I'll ask Doris about it later.

Tomorrow I think I'll help with the haymaking. There's not much else to do anyway.

14 JULY

Today I remembered to ask Doris about the pressed plants. I showed her the herbarium and she leafed through it and told me that it belonged to my mother's aunt Alina, who had died when she was young. She didn't know what the yellow flower was called either, but said that it grows on Vittermåsa marsh and blooms in early summer. Which is annoying because it means there won't be any flowers left there now, and it would have been cool to have a mystery plant in my herbarium. But Doris suggested that I press the leaves and describe its growth habit and location and simply draw the flower from Alina's herbarium. Good idea!

Doris promised to take me to the marsh on Sunday and show me where it grows, if she and Lovisa have finished collecting hay by then. She pointed out that they will probably be finished sooner if I help. I know she only said that to get free labour, but I don't mind. It was quite fun helping with the hay. Sweaty though. Soon I'll be so tanned that Mum will hardly recognize me!

16 JULY

Oh, boy, am I tired! My whole body is smarting, as Auntie Lovisa would say. First, we spent all Saturday hauling hay around. The weather was clear but ominous thunder rumbled in the distance. There was no time to cook so we lived on boiled eggs and bread and Auntie Lovisa's delicious cardamom buns. Speaking of Lovisa, she is such a hard worker! There was no way I could have kept up with her, even though I guess she must be well over sixty. I don't know if I was really of much help in the end, but we collected all the hay! And I felt pretty good about myself that evening when we fired up the sauna and scrubbed ourselves clean from all the seeds and husks.

I never thought I would be able to get up early the next day, but I was the one awake with the cows! I prepared sandwiches while Doris and Lovisa did the milking, then when Doris had washed herself, she packed everything in a bucket, which she put in the basket she uses for cloudberry picking. Then she balanced the radio on top! I brought a pair of scissors and a box for my plants, and we hopped on our bikes and pedalled off along the forest road. It was already hot early in the morning! I was wearing shorts and a vest top, and Doris wore shorts too, even though Lovisa obviously disapproved.

I took advantage of the opportunity to ask Doris if she was in love with Ilmari. Her eyes lit up, as they always do when she speaks or thinks about Ilmari. She said she doesn't know, but she wants to be with him all the time. Her brain

355

has stopped working, all it thinks about is *IlmariIlmariIlmari*, she said.

I said it sounds as if she is *attracted* to him, which is a word I've heard in films. Doris said, yes, maybe.

We cycled deeper and deeper into the forest. At first we passed small fields with grey barns next to them, but soon they ended and we were surrounded by nothing but tall fir, pine, birch and aspen trees. The road was mostly just two thin tracks with a strip of grass in between. I said that I used to think the forest was rather boring, but now that I think about it, it's cool and wild. That made Doris laugh so loudly that it scared a little woodpecker away from the pine trunk where it had found itself a meal.

The road ended in a turning circle, and we left our bikes there. Doris led the way into the forest through lingonberry and blueberry bushes. The blueberries weren't quite ripe yet, but I picked the ripest ones I could find and popped them in my mouth. We came to a place where a circle of tall fir trees swayed in the gentle breeze. We walked among the firs, and there was a little valley covered in the softest, greenest moss. Doris explained that it was an old tar pit. She used to talk to the spirits of the ancestors there, she said. I looked up into the tall, rustling fir tops and thought I could really feel those ancestors whispering to me about all the hard work it took to produce a single barrel of tar.

We should leave an offering, I said. To the ancestors. Doris thought for a moment and then agreed, but said in that case it must be a proper offering. Not a joke. She opened her backpack and pulled out the bottle of Pommac she had packed for us. I thought of the sweet, bubbly Pommac running down my throat and said it was perfect. We found a hollow under a spruce root and stuck the bottle in as far as we could. Then we bowed deeply to the spirits of the ancestors, and the forest, and the trees, and the green, green moss.

We still had a long way to go to the marsh, it was awfully hot, and there were lots of gnats and mosquitoes. But it was still fun. I don't know—the forest is cool and wild, but it's also welcoming somehow. Even though it sometimes seems a little *too* wild and sort of eerie. I don't know how to explain it.

We passed a dark little lake, then finally came to the marsh. Which was all golden with cloudberries! Doris' eyes lit up. I have noticed that Doris and Lovisa mostly eat things they have grown or picked themselves. There is always home-made blueberry, lingonberry or raspberry jam to eat with porridge or bread. They grow their own potatoes and carrots and onions, and their milk, cream and butter comes from their own cows. I think the only things they buy are flour, salt and sugar. Oh, and porridge and that sort of thing.

First we looked for the little yellow flower. Doris was right, it wasn't in bloom any more, but I carefully dug up a plant, keeping the roots intact, and put it in my box. Then I picked lots of other plants as well: wild rosemary and bog-myrtle and brambles, cloudberries and cranberries, sedges and other kinds of grass. My herbarium is going to be better even than Anne-Maj's this summer!

357

Then I helped Doris fill the basket and bucket with cloud-berries. We listened to the radio and were having a blast. It was easy-peasy, and there are still tons of berries left! Maybe we can come back another time. Then we drank a thermos of coffee (luckily we had brought something other than Pommac) and ate our sandwiches in the shade of some big fir trees. I asked Doris if she would say yes if Ilmari proposed. She said she would be very dubious of a man who proposed after only a few weeks. I like it when she says things like that. She takes my questions seriously and answers properly. I told her that I don't ever intend to get married. I want to travel instead! I want to see the whole world. I have been with Mum and Dad to Norway on a road trip, and to Åland and once to Stockholm.

Doris said she has been to Kokkola and Vaasa, but I said that doesn't count as travel. It has to be abroad. New York! Paris! London! Doris told me I should write to her on my travels, and I promised I would. I'll send her long, interesting letters about all my adventures!

Right, it's time to collapse into bed. I'm so tired! I'll press the plants tomorrow—I don't have the energy tonight.

17 JULY

Today I slept through the mooing of the cows! Imagine! I suppose you get used to it eventually, like how I got used to the sound of the trams back home.

Auntie Lovisa has made cloudberry jam, and I got my very own jar to take home to Helsinki! I like the idea of having a part of Nevabacka to eat with my porridge this winter.

There have been thunderstorms most of the day. Doris and I pressed all my plants early in the morning, and then she helped me look them up in the botanical guide, and I wrote notes about them all in my neatest handwriting. In the afternoon I sat in New Cottage and drew Alina's flower. I could have taken the herbarium into Old Cottage, but it felt like it belonged in New Cottage. Also, it was nice and peaceful sitting there in silence, all alone, drawing. I think it turned out pretty well. On the plant label I wrote "Orchid, unknown" and then its location. I hope Miss Sunnan will be impressed!

20 JULY

Rut and I have spent a lot of time in the church village lately. We've been out fishing in the river again, and her father told us stories about how they used to transport logs and tar along the river. In winter it was an important trade route. Now there are power plants and dams instead. "The river serves people," said Uncle Hasse. Which I think is a bit strange—are rivers really supposed to serve humans? Can't a river just be a river? Then Gustaf said that I'm too young to understand. He's such a jerk!

I am knitting a lilac sweater to wear this autumn, and Rut is knitting a similar one in forget-me-not blue. Then we will almost look like sisters! People say we are awfully alike. And there's something about being related—she already feels much more like a sister than my friends back home, even though I've known some of them since I started school. We *understand* each other. Next summer Rut and I have decided that we will take the bus to the sandy beaches north of town and stay there all day. Maybe even camp overnight! I would like to camp by the marsh too. There's a mysterious pile of rocks there that I want to explore—it might be an ancient tomb with real treasure inside! We have also talked about asking my parents if I can spend the winter holiday here too.

29 JULY

Tomorrow Mum and Dad will come and pick me up. I want to stay in New Cottage alone tonight. I could have invited Rut over, but for some reason it feels important to be alone this time. I want to get up really early and walk around and say goodbye to all my favourite places at Nevabacka. The sauna by the stream, the lilac arbour, the haystack and the kittens, my reading spot up on the stone cairn, the cows and old Freja in the cowshed, Auntie Lovisa's strawberry patch, the hedgehogs that live behind the barn. I want to do it alone, so I can really communicate with all the places and hear their answers. It wouldn't work with someone else there.

THE 21ST CENTURY

Only one thing is certain
And that is life's way
Of turning around
And starting again
And though our voices
Will fade into silence
New voices shall sing
New voices shall sing

MIKAEL WIEHE

DECAY

IT WAS A HAZY GREY MORNING when she tackled the potato field. She had eaten one row already this summer as new potatoes, and now there were three rows left. Her back wasn't aching, and her heart hadn't played up last night. She walked slowly across the yard to the shed, lifted the latch and propped open the door with a stick. She was greeted by the familiar smell of sawdust and resin. The potato hoe was hanging in its usual place. Its handle, made by her father, was cracked, and she had repaired it with duct tape. She put the hoe in the wheelbarrow along with the bucket. As she pushed the wheelbarrow over the threshold of the shed, it began to rain. She went back to the boot room in the front porch of the cottage to retrieve her yellow raincoat. It was from the nineties and had a tear on one shoulder, which she had also repaired with duct tape. Tape was handy for most things. She had patched a crack at the bottom of the kitchen windowpane with several layers of masking tape. And the mouldings that were splitting around the front door as well.

The tape had been her mother's idea at first, and she had just carried on. With her father gone, it became the simplest way to mend everything that had broken.

The soil in the field was wet and dense, and her back soon began to ache. She dug the plants up carefully, took hold of the leaves and pulled. She had planted Sieglinde potatoes, her favourite. She shook the potatoes, brushed off the soil and tossed them in the wheelbarrow. When it was half full, she rolled it through the mud to the cold cellar door. She used to be able to push a whole wheelbarrow full. Now she could barely manage half a load. She pushed against the muddy earth sucking at her boots; it was a hell of a job getting the wheelbarrow out of the potato field. Then it got easier. She didn't have to look at the path to know exactly where she had to curve around a rock, and where she had to drive the wheelbarrow onto the lawn to avoid getting stuck in overly wet, soft ground. The path snaked across the old meadow and up to the yard like a crooked spine. Every year along the same path, chopping and clearing and sowing and planting and fertilizing and digging and harvesting. For the last thirty years, alone. But at least she didn't have to grow as many potatoes these days. Just enough for herself. And an old biddy like her could live on very little.

After emptying the wheelbarrow into the potato crate in the cold cellar, she had to sit on the chopping block outside the shed door and rest a little. It was her heart. It protested as soon as she did certain activities. Chopping wood was okay, but sawing was difficult. Picking potatoes was okay, but pushing a wheelbarrow took its toll.

Rain dripped from the hood of her raincoat onto her nose and cheeks. The lilac bush was still green, but the birches and aspens had faded to yellow. They appeared soft and blurry in the rain. Massi the cat strolled across the yard without looking at her. He was hunting, always hunting, day or night. He was far too wild and independent an animal to make a good pet. Nothing like Matti, who never used to like going out in bad weather and would always sleep by her feet at night. Massi had never come to her bed.

She stood up. Her legs felt a little shaky, but she was all right as soon as she took hold of the wheelbarrow's handles. There were two whole rows of potatoes still to go.

She managed to get all the potatoes into the cold cellar, then she had to lie down on the kitchen sofa for a long time. When she woke up it was dark and she was confused. She didn't know how long she had slept—was it morning? The fire in the stove had gone out. The house had electric radiators as well so it didn't get cold right away, but it was cooler. She kept the heating on low to save money. Firewood was free, from her own forest. She got a fire going again and lifted the pot of porridge out of the bucket next to the stove. She had boiled the porridge oats in the morning and put the whole pot in a zinc bucket lined with straw. Then she let it cook slowly throughout the day; it saved on electricity. She added a big dollop of butter and a sprinkle of sugar and cinnamon to the thick porridge. She switched on

365

the radio on the kitchen windowsill and listened to the news and weather report while she ate. She saw her own reflection in the dark glass pane.

At eight o'clock she went to bed and read for a while. She was reading a detective story she had borrowed from the mobile library. It was windy outside, and heavy rain pattered on the roof. She hoped it would survive the autumn. The roof couldn't be fixed with tape.

The next day was dry, but foggy and grey, and she tackled the root vegetables. Massi sat on the stone cairn and watched her for a long time. Or maybe he was watching voles. The freshly picked carrots had a wonderful aroma, and she gave almost every bunch a good sniff. Carrot and earth. She had never bought a carrot in her life. The long yellow-orange roots slipped out easily, despite the wet soil, bunch after bunch, and they smelled lovely. Her family thought she was crazy for growing potatoes and carrots when they were so cheap to buy, apparently. Why labour in the field unnecessarily, putting strain on her heart?

But they were used to shop-bought potatoes. She wasn't.

If she didn't grow anything, the vegetable patch and potato field would be taken over by weeds. Just as the pasture had turned to scrub now that she no longer kept sheep. Dense shrubs everywhere. She had cycled along Stockmossavägen in the summer and seen that the two forest fields that no one wanted to rent were so overgrown with sedge and young birches that they were barely distinguishable from the surrounding forest.

She remembered how Otto especially enjoyed ploughing the forest fields. He said he always saw lots of animals around there. Foxes and badgers and moose. An otter once, on the brook bank. It had reared up on its hind legs and studied him fearlessly.

She put most of the carrots in sand in the cold cellar. That would preserve them throughout the winter. She carried the last bucket of carrots into the kitchen. She twisted off the greens, gave them a thorough rinse and got out the food processor that Eva-Stina had given her as a Christmas present one year. She couldn't hold the carrots firmly enough in her hand to grate them. Her fingers were crooked from osteoarthritis. The food processor made the work easier. She had the radio on while she worked and heard the music come in and out between the whirring of the food processor. She hummed along, loudly and thoughtlessly, to no particular melody. She shredded the whole bucket of carrots, taking breaks sometimes when the machine started to smell like it was struggling. Then she put the grated carrots in plastic bags to freeze. Good to have for soups and pancakes.

The beetroot needed more time in the soil. They were still quite small. There can't have been enough rain in early summer. She had already picked the onions, which were hanging to dry in the cold cellar. She had frozen batches of dill and parsley in August. There was also some moose meat from the village hunting team in the freezer. She could get by on what she had.

She noticed her mobile phone sitting on the windowsill next to the geraniums. A missed call, from Rut. She must have called when she was out in the field. She rinsed her hands and dried them on her apron. Slowly and carefully, she dialled Rut's phone number. She knew it by heart. It was good to keep things in your head, to know things by heart. It kept the mind young. It kept her away from Evening Sun.

"Oh, Doris, hello! I was about to give Nyjärv a call and ask them to drive out and check on you."

"I was only out in the field. I picked all the potatoes yesterday and all the carrots today."

"You managed to do all that?"

"Why ever not? I've harvested potatoes every autumn of my life."

"Is there anything you need? Pekka is going shopping in town tomorrow so he can get you anything you want."

Doris looked around the kitchen. "Cat food. The type that Massi likes."

"Three boxes?"

"That would be fine."

"Nothing else?"

"No, I have enough to make do. Old ladies don't need all that much, you know."

"There's a concert in the church on Sunday, would you like to come with us? We can drive over to Evening Sun to visit Astrid afterwards if you want."

Doris thought about her apple trees, and the lingonberries she hadn't picked yet.

"Call back on Saturday and we'll see."

368

"Okay. And Doris? Take your phone with you when you go out, so I don't have to worry. The ground will get slippery soon, and I get mental images of you stuck somewhere—if you fell and couldn't get up—I really worry."

"I walk very carefully. I do know where it gets slippery, you know. You shouldn't think such things."

They said goodbye and Doris sat and rested for a while. Talking to Rut took effort, a bit like sawing wood. Evening Sun loomed behind every conversation, a veiled threat. She had to bypass and steer away from anything that could possibly bring moving into the conversation. Uno had died a year ago, and Astrid had moved to Evening Sun. Doris had visited her a few times. Astrid was barely recognizable. She had withered. Like a tree that had been dug up and potted indoors, where it got too many pests and too little light.

All those old folk walking—no, *shuffling*—up and down the corridors, or occasionally being taken out in a wheelchair to be aired out on the church hill.

"Care home" were such heavy words. Like rocks. How was she supposed to deal with words like that?

She thought of her apples. They needed picking now, before the birds pecked at them too much. In order for the apples to last in the cold cellar, they had to be picked straight from the trees, but she was a little unsure of her legs these days and the ladder felt wobbly. Maybe if she had someone to hold it. She could have asked Rut if Tomas might come and help her, but she had a feeling that Rut wouldn't like the idea of her up on

a ladder at all. Maybe the whole family would come, Rut and
Pekka and Tomas, and then she would have to feed them and
it would become a whole to-do.

Anyway, she had never needed help picking the apples before.

She could spread a sheet under the tree and bat down as
many apples as possible and turn it all into apple sauce. Maybe
bake a pie with it. Or muffins, they froze well.

Tomorrow. Today she would bring in more firewood and
wash up after the carrot-shredding. Sometimes Rut asked her
if she ever got bored and lonely out there at Nevabacka. Bored!
She had always had the animals and the earth, the house,
food, sewing, all sorts of things. There was still plenty to do.
Her chores went more slowly now, of course. Same work, but
slower. Even something like lifting the wood basket out of the
shed and closing the shed door. She always used to do that in
one fluid motion, whereas now she had to slowly lift the basket
first, then step over the threshold while holding on to the door
frame. Then put the basket down and turn around. Remove the
door stop and place it against the wall. Shut the door and latch
it. Then lift the basket and walk across the yard.

So many little movements she never thought twice about
when she was young. Younger. When did everything become
so complicated? Ten years ago? Or more?

By the time she turned eighty, she had started touching
each knob on the stove in turn and confirming, "Zero, zero,
zero, zero" out loud. So she could be sure they were all off
before she went out. Not that she forgot things, she didn't have

dementia. She had been tested. She could still do the Sunday paper crossword.

At the care home, there was nothing to do.

She got the kitchen door open, lifted the wood basket in and closed it. She stepped out of her boots and carefully walked the basket over the rag rug. The rugs could suddenly slide away from under her feet. Falling was her biggest fear. Hip operations and such—then you ended up in hospital and then at Evening Sun.

She heard noises in the attic at night. Soft but distinct thuds.

She woke up early and swung her legs over the edge of the bed to get up and milk the cows. The room swayed, and she gripped the bedpost. She couldn't hear the animals mooing. Was something wrong? Her heart clenched.

There hadn't been cows in the barn since Maja died in 1983.

It was a bad start to the day. She sat there for a long time with her hand pressed to her chest, waiting for her heart to calm down. What was it she was going to do today? Her eyes rested on various items in turn; the watercolour of the marsh that she had saved from New Cottage; the fabric that her mother had embroidered with a red cabin and green firs, with the motto HOME IS WEAR THE HEART IS in red wool thread; the beige wallpaper she put up herself twenty years ago. The furniture: the glossy dresser with all the papers in and on it, the low bookcase full of photo albums and her gramophone. This had been her childhood bedroom. She hadn't felt like moving

371

when her mother died. Mum's room had become storage for everything that had no particular place.

The apples. That was what she was going to pick today. Before the night frosts came. Her feet felt around for her slippers. They had slid under the bed, and she couldn't reach them with her foot. Her bunions stopped her from pinching her toes to pick them up like she used to. She wore rubber boots and wide sandals. She couldn't wear ordinary shoes any more. She looked at her contorted bare feet. Toenails yellow and horn-like, skin flaky. She should moisturize them but couldn't reach any more. She couldn't apply anything to her back either. Washing her hair was also getting tricky, as she had difficulty raising her arms.

But never in her life had she spent a single day in hospital. It was a miracle. Not like her mother in her fading years. In and out of hospital and bedridden at home for long periods of time. Prolonged suffering was the worst.

The floor was cold on the soles of her feet. She got up and fetched the small footstool with the embroidered seat cushion and moved it over to the bed. Sat on it, held the edge of the bed as support and leaned forward. There were the damn slippers! She got them out with great effort and slipped them on. When she stood up, the room began to sway again. She stood dead still. Just don't fall. Anything but a fall. Once the room was steady again, she put on the red cardigan she had knitted for Mum when she was bedridden. It was a little chilly. She wondered if there had been a night frost. But there were no icy patterns on the window.

She came out into the kitchen and opened the door to let Massi in. Took out a packet of cat food, the wet kind, and squeezed some out onto a saucer. Massi nuzzled against her leg and mewed.

"Oh, sure, now you want affection." She filled the coffee maker and switched it on. Then she took a few bits of kindling to get a fire going in the stove, and added a couple of logs. Once it had got going, she fixed herself some crispbread with butter and cheese. The fire crackled and there was a faint smoky smell. She eyed the crack in the chimney breast, which Dad had repaired and plastered so many times. It wasn't smoking, was it?

She should get one of those box thingies. Not a smoke detector—she had one of those—the other one. For carbon monoxide. She sat down at the kitchen table, overlooking the pasture and potato field, and took a bite of her crispbread. She had good teeth. Her own teeth. Crispbread wasn't a problem.

Something fell into her coffee cup. A birch leaf, dry and brittle but still green. She looked up cautiously, her neck was stiff and she knew that if she tilted her head back too much it could trigger vertigo.

A birch twig was wrapped around the curtain rod. A midsummer birch. She must have missed it when she took down all the others. How could she have missed it? It had been hanging there for months. Hanging there gathering dust. She got up and carefully stepped onto the chair, holding on to the back. Then up on the table. It was large and flat, not rickety at all. But

373

reaching up for the twig was not easy—she wobbled, grabbed the curtain rod with her left hand and groped for the twig with her right, without looking up; the leaves got tangled in the curtain and there was a tearing sound. Damn and blast. The curtains were ancient, she knew she shouldn't touch them. They were disintegrating and too fragile to be drawn. She dislodged the twig, bringing down a piece of curtain, dust and cobwebs with it, stepped heavily back down onto the chair and collapsed onto the seat, scraping her leg in the process. She sat there, breathing heavily, twig and curtain still in hand.

The coffee had spilled over onto the wax tablecloth. She put down the birch twig, pulled a handkerchief out of her shirtsleeve and patted it dry. There was movement out in the meadow, something big and grey. She put down her handkerchief, thinking for a moment that Maja must have escaped from the pasture, but Maja was brown, it must be a moose, or was it? A reindeer. A large grey reindeer with antlers. Except it was too big to be a reindeer. And a half-grown calf came walking behind it, so it must have been a female, but females didn't have antlers that big, did they? The animal stopped in the middle of the half-wild pasture where sheep had once grazed, three of them back in the eighties. They were the last animals on the farm. She had named them after her favourite artists. Carola, Christer and Monica Z. Christer was very affectionate and always wanted his head scratched. Carola was timid and always followed Monica. Her eyes filled with tears, quite unexpectedly, and she wiped them with her shirtsleeve. The two reindeer had come to the edge of the forest now, and the mother looked around as the calf ran ahead.

She fumbled for her mobile phone and dialled Eva-Stina's number. She answered on the third ring.

"Hello, Doris!"

"Sorry to disturb you, but I just saw an animal. Two of them, and I thought I was going mad, but they were right there, and they went into the forest." She heard how choked up and weepy her voice sounded, and cleared her throat at once.

"Is everything okay?"

"Oh, yes." She groped around for her handkerchief to blow her nose but found it lying on her plate, soaked in coffee. "It was a mother reindeer and her young, but they were much too big to be reindeer. And the female had antlers, big antlers."

"Are you sure they weren't just regular reindeer and you were mistaken about the size?"

"No, they were much too big."

"Hang on a sec."

She heard Stina turn on her computer. She must have been at work.

"It sounds like Finnish forest reindeer. They match your description. Can you look it up in an encyclopaedia? Didn't Sven have one? *Rangifer tarandus fennicus* is the Latin name. I found an article: 'The last forest reindeer were shot in central Ostrobothnia in the late eighteenth century. They were also eventually eradicated from eastern Finland in the late nineteenth century during the famine years. Attempts have been made to reintroduce the species in several parts of Finland, and some animals have now crossed the eastern border. In the eighties, forest reindeer were bred in captivity in Perho and later released.' Seems like the herd must be thriving and multiplying, and now moving into your area."

"Finnish forest reindeer. Well, I'll be damned." She looked all along the forest edge but couldn't see the creatures any more. "I'll see if I can find Dad's encyclopaedia."

"Yes, do. Good that you called anyway. I was thinking I'd like to come and visit in October."

"Yes, come come. We can pick lingonberries."

"And see if any chanterelle mushrooms are growing by the marsh."

"That would be lovely. Everything good with you?"

"Yeah. Anna was just visiting with the baby."

"Hard to believe you have two grandchildren now."

"It's so much more fun than I thought it would be, I must say. I've become one of those grandmas who show off pictures of their grandchildren all the time."

"Well, you can certainly show them off to me."

"I'll bring lots to show you. Have you picked the potatoes yet?"

"Yes, and the carrots. It was a good harvest this year."

"I look forward to tasting them when I come."

"Are you driving?"

"Yeah, that was the plan. That way we're more mobile. We can go on a trip somewhere."

"That would be fun. Now I should probably let you get back to work."

"Oh, don't worry about that. I'm almost a pensioner myself! Speak soon, Doris!"

"Goodbye, Stina."

She found Dad's encyclopaedia on the bookshelf in the hall. As she pulled out the twenty-fifth volume, thick clumps of dust fell to the floor. She flicked to "Finnish forest reindeer" and read "See Reindeer, p. 1412." That entry didn't give her much more information. *In Finland, wild reindeer only appear occasionally in Karelia.* To find an image, she was referred to "the Polar countries". There wasn't a decent picture there, so she gave up. She sat down in the rocking chair for a while and caught her breath. Forest reindeer. Wasn't there a gimlet somewhere in the tool shed with a horn handle? That could be forest reindeer antler. Or common ram horn.

A flock of sparrows and a few plump red bullfinches fluttered by the living room window. It was too early to start feeding the birds, but she needed to make sure she had birdseed for winter. And suet balls. She carefully got out of the rocking chair and went into the kitchen. Put her mobile phone on the windowsill and wrote *Birdseed* and *Suet balls* on the small pad next to the geraniums. Above it was *Herring* and *Butter*.

She missed the taste of freshly churned butter. The co-op's butter just wasn't the same.

She thought about what else she might need. Sugar maybe. For the apple sauce. And citric acid.

It was a blustery morning. The lace curtains swayed gently in the draught from the cracked windowpane. The tape could only help so much.

The apples.

She went into her bedroom and got dressed. It took quite a while. Her leg ached where she had scraped it along the shin, but it wasn't bleeding so she let it be. Underpants and socks were the trickiest, but then getting her arms into her shirtsleeves and doing up all the buttons was a hassle as well. All these things she used to take for granted had become mini battles. Sometimes she thought she should just go to bed, fully clothed. Spare herself the trouble.

But that would feel like a slippery slope straight to Evening Sun.

Once she was dressed, she sat on the edge of the bed to recover, and her eyes came to rest on the aerial photograph of Nevabacka. It was from 1989 and already faded. Old Cottage was white with a red sheet-metal roof, and New Cottage had its old shingle roof, bowed in the middle like a bowl. The pasture, not yet overgrown, where the sheep had grazed only two years previously. Purple lilacs bloomed. Bleeding heart blossoms could just about be seen around the front porch. The irises must have been in bloom then as well, and though they weren't visible in the photograph, she knew exactly where they were. She knew that the strawberry patch was just outside the picture, and that she had grown a lot of onions and garlic that year.

She had been to Paris the year before that. She celebrated her sixtieth birthday there with Eva-Stina. Just the two of them.

It was all Stina's doing. She spoke French, and she booked all the flights and hotels and everything. It was extravagant, and Doris had a hard time accepting the gift. But she also understood. Stina's mother had died not long before. Doris was not a replacement, but perhaps a kind of consolation. Stina and Tilia had planned to go to Paris when Tilia turned seventy, but they never did, and then it was too late.

They had stayed in a small hotel with narrow staircases and no lift. The only breakfast option was sweet pastries. They saw the Louvre and those big paintings of water lilies. The name of the artist escaped her but he often came up in crossword puzzles. Monet.

Her most vivid memory of the trip was up on that hill with the big windmill that hosted cabarets. They didn't see a show, but they mooched around and admired the view. It was a windy day, clear, and everything was bright and dry; the facades of the houses looked like they were painted with chalk. A beautiful Parisian woman in a trench coat hurried across the street towards them, with black hair and red-painted lips. A strong gust of wind chilled their legs and lifted the Parisienne's coat, revealing nothing on underneath!

Stina thought Doris would be shocked. But she had found it interesting. And rather practical.

She went into the boot room and put on her jacket and rubber boots. Tied a headscarf around her hair, picked up her basket and opened the door. Massi slipped out and trotted to the barn. There were bound to still be mice to catch in there.

She went to the apple tree her mother had planted before she was born. It was huge and stood in the eastern corner of the yard between New Cottage and the woodshed. The trunk was gnarled and mossy. Really, it should have been pruned to prevent such unruly growth, but no one had done so in decades. She was "no one". She hadn't pruned it. All of this was her job to maintain. And much of it had been neglected. That was just the way it was.

Maybe if she had children. Someone to pass it on to. But now everything she couldn't manage on her own had fallen into disrepair.

Most of the apples were out of reach, but if she held onto the lowest branches she could grope for low-hanging fruit without bending her head back and getting dizzy and falling. She hung the basket from her arm and put the apples straight into it. Then she carried it slowly across the yard back to the vestibule, where the birds couldn't get at the fruit, and had a think. There was a tarpaulin in New Cottage, but she couldn't remember why she would have put it there and not in the shed.

The door into New Cottage was jammed. By the time she got it open, her heart pounding from even such a small task, she was almost angry. She stepped in and inhaled the damp, lonely smell. Tilia's painted birds in the vestibule still gazed at her, the paint faded and flaking. She walked carefully—the floor was rotten and there was a risk it could give way. Inside the cabin there was a soft grey light and an even stronger smell. She had removed everything that could be saved from the little cabin many years ago, when it became clear that Tilia wasn't going to do anything with it. The paintings, the sideboard, some old papers. One of Grandpa's old stuffed birds, shabby and horrible, cluttering up Lovisa's bedroom. She moved slowly forward, shuffling so as not to trip over something unexpected. It sounded like Astrid shuffling along the Evening Sun corridors. The floor up ahead was paler; there was a streak of light just below the skirting board. She moved forward cautiously, unsure what it was at first. The wall had somehow detached from the floor, and a large gap was letting soft grey daylight in. That couldn't be fixed with tape. She would have to discuss it with Stina. Now that Tilia wasn't around, this was Stina's house, and she really should do something about it.

Then again, she didn't want to start an argument. Stina had a job and was a grandmother now, besides.

She found the tarpaulin on a bench by the wall, but when she lifted it up something rustled and squeaked—movement, flying in all directions, her chest clenched, her breath caught in her throat, and as she dropped the tarpaulin, little creatures scampered away in the dark, claws on bare floorboards, and she collapsed onto the bench, kicking the tarpaulin away, pressed her back against the wall and tried to catch her breath again, her heart was beating wildly, *thump thump thump* in her chest and throat and ears, she gasped for air and tried to take calm, even breaths. But her chest, heart, breathing refused to calm down, she needed her nitro pills, she fumbled around in her pockets but the box must have been in the house on the kitchen table as usual, she got up, leaned against the wall with her left hand and stood up, gasping for air, quick short sharp steps, the porch steps yet another battlefield, got down without falling, and her eyesight was flickering now, or was it the mist, wet leaves beneath her boots, slippery, dangerous, don't fall, Evening Sun, there was the kitchen door knob, she clung to it like a lifebuoy, then into the kitchen, the nitro box on the wax cloth, the lid was stiff, pills everywhere, one under her tongue and then the sofa, where she collapsed and lay still for a

long

long time.

Finally the room stopped spinning. She could focus her eyes. Her chest still felt bad, but better. She managed to sit up, moving as slowly as possible. Made her way to the sink and drank a glass of water.

Maybe she should call someone. Rut. Stina. Rut was closer.

But Evening Sun.

She would just have to be very careful now. No unnecessary strain. As soon as she felt any dizziness or chest pain, she would sit down to rest.

She turned on the radio for company, as a distraction, so she wouldn't have to think too much. Then she noticed the state of the kitchen: the butter was out, and the coffee-soaked handkerchief had got her crispbread wet. Had she not eaten her crispbread? No wonder she felt strange. The birch twig was still on the table. Pills on the rag rug. She tidied up, very slowly, threw the twig into the stove, wiped the table down carefully, washed the cup and saucer and butter knife. Swept up all the pills, blew them off and put them back in the box. There might have been a few left on the floor, but she didn't think Massi would be silly enough to try to eat them. Then she swept the bark and birch leaves off the floor. Pulled the dead leaves from the geraniums and watered them.

Then she felt as though she may have overdone it, so she lay down on the kitchen sofa as a precaution and fell straight to sleep.

Woke up, radio still on, afternoon. Time for coffee. She made some coffee, got out the biscuit tin and drank two cups with a lot of sugar and ate a few biscuits. There, she felt much better already. Then she thought about the nitro and whether she had any left in her prescription. She went to her bedroom to search the dresser. As soon as she stepped into the room, she was struck by its smell. Old lady smell. Sickly and musty and sweet and disgusting. Decay. It smelled like Evening Sun.

Was it Friday? She used to use the sauna with Mum and Dad on Fridays.

She went out into the vestibule, put her feet in the rubber boots and went back out. The sun was low over the treetops now and the wind had stilled. As she walked down to the sauna, the evening sun shone golden in the house windows. But one was dark. The little one, up in the attic. She moved closer, squinting. She remembered those thuds at night. The window was broken. Something had got in. She thought of the tarpaulin in New Cottage and sighed. Hopefully it was something small that Massi could take care of. A little bird.

The sauna down by the stream was in pretty good nick. That was thanks to her father, who had built it himself, from logs he cut and sawed at his sawmill. He had also sawn all the boards himself, and the sheet-metal roof was still new-ish. She vaguely remembered his sawmill. The saw. Dad at the saw. Ant with Dad at the saw. She opened the sauna door and thought of Ant, of his kind grey eyes and how tongue-tied he became whenever he tried to speak to people. But not with her. He could speak to her. He was her first ever crush.

Then the war came and claimed them all. Ant and her brothers. She was the only one left: one stay-at-home spinster.

There was wood in the sauna changing room, old but dry. The matches were in their place on the windowsill among dead flies and the beautiful stones Stina had lined up there when she was a child. The fire took straight away. The stove and the wooden walls smelled so good—that special scent of a wood-burning sauna. She took a deep breath. She felt better already. She wouldn't make it too hot. Just enough to get clean. She took one of the buckets and stepped outside, leaving the sauna door open to get a good air flow. The bank of the stream wasn't steep so there was no fear of slipping. As long as she walked carefully. There was the rope, she tied it around the handle and threw the bucket into the stream. It was high and foamy with autumn water and the bucket filled quickly. Once when the pump had broken, she had drunk stream water for a week. But she told Rut she only used it for washing dishes.

She poured a little water out until it was light enough to carry

384

and walked slowly back to the sauna. Soon it would be dusk. She set the bucket on the lower bench and went outside, closed the sauna door, went to the porch of the cottage and turned on the outdoor light. So she would be able to see when she went back.

Then she undressed in the cold of the changing room. Buttons and sleeves and socks and the whole damn to-do yet again. Finally, she threw in some more wood and carefully climbed onto the top bench. She leaned against the warming wall and looked out the window. She could see part of the road, the mailbox and the stream where the bird cherries bloomed in May.

"It's like in a Finnish film," Stina had said in amazement that first summer she had come to stay with them, sitting on the bench and looking out the window. It had been a hot summer, she remembered. Haymaking was early that year.

The fire crackled and sparked and the metal of the sauna oven clunked as it expanded. She closed her eyes. She thought about that first summer with Stina. The summer with Ilmari.

They had made love in the sauna once, without lighting it; otherwise Mum would have seen the smoke. It was the only time they did it anywhere other than the woods. There was nowhere else for them to go. Thorns and ants in her clothes. His hands on her breasts, in her hair. That voice, deep and warm. The most beautiful man she had ever seen. Married, of course. She only found out later.

Otherwise. Otherwise she might have left Nevabacka.

She slid her fingers over her collarbones and down to her chest. She didn't feel the wrinkles, the jagged ribs, the sagging breasts. She felt what Ilmari had felt. Stiff nipples. Thick hair, slender neck. No man had touched her since Ilmari.

People can't live without touch. Sometimes, when Astrid had pursued her, she had given in. When Uno was out hunting. Or in town. Or out with the tractor.

Between milking cows and washing dishes, there were plenty of occasions for the two women to be alone. She tried not to let it happen too often. Astrid always became unbearably clingy afterwards. And then came the anger, the accusations, the tears.

But loneliness is hard to bear. To never be touched, held, caressed.

She should go and visit Uno and Astrid. Maybe bring them an apple pie? She could go over tomorrow. Maybe Uno would go out for a while.

No, Uno was dead.

She winced, sitting on the sauna bench. How could she forget something like that? Uno was dead. Astrid had moved. To a place where there were no opportunities for privacy.

The sauna was very dark, and a small window of faint red light spilled out through the ventilation hatch and onto the duckboard. The fire had died down. She heard a pattering sound against the tin roof; it had started raining again. She climbed down carefully in the dark, poured water from the bucket into a basin and slowly washed all the places she could reach. She rinsed off the soap and shampoo. Then she went out into the changing room and dried herself with the towel that hung there, groped for her robe and found it on its peg. It was difficult to

386

get her arms in with her skin still damp and sticky, and the terry cloth got stuck. Finally she got it on. She gathered up her clothes and stepped into her boots.

Her stomach growled. Had she remembered to eat? It wasn't like her to forget something like that.

Except, how do you know what you have forgotten? Why was her shin aching? Had Maja kicked her? No, not Maja, she was too sweet, she would never kick. Alice was the difficult one. Once she kicked Mum so hard that she had to go to the medical centre for stitches.

As she crossed the yard, she heard humming on the road and saw a couple of lights glinting in the darkness. It was the mobile library. She hurried into the vestibule, dropping something from her pile of clothes on the way, but oh, well, she could pick it up tomorrow—she couldn't be seen like this, in her bathrobe! She pulled the door shut behind her just as the bus turned into the yard. Gasping for breath, she stumbled into the living room with her boots on, groping for the light switch, she would never have time to change, and Rufad didn't like to hang around for too long, so she took off her bathrobe and pulled on her winter coat, found a hat to hide her hair, then located the pile of books she had borrowed; they were on the dresser in the living room, and she came out with them under her arm, and there was the bus with lights shining from all the windows. Rufad opened the door when he saw her. She hoped she didn't look too dishevelled or batty. Else he might call someone, and they would come with worried expressions and talk of Evening Sun. Rufad got out of the driver's seat, came to the steps and took the books. She walked up the steps herself, while Rufad looked on with concern.

"Hi, Doris! I can always come to your door if you want," he said. "And carry the books."

"No, no, there's no need." She waved her hand dismissively. "I can carry a few books. I picked ten kilos of potatoes yesterday!"

"Wow!" Rufad scanned the bar codes. "What would you like this time?"

Doris sat down on the small bench inside the library bus and caught her breath. The bus was swaying and vibrating, while her heart swayed and fluttered. She closed her eyes. She had hurried even though she had promised herself to take it easy. The wool coat itched against her bare skin. *I'm not wearing anything underneath,* she thought with a chuckle.

"Are you okay?" A voice, nearby, worried.

"I'm fine, it was just the stairs. I'll be all right in a minute." She opened her eyes, pretending to look around for something to borrow. The bookshelves, the box of picture books, the shelf of new books, placed with their covers showing. Gilded letters danced before her eyes.

"I don't think I need anything just now," she said slowly.

"But you always borrow something!" Rufad leaned closer. "Are you feeling okay, Doris?"

"Yes, yes. But I have so much to do at the moment, you see. I have to make apple sauce, and there are so many leaves to rake. And…" She searched her memory. There were always lots of tasks in autumn. But what were they? "Lingonberries. I have to pick lingonberries. I usually pick several bucketfuls. For my porridge."

"Impressive." Rufad shook his head. "Astrid sends her regards. She always asks after you when I go to Evening Sun on Thursdays."

She stood up, holding on to a shelf for support. A book about farming fell to the floor. Rufad bent down to pick it up and placed it back on the shelf.

Doris stood by the steps and looked out into the darkness. It was hard to even see where the ground was. Everything was so dark and wet, glinting in the headlights of the bus.

Rufad took her by the arm and helped her down, one step at a time.

A hand holding her arm. She felt his body heat through her coat. When they got down she used her free hand to pat him on his. Human skin, soft and alive. Rufad smiled and squeezed her hand. Then he went back up the steps.

"See you in two weeks!"

Doris waved. The bus reversed and drove slowly out of the yard. She watched the red tail lights disappear into the darkness. Rain pattered against the grass, and the stream gushed on the other side of the track. The sky was black overhead. She walked up the two front steps and closed the door behind her. Turned off the outside light, stepped out of her rubber boots.

She was very tired. It would be nice to go to bed. She had always slept well.

*

In the morning, the mobile phone on the kitchen windowsill rang. The sound carried out to Massi, who was sitting in the barn loft, scouting for swallows. It carried out to the small birds that flew around the empty bird feeder hanging among the lilacs. It carried out to the apple tree where fruit was still hanging, waiting to be picked.

It rang and rang.

INVENTORY

T HE FARM LOOKS THE SAME AS it always has. Stina parks
outside the cottage and sits in the car for a while. A broom
is leaning against the wall next to the door, as if someone were
home and had just swept the front steps. But there are no foot-
prints in the weary March snow. And something about the white
house exudes emptiness. The windows feel dead.

She gets out of the car and stretches. Stiff after the long drive.
Rut wanted her to pop in and say hello on her way through the
church village, but Stina didn't want to stop. Get on with it. Get
it over with. She lifts her bags out of the car and unlocks the
front door. The boot room smells the same as it always has. Of
her childhood. She sets down her backpack and cool box and
takes off her winter boots, but keeps her jacket on. Everything
looks the same as it has her whole life. The small table with
the embroidered cloth, the wicker chair, the coat stand. She
unlocks the inner door and enters. The floor is cold through her
woollen socks. Rut has been by to turn the heating on, but all
the rooms are still damp and musty. And so quiet. Not even a

ticking clock. All that can be heard in the sleeping house are the little birds chattering and chirping out in the yard. Stina walks through the rooms, sees the dust, the dead flies on the floors, the withered geraniums in the kitchen window. Faded rag rugs, faded wallpaper, faded bedspread. The kitchen curtain is torn. Windowpane cracked. An old calendar open to September last year. In the living room, the dining table, sofa, rocking chair, TV, low bookshelf full of encyclopaedias and a Bible. In Doris' room, the gramophone and small transistor radio, the same one as when Stina was young. The paintings still hanging in the same places: the marsh scape, the portrait of a girl, the embroidered tapestry with the spelling mistake in its motto. And framed photographs everywhere: Stina's grandmother and her sisters all in a row, serious; Doris' brothers in uniform; Lovisa and Sven's wedding photograph. More recent photos: Stina with a bow in her hair and a gap between her teeth; her wedding to Björn; her on a park bench wearing big sunglasses with baby Anna in her arms. And then a grown-up Anna with Adrian in her arms on Adrian's first birthday.

Even just these photos. What was she going to do with them all?

Yet another home to clear out. And once again, her job to do it.

First it was Dad's flat, with Mum's things still left in cupboards, wardrobes and drawers. Ten years after her mother's death, he had barely got rid of anything. She had to go through old passports, diaries, clothes, postcards, knitting, research reports, watercolours, jewellery, photo albums, handbags, letters. Not to mention Dad's personal belongings. And then everything else that makes up a home: clothes, housewares, books, furniture. An awful lot of things. Anna only took a few small souvenirs. Anna already had a home of her own, with Sam and Adrian, and now little Moira, and plenty of things of their own.

It took Stina months to go through it all. Months of agonizing over each and every thing: can I really throw this away? Give this away? Sell this? Sometimes she still lies awake at night, feeling guilty about some of the things she threw away. Mum's art supplies. Old board games with pieces missing. Nothing of any importance. But still.

She held on to too much. Björn thought so. Their two-bedroom flat was already filled with their own lives. Now it was cluttered up with extra stuff. Some boxes were still unpacked. Still, she hadn't saved as much as she thought she should.

What she actually *wanted*, she had no idea.

Shortly after Doris' death, Björn fell ill. Stina didn't get around to travelling up to Nevabacka to go through the house.

She and Björn came to the funeral, of course, and slept at Nevabacka. Talked about how strange it was that she, Stina, now suddenly owned a house. Doris had left everything to her. The whole farmstead, with land and forest. To someone who had only ever rented before. Never owned anything bigger than a car.

She knew that Björn thought she should sell. They could use the money to travel, buy a new car. Maybe help Anna with a deposit on a house, if that's what she and Sam wanted.

It sounded sensible. Maintaining a property with several old buildings would cost a lot of money. They were pensioners, there was no money to spare. And Nevabacka was so far away. Björn didn't have any connections to the place. Neither did Anna. Selling was the logical thing to do.

She wasn't even sure she liked the idea of owning anything. The whole time Björn was ill, she could feel the farm waiting for her. Expecting things from her. It was more like *it* owned *her*. Rut and Pekka helped out with the buildings, reported broken windowpanes, cleared snow from the roofs and generally kept an eye on things. But she couldn't ask too much of them. Doris left Nevabacka to her. It is her responsibility.

Now here she is, walking around and picking through items aimlessly. Folders with recipes cut out from *Allers* magazine in the cupboard in Doris' room. A box under the bed with winnings from the parish bingo evenings. A scrapbook full of bookmarks and verses from Lovisa's childhood on the bookshelf in the front room. A shelf full of home-woven, completely unused linen towels in the closet. An old sweets tin full of trinkets. Records next to the gramophone, glass and porcelain ornaments, crocheted doilies and cracked coffee cups. All of it hers to sort. Save, sell, throw away, what might Anna want, what might Rut want, could she just sell the house as is, with everything in it?

It feels like déjà vu. Like no time has passed since her father's death. She is stuck in a quagmire—the same burden, the same commitments, over and over again. As soon as she frees one foot from the mud, it gets stuck again on the next step. Going through other people's lives, making decisions about their memories. Being the only person left to carry the torch.

What would she do with the money from the sale? There would be no trips with Björn now. But if she doesn't sell, how could she ever take care of Nevabacka on her own? With everything in need of maintenance and repair. Impossible.

All of Björn's things are waiting for her at home too. She can live surrounded by them for as long as she wants. But one day she will have to go through them too. She can't leave everything to Anna, shift the responsibility onto her.

She makes up Doris' bed with the old embroidered sheets. Everything is clean but still smells stale somehow. Someone else's ancient pillows and quilts. She wishes she had brought her own. She drinks herbal tea at the kitchen table with the radio on to keep her company and banish the silence. Outside the window, the March night is so black, a void. The house feels like a spaceship floating in unknown, empty space, completely alone and cut off from everything and everyone. She wants to call Björn, to hear his deep, comforting voice, and almost picks up the phone before she remembers.

At night she lies awake, flinching at every click, every sound. She's not sure what she is scared of. Wild animals? A murderer?

She's just scared. She dozes off and when she wakes up, bright light is flooding into the bedroom. She lies still, her heart pounding. It's a car. Someone has parked in the yard with beaming headlights. No one who turns up at this time of night can have good intentions. She is terrified, petrified, doesn't know if she has ever been this scared before. She notes her body's reactions to the fear: dry mouth, heart pounding, blood rushing in her ears so loudly she can barely hear.

The light neither fades nor moves. Finally, she sits up as quietly as she can. The sheets rustle, the bed creaks. She sits still, listens, hears nothing. She gets up, tiptoes over to the window, hides behind the curtain and peers out.

It's the moon. A near-full moon shining over the trees and directly into the bedroom. She can't recall ever having seen such bright moonlight before. The shadow of New Cottage is sharp and deep black, the shadows of the trees are long and narrow over the coarse snow, softly sparkling in the moonlight.

She crawls back into bed, feeling sheepish. Thinks about how to relate this anecdote to Rut. I was terrified of the moon, she will say, and they will laugh together. See why I can't keep Nevabacka? I'm too scared of the dark! And Rut will say that she can ask Tomas or Marina if they might be interested in buying. But they both know that Rut and Pekka's children can't or won't. Marina lives in Oslo, and though Tomas only lives in Forskant, he has a new build by the river and works for an advertising agency in Kokkola. What is he going to do with an old farm in disrepair?

*

The next day, the man from the Forest Association comes early, but she is ready and waiting for him when he arrives. She had breakfast at dawn, made coffee and filled a thermos. She is tired after a restless night, her movements feel sluggish and her head is aching. She waits in the entrance hall wearing rubber boots, a windbreaker and headscarf, with Otto's old backpack by her feet. It started to rain in the wee hours and is drizzling still. When he gets out of the car, wearing a black cap and a jacket that reads Metsä Group Forestry, she is surprised by how young he is. She comes out to say hello. The rain has made the snow even more compact, and the grey sky looks as tired as she feels. They take his car out to the turning circle—it's a four-wheel drive so there's no danger of getting stuck.

The forest is hers now too. It also requires care, maintenance, decision-making. She needs an inventory to get the forest valued, if she is going to sell.

The man from the Forest Association has been here before and is familiar with the place so he knows what to do. He has an app on his phone too, with a detailed map.

He comments on the different species of trees they pass and patiently answers her questions. She is embarrassed by her ignorance. What with her mother being a forester and everything. She doesn't mention Tilia. Else he might expect her to understand all the forestry terms he is using. He points to some small pines growing densely beside the path and says they need to be cleared. When they get to the ridge where she and Doris and

Lovisa used to pick lingonberries, he says that this part of the forest will soon be ready for felling.

The lingonberry bushes are sprouting out of the March snow. Dark, glossy leaves and a few limp berries. After Lovisa died, she and Doris were the only ones who picked them. They always brought a thermos of coffee and sandwiches. Maybe a few buns. They would spend the whole day picking. Then Stina married Björn and Anna was born. The whole family came up a few times when Anna was little. Björn's parents had a summer cottage in east Uusimaa, by the sea. Only about an hour from Helsinki. They started spending their summers there. It belongs to Anna now. Björn's parents left the cottage to Anna, and she and Sam go there a lot. Sam is into sailing, and they have a sailboat and a motorboat. Anna likes to fish. Björn's parents taught her how.

Nevabacka isn't even by a lake.

The guy from the Forest Association thinks the lingonberry ridge is the area that should be felled. Chopped down. Forestry machinery ploughing forward, crushing crowberries and lingonberries, devouring pine trunks. Then the land must be cultivated. Seedlings planted. No lingonberries for many years. He looks at the trees, appraising them, over a hundred years old, he says. It will all be turned to pulp, she thinks. He mentions how much she could get for the wood. It's not a lot. Ostrobothnian pines grow slowly on rocky ridges and they don't grow large. Even in a hundred years. Still, it's money.

Do they really have to strip everything away? Couldn't they... leave a section of trees, let the forest repopulate itself? She heard

398

Mum say that people used to do that in the past, but she can't remember the technical term. She knows how she comes across: an ignorant urbanite.

Selective logging, he says with a frown. It only recently became legal. But it's difficult to carry out continuous forestry on land like this. Pine trees need a lot of light to grow.

He knows where the tar pit is; he has already marked in his app that he thinks it should be protected. They go there and admire the huge fir trees. This is a big tar pit, he says. The firs must be very old. This year, something has bored holes into one of the trunks from several directions. A woodpecker perhaps. The tree won't live long after that, she thinks. But when it falls, it should be allowed to remain. Become food for insects, mosses and lichens. An important part of the life cycle.

Then it dawns on her: if she sells, she doesn't get a say in what happens to the tree. Or to anything else. The lingonberry ridge might be stripped bare, and there would be nothing she could do about it.

Her childhood and youth were stormy at times. Dad moved out when she was a teenager. He lived in a studio apartment in another neighbourhood for a few years. But her parents never divorced, and he moved back home shortly before she herself moved out. He had several girlfriends during that period. It was never talked about. Not at the time, and not later. New people came into her life and left again, and her once secure and predictable life was ripped away from her, never to return. The only thing that felt permanent was Nevabacka. The paths.

The little dell full of heartsease pansies. The lingonberry ridge. Everything is the same as it has always been: welcoming her, familiar, demanding nothing of her. Her relationship with this place is simple and straightforward.

The thought of never coming here again, never picking lingonberries on this ridge again, hurts more than she anticipated.

She has never been to the other side of this valley. There, overgrown with brushwood, she sees the place where the tar pit was drained for the first time. The wooden structure is still there. How old must it be? Three hundred years? When did they stop tar burning? How hard they must have worked, she thinks. Everybody who lived and worked here. She has heard Nevabacka referred to as "newly built", because the land only started being cultivated in the second half of the seventeenth century. Not during the sixteenth century, like the oldest homesteads in the parish.

She lurches clumsily over a ditch as he strides ahead on his long, youthful legs. They amble through the brushwood behind the tar pit and then back along a logging road that runs straight through her land.

"Shall we walk around the lake? Do you have time?"

She has time and is happy to have company walking around the lake. She wishes she were the type of person who would enjoy walking alone through woods and fields. Her mother was a forester, after all, and she herself spent plenty of time in the woods when she was young. But it's like the dark. With age, she has grown afraid, and shameful of her fear. There are bears here, and maybe wolves too. She trusts wolves to stay away. But a female bear with cubs… She asks him if he has seen many animals in the forest. Moose, he says. Nothing else.

"But I have a friend who flies a helicopter and keeps records of the bear population. He says that if people knew how many there really were, no one would dare go into the forest at all."

She looks around anxiously. She and Doris have found bear droppings here before. And seen deep scars in tree bark where a bear had sharpened its claws on the trunks.

Doris' land—now her land—is a large territory, but most of it is not really forest: there is a lake and several areas of marshland, the largest of which takes up about two-thirds of the property and is part of a vast marsh. It stretches north, mysterious and completely unknown to her. She has never gone there. Just picked the cloudberries at one edge. But she has heard that people drowned there, long ago.

They cross a smaller marsh with spindly pines and climb up a steep hill. They joke that it hardly feels like Ostrobothnia any more, it being a famously flat region. Up on the hill is a stone circle that has collapsed in the middle, giving home to a large anthill. It could have been a burial mound, she thinks aloud, and he says the same thing occurred to him. The location is appropriate, up on a hill, and she knows that the remains of an ancient stone construction have been found not far from here.

They make their way down the hill. The sun has come out now, and she takes off her sweater and ties it around her waist under her jacket. She is sweaty under her blouse. She points out

401

the two fire pits on this side of the lake. People have made fires and left split wood and crushed beer cans behind. This feels extra offensive because the pine trunks here are still black and sooty from the forest fire that ravaged the land one dry summer a few years before Doris' death. Someone had started a fire despite the warnings and hadn't bothered to extinguish it properly afterwards. That's when Pekka set up the camera. He set it up so that she would get photos emailed to her as soon as the sensor picked up motion in the forest. Doris didn't have a computer, of course. The camera has caught a lot of people, dogs, and once a couple of young men making an illegal campfire, but thankfully that was in autumn when the forest was damp.

She hasn't captured many pictures of wild animals. Mostly small birds flying past or hovering in front of the camera. Once a hare with eyes shining in the camera flash. The best pictures have been of cranes. They appear in spring sometimes. One or two. The large birds resemble prehistoric animals with their curved necks and long beaks.

It has struck her that she is the first person to ever own this land, this farmstead, and not live here. She isn't party to the cycles of the forest or routines of parish life. She spent her childhood summers here, and many of the older folk in the church village know her. But the younger generations don't know who she is. She is a stranger. An outsider. To both the people and the land.

But the forest enters her home via the camera. She studies the pictures carefully, as if searching for something. The answer to a question she can't quite put into words. Most of the pictures show nothing in particular, the camera's motion sensor being triggered by the flight of a small bird, or the sun hitting the lens at a certain angle. All that can be seen in the grainy pictures are pine trunks, small aspens, a corner of the marsh in the distance. Still, she studies them for a long time. Looking for what might have triggered the camera. Is that an animal? Are those pointed shadows the ears of a fox? Every time a picture captures something living, even if it's just a stray dog, adrenaline rushes through her body. She sits at her desk at home in Töölö, hearing the local trams screech past, looking at a crane gazing out over a lake 600 kilometres to the north. The forest steps into her flat.

They sit for a while by the remnants of the illegal campfire and she offers him coffee from her thermos. She has brought an extra cup. They discuss camera models and whether it would be a good idea to build a wind shelter on the lake shore. She wants to know more about his map app. How to use it. Wants to see the forest in detail. He shows her and tells her all about it, advises her on other map services that provide different information. There is one that tells you about historical events in the region as well, he says.

She has lots of similar apps on her phone. One to identify birdsong and one that recognizes plants. She doesn't mention them. She feels like she should know these things by heart. Recognize the woodpecker's call and what common weeds like silverweed look like. But she doesn't. Sure, she pressed plants in herbariums as a child, but she can't remember the names any more, not even the common ones, let alone the Latin.

But with the help of the apps, she has started to learn.

They don't go all the way to the large marsh, but she tells him the story of the time her mother got lost there when she was very small and encountered a bear. And that there is some sort of yellow orchid growing there that she doesn't know the name of.

Finally, they pass by something she never knew existed, despite its proximity to the turning circle: six small rock fields from the Ice Age. They are marked on the Forest Association's app as protected areas. They must not be disturbed, he says. Now only parts of them are visible under the snow. She takes photos on her phone and thinks that of course they must not be disturbed. She imagines the ice that dragged the rocks here, ice tens of metres, no, probably several kilometres thick!

They have been out for three hours. When she comes back to the farm, she is ravenous and completely exhausted. She heats up some soup, eats, then collapses on the kitchen sofa.

She thinks about the marsh. About the cranes that walk there, lifting and lowering their slender necks. Whether she captures them in a picture or not, there they are. And the monuments: built by human hands or created by nature itself. Burial mounds, rock fields, tar pits. There they are, whether she thinks about them or not. Independent of her. The forest can take care of itself. It doesn't need her to maintain, organize, protect it. It requires nothing from her. Not like the house, the farm. She owns the house, and it owns her. But she and the forest have a relationship free from obligation.

She sits up, thinks she might as well get on with it. She decides at random to start with the pantry. Sifts through the various jars and packets, looking for things that expired long ago. She finds a plastic bag and starts throwing things away. When she finds an ancient packet of crackers, she puts the plastic bag down, steps into Doris' clogs, which are standing by the kitchen door, and goes outside. Great tits are fluttering around the lilac arbour looking for seeds with bright, airy squeaks. A magpie flaps in the big apple tree next to the shed. She goes over to the tree and crumbles the crackers onto the snow beneath the branches. She knows anything she leaves for the birds will also feed the rats, but maybe there aren't rats here like there are in cities. She thinks of how, in the past, sacrifices were made to house elves, forest spirits, to the farm's guardian tree. Maybe that's what she's doing now. A gift. A prayer for understanding and forgiveness. She pours out the last crumbs as the magpie swoops down, curious, from the barn roof where it has taken refuge. Then she scrunches up the bag and looks around at everything that is now her property: the main house. New Cottage. The woodshed, cowshed, tool shed, the old granaries and barns. The cold cellar that Rut has emptied of Doris' potatoes and carrots. All the tools, all the objects.

All burdens.

I can sell, she thinks. It is allowed. I can put down this burden. I don't have to keep Nevabacka just because Doris left it to me. I don't have to continue with it, just because the farm has been in the family for so long. Maybe no one wants the house, but someone is bound to want the land for its forest. No doubt about that. And does it really matter if the house is left empty?

She imagines the forest marching closer and closer, taking over the fields completely, trees growing through the bowed roof of New Cottage, animals moving into the empty rooms, moss covering everything like verdigris. The collapsed sauna. Brushwood around the porch dormer.

For you are dust, and to dust you shall return. Nothing is permanent. There are abandoned homesteads like this all over Ostrobothnia.

She follows the thought further. What if we all disappeared? If we were no longer here cultivating and felling and making decisions. Would this place miss us?

She imagines the neat, tidy, commercial forest rewilding as soon as people stopped logging. She imagines overgrown ditches around Vittermåsa, the water level rising, fallen trees left to lie, insect life flourishing, woodpeckers feasting on beetles and larvae in uprooted trees. The forest reindeer that Doris once saw walking through the marsh again with long strides.

We could all die out. Perhaps that is the direction we're headed in already. So many other species have. Why should humans be any different? But the land doesn't die. It changes, but life goes on.

She looks out over the field, which is covered in a tired, patchy layer of snow. Not yet completely invaded by brushwood. Just about big enough to play football on. Maybe have an inflatable pool.

She could come here with Adrian in a year or so. For winter break, when Anna and Sam have to work. Rut would turn the heating on for when they arrived, like now, but it would still be chilly. She imagines lighting a fire in the kitchen and one in the front room while Adrian keeps his jacket on to call his mother and tell her they have arrived safely. Then she unpacks the food, puts it in the refrigerator, which is working and contains a few basic items. Butter and lingonberry jam she made with fruit picked from the lingonberry ridge, which has not been cleared. For supper they eat porridge with lingonberry jam. She makes a bed for Adrian on the floor in Doris' room. The gramophone is still there, and the paintings, but she has bought a new mattress and pillows. Emptied Doris' clothes out of the closet and hung up her own. She leaves them here so she doesn't have to pack too much each time she comes. In the evening, when Adrian has fallen asleep, she sits at the kitchen table with a whisky and looks at the wildlife camera's black-and-white images from the forest at night. A raven has been captured. Or maybe, just maybe, a forest reindeer. It has wandered back to its old homeland. During the night, Adrian crawls into Doris' bed and they sleep side by side, close. It's dark, but she's used to it. Or she has got used to the fear.

In the morning, she skis through the field to make tracks for Adrian. The boy falls, but Grandma pulls him up and he tries again. He is a stubborn child who refuses to give up and eventually learns to ski. He finally gets to see masses of pure white snow. Not like the dirty brown sludge that occasionally lies on the ground for a few days in the capital. In the evening, they fire up the sauna, roll around in the snow and marvel at the wintry starry sky together. She shows Adrian her stone collection in the sauna window. This summer you can add your own stone to it, she says. When we come here on summer holiday. Then I will show you the best swimming spots.

Both paths seem equally plausible. The property abandoned. Or a place of her own. The choice is hers.

INSTRUCTIONS

Hold the memorial service at Nevabacka
Granholm's bakery does good sandwich cakes
serve champagne
some decent food
But don't go overboard!
Remember me, don't mourn
No begonias on my grave,
or I'll come back to haunt you!
Cremation please.

You know you mustn't sell Nevabacka

Open the damper
open the summer damper
and the draught regulator
empty out the ashes if there are any
close the summer damper slowly once the fire is lit
The firewood should last a couple of years

if you don't come down too often
—though I hope you do

The key to the basement is in the right-hand drawer in the
    kitchen

There is a leak in New Cottage again, it needs a new roof
assuming it's still worth saving
The battery for the strimmer is in the shed
The mower still works,
it just needs a steady hand and perhaps a little oil
but I've been thinking for a while now that it might be time
    to give up on the lawns
let there be meadows instead
biodiversity and insects and all that
and less work

The rowan is our guardian tree
It would be bad luck to cut it down
Call in the chimney sweep once a year
The number for the hunting team is in the logbook in the
    bureau
You're responsible for forest tax declarations
Anders has the keys to the bollard
Johannes Oskarsson is chairman of the road association

Hannele S has rented the fields
Ask her to keep the meadow closest to the house as it is
I've sown so many wildflowers
and wild cumin grows there
because someone planted it at some point
The swallows have returned, they are nesting in the barn
This is thanks to the meadow, I'm sure
there are plenty of insects for them now

The mobile library comes every other Thursday
Don't forget to close my account at the general store
If you want to get rid of my old records, call Tomas
he collects them

I owe Anders a bottle of whisky
for helping me with the firewood
Pour one out for me

Take care weeding the flower beds
lilies usually grow in the far right
and irises by the wall
Doris planted them
Wild currants grow behind the barn
Someone planted a lot of berry bushes here
long ago

Before you go back home:
Unplug the water heater
Turn all the radiators down to 10 degrees
Take out the rubbish and compost
Don't forget to empty the water barrels before winter

I've been taking part in a forest preservation programme
you're not allowed to fell anything for another ten years
The forest reindeer are thriving
and the badgers
and that strange orchid
insects and fungi live in the uprooted trees

But do what you like
with all of it
It is your turn now

I hope you will be happy here

AVAILABLE AND COMING SOON
FROM PUSHKIN PRESS

Pushkin Press was founded in 1997, and publishes novels, essays, memoirs, children's books—everything from timeless classics to the urgent and contemporary.

Our books represent exciting, high-quality writing from around the world: we publish some of the twentieth century's most widely acclaimed, brilliant authors such as Stefan Zweig, Yasushi Inoue, Teffi, Antal Szerb, Gerard Reve and Elsa Morante, as well as compelling and award-winning contemporary writers, including Dorthe Nors, Edith Pearlman, Perumal Murugan, Ayelet Gundar-Goshen and Chigozie Obioma.

Pushkin Press publishes the world's best stories, to be read and read again. To discover more, visit www.pushkinpress.com.

THE PASSENGER
ULRICH ALEXANDER BOSCHWITZ

TENDER IS THE FLESH
NINETEEN CLAWS AND A BLACK BIRD
AGUSTINA BAZTERRICA

AT NIGHT ALL BLOOD IS BLACK
BEYOND THE DOOR OF NO RETURN
DAVID DIOP

WHEN WE CEASE TO UNDERSTAND THE WORLD
THE MANIAC
BENJAMÍN LABATUT

NO PLACE TO LAY ONE'S HEAD
FRANÇOISE FRENKEL

FORBIDDEN NOTEBOOK
ALBA DE CÉSPEDES

COLLECTED WORKS: A NOVEL
LYDIA SANDGREN

MY MEN
VICTORIA KIELLAND

AS RICH AS THE KING
ABIGAIL ASSOR

LAND OF SNOW AND ASHES
PETRA RAUTIAINEN

LUCKY BREAKS
YEVGENIA BELORUSETS

THE WOLF HUNT
AYELET GUNDAR-GOSHEN

MISS ICELAND
AUDUR AVA ÓLAFSDÓTTIR

MIRROR, SHOULDER, SIGNAL
DORTHE NORS

THE WONDERS
ELENA MEDEL

MS ICE SANDWICH
MIEKO KAWAKAMI

GROWN UPS
MARIE AUBERT

LEARNING TO TALK TO PLANTS
MARTA ORRIOLS

THE RABBIT BACK LITERATURE SOCIETY
PASI ILMARI JÄÄSKELÄINEN